Hear[illegible]
HANDOFF

USA TODAY BESTSELLING AUTHOR

LEX MARTIN

This adult contemporary romance is recommended for readers 18+ due to mature content.

Copy editing by RJ Locksley

Proofreading by Julia Griffis, The Romance Bibliophile

Cover by Najla Qamber Designs

Model Photograph by Lindee Robinson

First Edition

ISBN 978-1-950554-16-4

ABOUT THE BOOK:

Billy's not my baby daddy, but he doesn't mind pretending to be...

I'm a Division I cheerleader with hopes of becoming a sports broadcaster. None of my plans for college include getting knocked up by a cheating ex who just got engaged to another girl.

When my father finds out I'm pregnant, he goes ballistic. That's when my BFF, bad boy Billy Babcock, comes to my rescue and agrees to "take responsibility."

Billy and I solidify our contract on a napkin—he'll pretend to be my baby's father, and I'll help him clean up his image. The only problem is my father, the football coach, hates Billy. He warned me off dating players a long time ago, and he thinks Billy's the biggest *player* out there.

Now that we're in a "relationship," Billy thinks we should spend some quality naked time together, but I'm worried about crossing that line. Because athletic guys with big muscles, intricate tattoos, and sexy smirks are my biggest weakness, and Billy ticks off all those boxes.

Can my football player "boyfriend" walk the straight and narrow for me?

Or did I just get handed off from one heartbreaker to another?

***Heartbreaker Handoff* is an angsty, friends-to-lovers, forbidden romance featuring a sassy cheerleader who's about to be a single mother and a criminally charming football player determined to prove he's the man for her, one sizzling kiss at a time. *Heartbreaker Handoff* is a dual-POV standalone in the *USA Today*-bestselling series Varsity Dads.**

"The course of true love never did run smooth."
—William Shakespeare, *A Midsummer Night's Dream*

1

ROXY

I'M HAVING A BABY. In about seven months, I'm popping out Ezra Thomas's child.

If he hadn't been sticking his dick in half the girls on campus, I probably wouldn't be freaking out right now.

He doesn't know I'm pregnant yet.

But given how that asshole won't return my calls, I'm likely doing this solo.

A basement party at some frat house isn't the place to have a panic attack, but between the sweaty bodies and the loud music, I'm starting to freak out.

I push off the exposed wood beam and make my way to the back door.

"Roxy. Wait up." Billy Babcock, resident bad boy and notorious flirt, sidles up to me. "Where ya going, biscuit? The festivities just got started." He tosses his muscular arm over my shoulder and shoots me a sexy smile.

My heart kicks in my chest, which I ignore because a pregnant girl probably shouldn't flirt with her best friend, who's *not* her baby daddy.

"I'm going to head home."

Billy turns me to face him. I finally give in and look into his beautiful eyes.

There's no question about it—Billy is a drop-dead gorgeous man. Confident on the verge of arrogant. Cocky but sweet. He has dirty blond hair, piercing blue eyes fringed with thick lashes, muscles for days, and just the right amount of scruff on his rugged chin. And don't get me started on those sexy tattoos all over his thick arms.

But I don't mess around with players anymore, not after what happened with Ezra.

Billy leans close enough that I can appreciate his spicy cologne. "It's too early to take off. We just won a National Championship," he says with cheek, like I don't know.

Kind of hard to miss when his coach is my father. "I'm not in the mood for a party."

Billy's a six-foot-two-inch defensive back. He's broad. Strong. Fearless on the field. Has quick feet. Could leap over me if he wanted to and easily bench-press three times my body weight. All reasons my father should love him.

If only Billy's mouth wasn't his worst enemy. This boy is always saying shit he shouldn't.

Coach isn't a fan.

I brush pizza crumbs off his Broncos t-shirt. "I'm tired."

Billy's usual carefree expression goes serious in a heartbeat, and he lowers his voice. "You feeling okay?"

I stare down at my shoes. "No. I mean, physically, I'm fine, but inside I'm..." I don't know how to explain the suffocation clawing at my throat right now.

"You're freaking out."

I nod, grateful he knows my secret. Not many people do.

He squeezes my shoulder. "Let's get out of here. Get some fresh air."

"Are you sure you want to leave the party?" At least three girls are eyeing him right now.

For some reason, the thought of him hooking up with some random woman makes me bristle.

He glances around and shrugs. "The football house is having a party tomorrow. And maybe another one the night after that."

Laughing, I shake my head. "You heathen. Of course you are."

He winks. "See, you're already feeling better."

After he grabs his jacket, we climb up the rickety stairs and step out onto the back porch. A brisk wind whips around us. January weather in the Texas Hill Country is so unpredictable. One day, it'll be seventy and the next, twenty degrees.

I zip up my coat and shiver.

He wraps his arm around my shoulders again. "Cold?"

"Yeah, but it feels good after being inside."

"Wanna get some hot chocolate?"

I check in with my stomach that's finally settled. "With those little marshmallows?"

"Is there any other way?"

I playfully pinch his side. "Nope."

We jump in his thirty-year-old tan Ford Bronco, a gift from his grandmother that runs surprisingly well, and head for the nearest convenience store since it's too late to go to a coffee shop.

After we load up on hot chocolate with marshmallows and whipped cream, we stop off at the park where we settle on the swings.

It's dark enough that stars peek through the clouds and so cold I can see my breath, but this is the most settled I've felt in months.

"Thank you, Billy. I feel better."

We turn so our knees are touching. "If you had dated me instead of Ezra, we could be doing this all the time. Actually, there's a lot more we could be doing." He shoots me a flirty smirk.

I snort. "I'd hate to curtail your extra-curricular activities." I love Billy, but his reputation is worse than Ezra's. His nickname is Billy *Bigcock*. Can't get much more obvious than that.

He almost looks offended. "There are no extra-curricular activities. We can put that blame squarely on No-Nut November. It threw me off my game."

I sigh dreamily and bat my eyes. "Gee, Billy, that's what every girl wants to hear. That you and your roommates didn't nut because you were afraid of losing a football game. Won't that make you lose your vision or hearing or something?"

"What? I can't hear you."

We both crack up.

Then he motions to his lap. "To be clear, I've jerked off since November. I just haven't hook—"

I throw my hand over his mouth. "Stop while you're ahead."

The second I remove my palm, he lifts an eyebrow. "What about head?"

I roll my eyes, but I'm laughing.

Until I remember what I need to do this weekend. "If I don't hear from him by Saturday morning, I'm driving down to San Antonio. I need to have this conversation before school starts next week."

"The whole team will thank you for not busting Ezra's ass before the championship game."

"I wanted you guys and my dad to dominate, and you needed Ezra to focus on winning. But it's been tough to watch the media fall all over themselves to praise that spineless weasel."

His voice goes soft. "I tried to warn you."

"I know, and I regret not listening." At the time, I wondered if Billy was letting his personal beef with Ezra taint how he viewed him.

But no, he was right. Ezra really is a dick.

I fiddle with the lid on my hot chocolate. "How flipped out do you think my dad will be?"

"Are you asking me if *The Saint* will shit a two-story brick house when he finds out you're pregnant?" The Saint was my dad's nickname in the NFL. "It's a distinct possibility."

"He'll never believe this, but I really try not to disappoint him." After partying too much last year, I buckled down in the fall and got better grades. But it won't matter once Coach hears I got knocked up.

"Aww, biscuit. I'm sorry. But welcome to the club. I'm a disappointment to my father too. You'll get over it."

Billy might act like he doesn't care, but doesn't everyone want their parents' approval to some degree?

"Does your dad really doubt your chances of getting drafted?"

Billy's so dynamic on the field, the kind of guy who puts his whole heart and soul into the game. If he could do that with a relationship, he'd be as swoony as those rakish dukes I love reading about in my historical romances.

He shrugs. "I don't think he cares now that I'm not quarterback."

That's the big rub between Ezra and Billy. Ezra gloats about being QB1, especially since Billy got switched to defense.

When I started dating Ezra last fall, I didn't know he was such a douchebag. He puts on a good show for his coaches. Unfortunately, my dad loves him.

"Tell me everything will be okay."

Billy takes my hand in his rough palm. "Rox, you're a tough little firecracker. You can do this. I promise everything will work out." Pausing, he tilts his head. "And if Ezra doesn't take the news well, I'd be happy to clear up his confusion."

My eyes sting, and I squeeze his hand. "I don't want you to get in trouble."

"Trouble's my middle name," he says with a crooked grin.

Flutters erupt in my belly from the look he gives me, but I ruthlessly stamp them out. Jumping from one player to another would be the height of foolishness, but I appreciate Billy's friendship, more than he knows. "He'll probably declare for the draft this spring, and then he'll be out of our hair. But he should know the truth before he goes."

"Do you want some company? I can drive you down to San Antonio."

Do I want Billy to take me to confront Ezra? That sounds like a terrible idea.

"It's something I need to do on my own."

He nods, then gets up to stand behind me. "Wanna push?" Nodding, I place my now empty cup on the ground and zip my jacket a little higher. Billy gives me a gentle shove, and my swing starts to move. "That pencil dick wouldn't know a good thing if it bit him in the ass. This is his fucking loss."

"Thanks for the vote of confidence."

"You know I got your back." The vehemence in his voice calms my ruffled feathers.

Cold air rushes past me as I rise higher and higher. Closing my eyes, I hang on to the metal links and kick up my feet and let my head fall back.

That brief moment of weightlessness when the swing reaches the peak feels so good.

I can almost forget that my whole life is about to change.

Because next fall, instead of making captain of my Division I cheer squad, I'll be nursing an infant.

2

ROXY

Don't chicken out.

After I lock my car, I stare at the house across the street.

I'm starting to regret not taking Billy up on his offer to come with me.

I text him an update like I promised I would.

Looks like Ezra's family is throwing a party.

Probably to celebrate his win last week.

Billy's response almost makes me smile. **You love crashing parties. You can handle it.**

A second later, he sends another one.

Don't let him off the hook. You got this. And if you don't, like I said, I'm happy to relay the message.

When Billy's message disappears, I stare at the dark screen.

That sinking feeling in my belly makes me wonder if I picked the wrong guy last fall.

How did I get tricked by Ezra's bullshit?

He and I were supposed to be more than friends with benefits. Except he was secretive as hell with his phone.

Some of his teammates call Ezra "Easy" because of how well he plays QB.

Well, that's not the only easy thing about him.

Despite my growing urge to tuck tail and run, with the draft looming I can't hold off telling him about my pregnancy any longer. Not that I expect him to stick around for me, but maybe he'd want to for the baby.

Or you're being delusional, Roxanne. That's a strong possibility.

Shoving that thought down, I zip my jacket as I wonder how much longer this coat will fit me. *How am I going to do my broadcast journalism course next year while toting around a baby?* I've already given up cheerleading, and if I look like a beached whale when school starts next fall, that doesn't bode well for my future in front of a camera.

Dreading every step, I make my way up the long driveway lined with cars. Ezra's parents have a pretty two-story colonial in a nice part of town.

A wave of nausea washes over me, and I swallow hard. Cold sweat builds along my back and under my arms, and my stomach feels like it might drop out of my ass at any minute. I say a prayer I don't shit my pants in front of Ezra's family.

After I knock, an older woman wearing Ezra's jersey opens the door with a smile. "Hi! Welcome! You must be one of Ezra's friends. I'm his mom Beth."

"Hi, Beth. I'm Roxy."

"Come in! I'm so glad you could make it. My son swore none of his friends could come to our little shindig, which seemed so strange. I mean, our boy just won the big game!"

It is strange Ezra didn't invite his teammates to his party. He's the damn captain, the starting quarterback, one of the best in the country, and one of the most popular guys on campus. People kiss his ass everywhere he goes.

I'm caught off guard by his mother's warmth. Ezra always goes radio silent when he's gone home over breaks, and I've wondered if his parents were strict. But judging by Beth's welcoming smile, that's not the reason Ezra blew me off.

"Everyone's in the den," she says. "The beer is in the cooler. If you're over twenty-one, feel free to take one. If not, there's one full of soda too. I'm so glad you could make it to his special day."

Special day? I thought his birthday was in the spring.

"Thank you." I force a smile and make my way to the back of the house. I expect to see Bronco stuff everywhere, not pink and gold balloons.

About twenty people mill around, and along the back is a long table with a huge cake and tons of food.

Standing next to the cake is Ezra.

With his arm wrapped around a woman.

I freeze when I see them. Because based on the way he's holding her, she's not family.

This was a bad idea.

I start to back out of the room, but bump into a large man with a barrel chest. "Hey there! My wife said you're here to see the happy couple."

Dear God, what did I walk into? Before I can say anything, Ezra's dad shouts across the room. "Son! You have a visitor! Come say hi."

When Ezra spots me, all the blood drains from his face. But his date gives me a beaming smile and drags him across the room.

She's not exactly who I pictured Ezra with. Her dirty blonde hair is pulled into a tight bun, and she's wearing wire-rimmed glasses and baggy clothes. Even though she has an awkward vibe, she's really pretty.

And probably too sweet for that asshole.

She waves at me. "Hi. I'm Abigail."

Say something.

"I'm Roxy." Um... What the hell do I say? "I'm one of the cheerleaders on the squad." Or at least I was.

Ezra frowns and points at me like I'm an equation he needs to solve. "This is Coach's daughter. She, uh, she always checks on everyone."

I raise an eyebrow. That's what he's going with?

She snorts and smacks his chest. "If you had just let me visit you at school to meet all your friends over the years, this wouldn't be so weird."

Over the years?

I turn that statement over in my head. Over the fucking *years*?

"So tell me, Abigail, how long have you two been dating?" I watch the asshole's face as I ask the question. He has the decency to look like he wants to hightail it out of here. He shoves his pitch-black hair out of his eyes and glances away.

I used to be so enthralled with his eyes. They're a unique shade of brown that turn green at the edges. Now I look at them and see lies piled on more lies.

Abigail gives him a sweet smile. "Since high school. I always knew he was the one." She waves her left hand at me where a diamond sparkles on her finger. My mouth drops open, and she giggles. "I know! Isn't it awesome?"

I peel my tongue off the roof of my mouth before I choke on it. "Congrats. That's..." Unexpected. Twisted. Fucked up beyond belief. "So cool."

She hops up and down and hugs me. I pat her on the back awkwardly, and when Ezra sees us, he flinches. *Yeah, you should be uncomfortable, asshole. You made me the other woman, and I hate cheaters!*

I narrow my eyes at him and hope he can read the curses exploding in my head.

I clear my throat. "I just wanted to drop by to say congrats." I look Ezra straight in the eye. "I'm sure my father will be delighted when he hears the news." *You're going down, motherfucker.*

His Adam's apple bobs as he swallows.

Turning, I hug Abigail again. "You know what? Why wait for an invite from Ezra to visit Lone Star State? We should swap numbers, and you can come and stay with me."

She flails her arms. "That would be amazing!"

Ezra's nostrils flare, and I smile. He fucked with the wrong girl.

Poor Abigail needs the truth before she marries this douchebag. I'm not the only girl he slept with last semester. According to the report the clinic sent me, he didn't give me any STDs, thank God. But I always made him wear a condom even though he whined about wanting to rawdog it.

For the record, any moron who says things like "rawdog it" should be immediately kicked out of your bed. I know this now.

I'm not sure how one of his swimmers got through, but since he's the only person I've been with in the last year, I don't have any doubt he's the donor.

After Abigail and I swap numbers, she wanders off to greet other guests. Pausing in front of Ezra, I lower my voice. "You are dead to me, asshole."

"I can explain, Rox." He leans down, trails his finger over my wrist, and whispers, "Let me stop by your place tomorrow night. We'll grab a bite. Maybe go for a drive."

Is he really propositioning me for sex at his damn engagement party? "Go for a drive" was our code for naked activities.

Laughter spills out of me. I can't explain why, but all I can think is that I'm possibly hysterical and definitely hormonal. "Fuck you. I hope your dick falls off."

I mean every word.

3

ROXY

I'M BACK in my car and on my way back to Charming when I realize I never told Ezra I'm pregnant.

I let out a string of curse words that would make my father send me straight to church.

Once I stop hyperventilating, I call my bestie Charlotte, who was briefly my roommate last semester.

She answers on the first ring. "Oh my God, what happened? Did you drive down to San Antonio?"

"You're never going to guess what that lying asshole was up to. Ezra got engaged. To his *high school* sweetheart. Some girl he's been dating for *years*."

"You're kidding."

"Nope. And here's the worst part—she's actually really nice. Like, I could see myself being friends with her if she wasn't dating that tool. I made sure to get her number and told her we should hang out. Right in front of Ezra. I hope he has nightmares about the things I might tell her."

She hums. "You're taking this really well."

"I'm stuffing it all down for later, and not because I loved that idiot. I didn't. I mean, I had feelings for a while. Until he started showing his true colors." I wonder if I went for him in the first place because my dad likes him so much.

"I'm sorry you're going through this," Charlotte says.

"I had to quit cheer because of that asshole. I can't exactly tote my baby to football games. Even if I could, who knows how long it'll take to get back to that level of athleticism?"

I was on track to be cheer captain, and now I'll be elbow deep in baby vomit and poopy diapers.

She lets me rant. "How am I going to do my broadcast course next fall right after I push out a kid?"

Charlotte will be gone by then because her boyfriend Jake will get drafted to a great team, and they'll be off living their best lives.

I'm thrilled for her.

And terrified for myself.

"Take things one day at a time," she says calmly.

"One day at a time. I can do that." I nod, talking out of my ass. "Do you want to go for pizza? I could use something with cheese and lots of carbs."

"Jake and I were about to head to the movies. He got a babysitter and everything. Want to come with us? We could pick up a pizza on the way."

"No, go enjoy your date." As much as I love Jake and Charlotte, I don't want to be a third wheel. Those two just started dating last semester after a whole whirlwind of drama. They deserve some time to themselves. "Let's grab lunch on Monday, though. You can help me plan my revenge."

Ezra deserves my A-game.

I don't really want to be alone, though, and while I love my parents, I'm not ready to face them.

And even though I threatened Ezra with telling my father about him two-timing me, I don't have the faintest idea how I'll broach the subject.

That's how I end up at the Stallion Station. Because I could really use a hug from Billy.

The driveway is packed with cars, which is no surprise for a Saturday night. The football guys are crazy. On any given night, they might have a swim party, poker night, rave, or dart competition. Though they haven't played darts since Jinxy got nailed in the ass.

I park down the street and head in when I reach the front door. Music blares from the speakers, and when I reach the living room, it's packed wall to wall with bodies. Championship banners line the walls.

Even though it's been a rough day, seeing those banners makes me so proud of my friends on the team and my father. Of their sacrifices to be the best. No one knows better than I do how hard they worked to get to this point.

Movement on the makeshift stage catches my attention. Billy's up there shaking his ass and smiling at the crowd like he's Travis Kelce working the crowd after a touchdown.

As I watch him dance, I have to admit he's sexy as sin. He's donning that killer smile, and I'm pretty sure all the girls in the room are swooning right now.

Watching him makes me wonder what would've happened if I'd gone out with him when he asked last fall instead of Ezra.

I sigh. If only my dad loved Billy the way he loves Ezra. While everyone thinks Ezra is the good guy, Billy's the bad boy with a chip on his shoulder.

Jim Jankowitz—Jinxy to his crew—sidles up to me and lifts me in a hug. "Foxy Roxy!"

I hoard the nickname for later. For when I don't fit in my clothes anymore and my feet are swollen. For when I'm depressed that I can't cheer anymore. For the nights I have to stay home with the baby instead of partying with my friends. "Hey, Jinxy. Is there a theme tonight?"

"Just some karaoke. Billy's warming everyone up first."

I can see that.

Billy's snug black t-shirt hugs his broad shoulders and chest as he moves. I'm getting hot, and I'm not sure if it's because the room is warm or because Billy's up there looking so damn handsome.

When the music ends, Billy grabs the mic. "Who wants to sing with me? Let's kick off karaoke night with something retro."

I'm debating whether I should join him when Vicky Mitchell, Billy's former friend with benefits, hops on the stage. They hug and the first notes of "Summer Loving" from *Grease* blare from the stereo.

Vicky's gorgeous. A bottle blonde with long legs, a modelesque figure, and blindingly white teeth. Basically what you picture when you think of what kind of woman a guy like Billy would be into.

In a nutshell, the opposite of me.

I'm short and muscular. I have boobs thanks to genetics and a decent ass from gymnastics and cheer, but no one would confuse me for a leggy blonde. My hair is coffee brown and frizzes out like I've been plugged into an electric socket on humid days.

Don't get me wrong. I love my body and the things I can get it to do. I kick ass in cheerleading. I'm the girl who climbs to the top of the pyramid and flips to the ground. I'm balls-out like that.

I'm just not Vicky.

Watching her dance with Billy while they pretend to be a couple as they act out the lyrics makes my skin itch. She's flipping her hair and shaking her ass at him, and he's crooning and flirting back like he's Danny who's hot for Sandy.

Billy says they're over. That they were fun for a while, but he's not into Vicky like that anymore. Judging by how good they sound together and their off-the-charts chemistry, that might not be the case anymore.

My stomach twists uncomfortably.

I'd rather not witness Billy break his dry spell tonight, so I turn and head back out the door.

He's still a player, a little voice in my head whispers.

This is the reason I didn't go out with Billy in the first place.

And why I never will.

I've had my fill of players for a lifetime.

4

BILLY

Are you sure you're okay?

When Roxy doesn't respond to my text, I squint harder at my phone, like glaring at it will make her talk to me. Jinxy said he saw her at the party last night, but what the fuck? If she came to our house, why did she leave without saying hi first?

She does this. She clams up when she's upset.

I almost stopped by her apartment this morning to check on her, but then I remembered who I'm dealing with. Roxanne Santos does shit on her timeline. She'll talk to me when she's ready.

This woman is stubborn. It's one of the things I like about her. It also drives me batshit crazy.

I'm morbidly curious how her conversation with Ezra went down. If he was an asshole to her, he and I will have words.

Then again, maybe he had a change of heart and wants to be with her.

My jaw tightens. I hope Roxy doesn't take him back. That pencil dick doesn't deserve her, but I know what women sometimes do for the sake of their children, so nothing would surprise me at this point.

After I jam my phone in my back pocket, I take a deep breath and head inside my house. Second semester starts in two days, and I promised my mom I'd visit. I sure as hell didn't drag myself to Austin to see my father.

He's camped out in the living room with his designer coffee in hand, ESPN on the flatscreen, and the *Wall Street Journal* in his lap.

"Hey."

He barely glances at me. "Nice of you to finally come home."

We haven't spoken in weeks, and that's what he says? "Did you watch the game?" I *did* just play football on national television.

"You missed a pass in the third quarter that you should've intercepted, and you really need to do more footwork drills. You got tangled up with Markowitz more than once."

No mention of my interception, the forty-one-yard return, or the ten tackles.

My hands clench at my side. I know I'm a disappointment to him, but you'd think he'd say something nice for once. I don't know, like maybe "congratulations" or "good game?" I don't have the grades for law school like my two older brothers, and I don't play quarterback like he did in college. That means I don't land on his radar anymore except to criticize.

He finally turns my way. "I spoke to Randolph Klein last week. He said he'd rep you if you got your shit together. I told him you'd be on board if he thought he could get you drafted."

Randolph Klein. As in one of the most sought-after agents in the country?

I can't deny the excitement that zips through me. Fuck yes, I wanna get drafted. I've had to switch positions twice since I became a Bronco, which doesn't help my odds of making it to the NFL.

The guys who go pro have been playing those positions for

years. They didn't just hop over from offense to defense last year like I did. Sure, I had a good game last week, but I need a stellar senior year to really stand out, and with Coach Santos on my ass every two seconds, what are the odds that'll happen?

"Isn't it illegal to verbally commit to an agent?" If I get busted for making a verbal agreement, it'll make me ineligible to play next year. Coach might be an asshole, but he's given us several lectures about this.

My father rolls his eyes. "You do know I'm an attorney, right? What the school doesn't know won't hurt you. Klein says you need to clean up your rep. To cut the parties and the women. Maybe get a nice girlfriend. Someone the media will like. Doesn't mean you can't have some fun on the side. Just don't do it publicly."

Did my father just encourage me to get a girlfriend and cheat on her? What the hell?

Reaching for his coffee, he adds, "And for fuck's sake, don't switch positions again." He says it so nonchalantly, like I have any say in what I play.

But the Broncos have had several coaching turnovers since I've been at Lone Star, and every coach has his own philosophy about how he wants shit done, which usually means I get the short end of the stick.

They say things like, *Babcock, you're versatile and have good hands. Play wide receiver. Babcock, you're big and fast on your feet. We need you on defense.* None of them give a damn that I wanted to stay at quarterback, which is what Coach Sullivan recruited me for. But since he retired, and his replacement, Coach Krud, was a huge asshole, I got screwed.

My father shakes open his *Wall Street Journal* again, and just like that, I'm dismissed.

"Where's Mom?" I ask, knowing how much he hates talking while he's reading up on the stock market.

He shoots me a look of irritation. "Brenda's in the kitchen."

When I turn away, I smile. There's nothing I love more than getting under his skin, but he's a cutthroat bastard, and I'd rather not incite his wrath. So I can't really live up to my full asshole potential with him.

"Billy," he barks behind me. "Figure out your shit. Because once you graduate, I'm done paying for your crap. You're on your own."

He's just pissed I won't go to law school and become one of his minions.

Graduation always seemed so far away. I thought I had time to figure it out, but I guess I don't. I have one more season of eligibility, and then I'm done. Who the hell knows what I'll do if I don't get drafted?

My parents are one of those perfect couples on the outside with expensive cars, an enormous house, and generous bank accounts. But my mother is a functioning alcoholic, and my father is a ruthless litigator who'd rather hang out with his colleagues than spend time at home.

There's no pleasing him, so I stopped trying, which makes me the black sheep of the family.

Unsurprisingly, my mother is camped out at the kitchen table with a mimosa. "Hey, Mom."

Her bloodshot eyes brighten when she sees me, and guilt pinches my chest. I should visit more for her sake. Just because I can't stand my father doesn't mean I don't love my mother. I lean over to kiss her cheek.

Her eyes are swollen like she's been crying. "Goodness. I didn't know you'd be by today." She pats her hair like she's worried it's a mess. My mom is beautiful even though she's wearing a house dress and slippers.

"Sorry. I should've given you a heads-up. Want to head out to grab a bite to eat?"

"Oh, honey. I need to make your dad some lunch. You know how much he hates takeout. He always goes on and on about how bad seed oils are for you."

"Let him make his own damn sandwich. Come on. My treat. Then we can stop by Grandma's because I have some things I need to drop off. Actually," I say, reaching into my backpack, "I have something for you too."

I pull out a calendar and some glossy black and white photos of me playing football that my friend Charlotte took.

"Billy, these pictures are so good!" She presses her hand to her chest. "You look just like your father at his age."

The smile on my face falls. More and more, I'm realizing I don't want to be anything like that asshole.

She flips through the calendar, chuckling when she sees me holding the puppy from the animal rescue. "How sweet. I bet all the girls are crazy about you. Speaking of pretty girls, you're never going to guess who I just saw. Do you remember Samantha Schilling?"

My mom goes on about some girl I went to high school with.

When it comes to women, my head's pretty fucked up these days. I used to be a "party hard and fuck harder" kind of guy. Then my best friend Cam and I got outed by a gossip blog for tag-teaming our dates. It was all true. Cam and I shared women. So what? They were more than willing. But the really fucked-up part was that one of the women we hooked up with posted all that shit on the blog.

I guess you could say it scared us straight, and it made me a lot more selective about my hookups.

For the record, Cam and I never crossed swords. That's always the first question our idiot friends ask. Cam and I aren't like that, but I'm not uptight about it. I shower in a room full of naked dudes. There are dicks swinging everywhere. A body is a body. Cocks don't do it for me, though.

The part that sucked was how Coach Santos flipped out about the blog post. He sat our asses down and reamed us out for a solid hour. You'd think Cam and I had lit Mother Teresa on fire. I've been on Coach's shit list ever since. Cam's more chill than I am, so Coach didn't stay pissed at him for long. Me? I'm another story.

And since Roxy lives for her father's approval, I'm literally the last guy she'd ever date. She'd rather sleep with Ezra Thomas, Lone Star State's biggest fuckboy, than me.

The fact that she's having his kid? Yeah, that gets under my skin, more than I'm comfortable admitting.

When she told me that Ezra had knocked her up? Fuck. It felt like a roundhouse kick to my sternum.

But only two people know she's pregnant, me and Charlotte. That has to mean something, right?

I shouldn't be so wrapped up in this drama, but it's no secret I'm wickedly attracted to Roxy.

Ever since I spotted her flying off the top of that pyramid like some cheerleader goddess at one of our football games last year, I've had a thing for her.

Roxy is a beautiful woman. Like if Gina Rodriguez and Zoe Saldana got spliced into a little sister. That's Rox. Sassy, funny as fuck, and always optimistic. She'll bend over backwards to help anyone. I love that about her. She's my favorite person to hang out with, even more so than the guys on my team, and that's saying something 'cause I love those fuckers.

But I should probably start distancing myself from her because, at the end of the day, nothing good will come from hooking up with Coach's daughter.

And let's be honest—I'm only good for hookups.

When my mom's done flipping through the photos, she stands. "Let me make you some lunch. I'll feed you and your father, and then you and I can drive over to Grandma's."

I toss my backpack on the ground and sit. God forbid the man has to feed himself.

I have no idea why she stays with him. He treats her like his maid, and I have a sneaking suspicion he enjoys the company of his secretaries a little too much.

My parents are the main reason I'll never get married. I have no clue what a healthy relationship looks like. I had a couple of girlfriends in high school, but they were never serious. I'm not sure I can handle serious.

Maybe it's better that Roxy and I will never happen.

Because I'm probably the last thing she needs.

5

BILLY

TWO DAYS LATER, I'm back on campus. I head home to make sure the football house is still standing, drop off my stuff, and head to a team meeting. After I sit my ass down next to Jake Ramirez, I elbow him. "How's my girl?"

He gives me a look. "You mean *my* girl?"

I love giving this guy shit. "Always so sensitive. You do know the only reason you and Chuck are dating now is because I'm such a damn good matchmaker, right?"

"*Charlotte* is great."

My little nickname for his girlfriend gets under his skin. "And the kid?" He has a cute son all the girls in our group are nuts about.

"Asher's great." He finally cracks a smile.

"Just razzing you, dude. You know I got your back. I ain't gonna steal your girl."

"Not that you could."

I lift my eyebrows in challenge, and then we both crack up. As sweet and beautiful as Charlotte is, she's not my type. I need someone who can hold her own with me. Someone with more fire.

Someone more like Roxanne Santos.

The room fills with the team, and I hold out my fist to Cam, who's smiling ear to ear.

"How's your gamer girl?" I ask after he taps me back and sits next to me. He's been talking to this chick he games with for the last several months. They finally met up last week, and he's had dancing stars in his eyes since.

"Kelly's amazing."

I lower my voice. "Gonna share her with me?"

"Fuck you."

Good for him. "Just testing your seriousness."

He covers his jaw with his hand like he's embarrassed. "I'm pretty damn serious."

"Bro." I chuckle.

"I know. It's crazy, but I really like her."

"Cam and Kelly sitting in a tree, f-u-c-k-i-n-g." He gives me a look, and I laugh again. "Kidding. Mostly." The guy's sex drive is as high as mine. They'll be fucking like bunnies in no time. And if they're serious, hearts are gonna break all over campus when the news gets out.

Some white Nikes with a gold stripe along the side come into view. Shit. "Hey, Coach."

Coach Santos gives me a look like he overheard me. Awesome. Just what I need. This guy always walks in on the worst part of my conversations. I tend to have a big mouth.

Whatever. If he wants to find reasons to hate me, there's nothing I can do about it.

He turns to Ezra, who struts in like he's God's gift to college football. "I want to talk to you about some suggestions your agent has."

Ezra has a strange look on his face, like he's bracing himself to get reamed out, but then the turd smiles. "Sure thing, Coach."

Santos pats him on the back. "I hear congratulations are in

order. I got engaged to my girlfriend in college too. Snagging a great woman before everyone comes after you for your bank account is smart."

What the fresh hell? Did Ezra fucking propose to Roxy? Jesus Christ, did she say yes?

My ears fill with white noise like I just got my bell rung on the football field.

Then I come to my senses. Coach would never be this chill about his daughter getting engaged.

Who did Ezra propose to? He's been sleeping his way through sorority row all year. Unless he knocked up one of those girls.

Like he knocked up Roxy.

My nostrils flare when I remember all the shit she's dealing with. This fucking guy.

Ezra has a tight crew of friends who cover for him, half of whom are on the team. It's an even split of those of us who hate him and those who lick his hairy ass. Some guys want to win no matter the cost.

It's no secret that Ezra and I don't gel. That's why I got booted off offense. Because there was no way Coach was gonna oust his golden boy from QB, which meant I went from wide receiver to defensive back. Realistically, that marked the end of any hope I had to return to the quarterback position.

Coach heads to the podium and taps on the mic. Everyone quiets down. He leans forward and asks, "Am I looking at the national champs?"

The guys clap and yell, and I get up and bark like the idiot I am. My teammates and I high-five each other because we put our whole hearts and souls into last season.

Once we settle down, Coach gets down to business. "For those of you declaring for the draft in the spring, I want you to meet with me after this so we can discuss your combine training plan." The combine is a four-day event thrown by the NFL where prospects run drills for scouts and bragging rights. Having a great performance is key to going pro.

Some of the guys slap Ezra on the back because he's going to declare for the draft as a junior.

I'm not bitter.

Who the fuck am I kidding? Of course I'm bitter. This dick got my spot with his slick words and bullshit.

And fine, he's a damn good quarterback. Probably better than me, but since I never really got a shot, it bugs me not knowing if I could've hacked it.

Coach hands some papers to his assistants. "The rest of you will get a calendar for the week. I hope you got the parties out of your system, gentlemen, because doing well this semester is imperative. You all had light semesters in the fall to accommodate our season, but now you'll need to focus on the more challenging classes. Don't underestimate the work required to do well in those courses."

I'm yawning when Coach shoots me a dirty look. Damn, now he thinks I'm commenting on what he's saying when I'm just tired. My grandmother wasn't feeling well this weekend, so I bunked at her place and fixed all the shit that had broken in her house over the last few months.

He continues. "The offseason is not the time to rest on our laurels. Now is the time to defend the title. *Now* is the time to go even harder than we did last fall. *Now* is the time to envision the season you want to have next year. Every college team in the country will be gunning for our spot come September, but I have a dream. It's called domination."

We all howl in approval, and Coach smiles. "I want to do what very few other teams have accomplished—back-to-back titles. In recent years, Alabama did it. So did Georgia and Nebraska. I say this year is our turn." He pauses while everyone claps and stomps in approval. "But the media will tell you that our day in the sun is over. That our season was a fluke. That we're a flash in the pan. That we're losing players to graduation and the best quarterback in college football to the draft and won't have what it takes to repeat."

Coach leans over the podium. "But I have a plan. You haven't heard the news yet, but we managed to snag two excellent quarterbacks next year thanks to the transfer portal." He probably never considered that I'd love to try out for the position. "And I'm also happy to say that my son Deacon Santos will be joining us as well."

That's a surprise. The kid is a star wide receiver at Notre Dame. Weird that Roxy didn't mention it.

After our meeting, we have a light workout. I'm toweling off when my phone dings in my locker. It's Roxy.

My heart speeds up for some reason.

Sorry I'm just now getting back to you! I had a lot to process. Want to come over, and we can grab dinner? I need someone to vent to.

I smile, my chest swelling with a weird kind of pride because she wants me to come over instead of one of her other friends.

Be there in twenty.

6

ROXY

THAT DEVIL SMILES back at me on the TV, and I curse. Why is this man always on ESPN?

"Ezra, how did it feel to cap off your junior year with the biggest game of your college career?"

Ezra gives the reporter his *oh, gosh, are you talking about me?* expression that makes me want to punch him in the face. "I'm just so honored to have played a role in our victory. Coach always tells us to put our best foot forward and envision the possibilities..."

Gag.

"I've heard you're superstitious. What's one pre-game ritual you have?"

He chuckles like this is no big deal, but if you come between Ezra and his pre-game habits, he flips out. He has to eat the same meal. Before *every* game. He even weighs the chicken breast on a scale. He has to wear the same wristband he's had since high school. And God forbid you wake him up even a minute before his game-day alarm goes off.

Ezra smiles and brushes his black hair out of his eyes. "I

don't really do much. Mostly I make sure to say a prayer so I can stay focused."

I change the channel before I hurl. After a few minutes, I settle back and watch *Friends* while I wait for Billy. But by the time he knocks on the door, I'm a hot mess.

When I answer the door, his eyebrows furrow as he looks me over. Before I can say anything, he opens his arms and I rush into them.

"What happened, my little biscuit?" he asks as he squeezes me in a tight hug.

Tears burn my eyes, and I push my face into his chest. "I don't know. One minute I was fine, and the next, this commercial came on about baby food. And the baby was hungry and started to cry, and..."

"And that made you cry."

I nod against him as more tears flow down my face. "I know that sounds crazy, but now everything makes me cry. I want my hard shell back."

He chuckles and kisses the top of my head. "You don't need your hard shell with me. I got you."

Closing my eyes, I take a deep breath and try to calm down. Once I have a hold of my emotions, I step back. "Sorry about that."

He gives me a sweet smile. "No worries, Rox. Come on. Let's go grab some dinner. How does pizza sound?"

My mouth waters at the thought of hot cheese and sauce, but then I realize I probably have smeared makeup on my face since I just smashed it to his body. "Let me go clean up first. I'm sure I look scary."

"Don't do it on my account. I always think you look beautiful."

A tightness wraps around my throat, and I sniffle. "You're not allowed to say anything else that nice to me today unless you want me to cry again."

He chuckles. "Deal. Now get your ass in gear."

That's more like it.

We reach the pizzeria half an hour later. When the hostess finally seats us, we get separated from her because this place is packed. So Billy grabs my hand and takes the lead, easily parting the crowd for us.

I shouldn't like how good it feels to hold his hand. This isn't a date. We always nab dinner together. This is just two friends enjoying a meal.

As I trail behind him, I give in and check him out. His hair is damp from a shower, and he's sporting some dark wash jeans that mold perfectly to his ass. And although he's not wearing cologne, I can still smell the spicy scent on his letterman jacket. I love his cologne. It's doing things to my insides.

People yell out to us, but Billy tightens his hand on mine and waves with the other, never stopping to chitchat, which I appreciate. I'm not in the mood to socialize tonight.

We scoot into a booth in the back and order drinks. When the waitress walks away, he leans back and drops his arm over the back of the booth and watches me. I love his intensity. It's one of the things that really draws me to him, but having it focused on me right now makes me squirm.

I try to hand him a menu, but he shakes his head. "I already know what I want." Our eyes lock, and the way he looks at me makes me feel like *I'm* on the menu. Breaking his stare, I scan the pizza toppings as he slouches back. "Are you excited about your brother?"

I wrinkle my nose. "Deacon?" My younger brother is a wide receiver for Notre Dame, which is my father's alma mater.

"Yeah. You know, since he's transferring to Lone Star."

My head jerks up. "What are you talking about?"

His eyes widen, and he looks away. "Well, this is awkward. Uh, your dad announced that your brother is coming to play for the Broncos."

"Are you serious?" I don't give him a chance to respond before I break out my phone and text Deke. **WTF? Why am I hearing that you're transferring to my school from one of your teammates instead of you?**

When I don't say anything else, Billy ducks his head until our eyes meet. "Sorry, Rox. Didn't mean to drop that on you."

"The people who should be apologizing are in my family."

He frowns. "Why would they keep this from you?"

"Honestly, I don't know. I haven't been home much lately because Dad's been busy with the playoffs. My mom went to Florida for a few days to see her aunt. Deke didn't come home for Christmas, but I didn't think anything about it because my parents said we'd do gifts over spring break so Dad could focus on the team."

Everything about our family revolves around my dad's coaching. I've never resented it before, but I'm starting to now. How difficult would it have been to pick up the damn phone and let me know? Or text me?

Seeing how I won't be on the field cheering anymore, at least Dad will have his mini-me to keep him company during games.

Billy waves a finger around my head. "There's steam coming out of your ears."

"I love my little brother, and he'll be a great addition to the team. It's just..." Being the last to know hurts my feelings.

"I get it."

I'm starting to sweat, so I shove off my coat. "Deke is only ten months younger than me and twice my size. I can't exactly call him my little brother anymore. Do you get along with your brothers?"

"We have nothing in common. One's a lawyer at my dad's firm, and the other one is about to graduate from law school."

"You didn't want to join the family business?"

"You're thinking I'm the last person who should be shaping young minds, and I agree. I picked education because I like history, not because I want to sit in a classroom all day. But I'd rather wax my balls than work for my father."

I bark out a laugh. I can always count on Billy to make me smile.

After the waitress drops off our drinks and takes our order, I decide to get down to business. Enough with this pussyfooting around. It's really not my style, but pregnancy has messed with my head. "I'm sorry I didn't call you after I drove to Ezra's. I had a lot to think about."

"Understandable."

This part is embarrassing. I fiddle with my napkin. "Did you hear he got engaged?"

He nods. "Coach told everyone today."

"I basically crashed his engagement party. His parents were like, 'It's so nice you could come! Ezra said none of his friends could make it!'" I snort. "They're so nice. They have no idea they spawned a monster."

I look down, but I can feel Billy studying me. "Are you doing okay? How did he take your news?"

Hot shame spreads through my chest. "I didn't tell him. His fiancée was right there, and she's so sweet. Get this—Ezra wouldn't let her visit him here. Gee, I wonder why."

"Because he didn't want her ruining his fuck fest on campus." I flinch, hating that I contributed to that. Billy winces. "Sorry, Rox. I don't mean anything by that."

"I am now *well aware* I wasn't the only girl." Lowering my voice, I make sure no one is close enough to hear me. "I'm over Ezra Thomas."

"When do you plan to tell him about the baby?"

I fold in my lips. "This might sound evil, but I got his fiancée's phone number. I made sure to do it right in his face and invited her to come stay with me. I think I want to start dropping hints to him just before I hang out with Abigail."

Billy chuckles. "Savage."

"Short of breaking both his legs, I don't really know how else to make him suffer. The part that sucks is I don't want to hurt Abigail. She seems like a sweet girl."

"Think of it this way. You're doing her a favor by showing her what Ezra's all about. This way she won't waste twenty years of her life and wake up one morning with a raging STD because her hubby banged the wrong side piece."

I take a quick breath. "That could've been me. I feel like I dodged a bullet. And thank God, I got a clear bill of health from the clinic last month."

"Why don't you tell your dad? Coach would rip off Ezra's balls and shove them down his throat."

"And land himself in a maximum-security prison."

"Just make sure you tell him at home so he has time to calm down. Your dad is smart. Give him some credit. He loves you. Let him take care of this for you."

"Maybe you're right." Emotion makes my throat tight, and I wave a hand in front of my face to keep the tears at bay. "To be clear, I'm upset right now because I was dumb enough to buy into Ezra's bullshit, not because I have feelings for him. That man is dead to me. I just don't know how I'm supposed to navigate the next eighteen years by myself. Honestly, I'm terrified."

He nods slowly. "It's okay to be overwhelmed." Reaching across the table, he takes my hand in his giant paw. "I know you're afraid to tell your parents, but they've got your back. Your dad might hate me, but you're his pride and joy."

I question whether my dad will feel that way after I tell him I got knocked up by one of his players.

Billy squeezes my hand. "You've got me and Charlotte and Jake. Hell, my whole household will be there for you and your baby. And what about your roommates?"

"Debbie made them take me in after the fire." Charlotte and I briefly lived together before our apartment went up in flames last fall due to our negligent neighbors. When my squad coach Debbie encouraged me to move in with some of the cheer girls, she was only trying to help. But my current living situation isn't the best. "The girls are nice, but I competed against them for the last year and a half. And..."

"And you always won, so now they're butthurt."

I nod. We might be a team, but there's a lot of individual competition that goes on to make mat for certain events. "Plus, I got a spot because I was basically a package deal with my dad. He worked it into his contract because he knew I'd go wherever he and my mom moved. So Lone Star had to make a place for me on the squad. I sent in my tapes, so they didn't exactly accept me blind, but I didn't really understand what bypassing the official tryouts would mean for the camaraderie on the squad until some of the girls started throwing me shade." I groan, hating the drama.

"But you tried out for Indiana, right?"

"Yeah. I made that all on my own as an incoming freshman, which is why Lone Star agreed to the terms. My dad was already coaching at Indiana when I tried out there, but he said if I wanted to cheer at a collegiate level, I had to have what it takes. He said he wasn't going to pull any strings. With the transfer here, though, he said I had already proven myself by making the Indiana squad. I don't think he liked the idea of leaving me behind."

Billy's lips tilt up. "Your dad's protective of you. I'd be the same way if I had a daughter."

That statement makes me pause.

Billy with a daughter? The image of him holding a baby girl makes me weak-kneed.

Focus, Roxy. Even if Billy was into relationships, you don't have time for anything but the baby you're gestating.

"So yeah. I'm not close to my roommates. It's tough being a transfer. It was so much easier to make friends as a freshman at Indiana, but I wanted to go wherever my dad coached. You know how much I love football. Can you imagine me cheering for a team after my dad had just left the head coaching position?"

"Not really."

"It broke my heart when he said he got the job down here. As much as I love the Broncos and the school spirit here, uprooting your life sucks. We moved my entire childhood for his teams. First when he was in the pros and then coaching. I was so ready to settle down somewhere, and I thought I'd get that chance in college. I was good friends with the girls on my old squad, but I don't have the same camaraderie here. And maybe that's why I went a little off the reservation when I transferred."

It's embarrassing to admit, but my dad put me on lockdown for a while over the summer to "settle down" and stop partying.

The waitress brings our food, and we chow down for a few minutes. I'm mid-bite when Billy pushes his plate back. "What do you need from me? I can help."

My eyes sting, and I slowly chew, overwhelmed. It chokes me up to ask this favor. "You can say no."

"I won't."

I give him a wobbly smile. "Could you take me to my doctor appointment next week? I'm anxious about going by myself. Charlotte has a meeting with her counselor that she can't reschedule, or she would take me. She already tried, and I'm—"

"Done. What day and time?"

7

ROXY

RAIN PELTS THE WINDOW, and I take in Charming as Billy drives me to my appointment.

The cobblestone streets are slick and glisten in the early morning sun that peeks out from behind the clouds. The holiday lights are still up and wrap around the great oaks along Main Street.

Charming is so quaint. I love the postcard-pretty downtown area with its vintage storefronts and historic buildings. Even though Lone Star is an enormous school, there's still a small-town feel. The baristas at the Rise 'N Grind know my name and order. Sometimes, when I miss my friends in Indiana, I grab a coffee or chai tea there. I like talking to the staff and curling up with a book. It makes me less homesick. Not that I lived in Indiana that long, just a few years, but of all the places we've resided, that felt the most like home.

"So what did your brother say about not telling you he was transferring to Lone Star?"

"He thought my parents would tell me. Which, yeah, I get that. But they're in their own little world right now. My dad's still on some post-game high, and my mom just got back from a trip.

I asked if I could come over last weekend, and they said no because they wanted 'time to reconnect.' They're probably making out all over the house. Gross."

Billy chuckles. "It's great that your parents are still into each other. I have a hard time thinking mine ever liked each other, much less loved one another."

I guess I'm lucky that my parents are still in love. But I can't think about them without feeling nauseated. Because they're going to flip out when I tell them I'm pregnant.

All of a sudden, I feel Billy's palm on my knee and realize I've been jiggling it.

"Everything will be okay," he says as he returns his attention to the road.

"It's my first OB-GYN appointment."

"Any idea when you're due?"

"This summer. Probably late July? Pregnancy calendars are weird. You can figure it out from the date you did the deed or from your last period. I'm not sure which is more exact." I laugh awkwardly. "Sorry. You probably don't want to hear about periods."

He shrugs. "If a guy can stick his dick in a pussy, he should be able to deal with periods. It's part of life."

Billy always has a very blunt way of saying things. He cracks me up. I just wish my father found him humorous. "That's a very mature outlook." He clears his throat, but doesn't say anything. "What?"

"How'd you know I was gonna say something?"

"Because you always have something to say."

Chuckling, he nods. Then goes quiet. "Just wondering when you were gonna tell me you stopped by the football house during karaoke. You know, after you went to Ezra's." He side-eyes me. "Why didn't you say hi?"

Heat crawls up my neck. "Jinxy told you."

"Let me guess. You didn't like my singing."

"You have a great voice. I love how you work the crowd." *And you looked* really *sexy doing it.*

"But?"

I nibble my bottom lip, debating what to say. God, this is embarrassing. "Don't make an issue of this, okay? I'm not myself right now."

"Just spit it out. I can take it."

Taking a deep breath, I turn my head to stare out the window. "Watching you sing and flirt with Vicky was hard to watch."

He's quiet for a long stretch, and I brave a glance at him. His brow is pinched. "I told you we're just friends. I meant that. She didn't come upstairs with me that night." I give him a look, and he chuckles. "And we didn't do anything in one of the downstairs bathrooms or hot tub either. I went to bed by myself. Scout's honor."

"You were never a Boy Scout."

"True. But I haven't gone there with Vicky in a while."

"Since homecoming." *Jesus, Roxanne. You sound like a stalker. Why are you bringing this up? Drop it already. That was over two months ago.* Billy looks really focused on driving all of a sudden, and my heart sinks with that confirmation. I try to play it off. "It's okay. You're a twenty-year-old dude who likes to fuck. I get it. But you wanted to know why I left? That's why. I know you and I are just friends, and that's really all I can handle right now anyway. I have no claim over you, Billy. Go fuck around and play the field. I just don't want to know about it."

I have no room to be critical of this man. If Ezra hadn't been such an asshole that week, I would've gone to homecoming with him, and we definitely would've had sex.

This conversation is freaking me out. I'm the last person who should be angling for a relationship with Billy while I'm pregnant with Ezra's kid. *My life is so screwed up right now*, I think as my heart hammers in my chest and sweat breaks out under my arms. I'm jittery all of a sudden, like I have low blood sugar.

Having Billy bring me to my appointment was a mistake.

He pulls up to the medical complex, and I gather my bag. "Thanks for the ride. You can just drop me off. I'll call an Uber home."

Ignoring me, he parks. I reach for the door handle, but he puts a hand on my elbow. "Can you give me a minute?"

"I don't know why I said all that crap. Just ignore me, okay? I'm hormonal and hungry. I can't explain why else I feel possessive about you. I have no right to feel that way."

Finally, I brave a look at him. His blue eyes are dark and positively feral. I suck in a breath as he reaches for me and crashes my mouth to his.

The first swipe of his tongue against mine shoots an electric current through my entire body like I've been struck with a live wire. Every part of me comes alive under his touch.

I jam my fingers in his thick hair and bite his bottom lip. He groans and yanks me into his lap, where his enormous bulge presses into my thigh. His huge hands cup my face as he controls the kiss.

I've never felt anything like this before. It's cataclysmic. Like the planet has stopped moving, and his kiss has redirected the tides.

His lips are firm but soft, and my heart melts as he dips his head to my neck where he nibbles on my skin. "Roxy Santos, you make me fucking crazy."

I laugh, but then he sucks on my throat, and it turns into a moan. "You'd better stop. My doctor will be able to tell I'm turned on."

His head pops up, and he lifts an eyebrow. "Really? You're

wet?" He looks like he wants to tear the clothes from my body to check.

"Yes, I'm wet." Like, embarrassingly so. "Are you happy now?"

He laughs and kisses me again. "I am rather pleased with myself, if you must know. And grateful there's no center console in my ancient Ford Bronco."

I won't deny how good it feels to be wrapped in his arms. "We can't do this, Billy. As much as I like you and as much as I'm attracted to you, I have so much going on right now. But I really can't handle seeing you date other people. I know that's not fair. So if you're banging someone, please don't tell me about it."

His eyes go soft as he runs his thumb along my jaw. "What if we took this slow? Like, sex is off the table for a while, but we hang out."

I smile. "We already hang out."

"This would be different. We could hang out with the *intention* of having sex at some point. I mean, no pressure. But I like you, and I definitely wanna fuck you."

I cover his mouth before he says anything else obnoxious. "So you mean we should date? Old school-style where we wait a while before we get naked?"

He plays with a lock of my hair. Runs it through his fingers. "Yeah. Like that."

"And we wouldn't see other people?" Mostly, I mean him. Because who the hell is going to date the pregnant cheerleader?

"We'd go full-on monogamy."

"Even if it means extending your no-sex streak? Assuming that's still intact." My stomach flips at the thought of him being with other women.

"It's still intact." His expression turns playful, and he winks. "For now."

The relief that hits me is so strong, I press my hand to my belly.

I'm tempted to say yes, but I still have questions. "What's the longest you've ever gone without getting laid?"

"You question my ability to stay on the straight and narrow?"

"Pretty much."

"One, I would never cheat. Sometimes I think my dad cheats on my mom, and I would never do that to anyone. Two, if you're the prize at the end of the road, I can wait. And three, you underestimate the power of my left hand. As I've mentioned, I'm well versed in jerking off."

I brush his hair out of his brilliant blue eyes. "This sounds messy."

"Hopefully, it will be. I plan to lick you all over and slurp you up. And then maybe come on your tits, if you must know." My mouth drops open with lust as that image takes over my brain. He laughs. "I can see you like this plan."

Cradling his rugged jaw in my hands, I kiss him. "Are you sure you want to deal with my baggage? At some point, I'm going to have to tell Ezra I'm pregnant. You two are contentious enough as it is. And my dad is going to bust an artery when he finds out we're dating on top of everything else. You have your senior year of football and the draft to worry about, and I know how intense that is. Maybe you should count the cost before you give me an answer and take some time to think about it."

He levels me with one of those dangerously sexy smiles. "I already know my answer. The question is, what's *yours*?"

For his sake, I should say no.

For my sake, I'm dying to say yes.

But I go with the safe answer. "Let me think about it."

8

BILLY

GRUNTING, I place the weights on the rack. Out of the corner of my eye, I spot Ezra joking with his friends by the treadmills.

Cam motions to me. "You have murder in your eyes, bro."

"Pretty much what I was fantasizing about just now, but I'm trying to avoid jail time before the draft."

Laughing, he nods. "Solid decision." He lowers his voice. "How did Roxy's appointment go?" Cam is the only one of our friends besides Charlotte and Jake who knows Rox is pregnant.

A smile erupts on my face. "It was crazy. She had the nurse call me into her exam room at the end to see the ultrasound. I got to hear the heartbeat. It was just whirring away." I hold my hand over my chest because that moment will go down as one of the coolest in my life. "She's due in August."

"Girl or boy?"

"Too early to tell. It looks like a bean, though." I hold my fingers apart by a centimeter. "Like this big."

"Y'all gonna make it official or keep pretending you're just friends?"

"We're definitely not 'just friends,' and I think she's starting to figure it out."

He smacks me on the back. "Happy for you." His eyes travel across the room to Ezra, but his voice lowers to a whisper. "You're obviously a better candidate than that jackass."

Frankly, I think so too.

I never told him Ezra is the father, but Cam's pretty damn perceptive. When he heads to the locker room, I reach for my water bottle.

Jinxy pops up next to me out of nowhere, his eyes wide. "Roxy's pregnant?"

Water almost shoots out my nose. "Lower your fucking voice," I growl as I glance around to make sure no one else is around. Jesus, where the hell did Jinxy come from? I would've sworn Cam and I were alone on this side of the weight room. "Forget you heard anything."

"I swear on my PlayStation."

He crosses himself, and I smack his hand away. "The condition isn't contagious. You don't have to ward it off like a vampire."

Jinxy laughs. "Says you. I'd rather run through campus naked than knock up some girl."

"First off, Rox is not just 'some girl.'"

A guilty look crosses his face. "Yeah, yeah. I know. Sorry."

"Second, she's pregnant. She's not infected by zombies. Third, it's a baby. Women have them every day. It's not the end of the world."

His eyebrows lift. "Have you ever been around babies?"

Not much except for my former teammate's twins. Olly's girlfriend had them last winter. I babysat a few times since I sublet a room in her house, but the boys usually just slept. It wasn't a big deal. I could probably handle one small child on my own. How hard could it be? Olly's boys Levi and Jude are great. And Jake's three-year-old son Asher is awesome. Really, I don't know why people freak out when someone gets pregnant.

Jinxy points at me. "Babies smell, they vomit, they shit everywhere. They cry at all hours of the day and night. They're like wild animals that never stop pooping. No offense, Daddy, but I'll pass."

Daddy. The word gives me pause.

Does Jinxy think I'm the father? I almost laugh. But the paternity of Roxy's child isn't my news to share, so I wrap my arm around his shoulders and glare at him like he's an opponent on the line of scrimmage. "Say a fucking word to anyone, and I'll piss in your Gatorades at home, the ones you leave everywhere half empty but still drink randomly."

He shivers comically and shakes his head. "I swear, my lips are sealed. I'm a vault."

We'll see about that.

After I let him go, he scratches the back of his head. "Serious question, man. How are you gonna juggle everything? School, the baby, football. It's a lot. And Coach is gonna go ape shit when you tell him. Although that might solve your problem."

"What do you mean?"

"He'll kick you off the team, and then you'll have plenty of time for a kid."

Out of the corner of my eye, I catch Coach Santos down the hall, talking to one of the trainers. As usual, he's frowning. The man will definitely lose his marbles when he finds out Roxy got knocked up. Good thing the hot seat belongs to Ezra, king of the douchebags. And while I hate the idea of Roxy catching heat from her father, I can't fucking wait for Coach to find out the truth about his precious quarterback.

Too bad Ezra's declaring for the draft. He's due some retribution from Coach. If he was sticking around another year and Coach got wind of what Ezra did, there would be hell to pay.

9

ROXY

"ROX, LOOK AT THIS ONE." Charlotte holds up the cutest onesie I've ever seen. It has a football stitched into the blue fabric and a number one on the back.

I sigh dreamily. Retail therapy always makes me feel better. Too bad I can't afford to buy anything. "I hope it's a boy. My dad will give me grief about being pregnant, but I'm pretty sure he'll suck it up if I have a boy."

She gives me a sympathetic smile. "Don't you think he'll love your baby, regardless of the sex?"

"He'll be more excited about the prospect of teaching his grandson the ins and outs of throwing the perfect spiral pass. Trust me, he'll want a boy."

Asher's bushy head pops up between us. "Imma boy!" He points at himself, and we laugh.

"Yes, you are, handsome." I hold out my hand, and he takes it before he grabs Charlotte's.

We swing him between us as we stroll through Target. We drove to the farther one to avoid anyone from school.

I pause in front of the cribs. "Ugh, I've been fantasizing about a Pinterest-worthy nursery, but I can't even afford cheap furniture." If I want to have any hope of having my parents respect my decision to have this baby sans father, I can't go crying to them about money.

"Don't stress. We'll have a baby shower, and I bet we can get all of your essentials. Are you sure you don't want to start scanning items for your registry?"

"I don't want to jinx myself. It's still early. Let's wait a bit." As much as this pregnancy is flipping my life upside down, I suddenly feel fiercely protective of this baby. I get the mama bear references now.

I'm also one hundred percent fine if Ezra flies off to whatever team that drafts him. I don't need a man to raise a kid. I've always been a self-sufficient girl. I'll figure it out.

I've been debating how to tell Abigail that her fiancé is a manwhore. She texted me yesterday and told me how happy she was to meet one of Ezra's friends. It made me feel so guilty. When she finds out I'm pregnant with his baby, it'll devastate her. I barely know the girl, but I don't take any pleasure in ruining her life.

I stop in front of the breast pumps and nearly fall to the floor from the price tags. Do I even need a pump if I breastfeed? God, I know nothing.

Charlotte nudges me with her elbow. "You never told me how your appointment went. Billy took you, right?" Now there's a topic that's more exciting than breast pumps. I bite my bottom lip to keep from smiling, and she laughs. "You should see your face right now."

We turn the corner and enter the toy section. I wait until Asher is busy ogling the toy cars on a shelf before I whisper, "Billy kissed me."

Her eyes bug out. "Oh my God. Tell me everything! How was it?"

"Earth-shattering." That's no joke. I've kissed a few boys, and

Billy is, hands down, the best kisser I've ever locked lips with. There was something so thrilling in the way he pulled me into his lap and kissed me breathless.

"So are y'all dating? You know how much Billy likes you. I've always thought he took me out on that 'blind date' last fall because he wanted to make you happy."

"He wants to date and offered to take things slow, but I'm worried he doesn't fully comprehend what he's agreeing to. I'm a package deal here." I wave at my belly that's still fairly flat.

She tilts her head and hums. "Billy strikes me as a guy who goes after what he wants, and he wants you. Maybe the baby thing really doesn't bother him."

"But it's Ezra's," I whisper. She already knows who my baby daddy is, but I feel the need to emphasize this point. "How could this not bother him? They *hate* each other. I feel like I'm just welcoming unnecessary drama if I date Billy."

"I see your point. But Billy is such a good guy, and I'd love to see you date someone who really appreciated you. Are you afraid he won't be able to commit?"

Charlotte is one of my few friends who loves Billy. He helped her reconnect with Jake last fall, and now she's his biggest fan. But she knows what I went through with Ezra and why I might be hesitant to jump into anything else.

I wait until a customer wheels his cart out of the aisle before my shoulders slump. "Billy promised we could be monogamous and everything, but I've heard that before. Ezra made all kinds of promises, and he broke each and every one. What if... what if I'm just handing off one heartbreaker for another?"

She loops her arm through mine. "A very valid concern. Has Billy ever seriously dated anyone?"

"Not that I know of."

"He just plays the field, right? All casual? Maybe some friends with benefits but no one serious."

"Right."

"That's why I know you're different."

"What do you mean?"

She scoops Asher up and puts him in the front of the cart with a toy. "Because Billy tells it like it is. If he just wanted to bone, he'd tell you that. He has no qualms about mincing words. In a way, that's refreshing because you always know where you stand with him. And I seriously doubt he made any promises to other girls. As I understand it, his paramours always know that he keeps things casual."

"Paramours?" I chuckle.

She holds her hands over Ash's ears and whispers, "Fine. Lovers. Fuck buddies. Whatever. The party girls he hangs out with. But you're different. You're the only one he dotes on."

"He dotes on me?"

She rolls her eyes and playfully nudges me. "As if you don't know."

"I kind of know, but it's nice to hear." We head to the checkout, and I finally come clean. "I told him I was jealous of him and Vicky singing karaoke. And that if he was out hooking up, with her or other people, that I didn't want to know about it. I one hundred percent blamed it on hormones."

Her eyes widen. "How'd he take that?"

"He pulled me into his lap and kissed me until I forgot my name and was so horny, I wanted to explode."

She chokes with a laugh, glances around, and covers Asher's ears again. "Maybe you should take advantage of the fact you're already pregnant? Go have wild monkey sex with him. Work off some of that stress. And who could blame you if you end up dating as a result?"

I give my friend a long look. "I feel like I've rubbed off on you in the last semester."

She nods. "You've definitely rubbed off. I never would've

moved in with Jake if it wasn't for you. And I highly recommend the wild monkey sex." Her face flames, but she chuckles and squishes me in a hug.

"I'm so happy for you guys."

"I am too. Please keep your fingers crossed for Jake. He's meeting with a big agent on Monday. Jake really wants this guy because he's repped a few single dads for the draft."

"Well, Jake ain't so single these days, is he?"

She laughs. "You know what I mean. Someone who's not with his baby mama."

Jake's baby mama, Charlotte's psycho older sister, is a total nut job. I'm glad he got away from that woman. "I know what you mean." I hold up my crossed fingers. "Jake's going to lock down that agent. He had a killer season, and everyone raves about what a hard worker he is."

Charlotte beams a proud smile. "I've been a nervous wreck. But enough about me. When are you going to let me take photos of you and your baby bump?"

I rub my belly and smile. There's no bump. Not yet. And even though I'm terrified, I'm also excited. "I want to wait until I'm showing more, but I would love to take pics."

And before I book a pregnancy photo sesh, I should probably tell my parents first.

The thought of that makes my stomach drop.

10

BILLY

WHEN ROXY EXPLAINED she wanted to think about us dating, I figured she needed a day or two, but she said she wanted us to take a full week to really consider things.

I just hope she's not bailing.

That would suck. I don't know how she can deny our chemistry. It's off the damn charts. I've been living off of our short make-out session in my car before her doctor appointment, but I'd really like to see her. Maybe take her to lunch or buy her some decaffeinated coffee.

That's how I know I have it bad. I've never once wanted to take a woman out for coffee, but Cam said he met Kelly for coffee on their first date. Then they went for dinner and ice cream. That sounded kinda nice. Sweet. Fucking wholesome, you know? Something I want to do with Rox.

But first we have to get through this stupid week to "count the cost."

Personally, I don't know why we can't just dive in and see how things play out. We're already good friends. We know we have insane chemistry. We enjoy spending time together. Why can't we do that naked? It's not like I can knock her up again.

After I take a quick shower, I'm about to pass out when my phone rings. I hope that's Roxy.

When I see the name on the caller ID, disappointment washes over me. It's Jake.

"What's up, man?" I ask as I toss off my towel and reach for some boxer briefs.

"I need a favor."

The man never asks for favors. He's a fucking island of stoic self-sufficiency. "Okay…" I say hesitantly.

"I need someone to watch Asher."

"And you thought I was the best candidate to babysit?"

"No. Not at all." He chuckles. "But I need to drive to Dallas to meet with an agent first thing in the morning, and Charlotte's sick. She has a stomach thing, and it would suck for her to have to watch Asher when she isn't feeling well. I need to take off tonight, but I should be back by noon tomorrow. Can I drop him off with you? I'd say you could just come over here, but Charlie's still puking. I think she had a bad corn dog or something."

"Yeah, I don't wanna go over there. You're sure Asher's not sick?"

"He's not sick."

Hell, why not? It's just one night. "Why don't you drop off the little dude? I'll watch him." This is the perfect time to prove that I have what it takes to date a soon-to-be single mom.

But a few hours later, when Ash leans over the toilet and hurls for the fifth time, I start to wonder if I'm cut out for this.

"I want Daddy," he cries. His lower lip is all quivery, and his eyes are bloodshot.

I take a towel and wipe his face. "Sorry, bud. He'll be back tomorrow. How about we wash out your mouth, and I'll change your sheets." Again. He was sleeping on the small couch in my bedroom when he flew into *Exorcist* mode and spewed chunks everywhere.

"My tummy hurrrts." Ash stomps on the floor, pissed. I'm pissed for him too. Poor guy.

"Let's go see if we have a ginger ale or Sprite or something bubbly. Then we can watch a movie." We have ten thousand channels. Surely, there has to be something the kid will enjoy.

That seems to brighten him up a little. I carry him downstairs, where we rummage around in the kitchen. "How about some crackers?" I ask. He shrugs. "We could add some jam."

His lips twist, like he's deep in thought, and then he nods.

I make a picnic in the living room with crackers, jelly, some bananas, and Sprite.

We're midway through *The Lion King* when I realize that giving a kid with a stomach bug some crackers with jam is a terrible idea.

"Oh shit." Cam and Kelly walk in just as Ash pukes all over me.

Oh shit is right. I look like a fucking crime scene with regurgitated raspberry jam splattered all over my white t-shirt.

Maybe I'm not cut out for kids after all, I think just before the smell of the vomit makes my dinner come up.

11

ROXY

WHEN I REACH the gymnastics room, I close my eyes and take a deep breath. I love how this room smells. Like sweat and mats with the faint hint of chalk we use so our hands aren't slippery.

You wouldn't think that scent would be appealing, but I love it. I grew up doing gymnastics and wanted to be the next Simone Biles or Laurie Hernandez, but that meant leaving my parents and relocating to a camp that trains Olympic hopefuls. I loved my parents and my dad's football teams too much to take that route. Cheerleading was the next best thing.

And now that dream is over, one year before I thought it would be.

I've been putting off clearing out my locker, but someone needs it, and I'm hogging up the space. I head to our locker room and jam everything into a tote bag before I return to the gym.

The squad is practicing a routine, and my heart aches at not being a part of it. I know every move like the back of my hand since I helped with some of the choreography.

Paige, the cheerleader replacing me at the top of the pyramid, hikes her leg up to her ear, but over-arches. The girls below her brace themselves. It's not enough to offset Paige's movement above them. I watch it happen in slow motion. The second tier gets wobbly, and Paige tumbles off. Fortunately, our male cheerleaders are awesome and catch her, but another girl, Carla, hits the mat hard.

I rush over to check on her. "Are you okay?"

Carla rubs her hip as we help her up. "We'd be better if you hadn't bailed."

My eyes widen. Every part of me wants to confess why I had to quit, but I have to talk to my parents first.

Paige shoots her a dirty look and limps off in a huff.

"Roxy." I turn to see Debbie, our coach, standing in the doorway of her office. "Can I have a word?"

As soon as I head toward her, everyone on the squad starts whispering behind me, and my ears burn. I stand straighter and take my time. I refuse to be ashamed. It's not like I got kicked off the team.

"Hey, Coach. What's up?" I ask when I duck into her office.

She gives me a sympathetic smile and motions toward the door. "Can you close that behind you?"

Okay, now she's scaring me.

I sit in front of her desk feeling like I got called to the principal's office. "I just stopped by to grab my stuff. That locker is empty now for whoever needs it."

She nods. "Thanks. Appreciate that. Listen, I was wondering if you've spoken to your father yet."

My face flames, and I shake my head. "No. I, uh, I was hoping to talk to my ex first..." Okay, Ezra isn't exactly my ex, except I feel weird giving my coach the details. "But that conversation didn't happen."

She folds her hands in front of her. "The reason I ask is because I got a call from the financial aid office. You're here on a scholarship for cheer, but now that you're not doing it..."

I close my eyes when I connect the dots. "My tuition isn't covered."

"Right."

"Damn." Flustered, I bite my lip so hard, it's probably going to bleed. "But I thought Lone Star covers tuition for students whose parents are faculty."

"It does, but that has to be determined in the summer, and you're dropping your sport mid-year."

I have a small savings account compliments of my grandmother, who sold her restaurant before she retired and split the proceeds between me and my brother. It's been keeping me afloat so I don't have to rely on my parents. After I got in trouble last spring for partying too hard, one of my father's stipulations was that I had to buckle down with my classes and pay my own way using that money. Because he felt like I was wasting my time here by not taking school seriously.

Debbie leans forward. "Look on the bright side. I'm sure the school will cover costs next year if you let the bursar's office know what's going on with you. But you might have to pay for this semester's tuition."

My dad's going to strangle me. He's big on covering your nut as you go and not over-extending yourself financially. He'll just view this as another screw-up on my part.

"Rox, didn't he notice that you didn't do any tumbling or stunts at the national championship game? Hasn't he noticed that you're not practicing with us anymore? Or gearing up for competitions this spring?"

"I don't live with him, and frankly, his head is all wrapped up with football."

"What about your mom? Can you talk to her about what you're going through?"

My eyes sting, and I blink and try to keep the tears at bay. "If

I tell her, she'll tell my father, and then they'll both be disappointed in me."

"Aww, honey." Debbie gets up and comes around to hug me. "This is just a bump in the road. They might not be happy with your decisions, but I'm pretty sure they won't love you any less. You're not the first young woman to get pregnant in college."

"I always feel like a disappointment to them, and this will only prove to them that I'm irresponsible."

She reaches for a box of tissues and hands them to me. "Would it help if I went to talk to your dad with you?"

"No. I need to do it by myself." If there's one person I want with me to have that conversation, it's Billy. I always feel stronger when I'm with him, but it would be unfair of me to drag him into my drama. It would only make my dad hate him more.

Tears fall faster as the truth of this situation really hits me. As much as I'm attracted to Billy and as much as I enjoy spending time with him, dating me would be disastrous for his football career.

And I won't do that to him.

When Debbie sits behind her desk again, she folds her hands. "I might have a way you could stay involved with the squad. It won't solve your financial aid issues, but I know you must miss this."

That gets my attention. I nod because I'd do anything to help. "What do you need?"

"Paige could really use some one-on-one tutoring. We have nationals coming up in a few weeks, and she isn't ready. You used to train high school kids over the summer, and you did such a great job helping with our choreography. I thought you'd be the perfect person to help Paige get her confidence."

A smile tilts my lips as I sniffle. "I'd love to help."

12

BILLY

"SORRY, MAN," Jake says to me as he picks up his son. "You okay, Ash? Did Uncle Billy take good care of you?"

Asher jams his thumb in his mouth and nods.

"I gave him some stomach medicine, the pink stuff, but he threw that up too." I scrub my hand down my face, exhausted. "The hurling finally stopped around five this morning."

"I owe you."

"It's okay. Ash was a trooper." I hold out my knuckles to the kid, and he pulls his thumb out of his mouth long enough to bump me back. "Hope you feel better, buddy." I look at Jake. "How'd your meeting go? The guy gonna lock you down?"

Jake's serious demeanor breaks, and he gives me a wide smile. "I got myself an agent. A good one too."

"Awesome. Happy for you, dude." Jake's been through the wringer in college, and I'm glad his hard work is paying off.

After they leave, I collapse on the couch. I have no idea how I'm supposed to work out today, but I have to get to the gym by one. Somehow I manage to drag my ass to the shower, where I catch another whiff of puke and almost lose it again. I debate skipping conditioning today, but if I call in, I'll just give Santos another reason to think I'm a slacker.

Where's my phone anyway? I search my room, high and low, and finally find it under a pillow.

I frown when I realize I have missed calls from Roxy. I'm about to buzz her back when I get a call from R. Klein.

Who the hell is that?

Hold up. Is this Randolph Klein, that agent my father mentioned?

I juggle my cell in my hands and almost drop it before I manage to calm the fuck down. "Hello?"

"Billy Babcock?"

"Yes." I clear my throat because I'm afraid my voice will crack like I just hit puberty. "Speaking."

"This is Randolph Klein from Endzone."

Endzone Elite is one of the best management companies in the country.

Be chill. Be. Chill. "Hey there. How's it going?"

"Your dad wanted me to call you to give you some pointers for the offseason and help you have a shot at the draft next year."

I'm almost afraid to ask, but the curiosity is killing me. "He mentioned that you two had spoken. How do you know each other?"

Silence. Then Klein sniffs. "Let's just say I owe him a favor."

Since he doesn't just come right out and say my father handled his divorce, I'm guessing maybe my father agreed *not* to represent Klein's wife.

"You had a decent season, Billy. Some great defensive plays and solid stats."

"Thanks, man."

"But that's not enough to get drafted. Especially with your history."

What the fuck does that mean? "Sorry? What do you mean by my 'history?'"

"You have a reputation for partying and women. Combine that with being difficult to coach, and—"

"Whoa. Stop right there. I'm a fucking slave to my coaches, even when they've sucked ass. And if you've been watching the Broncos for the last three years, you'll know we've been through a lot of bullshit. First, I got recruited by Coach Sullivan, who retired. His replacement my freshman year, Krugman, was a degenerate who was fired mid-season and is facing federal charges for accepting bribes. His replacement, Nicholson, accepted another offer after only half a season, and now we have Santos."

"And what's the problem with Santos? Why the beef between you two?"

I frown. "Why do you think we have a beef?" I mean, we do, but why the hell does Klein think this? I don't exactly advertise that I hate my coach. During game days, I'm on my best behavior, and at practice, I bust my ass. Isn't that enough?

He pauses. "You do know coaches talk, right?" Santos talks shit about me? "And even if they didn't, I have two eyes in my head. I watch all of the interactions on the sidelines during games. I've watched him yell at you and wave you away. I've watched him ignore you when you try to talk to him. I've watched the smile drop off his face when you interact. You never get any pats on the back, even when you have a great play, and he scowls when your name is mentioned by the press."

I'm a grown-ass man. I never cry, not even when I broke my hand in junior high from a bad tackle. But Klein's words choke me up a little. Not gonna lie—I feel betrayed. I leave my heart and soul on the field every fucking day, and the whole world apparently thinks my coach hates me.

I clear my throat. "I'll admit Coach Santos isn't my biggest fan, but I do everything he asks me to do in practice. His dislike of me is more personal in nature than professional. I'm a workhorse on the field. Ask any of my teammates." *Except Ezra Thomas. Don't ask him.*

"So what's the story? Why doesn't Santos like you?" When I don't say anything, Klein sighs. "If you want a glimmer of hope that I'll represent you next year, I need you to be honest with me. Think of me like your attorney. This shit stays between us. Your coach might blab, but I don't. I'll never badmouth you."

Fuck it. What do I have to lose? "Do you remember that blog, the Lone Star Stud Report? It listed out everyone's personal shit. Football players' girlfriends, hookups, parties, you name it."

"I remember your hashtag." Jesus Christ, that hashtag. You'd think I'd be flattered, but no one really wants to be nicknamed #Bigcock. "I also remember you being in the middle of that pool orgy."

Wincing, I rub the back of my neck. "No one had sex in the pool." I don't think. "It was mostly skinny-dipping." Did people hook up afterward? I mean, I definitely did, but that's par for the course. None of us are celibate. Except for my dry spell these last few months, but Klein doesn't want to hear about how I'm all hung up on a sexy little cheerleader. "Coach somehow thought I was responsible for the festivities, which was unfair. I'm the one who laid out a fishbowl of condoms. I encouraged safe sex. But ever since then, he thinks I'm out fucking prostitutes two at a time and snorting coke or some shit. For the record, I'm not."

Klein laughs darkly. "Listen to yourself. You sound like a raging hormone. If I'm being honest, you have a lot going against you. You party too hard, you fuck anything with two legs..." Not an accurate description of my sex life—I'm definitely discerning—but when I start to interrupt, he tells me to shut the fuck up. "Billy, you're your own worst enemy. If you want to get drafted, you need to take this seriously. I don't want to see any more photos of your face between women's bare tits."

Okay, yeah, that wasn't my best moment. I want to tell him that I'm not being a shithead anymore, that I'm over my fucking around phase, but he doesn't give me a chance.

"Get yourself a nice girlfriend." Roxy immediately comes to mind. "Someone homely." Uh, Roxy is *not* homely. "Be seen around campus going on quiet dates." Exactly what I want to do with her. "No more goddamn parties. No more random women." I can handle that, but his next words make me freeze. "And for fuck's sake, don't get anyone knocked up because your reputation definitely can't handle that."

Shit. If I date Roxy, people will assume the kid is mine. Jinxy did.

When we get off the phone, my stomach cramps, and I can't tell if it's from throwing up or that call.

I'm starting to see how limited my options are after graduation. I'd rather get my scrotum lopped off with a rusty blade than work for my father. He'd give me some shit job where all the assholes at his firm, including my idiot older brother, think they can boss me around because I didn't go to law school. Even if I wanted to be an attorney, I don't have the grades.

And I can't imagine getting a teaching job and spending my life in a classroom. Even if a school looked past what's out there on the internet about me, I don't really see myself hanging out with teenagers all day and instructing them on the finer points of history.

Never mind that I'm probably not the best candidate to play father figure to Roxy's baby. My sperm donor is an asshole to my mom, who bitches at her if she dares to cop an attitude because he's never home. I have no idea what a healthy relationship looks like, aside from a few of my friends who have girlfriends. But who knows if they're going to last?

Maybe Roxy is right. Maybe us dating would be a bad idea.

As much as I want to tell the world to fuck off and be with the woman I've been crushing on, what the hell do I bring to the relationship if I'm broke and jobless?

My one shot at any kind of success is getting drafted. I might not love football the way I used to, but it got me a full ride to a good school and out from under my father's thumb.

I collapse back in bed with a groan and toss my arm over my face.

I'm not sure what the future holds for me, but I have a sinking suspicion it does not include Roxy Santos.

And that's a goddamn shame.

13

ROXY

AFTER THAT TALK with Debbie yesterday, I decided I can't wait any longer. Because this will be ten times worse if my father hears my news from someone else. I can't hide anymore.

In fact, today will be the day I rip off the Band-Aid for everything.

With trembling hands, I try calling Billy again. When he doesn't pick up, I leave a message. As much as I want to text him and be done, that's not how you treat a friend.

"Hey. It's me. I just, uh... just wanted to touch base and let you know where I am with things. Can we grab coffee or something this week if you have the time? Let me know what works for you."

When I hang up, I take several deep breaths to calm down. Letting go of Billy is the right thing to do.

Then why does it hurt so much?

Not even the practice I had with Paige this morning can get me out of my funk, but I take heart knowing I can help. When I called her last night, she immediately agreed to do some extra training with me.

Paige has the skills to make mat for nationals. She just has to believe she can do it. Plus, she needs to trust that her spotters will catch her if she falls.

We're going to work on getting the right mindset. With a few more one-on-one sessions, I think she'll be ready.

I grab the hoagies I picked up on the way to the stadium and lock my car before I make my way through the back parking lot to my dad's office. A few of the players are hanging out in the hallways, and I give them brief smiles. I'm afraid if I stop to talk, I'll wuss out.

When I make it to Dad's office, he's chatting with two of the assistant coaches. I make sure to locate the trash can in the corner in case I vomit. It's a distinct possibility.

The other coaches greet me before they head out.

"Hey, Rox. How's my girl?" Dad gives me a one-sided smile where half his mouth tugs up but the other side doesn't bother making the trip.

"Hi, Coach." I know it's weird that I call him that, but I've spent a lifetime around his athletes, and it just comes out sometimes. "I'm good. Brought you some lunch."

That brings up the other side of his mouth as he types on his computer. "I'm starving. What did ya get?"

"Italian subs."

"Brilliant. Don't tell your mom I had processed meat, though. She's been trying to get rid of nitrates. Honestly, I don't understand it except that it has something to do with getting healthier. And after my hoagie, I am one hundred percent on board."

I chuckle. "No worries." After I place his sandwich on the desk, I toss him a Diet Coke.

Maybe this won't be so bad. Maybe I've blown this out of proportion and my father will take this in stride. And if we do this at work, he can't lose his cool. Everyone always says he's so levelheaded. So patient. That he lives up to his NFL moniker, the Saint.

Please, Jesus, let him live up to his nickname.

"You okay, kiddo? You're unusually quiet."

My heart feels like it might crash straight through my ribs. I'm definitely not okay. I take a deep breath. "There's something I wanted to talk to you about."

"Is this about Deacon? I meant to tell you. He said you were upset I hadn't mentioned he was transferring, but you know how crazy things have been with the playoffs."

My throat gets tight with the reminder that my entire family forgot to mention that my brother is transferring here in the fall. No biggie. When they disown me, at least they'll have Deke.

I nod with acceptance I don't feel. "You've been busy, Dad. I get it."

"I knew you'd understand. How's cheer going? I haven't seen you around lately. Busy with classes?"

Tell him. Spit it out. "Actually—"

His phone rings, and he holds up a finger. "Could be a recruiter. Can't keep those guys waiting."

Yeah, yeah. Because a recruiter holds the future of an athlete in his palm. I've heard the spiel a million times before.

"Yes, this is Coach Santos."

This call might take a while. I unwrap my sandwich and flick off a black olive that suddenly seems repulsive. I was ravenous a minute ago, but now the smell of food turns my stomach.

When I realize how quiet my father is, I look up and freeze when I find his eyes trained on me as he listens to whatever is being said on the other end of the call.

"That has to be a mistake," he says slowly. "She's on a cheer scholarship. Or maybe she's exempt because I'm staff. I can't remember the details, but I do recall that my contract specifically states her tuition is covered."

I feel the blood drain from my face.

Fuck my life. That had better not be about tuition.

"Hold on. Let me put you on speakerphone. She's right here." He motions to me. "Rox, tell Mrs. Connor in the bursar's office that you're still doing cheer. They must've gotten their wires crossed. She said you quit the squad." He chuckles like that's crazy.

A few months ago, I would've agreed.

My eyes flood. *Damn hormones.* I never cried before I got pregnant. Like, maybe once in a blue moon, or if I landed a stunt wrong sometimes my eyes watered. Nothing like this. I'm a damn watering pot now.

"Well, you see, Dad—"

"Oh, hell no. Mrs. Connor, I'll have to call you back."

Click.

Now my father's attention is one hundred percent lasered on me.

His nostrils flare. "I'm listening, Roxanne."

I swallow. "I quit cheer."

Silence.

A minute ticks by.

I clear my throat. "Dad, I quit the squad," I say a little louder.

"I heard you the first time," he says in that deadly soft voice that scares the crap out of me. It's the same one he used in high school when I stayed out past curfew after prom, and he caught me drinking beer with friends. He literally grounded me until college started. "I'm just wondering why you would do such a thing."

I almost forgot that quitting cheer isn't my biggest news. But one step at a time. "I wasn't feeling well."

That's true. Not the whole truth, but it's a kernel of what's going on. Ugh, this is not how I rehearsed what I was going to say.

His bushy brows furrow. "Are you okay? Why didn't you say anything? Did you see a doctor?"

He picks up his can of soda, pops it open, and takes a sip. I nod slowly and swallow past the giant boulder residing in my throat. I open my mouth but nothing comes out.

He tilts his head slightly. "Well, what did he say?"

"*She.* It was a she." *Do it. Just say it. Just blurt it out.* "She... said... I'm pregnant."

The Diet Coke drops out of his hand and splatters all over his desk. All over his charts and meticulously labeled file folders. All over his lunch.

But he doesn't move a muscle. Just stares at me like he has no idea who I am.

Truthfully, I don't recognize myself either.

And then he starts to yell.

14

BILLY

I'VE JUST COME off the field where I was running defensive drills. There's nothing quite like smashing your body into a blocking sled after puking on a night of zero sleep. Even though it's offseason and I could settle for the weight room and cardio on the machines, I'm relatively new to defense, and I need all the help I can get if I want to be a great safety. Offseason is where I stand to make the biggest gains, so I can't slack.

A wave of dizziness hits me, and I wonder if I could sleep in the locker room, maybe on a bench, until it passes. Damn, when was the last time I ate?

As I turn for the locker room, I pause when I spot my roommates huddled near Coach's office.

"What's up?"

Jinxy shushes me and leans closer to the door, which is cracked open just a sliver. Enough for us to hear what's happening in there.

"Roxanne, I'm so disappointed in you. I don't even have words," Coach's voice booms.

Suddenly, I forget that I'm sleep-deprived, dizzy, and irritable. Did Rox finally tell him she's knocked up?

When she doesn't say anything, it sounds like he bangs on the desk. "Who's the damn father? I want a name."

I glance around, looking for that weasel dick Ezra, but he's conveniently MIA.

"I'm going to ask you again," Coach bellows. "Who's. The. Father?"

Silence.

"Roxanne, do you even know who the father is?"

He did not fucking ask her that.

Then I hear it. The weeping.

I don't make a conscious decision to go in there, but next thing I know, I'm standing in front of Coach, ready to remove his head from his body. "Don't fucking talk to her like that." I must have a death wish.

Roxy has her face in her hands. Leaning down, I pull her into my arms. "It'll be okay, biscuit. Stop crying."

She wraps her arms around my waist and sobs against my chest as I glare at her dad.

Like an angry bull, his nostrils flare. "You." That's all he says.

He's doing some kind of deep breathing thing that makes me think he might keel over and die. Which would be bad. I might hate him sometimes, but I know he's a good guy. Deep, *deep* down. "Coach, it's not the end of the world. Women have babies every day."

"I should've known."

That Roxy would get pregnant? "Coach, you need to calm down before you say something you regr—"

"*You* fucking did this."

Me? "You're the one who made her cry."

He points at me. "You got my daughter pregnant."

I freeze. I don't budge an inch. He thinks I did this? That I knocked up this gorgeous girl and let her come in here to give him the news by herself? What kind of asshole does he take me for?

The biggest kind.

Of course he thinks I'm the culprit. Not Ezra, who's been cheating on his high school girlfriend for years and kisses Coach's ass at every opportunity.

Roxy's whole body shakes in my arms. Her father's a dick. What's he going to say to her when he finds out Ezra is engaged to someone else? He's gonna lose his shit.

What's worse? Me or the cheater?

I stare Coach straight in the eye. "That's right. I'm the father. So what? I'll take care of Roxy and whoever comes along."

Roxy stills. Sniffles. Looks up at me like I'm crazy. Maybe I am, but someone needs to stick up for her.

Leaning down, I kiss her on the forehead. "I got you, Rox. Everything will be okay."

I can only hope that my words ring true, because I have no fucking idea what I'm doing.

15

BILLY

Roxy looks so small huddled in a blanket on her bed. We're camped out in her room with some burgers I picked up on the way to her apartment. I would've brought her back to my place, but I'm not sure what kind of state it's in. I think I cleaned up all of the puke, but I'm not entirely sure.

Her roommates aren't around, so it's just us.

I finish eating my burger and toss the wrapper in the small wastebasket. It's very IKEA in here. All white linens and pink pillows. Rox has cheer photos everywhere in little collages that have been framed. I never realized how girlie she is, but it makes sense.

Leaning closer to one of the photos, I smile at the beautiful girl beaming back at me. "Is this high school?" I point at the pic, and she nods. She hasn't said much since we left her father's office. She has to be humiliated. All of the staff and half the team heard Coach bitch her out.

I sit next to her and wrap my arm around her. "Babe, you gotta eat something. Think of the bean."

"The bean?"

"Yeah, she's the size of a bean."

Her eyebrows crinkle. "You think it's a girl?"

I ponder that a moment. "I do. And she'll be as beautiful as her mother and every bit the heartbreaker." Roxy rolls her eyes, and I chuckle. "You're eating for two now, so you shouldn't skip meals."

"That's a myth. A pregnant woman doesn't actually need twice the calories."

There's my feisty girl. "But ya gotta feed her something, right? When was the last time you ate?"

She shrugs. "I had a smoothie this morning."

"And now it's almost four, so you need to eat. If a burger doesn't sound good, tell me what you want, and I'll run out and grab it for you."

Her eyes well with tears. "I can't handle you being so nice to me right now."

I laugh and kiss the top of her head. "And why's that?"

She looks down and whispers, "My family should be comforting me. They should be the ones who make sure I eat. They should be looking after me. But they're not. My dad doesn't care."

Damn. That hits me square in the fucking feels.

I squeeze her tight. "Your dad's just got his head up his ass right now. It might take a few days for him to extract it." Or weeks. "Give him some time. He'll come around. He loves you. If he didn't, he wouldn't give a shit what you're up to."

Rox grabs my hand and pulls it to her chest before she turns to me. "You have to tell Coach you're not the father. My dad will ruin you if you don't."

A part of me wholeheartedly agrees. It was the very reason I planned to tell her we shouldn't date after all.

But then I saw her dad bitching her out, and I couldn't stomach seeing her so brokenhearted and inconsolable. In a flash, all of my solid reasons for not dating her flew out the window.

I shrug with a nonchalance I don't feel. "What can Coach do? Bench me? The season doesn't start for months. Maybe he'll get over it by then. He can't exactly cut me from the team. I didn't violate any athletic or academic rules. Plus, my father is an attorney, and he'd sue his ass." Not because he cares about me, but he would flip the fuck out with embarrassment if I got kicked off the team.

Hearing myself spell out the specifics makes me feel better. Coach doesn't actually have a legit reason to kick me off the team besides the pregnancy.

But he might make my life hell.

I almost laugh at this lunacy. Here I am, taking heat for getting a girl pregnant I haven't even felt up.

After some coaxing, I manage to get Roxy to eat half of a burger and an apple.

I'm so tired, I'm fucking delirious. When she's done with her late lunch, I yawn. "I know we have a lot of shit to talk about, but could we possibly table that until later? I really need a nap."

Her eyes are droopy and swollen, and she looks drained too. "I feel like I could sleep into next year."

I point at her bed. "Can we crash? No funny business, I promise."

"Go for it."

As I strip off my t-shirt, I explain how I was up all night with Ash.

"Poor baby. Is he okay now?"

"Jake says he's better." He now thinks Ash and Charlotte ate a spoiled frozen pizza and that it wasn't a stomach bug. I start to unbutton my jeans. "This okay? I can't handle sleeping in denim right now. I can snooze on the couch in the living room if this is uncomfortable for you."

"It's fine. I'm gonna take a shower first."

"Wake me up in a bit, and we'll grab dinner or talk or whatever."

I kick off my jeans, leaving on my boxer briefs, and collapse on her bed. I'm asleep before she responds. There's no way I can untangle our situation before I get a nap.

It'll all make sense later, what I need to do.

Either that, or I'm screwed. It's a toss-up at this point.

16

ROXY

MY EMOTIONS ARE A MESS, I'm mildly nauseous, and I'm exhausted from everything that happened today, but the moment Billy strips out of his clothes, I forget everything. Like how flipped out my father is. How my ex will probably want nothing to do with his kid. How I have no idea how to balance school with a baby.

Because Billy is fucking gorgeous.

His muscles contract as he reaches behind his head and yanks his t-shirt off his body, leaving his dirty blond hair a tousled, sexy mess. He's a work of art with inked-up broad shoulders, a narrow waist, and an Adonis belt that leads into his jeans, which he unbuttons and slides down his legs before he flops face first on my bed.

I stare at his ripped back and tight ass while I try to not swallow my tongue. He's easily the most built guy I've ever dated.

Not that we're dating. I don't even know what we are at the moment. I guess we're friends. Really good friends, when I consider how he rushed to defend me to my father.

I can't help but compare Billy to the other guys I've gone out with. Ezra was leaner, almost lanky, whereas Billy has been carb-loading so he can hold his own on defense. And none of the other boys I dated come close to being as ripped as Billy.

What are you doing, Rox? Stop staring at the man.

I shake my head and head to the bathroom, where I take a quick shower. By the time I finish drying off, I'm so tired, I can barely stand. I throw on a t-shirt, undies, and a pair of flannel bottoms and return to my bedroom.

It's chilly in here, and Billy fell asleep on top of the comforter. He's going to be an icicle if I leave him like this.

"Billy," I whisper as I try to tug down the covers. It takes another few attempts to get him to wake, but he eventually cracks open an eye. "Let's get under the blanket. It's going to get cold tonight."

He grunts, but lets me yank down the bedding and pull it over him. "Thanks."

After turning off my reading lamp, I crawl into bed next to him, suddenly wide awake with awareness. I have a queen-size bed, and I'm pretty small, but Billy is massive.

Scooting to the edge so I don't accidentally bother him, I roll to my side and face away from him.

Billy Babcock is in my bed. Sleeping. Sprawled out next to me in his underwear, looking like some kind of beautiful action hero.

"Rox?" His low voice sends chills all over my body.

"Hm?"

"Wanna snuggle?"

My eyebrows lift with surprise before I grin. How I'm smiling after the day I've had is a surprise. I don't consider how it's probably not a good idea or that we should keep our distance until we figure out what the hell we're doing. Because the idea of being wrapped in his arms sounds amazing. "I'd like that."

That gets me a grunt before an enormous arm reaches

around me and yanks me to his hard chest. And then he buries his head in my neck and groans. "You smell good."

I chuckle. "Thanks. You do too." Like leather and spice and something masculine.

We're quiet for a while before he sighs. "Don't be nervous. I don't have any nefarious plans. I just wanna hold you."

Who would've thought that big, tough, defensive back Billy Babcock would be a snuggler?

"I trust you." Reaching back, I run my fingers through his hair. "I know we decided to talk after our nap or tomorrow, but I just need to tell you how much I appreciate what you did for me today. No one has ever stood up for me like that before. And no matter what happens down the road or what we decide to do about this crazy situation, I want you to know how much that means to me."

"I'll always have your back." He kisses my neck. "Go to sleep, biscuit."

This is supposed to be a nap, except we're both so tired, we're out for the count.

We fall asleep with only our top halves touching, but sometime during the night, I roll over. I wake up sprawled across his chest with one thigh tossed over his.

My eyes fly open when I realize I'm practically sleeping on top of the man. I start to slide off him, but his arms, which are wrapped around me, tighten. "Where are you going?" His gruff voice makes goosebumps break out on my arms.

"Sorry. I… I don't mean to maul you."

"That assumes I don't like it. Go back to sleep."

"I'm not invading your space?"

"I like you in my space. Now let me get my beauty sleep."

Grinning, I lay my head back on his chest and close my eyes with a sigh.

It's the best night of sleep I've had in a long time.

17

ROXY

THE NEXT MORNING, Billy holds open the door to the Rise 'N Grind as a gust of wind tries to shove me through it. He grabs my elbow with a chuckle. "Almost got blown away there, Dorothy."

I let out a laugh that promptly dies on my lips when everyone in the coffee house turns to look at us.

Everyone knows what happened with my dad.

The hottest commodity at this college isn't football, it's gossip. I look down and try to walk past Billy, but he tugs me back to him.

Leaning down, he whispers in my ear. "None of that. You have nothing to be ashamed about."

"People are staring."

"You're a beautiful woman. Of course they're gonna fucking stare. Let them."

I look at him. Billy has scruff on his strong jaw, and his hair is going every which way like he couldn't be bothered this morning to finger-comb it. "How do you always know what to say to make me feel better?"

"It's my special power." The corner of his lip tugs up as he stares down at me. "Sorry I almost impaled you with my boner this morning."

That laugh finally escapes. "It didn't bother me." It made me *really* horny, but he doesn't need to know this. "Want to hear a funny story?"

"Always."

We order our coffee and muffins and settle in at a table in the corner. "So Deke is a year younger than me, and when he was little, he was obsessed with his junk."

Billy chuckles. "I think all boys are."

"When he was little, I distinctly remember him yelling out to our dad something along the lines of, 'My penis is so happy! It's pointing to the sky!'"

Billy chokes on his coffee as his shoulders shake with laughter. Then he clears his throat. "I'll have to ask him about this when he joins our team in the summer."

"You should do that. It'll keep him humble."

He takes another sip of his drink. "Have you two talked recently?"

"Not since we discussed why nobody bothered to tell me he was transferring schools. I'm still irritated about the whole thing."

"I'm sorry, Rox. I know what it feels like to get left out of family shit. It's not fun."

I fiddle with my napkin. "I feel like this stuff shouldn't bother me anymore. Like I've aged out of getting butthurt by my family."

"I don't think there's an age limit for that. You feel what you feel."

A surge of affection wells in my heart for this man. "You're an idiot for stepping into that mess with my dad yesterday, but I also kind of adore you for it."

That gets me a full-blown smile. "I can handle adoration. Maybe on your knees if you're feeling up to it."

It's my turn to choke with laughter. "Billy!"

"Kidding." His eyes crinkle in the corners. "Kinda."

"What am I going to do with you?"

He lifts that eyebrow playfully. "I have a few ideas, but they all involve nudity."

"Okay, horndog. Seriously, what are we going to do?" I lower my voice to a whisper. "Everyone thinks you're my baby daddy!"

After peeling the wrapper off his muffin, he shoves half of it in his mouth. "Let them. I'm not gonna lose sleep over it."

"So you just want to let people believe it?" I figured he'd reconsider this morning, but nothing about Billy's devil-may-care attitude suggests he's backtracking.

"Why not? If it helps you out and you don't have to deal with pencil dick for a while, I'm cool with it."

Crazy, crazy man. "I'll have to tell Ezra eventually."

"On your timetable, sure. He's busy with the draft, getting engaged, and probably fucking sorority girls left and right, so I don't think there's any rush. And if he decides he wants to be a dad..." Billy shrugs. "Then let him."

I'm almost afraid to ask, but I want to know. "Was he... was he always a player?"

His eyes go serious. "Yes. And don't come at me like I didn't tell you he was bad news."

"I know you did. I just... I bought his lies. That people were trying to give him a bad rep."

"I'm sorry he hurt you, biscuit."

"Strangely, I'm okay. Yes, I was hurt initially when I found out he was saying one thing to me while playing the field behind my back. But I wasn't in love. Honestly, I don't think I have it in me to fall in love."

His brows furrow. “Why’s that? I thought all girls lived for romantic crap.”

I sigh and sink deeper into my chair. “We moved so much when I was growing up. When I was little, I cried when we left whatever town we were living in, and I would promise to stay in touch with the girls who had been my friends. But when you’re a kid, that’s not as easy as it sounds. After several moves, I stopped crying, and I stopped making those kinds of promises. And now it’s harder for me to be vulnerable with people. It’s good because I don’t get hurt that easily, but I wonder if it’s harder to love.”

“Makes sense.”

I blow out a breath. “So what are we going to do about this baby business?”

His phone buzzes on the table. And buzzes. And buzzes.

“Are you going to get that?”

“Nah. It’s all bullshit anyway. Teammates wanting gossip from the horse’s mouth. Or so-called friends wanting to be in the know.” He looks at me over the rim of his coffee. “What about you? Have you heard from your parents yet?”

“I’m almost embarrassed to admit this because I’m not usually the type of person to avoid confrontation, but my parents seem to be the exception to the rule.” I fold my lips. “Uh, my phone died last night and I never bothered to charge it.”

“That’s one way to avoid the inevitable.” He leans down until our eyes meet. Then he reaches across the table and takes my hand in his. “Your parents love you, Roxy. They’ll be upset for a while, but your dad will get over it.”

“He’s just so traditional. He has a thing about getting married before you have kids, something about the baby getting the husband’s last name, which I know sounds archaic. It probably has to do with his father taking off when he was little. Apparently, my grandfather was a truck driver and an alcoholic, and his womanizing ways did not sit well with my grandmother, who got an annulment shortly after they were married. Only she didn't know she was pregnant. Santos is actually her maiden name."

Billy watches me for a long minute. Sips his coffee. "So give the baby my last name. On the birth certificate. If you want to."

"Billy, come on." I snort. "I can't just name you as the father. There are ramifications for that." I mean, aren't there?

"I'm not joking. If it'll help you save face with your dad, I don't mind."

I squeeze his giant paw. "You're doing all this stuff for me—standing up to my dad, pretending to be my baby daddy, letting me put your name on the birth certificate. Surely there's something I can help you with. Do you like home-cooked meals? I can cook for you. Or bake. Do your laundry?"

"You don't have to do my laundry, biscuit. Thanks for offering."

"What about the home-cooked meals? My grandmother taught me a thing or two in the kitchen."

"I remember that killer Thanksgiving spread you made for us last fall." He rubs his hands together. "Let's just say I wouldn't reject anything you made me."

I smile, loving the idea of cooking for him. "Great. What else?"

He jams the rest of his muffin in his mouth. "Cheer for me at my games next fall?"

"I already do that, silly. Even without the uniform, I'll always be your biggest fan." I motion with my hand to give me more. "This has to be fair, Billy. I won't accept what you're offering if it's not."

He runs his hand over his face. "Um... Okay. I got something. My agent says I need to date a nice girl and be seen going out on dates. He's been on my ass about taming my image."

After I glance around, I whisper, "You're not supposed to have an agent yet. It'll mess up your eligibility."

"It's nothing official. I promise. But he said I have to stop looking like a dumbass. And apparently that means settling down with someone." He holds out his hand. "You're a nice girl with a great personality... and a hot-as-fuck bod. We can totally make this work."

I roll my eyes. "Okay, so, what? We pretend to date?"

"You already know I want to date you. We don't have to pretend."

My shoulders slump. "I thought long and hard about your offer this week, and I don't think I'm ready for that. I need to get through this pregnancy and see if I can deal with my life when it includes a baby. As much as I'm attracted to you and as much as I like you as a friend, I shouldn't add a new relationship to my situation."

"That's fair." He sits back and looks away.

Damn. I don't want to hurt his feelings. "Maybe we revisit the topic in a few months."

"Sure." He might be agreeing, but he doesn't look excited.

Suddenly, I think about him lying in my bed, and my nipples tighten. I won't deny how good it felt waking up in his arms this morning. Billy is easily the most handsome man I've ever been with. I blurt out my idea before I can change my mind. "What about friends with benefits?" I swore I'd never do that again, not after Ezra and I went up in flames, but maybe this would be different. "You're already pretending to be my baby daddy. I'll pretend to be your girlfriend, and privately we just do the sleep-over thing like we did last night and see where it goes."

His mouth tugs up as his stare gets heated. "I can tell you where it'll go."

I feel my face flush and let out a laugh. "Slow down, you animal. Let's make this official." Reaching into my bag, I pull out a pen, but I don't have any paper, so I take a napkin, open it, and press it flat.

His eyes twinkle with humor. "Whatcha doing? Writing a contract on a napkin?"

"Exactly. That way we have a plan." I list out my end of things.

WHAT ROXY WILL DO:

1. Be the best fake girlfriend Billy's ever had and go on dates to fix his rep.

2. Cheer for Billy at his games and be his number one fan.

3. Cook him delicious meals when her schedule allows.

4. Offer unlimited snuggling.

5. Maybe explore friends with benefits.

THEN I SLIDE the napkin over to him. "What do you think?"

He looks like he's trying not to laugh. "Unlimited snuggling?"

I nod, suddenly feeling shy. "You're a good snuggler."

He smiles and returns the napkin to me. "I'm down for all the snuggles. What about me? List out what you expect from me."

I grab my pen again.

WHAT BILLY WILL DO:

1. Snuggle Roxy every night and tell her she smells good.

2. Sleep without a shirt so Roxy can appreciate those big muscles.

3. Let Roxy name him on the birth certificate of the baby.

I'M NOT a hundred percent convinced that last one is a good idea, but he did offer. I can always reconsider.

Tapping my bottom lip, I shake my head. "Almost forgot something."

Under "Roxy," I add another item.

6. NEVER ASK Billy for child support or anything monetary.

I RETURN the napkin to him. "So when you're a hotshot NFL player, you won't have to worry about me trying to empty your bank account."

"I know you'd never do that." He looks my list over. "Why do I only have three requirements and you have six? Doesn't seem fair."

"My number three is a doozy, and we both know there's nothing I can do to repay that favor."

His eyes go soft. "I just want to help, Rox. Whatever that means."

"I know. And I'm really grateful." I sign and date the napkin and hand him the pen. He does the same.

"We really should start saving for the bean's college fund," he teases. "That shit will cost an arm and a leg by then."

Smiling, I get out of my chair and walk around the table until I'm standing next to him. If we're friends with benefits, then I can do this. "Thank you." I lean down, grab his handsome face, and plant a kiss on his full lips. "I'll always owe you."

Before I can back away, his arm whips out, and he pulls me into his lap. I let out a squeal of laughter when he wiggles his fingers against my ribs and whispers, "How soon before I can introduce you to my boner?"

18

BILLY

ROXY'S PUTTING on a brave face, but her hand is clammy. As we walk up the driveway to her parents' house, I squeeze it. "Everything will be fine."

Santos might strangle me and bury me in a shallow grave, but he won't hurt his daughter.

She nods but doesn't say anything. It's been twenty-four hours since we wrote that ridiculous contract, and even though it was kinda fun to do, I'm not really taking it seriously. Roxy is stressed out, and if writing that made her feel better, great. I'll go along with whatever she wants, but I wouldn't be surprised if she backs out once things calm down.

She's been really… chill. Almost numb, if I had to guess.

Coach took two personal days off, which is weird as fuck. The man never leaves the athletic department. I almost wondered if he slept there.

But no, he has a nice house with a huge yard in a quiet part of town. His sleek black Lexus and a shiny silver BMW sit in the driveway.

When we get to the porch, I whisper, "If you get freaked out, just think about that time Jinxy laughed so yard, he puked Jell-O through his nose."

Smiling, Roxy shakes her head as she pulls out her keys and unlocks the door. "Here goes nothing." Then she yells, "Mom! Dad!"

"We're back here!" a female voice shouts back.

"Have you spoken to your mom yet?" I ask her quietly.

She shakes her head. "She called, but I wasn't ready to talk."

So Rox does that to everyone and not just me. Good to know. I'm learning that every woman has their quirks. Roxy likes to "process things" in her head.

The two-story house has a grand staircase, vaulted ceilings, and a marble floor in the entryway. Roxy leads me through an airy great room and kitchen, back to a dark den, which is obviously her father's man cave. A beautiful woman with Roxy's thick hair and smile greets us.

Mrs. Santos opens her arms to her daughter. "Oh, baby. Come here."

Roxy rushes to her and they hug.

I start to relax. Mrs. Santos is clearly the more rational parent of the two.

Hanging back, I shove my hands into the pockets of my letterman jacket. I wore this today because I figured it couldn't hurt to remind Coach that I'm one of his players. That I'm not some rando off the street, hoping to lure his daughter down a path of destruction.

With an ominous creak, the executive leather chair behind the enormous mahogany desk slowly turns, and there's Coach, glaring. At me.

I fight like hell to keep from smiling. I won't deny a part of me enjoys getting under his skin. It probably stems from all the shit my father and I have argued about over the years.

There's one thing my father and Santos have in common—neither of them like me.

I haven't even had sex with Roxy and I'm standing before the firing squad for a crime I didn't commit. I'm a fucking idiot. Who gets themselves in these kinds of situations? Me. That's who.

Mrs. Santos keeps one arm around her daughter as she extends a hand to me. "Hi. I'm Marlena, Roxy's mom."

"I'm Billy. It's nice to meet you, ma'am."

"Aren't you adorable. I can see why my daughter likes you."

Roxy laughs, and I turn on my full-wattage smile. "Well, she's an amazing woman. She must take after her mother."

"Cut the crap, Babcock," Coach barks from behind his desk, making us all flinch.

"Richard," Marlena warns. *"Cálmate, mi amor."*

I can't speak Spanish for shit, but I took four years of it in high school, so I understand it well enough. And I think she just told Coach to calm down. And she called the old goat her love.

Marlena holds out her arm to usher us to the dining room. "Why don't we have some dinner, and we can get to know you a little bit, Billy."

I'm sure there's nothing more Coach wants than to have dinner with me.

We file into the other room, where Marlena has a pot roast steaming in the middle of the dining room table. Giant windows look out to the backyard where there's a pool and pool house. I have to admit that Coach's place is pretty dope.

Roxy and I sit next to each other. Coach takes a seat at the end, next to Roxy, and his wife sits across from her daughter.

"So Billy," Marlena says. "What position are you on the team?"

"Growing up, I played quarterback, and then I got switched to wide receiver my freshman year at Lone Star, and most recently defensive back. I'm the safety."

"Goodness, that's a lot of movement. That's not typical, is it?"

"No, ma'am. It's not."

She frowns and glances at her husband, who slices the pot roast like it personally offended him. Then she turns back to me. "Which position do you like the most?"

"I loved playing quarterback, but I'm trying my best to give defense everything I've got."

She nods, but her lips twist, and she side-eyes her husband again.

Roxy places her hand on mine and gives me a sweet smile. "Billy is being modest, Mom. He killed it at all three positions. He was an all-state QB in high school, which is what Coach Sully recruited him for, broke a school record for most receiving yards in one game as a wide receiver, and had five interceptions, the second highest in the conference, last year as a safety."

When she says it like that, I don't feel like such a damn loser. "Thanks, biscuit."

Her mom chuckles. "What a sweet nickname. How did that come about?"

"Rox made these incredible biscuits last fall for the football house. They were rich and buttery. Super flaky. We loved them so much, my roommates and I almost came to blows over who was gonna get the last one."

Marlena laughs. "I'm guessing that was my mother-in-law's recipe. She was a fine cook, and she and Roxy spent a lot of time together in the kitchen."

Coach takes the stack of plates and slaps slices of meat on each one before his wife hands them out. Then she tells us to serve our own sides. There's mashed potatoes and gravy, creamed corn, steamed broccoli, and cornbread. Jesus, the women in this family can cook.

My mouth waters as I stare at the mountain of food on my

plate. I start to slice the roast when Coach clears his throat and offers me another glare. "In this family, we say grace first."

He isn't gonna make tonight easy for me, is he? I nod and put down my silverware.

When he bows his head, I follow suit.

"Dear Lord, thank you for this great bounty. Please bless this food and keep me from committing a homicide."

"Richard!" Marlena smacks his arm. "What has gotten into you?"

His jaw tightens. "It's not what's gotten into me. Shouldn't you be asking what got into your daughter?"

Roxy gasps. "Dad!"

Holy shit. He's flipped his fucking lid.

"That's enough!" Marlena throws down her napkin. "You're acting like a damn child. If you're going to be this way, I'm taking the kids out to eat, and you can sulk by yourself. We waited to have this dinner so you could calm down, and now you're ruining everything."

Marlena starts to sniffle, and Coach closes his eyes. "*Preciosa*, I'm sorry." He clears his throat and then looks at Roxy. "Please forgive me, Roxanne."

I stare at my plate of food, wondering if I'm ever going to be able to enjoy this roast.

Roxy angles her head toward me. "Don't you want to apologize to Billy?"

"Not really, no."

"Dad!"

Fuck it. I shovel some of the most delicious pot roast I've ever tasted into my mouth. The man is ridiculous. "Coach, get a grip. You're offending your wife and daughter. Talk to me however you want, but have some care for them. Aren't you always going on and on about being respectful?" I point my fork at him and talk around the huge bite of roast in my mouth. "You, sir, are being a hypocrite."

I should remember my manners, but what does it matter? The guy already thinks I'm a savage. Might as well meet his expectations.

An angry vein in his forehead pulses, and I wonder if I've gone too far, but he takes a deep breath. Slowly nods. Swallows. Clears his throat. Tugs at the neck of his button-down shirt. "You're right. My apologies, Babcock."

The man has never apologized to me. Not once. Now that I think of it, I don't think I've ever heard him apologize to anyone besides his family here tonight.

I'm too stunned to say anything, and I sit there with a forkful of food in front of my mouth, frozen.

He places his hands on the table and looks down and starts muttering something in Spanish. I can't quite make it out, but his wife's eyes go soft, and she reaches over and hugs him.

His whole demeanor changes when he looks up again. Like I've taken the wind out of his sails. He looks defeated.

Shit. I broke Coach.

He sighs. "We, uh, my wife and I wanted to let you both know we'll help however we can with the baby."

That's all it takes for Roxy to burst into tears.

I really can't fucking deal with women crying. Reaching around her, I tuck her under my arm. "I told you it would be okay, biscuit. See how much your parents love you? Don't cry."

She squeezes me tight, and her father stares at me like he's never seen me before.

He clears his throat again. "We love you, Roxanne. We're disappointed—ouch." He gives his wife a look. She might've kicked him under the table. "Let me rephrase that. We wish you had finished college first, but we're here to support you however we can."

"I know, Dad. I'm disappointed in myself too." She's still sobbing against my chest, and I lean down and kiss the top of her head. "I'm heartbroken I can't... can't... cheer anymore. That I'm losing everything I've worked so hard for."

I'm in touch with that. When Coach Krud switched me from QB to wide receiver, I thought my world was ending.

Coach blows out a big breath. "Rox, I'm sorry I lost my temper." His eyes lift to me. "My apologies, Billy." There it is again. Another apology. I glance out the window, bracing myself for a plague of locusts or killer frogs. "As I'm sure you can tell, my family means everything to me, and I'm not handling this situation as well as I'd like."

I'm used to getting yelled out by the men in my life. Coach yelling at me isn't all that different than the way my father bitches me out. But my father never apologizes, not like Coach has tonight.

"It's okay, Coach. I understand. Roxy's awesome, and I'd hate for anything to derail her life too. But I think we have to have more confidence in her abilities because she's an amazing woman who'll be an incredible mother."

Santos swallows several times and nods. "You're right."

The table gets quiet as Roxy calms down. She reaches for a napkin, wipes her eyes, and then starts laughing. "Oh my God, I'm so glad this conversation is over. The idea of talking to you guys has been making me sick for months. I've been such a big chicken. It's embarrassing. Billy kept telling me you two would come around, but I felt like the sky was falling."

Roxy found out she was pregnant on a fluke in late November. Charlotte needed to take a pregnancy test but was freaked out, so Roxy took one with her in solidarity. Turns out, Charlie wasn't pregnant, but Roxy was.

Coach tilts his head. Pauses. Narrows his eyes at Roxy. "This is why you didn't do any stunts or tumbling at our championship game?"

She nods with a sad smile before she hops up to hug him and then her mom.

Marlena wipes her eyes. "We love you, darling. I'm sorry you didn't feel like you could talk to us. I do have a bone to pick with you, though. I'm not sure I'm ready to be called Grandma. It makes me feel old."

Roxy laughs again as she sits in her chair. "We'll come up with a cool name for you, like Gigi or Mimi or some short version of *abuelita*, like *Lita*."

"Those are cute!" Marlena holds her hand to her chest. "That's much better. Thank you, *mija*."

Coach clears his throat again. "Roxy, I spoke to the bursar's office. I'll cover tuition for you this semester, and you can pay me back after you graduate and get a job."

Marlena sighs. "You want her to repay you? Really, Richard? It's for college."

"Repaying that money is the responsible thing to do. I'm not a bank. Roxanne has to learn how to manage her money and keep herself out of trouble. Between that and the money her grandmother left her, she should be able to get by until she graduates. One zero-interest loan from her father is better than most college kids are faring right now. I'm not asking for her firstborn, though if she wants to name her baby Richard, I won't complain."

Roxy grabs his hand. "Thanks, Dad. I promise I'll repay you."

"Before I forget, your mom and I found you a place. It's a nice two-bedroom between here and campus. It has enough room for a nursery. We'll cover the cost. That way you two can save for the baby. They're expensive. And we'll be close to lend a hand when you need it."

Roxy's eyes widen. "You got me an apartment?"

Coach waves his fork at me. "For both of you, yes." Then his eyes drill into me. "Billy, you're not planning to stay at the football house, are you? While your girlfriend raises *your* child?"

How pissed would he be right now if I admit the bean isn't mine?

Like water rushing on the *Titanic*, the reality of this situation sinks in. I may have offered to help Roxy with my last name, to maybe buy her some time with pencil dick, to help her save face with her dad, but her parents now expect me and Rox to move in together.

"Dad, Billy doesn't have to do that." Roxy's eyes widen as she gives me a look. "I can manage on my own."

"The hell you can." That vein in Coach's forehead pulses again as he aggressively saws at the food on his plate with his utensils. "If Babcock plans to play football next fall, he'll move his crap into your new apartment by the end of next week. It's non-negotiable."

That delicious roast suddenly feels like a block of lead in my gut.

19

BILLY

Now that I've had some time to chill, I don't think this move is such a big deal. I can always party at the football house if I want. Nothing really has to change.

"Thanks for helping me." I toss the box of pizza in the middle of the coffee table, along with a stack of paper plates. I grab a piece and scarf it down while Jake and Cam eat.

They're unusually quiet. We're having lunch at the football house before we haul my shit to the new apartment.

"This is weird, dude," Cam says. "You guys aren't even dating, and you're moving in together."

I laugh. "It's totally weird, I agree. But hey, gotta roll with it, right? I mean, what else am I supposed to do?"

"How about *not* move in with Roxy?" Jake says quietly. "Look, we all love her, and I know you're watching out for her, but this is nutty, even for you."

I shove another slice in my mouth. "How is this any different than the year Cam and I lived with Maggie?"

Cam laughs. "We rented rooms in her house. We didn't *sleep in her bed*. Olly would've had a problem with that anyway."

"He would've kicked our asses into the next county." I

chuckle, thinking of how protective our buddy was with his girlfriend. "Okay, I'll admit this is a little extreme."

Jake's eyes bug out. "Then why are you doing this? Just tell Coach the truth. It'll cause fewer problems for you and Roxy down the road."

It sounds so simple.

I reach for a can of soda and pop it open. "After dinner at Coach's house, I realized how serious this has gotten. When we got back to Roxy's apartment, she said we should tell her father the truth. She said she knew this had gotten out of control and wanted to make things right between me and her dad." I lower my voice so my other roommates upstairs don't overhear me. "But later that night, she started spotting."

"Oh, shit." Cam pauses with a slice halfway to his mouth. "Is she okay?"

"Yeah, but I took her to the ER just to be safe. The doctor said she needs to relax. That high levels of stress are not healthy for her or the baby." I look between my two best friends. "You heard Coach yell at her in his office. How flipped out do you think he's gonna be if he finds out I'm not really the father and Ezra, who just got engaged to his *high school* sweetheart, is?"

They both hiss.

"Fuck."

"Shit."

"Exactly." I hold out my hands. "So tell me. What do I do? Do I risk Roxy's health and maybe the health of her baby? Because that sounds kinda selfish."

Hearing Rox cry at dinner with her parents broke my fucking heart. But then seeing how relieved she was afterward? That weighs on me. I don't want to take that peace away from her. Honestly, what's the big deal? I'll help her out when she needs it, maybe babysit her bean sometimes, and Roxy and I can fuck this out of our systems until we graduate. Plus, I'll get to spend time with one of my favorite people. That doesn't sound like such a hardship.

Jake nods slowly. "Then wait a few weeks. Maybe a month. Let Coach calm down. Give him time to come to terms with this pregnancy."

I'm guessing this charade might go a little longer than a month—just my gut instinct—but I nod, because there's no reason to get my friends riled up when they're nervous Nellies about the whole thing. "That's what I was thinking. It just means I have to move in with Roxy in the meanwhile."

"*Chingao*, Babcock. You really know how to get yourself in some deep shit."

I look at Jake, then Cam, and chuckle. "You guys think I'm fucked, don't you?"

When neither of them say anything, I shrug and grab another slice.

"Since you'll be living together, does this mean you're officially dating now?" Cam asks.

"Define 'official.'"

That's the only rub. Roxy won't date me.

The food gets lodged in my throat, and I cough. I'm definitely not telling my friends about Roxy's offer to help me clean up my rep. When Klein hears I'm dating the coach's daughter, who's knocked up, presumably by me, he'll blast my number from his contacts.

Well, it's too late now.

Rox is right about us keeping things casual. We both have a lot on the line. Keeping things uncomplicated is probably the best thing to do. It's not like we're gonna run off and buy a house with a white picket fence after college and actually be together once she comes to her senses and ends our agreement.

What I don't mention to my friends is how much I like the idea of living with this girl.

Chill, man. You and Roxy will have some fun, her parents will get on board with this baby, and then you and Rox will go your separate ways.

She even told you she's not the falling-in-love type.

I'm not sure why that bothers me, but it does.

It makes me wonder what it would take for a girl like her to fall for a guy like me.

Probably the biggest Hail Mary of my life.

I haven't thrown one of those in a while and likely won't get another chance to anytime soon.

20

ROXY

"Do you need another blanket?" Billy asks from the hallway.

"No. The last one you brought me is enough." I'm curled up on the couch in the living room of our new apartment. On one side of the living room are two side-by-side bedrooms and on the other is a galley kitchen. Thinking about how supportive my parents are being chokes me up, so I don't let myself think about it. Not after that spotting scare the other day.

Billy says I need to relax. That we'll figure out how to tell my dad the truth about the baby's paternity once my health isn't a concern.

We spent the last two days moving in, and when I say we, I mean Billy, his friends, and my dad because they wouldn't let me do anything to help. It was funny watching Dad and Billy try to be nice to each other for my sake. Even though this situation is bonkers, I'm hoping Billy uses this as a chance to get to know my father. I think if they gave each other a chance, they'd really like each other. And while that's not officially listed on our agreement, if I can get Coach to see Billy for the great guy he is, I won't feel like I'm getting the better end of this deal.

"Are you sure you're not hungry?" I call out. "I can make you dinner."

"The doctor said you're supposed to stay off your feet as much as possible." He pops his head around the corner. "Why don't I grab us some takeout?"

"How about we go *out* for dinner? It's my treat for all of your hard work and… well, inconvenience."

So much damn inconvenience. Now that I've calmed down, I can appreciate how utterly insane this whole situation is. Can I blame this on pregnancy hormones?

"*Or* you let me carry you to my truck, and we'll do drive-thru."

I let out a huff of annoyance. "Billy, I can walk perfectly well on my own two feet. The doctor told me to take it easy. I'm not on bed rest. There's a big difference."

He sits on the coffee table in front of me. He's wearing a snug black t-shirt that shows off all of his muscles and jeans that cling to his thick thighs. "Will you let me drop you off at the front door of a restaurant so you don't have to walk too far?"

"Yes, you crazy man, but I'm back to my normal schedule next week. My classes are all over campus."

"Right, but until then, humor me and let me do what I can do to make it easier for you."

"Okay, but this has to be one of our official dates, you know, to help you look respectable and all that."

He chuckles. "I'm probably a lost cause."

"You'll never be a lost cause. How about the Yellow Rose Bar & Grill? Sometimes they have live music, and I like watching the couples dance."

"If you promise to take it easy."

"I swear!" I head into the bathroom, where I slick on some berry-flavored lip balm and swipe my lashes with a little mascara. Then I grab my jacket, excited to get some fresh air.

"Ready?" he asks as he locks the door.

Before I can respond, I'm in his arms. The man freaking cradles me as he stalks off to his truck. "Billy."

"Rox." He stares straight ahead, like this is an everyday occurrence.

"You're being weird."

"You're pregnant. You're literally growing a human. I don't know—it makes me feel fucking protective of you."

"Thank you." I grab his scruffy face, and he shoots me one of his flirty smiles. "Really."

"Not a big deal. I can weightlift like five of you."

"No, I mean for everything. For helping me work through my stuff with my parents. I realize this situation is not ideal for you. You should be living it up after the championship, enjoying that single life and gearing up for your senior year in the fall. Instead, you're stuck with me."

"Then I guess we're both lucky I enjoy hanging out with you." He tucks me into my seat, snaps my seat belt, and closes my door. When he's settled in the driver's seat, he turns to me. "I know what it's like to have a fucked-up relationship with your parents, and if I can help you avoid that, I'm game." He nods slowly. "I get why your dad's protective of you. If some punk like me messed with my daughter, I'd lose my shit too."

"You're not a punk."

"We both know I'm an asshole on a good day. That I say things I shouldn't and open my mouth before I think things through."

"Which is how you ended up with me." I'll never forget him busting into my dad's office and defending me, but now he has a fake girlfriend and a baby that's not his coming in the summer.

He side-eyes me. "Not the worst punishment in the world, if you wanna know the truth."

With a tired smile, I shake my head. "For the record, I'm not going to let this go on forever. Give me a few weeks to let my dad settle down, and then we'll tell him." I nibble my bottom lip. "Or should I wait until Ezra gets drafted? If he's gone, then my dad can't get arrested for beating him to death with his own cleats."

Billy shrugs as he drives and glances at me. "Or you tell him now and let *me* beat him up *for* your father."

"There will be no fighting. Promise me."

"I don't know if I can do that, biscuit. That fucker has it coming."

"Maybe, but I don't want you to get in trouble." I stare out the window. Night is falling, and mist gathers along the side of the road. "I thought I wanted to torture Ezra by hanging out with his fiancée, but I don't know if I have it in me to be vindictive like that. Abigail is innocent in all of this. I don't want to pretend to be her friend only to drop some huge bomb about Ezra."

Reaching over, Billy laces his fingers through mine. "You're a good person. I like that about you. You always see the best in people and want to do the right thing. I don't operate that way, but I'm trying to be better."

"You don't have to change for me. I like who you are."

That gets me a crooked smile. "Thanks. That means a lot to me. But I know I could be more responsible and less of a loose cannon."

I run my finger over his scarred knuckles. "I like that you're never scared of anything. You're the only man who ever goes toe to toe with my father. It's kinda hot."

He laughs. "We all have our kinks."

When we get to the Yellow Rose, he pulls up to the front and lets me out.

"I'll get us a table," I tell him before I shut the passenger door. Even though the parking lot is full, it only takes a few minutes for him to grab a spot and make it inside. "That was fast."

"Something no man ever wants to hear."

I snort and cover my mouth. When I stop laughing, I whisper, "I have a feeling that's not a problem for you."

"We'll have to test your theory, huh?" The look he gives me sets my ovaries on fire. But then he has to go and ruin it. "When you're feeling better, of course, and the doctor gives you the go-ahead."

"You're such a buzzkill."

He tosses his arm over my shoulder and hugs me. "What kind of fake boyfriend would I be if I didn't look out for my biscuit?"

I wrap my arms around his slender waist. That's when I notice all the looks we're getting. It gives me an idea. I tug him down to me. "How real do you want to make this *relationship*?"

His gorgeous blue eyes stare into mine as he considers. "Are we talking about public displays of affection?"

"Yeah, I was wondering if you wanted to—"

But I don't get a chance to finish before he cuts me off with a kiss. Just like the time we made out in his truck, my whole body comes alive with his touch. I reach up and run my fingers through his hair. I've almost forgotten my name when he pulls away slightly.

"I'm sorry, Rox. What were you going to say?" He smirks.

I nip his bottom lip. "You're a beast."

He laughs and kisses me again. "That I am. And you're my Beauty."

"You're such a charmer."

"I know." The handsome bastard winks.

The waitress calls my name, and Billy grabs my hand as we follow her to the table. She seats us next to the dance floor. We order some po' boys and iced tea.

As we wait for our food, we talk about the upcoming season.

"Tell me more about your position on the team. I've looked up your stats, obviously, and I know you're a defensive back, but what's your focus as a safety?"

"I'm basically the last line of defense and cover the eligible pass receivers."

I think about that a minute. "For a guy who just switched to defense, you had a great season last year. Five interceptions is nothing to sneeze at. You were an all-conference player with the second highest number of interceptions. I know you miss offense, but you might be really well suited to play safety." I hold up my fingers as I count off all the reasons he could kick ass next year. "You excelled at QB, so you know what you're up against. You played wide receiver, so you know those routes inside and out. And if you could bump your interceptions up to, say, seven or eight, I don't think your personal life would matter all that much to prospective NFL teams as long as you keep the partying to a minimum."

He gives me a smile where his eyes twinkle. "You're right, Coach. I'll try to have a good attitude about defense and shoot for eight interceptions."

That gives me an idea. "We could even do a reward system. Like for every interception you make, I could—"

"Give me a gold star?"

I chuckle. "I like the star idea, but I was going to say a back massage."

His eyes roll back in his head as he clutches his chest dramatically. "Jesus, yes. I'll take all the back massages you want to dole out."

The way he groans sends shivers through me, as though we're talking about a sexy massage with lots of body oil and very little clothing. A slow, needy ache pulses between my thighs at the thought.

When dinner arrives, we scarf down the food. The whole time I watch couples two-step around the dance floor.

"You miss dancing, huh?"

I sigh and return my attention to Billy. "So much."

When we're done eating, he glances at the couples swaying together and clears his throat. "Wanna join me out there?"

"Aren't you afraid I'll overdo it?" I'm honestly shocked he's suggesting it.

"How stressful will one slow dance be?" He stands and offers me his hand.

I place my hand in his and smile as the song switches to "Next Thing You Know" by Jordan Davis.

We walk out onto the floor, and he pulls me close and starts to sway. I drape my arms over his broad shoulders and lay my head against his chest. I breathe in his spicy cologne and smile when he rests his chin on the top of my head as he sings the song.

His voice is raspy and so damn sexy. Being wrapped up in his arms sends a delicious warmth through me.

By the bar, I spot Vicky, Billy's former friend with benefits. When our eyes connect, her jaw tightens and she turns away to talk to her friends.

Billy might say they're over, but I get the impression that was his decision, not hers.

As the song ends, he leans over to murmur in my ear. "Wanna go home and snuggle?"

I tilt my head way back to stare up at him. "Can I be the little spoon?"

He chuckles and looks me over. "Kinda think that's the only way this works, biscuit."

21

BILLY

AFTER A QUICK SHOWER, I towel-dry my hair and brush my teeth. I glance at Roxy's toothbrush that sits in a mug next to mine on the gleaming white counter in her bathroom. This is so domestic. Typically shit that would terrify me, frankly.

Even though this place is technically ours, I'm not an idiot. I know everything in here belongs to Rox and her parents, who were nice enough to not bury me in a shallow grave.

When I'm done brushing, I tear off a paper towel, replace the roll in the cabinet, and wipe down the counter.

I feel compelled to be the opposite of what I am when living at the football house. Which means I can't drink straight out of the milk container, scratch my balls whenever I feel like it, or burp loudly after I eat.

It's called having manners, dumbass.

I'll admit I don't know what I'm doing, and I have no plan for tonight besides curling up around Roxy in bed and enjoying that time together.

It can't lead to more. The girl just went to the hospital last week. Don't think with your dick.

I seriously thought about jacking off in the shower, but then

I remembered I told her I'd be fast. I moved our stuff all afternoon and felt it was only polite to clean up before bed.

I'm only wearing black boxer briefs, which is more than I usually sleep in. I already asked her if this was okay, just to double-check, and she said whatever I wanted to wear to bed is fine.

After clicking off the light, I pad out into the bedroom where she's tucked in bed, flipping through a book. She has reading glasses perched on her little nose. Her thick hair is tied up in a huge, messy bun on top of her head. I can't tell what she's wearing because she has the covers pulled up under her arms, but spaghetti straps peek out.

"Hey." She smiles over the top of her book and pulls down the comforter so I can crawl in. I catch a glimpse of her thin tank top and pajama bottoms. I don't know how she makes something so simple look so damn sexy, but she does.

"Whatcha reading?" I ask as I stretch out next to her.

"Historical romance. My guilty pleasure."

She hands me the book, and I scan the cover, which features a woman in a fancy ball gown all tangled up with some rich guy. "*The Viscount's Vixen*. Sounds steamy."

"So steamy." She fans herself, and I laugh.

"Oh, yeah?" I twist toward her and rest my head on my hand. Her face is flushed. I run my finger over her soft cheek. "You turned on, biscuit?"

She nibbles her bottom lip and nods slowly. "Yeah. I blame the pregnancy. I'm basically a walking hormone."

I can relate. "Tell me what you were reading. Describe it."

"Oh. Um." She swallows. "The couple has to sneak around because her older brother hates the viscount, who's in love with the younger sister. The title is ironic because she's actually quite prim and proper, but this guy tempts her to be bad. And during a ball, they sneak off to the study where they hook up."

"What do they do?"

"They kiss in a dark corner. Then he scandalously lifts her skirts. Sinks to his knees. Makes her come. It's all very shocking for her because she's never gotten off before."

Damn. That does sound hot.

"How does he make her come?" I ask as I play with a long tendril of hair that's escaped her bun.

Her sharp inhale makes me smile. I am one hundred percent getting off on watching Roxy squirm. "He, uh, he uses his fingers and then his mouth."

"Does she return the favor?"

Roxy laughs. "Pretty sure she wouldn't know how, but they hear someone in the hall and have to hide before they're caught."

Leaning over her, I run my nose up her neck. "I know you can't have sex, but do you want me to take the edge off for you? Make you come?" I close my eyes as I breathe in her sweet scent. "You can say no, and I'll spoon you, and we'll go to sleep. Totally up to you. No pressure."

She doesn't bother with words, just wiggles closer, and I toss the book and reach for her. As I lean down to kiss her, she pauses. "Can I get you off too?"

"Like I'm gonna say no? You have a standing invitation to rub my cock."

She laughs. "You always have a way with words."

I groan when she tosses her thigh over mine and presses her tits into my chest.

She lifts her chin, and I lean down to kiss her. Her tongue battles with mine as I take a large handful of her ass and pull her closer. Until I can fit my hard dick between her thighs.

Christ, she feels good, but if we grind any harder, we're both gonna chafe.

"This will never do, my little fox. You have too many clothes on. If you want my best work, I need complete nudity and the lights stay on."

"Billy, you know I'm not shy. Look all you want," she says as she strips off her tank top and treats me to her incredible tits. "But so you know, my body is getting swollen in different places, so I'm not as thin as I used to be."

I watch as she flops back in bed and kicks off her pajama bottoms, which leaves her in pale pink panties.

"I have a feeling I'll love your body no matter what it looks like." I rub her belly, which is still pretty flat. "How's our little bean?"

That gets me another smile. "Good."

Leaning over, I kiss her again. She tastes like toothpaste and some kind of fruity lip balm.

I drag my finger between those gorgeous tits before I take a hard nipple between my lips and suck. Roxy squirms as I gently squeeze her other breast.

"Roll over so I can appreciate your ass. I've been wanting an up-close-and-personal introduction to it for a while."

"I had no idea you were an ass man." She gives me a flirty smile.

Pulling down the blankets, I make room for her to reposition herself. She's wearing these cheeky panties and fills them out to perfection. Roxy has an incredible body with lean, muscular legs that lead to a round butt.

"Fuck, you have a nice ass." I lean over and bite one cheek, making her squeal. "Sit still. It's a shame I can't spank you." If ever there was an ass that called out for a nice big print of my palm, it's this one.

She wiggles her behind at me and smirks over her shoulder. "You going to stare all night? Or are you planning to get me off sometime soon?"

I definitely wanna spank this ass.

When I grab her with both hands and massage those muscular cheeks, she lets out a squeak of surprise. I smile because she has no idea who she's dealing with.

I tuck a pillow under her hips. "Is this comfortable?"

"Yeah."

She looks so fucking good with her ass up like this. I reach down and squeeze my dick before I pull down her panties and nudge her legs apart.

When I drag my thumb through her pussy, I groan at how wet she is, but then she lifts her rear to me. She showered this afternoon, which makes my choice easy.

I drag my wet thumb up to her clit as I lick her asshole.

"Oh God," she says, panting.

That's when I gently push one finger into her tight pussy. After a minute, I add a second finger, making sure to rub against her G-spot. Her whole body trembles as she comes apart and screams into her pillow.

Once I've worked her through her orgasm, she flops onto the bed. I smile, pleased at how fast I could make her come. I've never been with a woman who was this responsive.

She turns to me with sleepy eyes. "That was amazing. Thank you."

I collapse next to her and pull her to my chest. "My pleasure."

I hold her for a few minutes. I'm about to tell her to go to sleep, that she doesn't have to reciprocate, when her small hand wanders down my chest and stomach and straight into my boxer briefs, where she thumbs my weeping tip and makes me groan.

"Take these off," she whispers.

She doesn't have to tell me twice. I kick off my underwear and lie back with her in my arms. She takes hold of my cock, lets out a sigh, and...

A little snore escapes her as I throb in her palm.

What the...

There it is again.

I half laugh, half groan.

No one had better hear of this because my buddies will have a field day if they find out the first time my fake girlfriend-slash-friend with benefits got introduced to my dick, she promptly passed out.

After I pull her hand off my dick, I yank the blankets over us and kiss her forehead. "Sleep well, my little biscuit."

22

ROXY

SMILING, I snuggle deeper into the blankets.

I had the sexiest dream last night. Billy went down on me *from behind* and did some dirty things to my body. That man made me come so hard, I almost passed out. Then I dragged my hand down his incredible chest, along his washboard abs, down to the biggest d—

I sit up in bed, suddenly wide awake. My heart pounds as I blink into our bright bedroom.

Please tell me that was a dream.

Because if it wasn't, that means...

That means...

I groan and flop back in bed and pull the pillow over my head. *That means I fell asleep on Billy right after I wrapped my hand around his enormous dick.*

His enormous *hard* dick.

Maybe I could stay in bed today. There's really no need to move from this very spot. And then maybe I'll disappear from sheer mortification.

My phone rings, and I cringe. If that's Billy, what do I tell him? *Sorry I passed out on you when I was about to pounce on your junk?*

Ugh. Moving to the pool house in my parents' backyard sounds pretty good right now.

Reluctantly, I pick up my phone and see it's Charlotte. "Hey. What's up?"

"Are you okay?" she asks. There's an echo to her voice like she's in the bathroom or somewhere cavernous.

"Yeah. Why?"

"Weren't we going to meet for breakfast today?"

"Oh my God! Charlie, I'm so sorry! First I fall asleep on Billy and now this." I glance at my clock and groan. "I must've slept through my alarm clock and now I only have half an hour to get to class."

"It's totally okay. I'm just relieved nothing's wrong."

After I get off the phone, I rush around my bedroom and get dressed. I toss on a t-shirt, jeans and sweater and lace up my hiking boots since it's dreary outside.

I barely make it to my sports journalism class on time. Afterward, as I hustle to the counselor's office, my phone buzzes with a text from Billy.

Hey, Sleeping Beauty. How's your day going?

Do I just come out and apologize? Or do I pretend it didn't happen?

Ugh, no, Roxanne. Don't be a wuss. It's not your style.

OMG, Billy, I'm SOOOO sorry I fell asleep on you last night!

He responds with three laughing emojis. **I won't take it personally.**

If it means anything to you, I woke up thinking I'd had the best dirty dream ever.

As long as I can keep your spank bank full, we're good.

I smile down at his response. **Can I make it up to you? I**

have a busy week, but maybe Friday night we could hang. How do you feel about Netflix, homemade enchiladas, and... I add an eggplant emoji and a splash.

Count me in, gorgeous. I'm about to put my phone back in my bag when he adds, **I had fun last night.**

I did too. Thanks for the date! See you at home. :)

He sends one more text. **I'm shocked to admit this, but I like living with you, biscuit. You smell much better than the guys, and you're a great little spoon.**

I'm still smiling when I reach the admin building. I'm hoping to switch my broadcast course from the fall to the spring semester next year, so I have to meet with my counselor.

After I knock on Mrs. Lockwood's door, she waves me in. "Roxy Santos?"

"Yes, ma'am. We've spoken on the phone a few times." I sit in the chair and clutch my bag.

She types on her keyboard and scans her computer. "That's right. You're Coach Santos's daughter. How can I help you?"

"I was wondering if broadcast journalism was being offered second semester next year. I didn't see it listed online, but I wanted to double-check." *Please let it be available.*

The room fills with the sounds of her clicking the keyboard as she checks. "I'm sorry. It's not. Why can't you take it first semester?" She stares at me over the rim of her glasses.

I bite my bottom lip, hating that I have to admit my situation to a relative stranger. I glance at the open door, and no one is standing nearby, but I lower my voice anyway. "I'm pregnant and due in early August. So while I might be able to swing it, I'd rather take the course second semester." I'm hoping that gives me enough time to lose any baby weight I gain.

Her lips purse. "That will be a challenge. Do you have childcare lined up for the fall?"

Will I sound like the world's worst mother if I admit I hadn't even thought that far? "No. Not yet."

She digs through her desk drawer and hands me a pamphlet. "The school provides childcare to students, but it's need-based. I'm not sure you'll qualify based on your parents' income, but it's worth a shot."

My shoulders slump. "That's frustrating."

She gives me a sympathetic smile. "We also have a free parenting class if you'd like to attend."

I babysat a few kids in high school, but they were all older. "Thanks. Yeah, I probably should." I jot down the info in my binder.

I'm feeling defeated and unprepared for the next few months when I walk out of her office. By the time I get to the student union, my eyes sting.

Damn it, I will not cry.

I duck into the bathroom to compose myself. After I splash a little cold water on my face and dry it, I step into a stall. Pregnancy seems to have shrunk my bladder to the size of a lima bean because two seconds after I drink anything, I have to pee.

A few people walk in when I'm zipping up my jeans.

"I heard he went out with her last night. Vicky said they slow-danced, and it looked like they were on a date."

Vicky? As in Billy's former friend with benefits? *They're not talking about you. Stop being paranoid.*

"The day Billy Bigcock actually takes a girl on a date, I'll be a born-again virgin," another girl snarks, and I freeze with my hand on the latch. "And even if he did, he'll be on to his new flavor of the month soon enough. The trick is to bump into him when he's in between hookups."

Cringing, I close my eyes and wait for them to leave.

I've always had a hard time reconciling the Billy I know, who does sweet things for me and makes me laugh, with the guy who hooks up at every party and leaves a trail of broken hearts in his wake.

It's a good reminder not to let myself get too invested in this game we're playing. Billy and I are friends. Really good friends who get naked sometimes. But that's all he'll probably ever want. There's no need to get completely wrapped up in him.

As I stand there, waiting for those girls to leave, I realize Billy and I never talked about being monogamous. Although we did last month, we never discussed it when we wrote out our contract.

Can I ask him about it now? He's already doing so much for me. I feel like I'm getting everything out of this deal we made, but the idea of Billy being with another woman makes my stomach hurt.

Once I'm sure those horrible girls are gone, I head out.

Only to bump into someone.

"I'm so sorry—"

"Oh. *Ohhh*. Hey!"

I come to a stop and stare at Abigail, who bounces on her toes. "I'm so glad I ran into you, Roxy! Literally!" She laughs nervously as she pushes her glasses up her nose.

"Hey, Abigail. What are you doing here?" I give her a hug.

She gives me the biggest smile and flaps her hands around. "I'm taking classes at Lone Star! It was really last-minute, but I found a few fun courses I wanted to take."

"That's great. I bet Ezra is *sooo* excited." That asshole is probably shitting his pants right now.

A frown forms on her pretty face. "Actually, he's been a bit grumpy. I figure he's just anxious about the draft."

"Probably. The guys always get freaked out before the big day." Her being in Charming makes me curious about the logistics of her situation. "Are you a junior like Ezra?" She nods. "So what's the plan next fall? Will you just switch colleges to a school in whatever city he's drafted to?"

"Exactly. Not all of my credits transferred here, unfortunately, but I wanted to be with Ezra to support him and make sure he doesn't get stressed out."

This woman is way too good for that dirtbag. "I'm sure he really appreciates that." Not in a million years.

"It's been so hard to do a long-distance relationship." She looks around to make sure we're alone and whispers, "We've had this weird energy lately, and I thought if we spent more time together before the draft, we'd be better off."

You're feeling weird energy because Ezra has been fucking every girl on campus and lying to your face about it. The words are on the tip of my tongue.

I take a deep breath. "Listen, Abigail. I know we don't know each other well, but—"

"Oh my God! Are you serious?" My eyes widen, and my heart pounds. Does she know I slept with her fiancé? I need to tell her I didn't realize he had a serious girlfriend back home, but before I can say anything, she takes me by my shoulders and shakes me a little. "I'd love to hang out!" She blinks. "That's what you were going to say, right?"

She looks so excited to spend time together, and I feel like a piece of shit for sleeping with her fiancé. It doesn't make me feel any better that I was just as clueless about Ezra's philandering as she is. I cough. "Y-yes. You took the words right out of my mouth."

"Good, because I don't know anyone on campus, and Ezra has been too busy to spend any time with me. And I could really use a friend. You mentioned it when you came to my engagement party, but I didn't know if you were just trying to be nice."

"I... I'd love to be your friend." It's true. Abigail has this great energy about her and is super sweet. If we didn't have this huge issue between us, she's absolutely someone I'd want to be friends with.

She hooks her arm in mine. "Great! Let's be besties. We can share everything. Like our deepest, darkest secrets."

Like how I slept with your fiancé? Several times? And got knocked up? "That... that sounds great."

I'm pretty sure I'm going to hell.

"Are you seeing anyone?"

"Um. Yeah, actually, I am."

"Awesome! We should go on a double date. Wouldn't that be so fun?"

So, so fun.

23

BILLY

WHEN I UNLOCK the door to our apartment, I find Roxy curled up on the couch, asleep on her textbook, drooling a little. After I unload my gym bag and school crap, I grab a blanket and drape it over her.

"You're home." She yawns and smiles at me.

"Hey, gorgeous. Want some dinner? I have some chicken and pasta I snagged from the athletic caf."

"That sounds good. Are you sure you have enough? I don't want to steal your food."

"I have enough for both of us. You think I'm gonna bring home dinner and not have enough to share?"

"Thank you. That's really thoughtful." She hops off the couch and flings herself into my arms. Tilting her head back, she gives me another sweet smile. "How was your day, dear? Was it ruined by my failed attempt to jerk you off last night?"

I bark out a laugh and hug her. "Feel free to sleep with your hand wrapped around my junk anytime."

She snort-laughs and covers her mouth. "I'm sorry. I'm honestly so embarrassed."

I hoist her into my arms and hold her by her ass. "No

apology necessary." I stomp over to the kitchen and place her on the counter before I take her beautiful face in my hands and kiss her. "We said we'd see where things go. There's no rush or pressure to do anything. Let's just have fun."

For some reason, she frowns. "Have fun?"

I shrug. "Yeah, I mean, if you can't have fun with your fake girlfriend with benefits, who can you have fun with?"

She chuckles. "I was just thinking the same thing."

"It's eerie how similar we are, isn't it?" I ask as I palm her boob.

She reaches around and smacks my ass. "Totally."

I kiss her again before I help her off the counter. After I grab the takeout containers and silverware, I set everything out on the bar. She gets us two glasses of ice water, and we both sit.

"How did your appointment with your counselor go?" I ask as I shovel chicken into my mouth.

She groans. "Not well. I have to do the broadcast class in the fall, and I'm worried I'll still look like a beached whale. The camera adds at least twenty pounds."

After I swallow my bite, I turn to her. "Roxy, you're a stunning woman, regardless of your weight. I know you're used to being super fit for cheer, but don't be too hard on yourself."

Nodding, she stares at her pasta as she pushes the food around with her fork. "I am one hundred percent about body positivity. But now that I'm facing a situation where I can't just work out and eat super clean until I look a certain way, I'm realizing that I don't extend that attitude to myself as much as I thought I did."

"Understandable. I'm sure it can't be easy growing a gremlin and then having to go about your daily life like you didn't just spawn."

She laughs. "A gremlin?"

"Did you ever see that old eighties movie? They're super

cute. Well, the good one. The bad ones are evil little fuckers, but that's not the one I meant."

"I must've missed that movie."

"What I'm trying to say, and obviously not doing a good job of it, is that you're, what, almost four months along now? And you don't look pregnant. And I've seen all of you." Her pretty cheeks flush. "I'm guessing that because you're in such amazing shape, hopefully, your recovery time will be easier."

"Thanks. That's really nice to hear. I hope that's true." She crosses her fingers. Why is everything she does so damn cute?

"Wanna study together after we eat? I have a paper I need to write."

"Yeah. I'd like that. Oh, before I shove this deep into my brain and forget I agreed to this... I ran into Abigail today, Ezra's fiancée."

"No shit. How did it go?" We toss our dirty dishes in the sink and head for the couch, where we sit side by side.

"Ugh, Billy, she's so freaking nice. How am I supposed to tell her the truth and break her heart?"

I toss an arm around her. "It's gonna suck big hairy donkey balls, but at the end of the day, she'll probably wanna know the truth."

"She just transferred here and told me she doesn't have any friends and wants me to be her bestie." Roxy's whole face contorts like she just sucked on a lemon. "And she wants us to go on a double date with her and Ezra."

"You're kidding."

"I would never joke about something like that."

I rub a hand over my face. "This will be memorable."

"I feel like I've already asked you for a million favors, but would you do this for me? I was thinking maybe this would help me figure out how to tell him about the baby."

Ezra and I never hang out. We never eat together or shoot

the shit. Because the day he got QB1, he turned to me with a smirk, smacked my back, and told me to enjoy being wide receiver. To anyone else, it would've sounded like congratulations. But he knew I was gunning to return to the quarterback position, even if I had to ride the bench for a while. And when I got switched to safety, he offhandedly said that some people can't hack offense. Again, not a direct slight, but he was looking at me at the time.

Ezra's slick like that. Slimy. Never really owns up to his shit. He lets everyone think he's this great guy when he's anything but.

I was ready to kick Ezra's ass both of those times, but then that would just feed Coach's perception that I'm out of control.

Blowing out a breath, I nod. "For you, sure." I can admit I have a hard time telling Roxy no. "Are you still thinking you want to wait for the draft to tell Ezra about the bean?"

She groans. "Sometimes I want to rip off the Band-Aid and get it over with. Other times, I'm worried the news will get back to my dad, and he'll have a coronary that his golden child betrayed him. To be clear, the golden child is Ezra and not his literal offspring."

"Aww, Rox."

"How have things with Ezra been at practice? I know you guys don't have the same kind of schedule in the offseason as you do in the summer or fall, but have you seen him around? Has he said anything to you about my... situation?"

She might as well hear it from me. "I'm in the gym in the morning, and he does afternoons, so fortunately, I don't have to see that turd often, but we had a team meeting last week, after you and your dad had your big blowup."

"And?"

It sucks to be the messenger. "He was sitting with a few of his friends when I walked by, and he motioned to me and said,

'Looks like I dodged a bullet.' I'm not sure anyone knew what he was talking about because it was kind of a non sequitur." But I knew he meant Roxy.

"Non sequitur?"

"Yeah, uh, out of the blue. Not really following the conversation he was having with the rest of the guys."

I watch her for any indication she still has feelings for that idiot. But when our eyes meet, she looks puzzled. "You're a smart guy, Billy, but you don't always do well in school. Why is that?"

Huffing out a laugh, I shrug. "I like to read, but I haven't always been motivated to study, especially if I'm not into a class. I'm trying harder this year, though, since I might not have a career in football."

She grabs my shoulder. "You're the best all-around athlete on the team. You have quick feet and sticky hands that can catch or intercept any ball. You leap like a damn jungle cat. And you have a stubborn coach who's determined to snag another national championship. I think that bodes well for you. Don't lose heart." Damn, this woman makes me feel ten feet tall. But then she pokes me. "To be clear, I'm not saying you shouldn't study."

"No, ma'am."

She chuckles and leans over to kiss my cheek, and I pull her into my lap. Her brow furrows. "You just need to remember why you fell in love with football and get back to basics. You know how my dad always says you have to focus on the immediate moment? Like, you have to catch the ball before you run, or you stand a greater likelihood of fumbling? That's what you have to do. It's the same thing with cheer. If I'm thinking about another part of the routine, I always screw up. My mind has to be on the move I'm trying to execute. Don't get so caught up thinking about the combine or draft next year. If you execute in the fall like I know you can, you'll be a shoo-in."

"That's great advice, biscuit."

For the first time in so long, I feel optimistic about next season. Maybe I should count myself lucky that I'm now on defense and don't have to deal with Ezra much.

I finger a long strand of Roxy's thick hair. "I'm sorry Ezra's an asshole."

"You don't have to tiptoe around this with me. My eyes are open. I'm not sitting around pining for that guy. *I'm* the one who dodged a bullet." She grabs her flat stomach. "You might not think that given my current situation, but at least I'm not heartbroken over that loser."

I place my hand over hers. "When's your next doctor appointment?"

"Friday."

"Have you had any more cramps since I took you to the ER?"

She shakes her head. "No, I've been good. Tired, but otherwise okay."

"Do you want me to take you to the appointment?"

"You wouldn't mind?"

"Of course not. Will we be able to see the bean on the ultrasound again?"

"I think so."

"I can't wait." Not a lie. Seeing that little life on the monitor is the coolest thing I've ever experienced. I waggle my eyebrows at her. "Make sure you ask the doctor if you can have sex."

"I totally plan to."

Our eyes connect, and the heat between us makes me groan. "Not that I'm expecting it or anything."

"Of course not."

"But it would be nice."

She laughs and shoves me again. "It would be."

24

BILLY

"SEVEN NATION ARMY" blasts from the stereo in the locker room as I head for the showers.

"Good workout," Coach Gates says with a slap to my back. He works with the defensive line. "I saw you pushing it in the weight room."

"Thanks, Coach."

My legs feel like wet noodles after all those leg presses. I head to the corner of the cavernous shower room, toss my towel on the wall hook, and crank the hot water.

"Hey, man. Those were some nice pics on your socials. You thinking of adopting?"

Cracking open an eye, I see Jake walk up to the showerhead two slots over. It takes me a second to figure out what he's talking about.

"You mean the photos from Second Chances?" Roxy encouraged me to do some volunteer work to beef up my good-guy image. But once I got to the animal rescue that Jake's girlfriend Charlie introduced us to last summer, I realized how much I liked it. Those animals are great, and I think that's something I'm going to continue doing, regardless of how it makes me look.

"We probably have too much going on to adopt a pet, but those little dudes are cool."

"How's the roommate situation going?"

"It's pretty damn good."

"Yeah?" He looks surprised.

I pump a handful of soap into my palm. "Roxy's a fun girl. She's so neat, and she smells incredible. And it's always nice to see her after a long day." Jesus, I sound like a dumbass.

He laughs and massages shampoo into his hair. "I love living with Charlotte too. She makes my apartment feel like home."

Huh. Yeah, I get that.

I soap all the important areas and rinse off. But when I glance at my junk, it makes me wonder.

"Dude, can I ask you something?" Since no one else is here, maybe I can pose this question to Jake. He's pretty good at keeping shit locked down.

"Sure. What's up?"

I shut off the water and reach for my towel. "Funny you phrase it like that, but I have a personal situation." I glance around to make sure we're still alone. "I'm not gonna look 'cause we're in the shower, and that would be awkward, but do you manscape?" After I finish drying off, I wrap the towel around my waist. When he doesn't say anything, I look at him.

He's staring at me with a brow raised. "Because you care what my pubes look like?"

"No, dude, I care what *Roxy* thinks about *my* pubes."

"Trim around the beast and call it a day. No need to obsess over it."

"That's what I do, but"—again, I look around—"Rox keeps falling asleep on me, and the first time it happened, she had her hand on my dick."

Jake's shoulders shake with laughter as he turns off the water. "She fell asleep while you two were...?"

"Something like that. Yeah. And since then, she's asleep the second her head hits the pillow. I'm starting to get a complex about it." When I told her there's no pressure to do more, I meant it. But for some reason, I can't shake the idea that maybe she didn't like what she found, and she's avoiding it.

Or maybe I'm too big?

I never thought that would be an issue, and it would suck if it was. Except she's tiny, and I'm packing. That shit usually makes me strut around like a damn peacock, but being with Roxy makes me all twisted up in ways I've never expected.

Jake schools his expression, but I can tell he wants to crack up. "Sorry. I won't laugh."

"My man pride is getting dented here. It made me wonder if she'd prefer it smooth down there."

He chuckles and wraps the towel around his waist. "Maybe she's just tired. I'd ask her about her preferences before you go to the trouble of trying to shave your balls and nicking something important."

I shiver. "Good point." No sense in doing all that if she doesn't care.

Rox is the first woman who's ever made me work for it, which is why I'm probably overthinking this. I've never really cared what my dick and balls looked like. I keep the area relatively neat, though, because who wants to give a blow job through an Amazonian forest? I can see the appeal of a neatly trimmed dick area.

We head back to the locker room. "Thanks for the talk, man." Jake's a hard nut to crack sometimes. He's so fucking serious all the time. Except when we're talking about shaving my balls, I guess.

"I'm sure your girl will be enchanted with your goods," he says. I'm about to laugh when he adds, "All the other women in your life seem to be."

I know he doesn't mean that to be a slight because Jake's genuinely a good guy, but being reminded of my manwhore past is starting to get under my skin. Like it's a role I used to play that I'm not comfortable with anymore.

It makes me wonder if Roxy has reservations about my past too.

My father says I'm a bad bet. Maybe he's right. Maybe Rox shouldn't count on me.

I finish drying off and throw on a pair of jeans and a t-shirt.

"Wanna grab a bite to eat?" Jake asks from his locker across from me.

"I can't. I'm taking Roxy to her doctor appointment. I'm kinda excited. I like seeing the bean on that monitor. The way the exam room fills with that little heartbeat is crazy. There's a whole life in there. It's wild."

He side-eyes me for a sec and lowers his voice. "You're much better at this dad thing than I thought you'd be."

I laugh and tug on my socks. "We'll see how long it lasts." It's probably easier to be chill when it's not your kid hurtling toward you like a bowling ball about to bash into those pins. "Probably until the first time the kid shits on me. That happens, right?"

Jake laughs and smacks me on the back. "All the time when they're little."

My stomach turns a little. "Great. Looking forward to that." Almost as much as I want to nick my balls with a razor.

25

ROXY

"I'M glad to hear you haven't had any more spotting." Dr. Irving smiles as she reviews my chart. "How does it feel to be officially sixteen weeks along?"

Scary as hell. "Exhilarating. And terrifying."

Billy squeezes my hand, and the tension in my shoulders wanes a bit. I'm grateful to have him standing by my side as I sit on the exam table.

"That's completely normal. I can assure you most soon-to-be mothers have felt the exact same way at some point during their pregnancies." She turns to Billy. "Daddy, how are you feeling?"

"Um." He blinks several times. "What?"

Billy might've come to the first appointment with me, but the tech only called him in at the end when we did the ultrasound. This is the first time he's talking to my doctor, and she obviously assumes he's the father.

She motions to my belly. "This is going to be a big change for both of you. How are you feeling? Have you been reading all of the daddy books to prepare?"

"Daddy books?" He looks like a deer caught in the headlights of an eighteen-wheeler. It's my turn to squeeze his hand.

It's not as though this is actually his child. Though, now that I'm getting to know him better, I wish it was. It would be so much easier to do this with him than my idiot ex.

The doctor rattles off a list of titles she recommends for first-time fathers. As she sits on the chair in front of me, she pauses. "You should probably read *What to Expect When You're Expecting* too. Although it's written for the mother, you'll get so much insight into the changes Roxy's body is going through. So if she's cranky or tired or really turned on, you'll understand more about what's happening to her body."

"Really turned on?" he asks, his voice husky.

I chuckle. That got his attention.

She nods. "A high libido during second trimester is one of the best parts of pregnancy, which might not make up for all the nausea Roxy experienced first trimester, but it's better than losing your breakfast every day."

Maybe this is a good time to ask... "Doc, speaking of libido, is it safe to have sex again?"

She flips through my chart and clicks her pen before she turns to me. "After today's exam, assuming everything looks good, you're free to go back to your usual routine, and yes, that includes sex. As long as there's no more cramping or spotting. Take it easy whenever you need to. I don't usually do a pelvic exam at sixteen weeks, but since you were spotting, I want to err on the side of caution."

"Can I start working out again? I mean, if I have the energy. Lately I've been crashing as soon as I get home."

"As long as you start slow and don't do anything too strenuous, you can do light workouts. You might consider yoga poses to help with the round ligament pain we discussed, like the pelvic tilt and cat-cow. If you're able to stay in shape during pregnancy, that might help you recover more quickly. However, if something is uncomfortable, be it during sex or any other daily activity, stop and assess how you're feeling. Continue taking prenatal vitamins and stay extra hydrated. Your baby needs those fluids for his or her placenta. And needing more sleep is normal."

"That's a relief." I laugh.

"She does sleep a lot," Billy says. "Kinda had me worried. She's usually a night owl."

I glance up at him, but he has an unusually stoic expression on his face.

Dr. Irving nods. "Pregnancy is very taxing on her body. I'm not surprised she goes to bed early."

The entire time she examines me, Billy stands there with his hands jammed in his jean pockets, staring straight down at his shoes, which is funny since he's seen me naked. Not in the last several days, since I can't seem to stay awake, which is bumming me out. I've been looking forward to taking things further with him. But he's a hell of a snuggler. Every morning, I wake up with him pressed to my back, and it's heavenly.

When my pelvic exam is over, the doctor tells me everything looks good, and she steps out of the room to get the ultrasound technician. I tug on Billy's arm. "You okay? You're awfully interested in your shoes."

His cheeks go ruddy. "I was afraid if I thought about you naked underneath that paper gown I'd get hard." I laugh, and he brushes a strand of hair out of my eyes as he grins. "There are probably some things we shouldn't surprise your doctor with."

The technician comes in, covers my lower half with a sheet, and squirts gel all over my belly. Then she gets the wand and rubs it on my abdomen. A few minutes later, the sound of the heartbeat fills the room.

"I love this part," Billy says quietly, almost solemnly. "Is it too early to tell the sex?" He turns to me. "I mean, did you want to find out?"

A huge smile breaks out on my face. "I absolutely want to find out the sex."

The technician nods. "Hopefully, we'll get a good look. Sometimes, the baby is too modest to tell." She's quiet as she waves the wand over my belly and takes measurements.

I stare at the screen. Tears burn my eyes, and I try to swallow as the technician points out ten little fingers and ten little toes.

"There." She points between the baby's legs.

I lean up on one arm to take a closer look.

"Congrats, Mom and Dad. Looks like you're having a girl."

I'm having a baby girl.

I don't care if my dad wants a boy. I'm going to love this little girl like no daughter has ever been loved before.

Tears stream down my face, and I bite my bottom lip to stop myself from full-on sobbing. Billy's arm comes around my shoulder as he hugs me to his side. "Aww, biscuit. I knew our bean was a girl. Think they make Bronco t-shirts for babies?"

Our bean.

My shoulders shudder with emotion as I try to breathe. Billy might only be pretending to be this child's father to help me out, but he doesn't know how much it means to me to have his support right now. I don't know many men who would offer to go to an OB-GYN appointment to help a friend. I love that Billy never gets squeamish or shies away from things that might make other guys run for the door.

I can't imagine Ezra sitting in the doctor's office holding my hand. And frankly, I would never want him here. It's too personal. I don't want to share these moments with him. I *won't* share these moments with him. Not that he would offer.

But I'm not going to think about that asshole because it'll ruin my mood. Today is a day to appreciate my little girl.

On our way home, I stare at the ultrasound images.

"You okay?" Billy asks as he drives. He has one hand on the steering wheel and one hand possessively on my thigh.

I pick up that hand and lace my fingers through his. "Yeah." I smile. "That was amazing, right? Seeing how big she's getting?"

"It's wild. Last time, she looked like something that fell out from one of your salads, and now she's a full-blown person."

"I haven't even met her yet, and this will sound crazy, but I'm totally in love with this baby."

"Pretty sure she's gonna be crazy about you too, biscuit." He gives me a crooked smile. "Wanna go home and watch a movie? Maybe order some Thai?"

"Ohh. I love Thai. But don't you have class later this afternoon?"

He shrugs. "I haven't missed any classes so far this semester. I think I can play hooky once."

"That would be really nice because I might actually be able to stay awake for a movie if we watch it early."

His smile widens. "It's a date."

The way he says that makes my heart race.

"Would it be better to go out? Do you need to be seen with that respectable girlfriend?" The idea of going out deflates my enthusiasm, which is strange because I'm usually a social butterfly.

"Nah. I'd rather just hang with you. Snuggle on the couch. Veg out. That okay?"

My excitement ramps up again. "It sounds perfect."

Spending some time alone with Billy? I'm definitely looking forward to this date.

26

ROXY

EMPTY THAI BOXES sprawl across the coffee table as some Tom Cruise movie plays on the TV. Frankly, I have no idea what's going on because I'm curled up on the couch with Billy. My legs are in his lap, and his hand is resting on my thigh. Every few minutes, he drags it up and down, just a little, almost like he just enjoys touching me. His attention is on the movie while he's slowly driving me out of my mind. Because that simple touch is going straight to my clit.

When I can't stand it any longer, I scoot off the couch.

"You okay?"

"Yeah. I'm fine." I motion behind me. "I need to take a shower and wash off all that goop the tech used for the ultrasound." Plus, I'm embarrassingly wet, and it's starting to get uncomfortable.

"Do you want me to pause the movie?"

Ask. Do it.

"No. It's fine."

Chicken.

His attention returns to the TV.

I clear my throat. "I was wondering if you'd like to join me."

"Join you where?" he asks as he takes a sip of his water, never turning away from that damn film.

"In the shower."

He chokes on his drink and then caps it. "Did you just ask me to shower with you or am I going mental?"

"Yes, I invited you to shower with me."

"Fuck yes, I'll join you." He tosses his bottle of water, leaps off the couch and picks me up, making me squeal with laughter.

The man carries me to the bathroom, where he stalks in there like a man on a mission. Reaching into the shower, I crank on the water. We're both smiling as we strip off our clothes. I pause to watch him yank off his t-shirt like it personally offended him. All of those beautiful muscles go on display like he's my personal thirst trap.

"You're too far away." I reach for him, and he lifts me by my ass. I wrap my legs around his waist as he kisses me breathless.

The way our tongues battle is animalistic. Primal. Like he's starving for me.

He smells so good, like spicy cologne and the masculine scent of his skin.

I tilt my head as he sucks on my neck. I usually hate hickeys, but it feels so good, I can't bring myself to tell him to stop. Not being with him this week while he slept in my own damn bed was pure torture. So tonight, I want everything he has to give. I want every mark, every bite, every hard thrust.

The bathroom fills with steam. I grab his handsome face and place a gentle kiss on his lips. "Let's get in the shower."

His pupils are blown out, and his cheeks are flushed. He nods and lets me slide down his body where I'm greeted by that thick rod in his jeans that presses against my belly.

I step away from him and flick off my bra. We watch each other as we finish undressing.

Billy is built like a machine. Tall with broad shoulders.

Muscles for days. Everything about him is hard. Especially that one part of his body that juts out the second he tugs down his black boxer briefs.

Holy thick cock, Batman.

I've never been with anyone that big before, and my clit throbs with anticipation.

It takes me another second of fumbling with my underwear before I'm naked. And then I stand there bare and let him look.

"Christ, you're gorgeous, Roxy."

"You're beautiful too." After a quick kiss, we step into the shower. I push him back against the wall and go to my knees. "I owe you for falling asleep the other night," I say as I take him in hand, which is a challenge because he's so thick.

I can't take my eyes off him as rivulets of water drip down his wide chest and over the hard planes of his stomach. Reaching up, I trace the same path, dragging my finger down his pec. Over his flat, brown nipple. Through the ridges in his abdomen.

He shakes his head. "You don't owe me anything. We're not keeping a scorecard."

I watch him as I lick up his long length. "Then this is just for fun."

He gives me a heated smile. "I'm at your mercy."

As he stares down at me, I lick his swollen cock head and flutter my tongue along his slit. He groans and fists my hair, leaning down to gather it all so he can watch.

Turning sideways, I treat him like my favorite lollipop to get him wet. Then I pump him into my mouth as I gently cradle his balls.

He tugs my head back. "Look at me when you suck my cock."

A shiver runs through me at his commanding presence. I eagerly do as he says. I'm not sure how deep I can take him. My stomach has been off with this pregnancy, but I want to make him feel as good as he made me feel when he delivered that mind-blowing orgasm last weekend.

After a moment, he reaches down, grips the base of his dick and rubs it across my lips. "Open your mouth. If something's too much, tap my leg."

I nod, grab his thick thighs, and open up.

"That's my girl." He places his dick in my mouth, and I move up and down. Deeper and deeper. After a minute, he pops out, and I gasp. "Is that too much, baby?"

"No. You can push me more."

His nostrils flare as he jams himself down my throat. Harder this time while he grips my hair tight. I love it. I love his roughness and the way he watches me with that feral edge as I stretch around him. I've never let a man fuck my mouth—one, because I've never trusted someone to not hurt me, but two, because I didn't really see the appeal—so I'm surprised by how much I'm enjoying this. Bringing Billy to the edge turns me on like nothing I've ever done before.

With my nails digging into his thighs, I swallow him down. All the way to the back of my throat. He grunts and groans and curses while I take him deep. I hold him to me when I feel him start to pulse in my mouth.

"Fuck. I'm gonna come."

I expect him to shoot down my throat, but he pulls out and spills all over my boobs, ribbons and ribbons of thick cum across my chest and belly.

He's panting, watching through slitted eyes, every muscle in his incredible body taut. "Was that too much?" he asks, his voice gravel.

I shake my head. "I'm not a doll. I won't break." I never thought I'd like it rough, but with Billy I do.

That ravenous gleam in his eyes makes me want to push him

further. I grip my breasts and hold them up to him. "Look at the mess you made."

His dick jerks again as he runs his finger over my wet nipple. He drags his finger through his cum, then rubs it across my bottom lip, where I lick it off and nip him.

"Jesus, Roxy. You make me want to fuck you until you can't walk the next day."

As I stand and stretch under the hot water, I smirk. "What's stopping you?"

27

BILLY

IT TAKES every bit of willpower to not hoist Roxy into my arms and fuck her against the shower wall, but I'm getting some post-nut clarity. I was rough with her just now. Much rougher than I intended.

She's pregnant, you asshole. You can't manhandle her.

I reach for her and hold her against my chest as I kiss her forehead. "You swear that wasn't too much? The last thing I want to do is hurt you."

She gives me a suddenly shy smile. "I like how you... how you control things. It's hot. You have my permission to fuck my mouth any time you want." Tilting her head, she bites her lower lip. "Except in the morning. I get nauseous then, and I don't want to puke on your pretty dick."

"Pretty dick?" I chuckle.

Wrapping her hand around my cock, she nods. "Yup. It's the most attractive cock I've ever seen. Thick and long with a beautiful head. I can't wait for you to fill me up."

Just like that, I'm ready to go again.

She looks down as I jerk in her hand and laughs. "So soon?"

I gently push her against the tile and kiss her. "I can't get enough of you." Words I've never said to any other woman. She melts against me. I reach down and squeeze her tits in my hands. Mold them together. Pinch her beautiful berry-colored nipples.

Stepping to the side, I get out of the way for the shower to rinse away the mess I made. Watching water spray along her perfect tits has me painfully hard. When I tug her nipples again, she moans and tilts her head back. I take that as an invitation to suck her into my mouth while I reach between her legs where she's dripping.

"Oh, baby. Look at you. Do you need to get off?" Of course she does. I just want to hear her say it.

"Since we were on the couch." When I give her a questioning look, she shrugs. "Being near you turns me on. When you were touching my thigh, I was going crazy. I almost ripped your clothes off then and there."

I laugh and kiss her as I rub slow circles over her swollen clit. "Since we're issuing invitations tonight, you have my permission to rip off my clothes any time you want."

Swallowing, she shifts, and her damp hair falls over her shoulders and over her gorgeous tits. I don't have words to express how enticing she is right now. Flushed, she pants as I move between her legs and slowly slide one finger, then two into her tight pussy. Working her over, I press the palm of my hand against her clit and revel in her pants and soft cries.

Leaning against the tile, she spreads her legs more and reaches down to circle her clit.

"That's it, baby." I move my hand deeper. "This okay? Tell me if it's too much."

She tangles her other hand in my hair. "Don't stop. It feels so good."

"What about this?" I remove my fingers and slip my dick between her thighs. She immediately grabs it and opens her thighs wider so she can rub my crown against her swollen flesh. "Fuck, that's hot."

Water drops cling to her lashes as she looks up at me. "Billy… I…"

"What do you need, baby?"

"I want you to fuck me. Hard. Right here. Right now."

Fuck yes. I'm about to turn her around and bend her over when I freeze. "I need to go get a condom."

She pauses. "Why? You afraid of knocking me up?"

Christ. She wants me to go raw? "Are you sure? I mean, I just got tested a few weeks ago. I'm in the clear."

She's nodding frantically and pawing at my shoulders. "The first time I went to the clinic, I got tested for everything. I'm good too."

"I've never gone without a condom," I say, almost to myself.

"I haven't either."

We stare at each other as some kind of primal male pride raises its head and roars in my chest. I want this first with her so fucking bad.

Grabbing her, I pull her into my arms and lift her until she wraps her legs around me. "Lean back. I got you." She braces herself against the tile as I angle my cock against her entrance. "We'll go slow."

Roxy wiggles in my arms. "Hurry."

Her enthusiasm isn't helping me put on the brakes, but I remind myself that she's pregnant, so it's not the time to fuck her through the shower stall.

I take her mouth. Kiss her slowly. Nibble her bottom lip. "We have all night, biscuit. No need to rush this. Don't want to hurt you."

She groans and writhes in my arms. "You're torturing me, Billy. Do it now."

Gotta say, there's nothing quite like getting Roxy this

worked up. Her nipples are tight, her pussy is dripping wet, and she's panting like she's going out of her mind. It's fucking hot as hell.

I'm gonna make my girl come so hard. Grabbing her by her ass, I bend my knees and notch my dick in her tight hole. She groans as I work my way in.

"Faster," she pants.

No, we're not going faster. She weighs maybe a buck ten. I'm basically twice her size. My dick looks enormous pressed up against her. I definitely need to take my time. If she wasn't pregnant, I'd take her up on the offer, but I can't manhandle her our first time together.

I grab her gorgeous face and kiss her as I let gravity take over. It's my turn to groan. "Holy shit, Roxy. You feel like heaven, baby. So fucking tight."

I'm still not in all the way. I glance between us, which I shouldn't do because seeing her pussy stretched around me makes me want to blow my load.

"Oh my God. Yes, Billy. More."

Finally, she sinks down fully and shudders in my arms.

"You okay?" I grit out. Frantic, she nods and reaches between us to rub her clit. "Let me do the honors." I take over for her, circling her clit with my thumb. Slow, then fast. Slow, then fast. She's moaning and thrashing, and I take a second to run my finger over her lips as they swallow my thick cock.

Then I lift her off me and let her slide down. She squeals and scratches my shoulders. "Again!" she shouts.

This time, she flutters around me so hard, my eyes roll back in my head.

I bury my face in her shoulder as I repeat the motion. Lift, drop, bottom out. Lift, drop, bottom out. My balls pull up tight, and I bite her neck.

Suddenly, she's shrieking and pulsing around me so hard, I

explode. That seems to set off another orgasm, and I hang on to her as we both quake.

It takes all of my strength to stay standing.

I've won a lot of football games. Thrown the winning touchdown in my high school state championship. Just won a national college championship.

But I'm not sure anything has felt as good as when Roxy, who's still impaled on me, opens her sleepy eyes, takes my face in her small hands, and kisses me long and slow under the hot water.

It's in this moment I realize how much I've been lying to myself.

About everything.

Because this thing with Roxy?

It's anything but fake.

Now I just need to prove to her I'm the kind of man she can count on.

28

ROXY

BRIGHT MORNING SUN filters through the blinds. I'm cocooned in warmth. Billy's spooning me from behind, but this time we're both naked. Feeling him skin on skin almost makes me moan with delight. He has one giant hand on my breast, one muscular thigh wedged between mine, and his morning wood is pressed against my ass.

His alarm goes off, but I don't want him to get up.

"Don't go," I whisper, my voice hoarse from all that screaming last night. I can admit I was embarrassingly loud, but bouncing on his monster dick made me have an out-of-body experience.

"Don't wanna go, biscuit, but I have to hit that morning workout."

I reach back to scratch the back of his head, which is tucked against my neck. "No one knows how hard you guys work." Twisting around, I burrow against his chest. "You're amazing. I love your dedication."

"Thanks, baby. That means a lot to me." He's quiet for a moment before he lifts my chin. I stare at his big blue eyes. "Are you feeling well this morning?"

"Yeah. I feel great, actually. Why?"

He studies me, a frown marring his handsome face. "Just worried I was too rough with you."

"Billy, I will never mince words with you when it comes to sex. If you ever push my boundaries, I'll let you know."

The furrow between his brows smooths out, and he lets out a breath. "Okay. Good. I was worried. I'd never want to do anything to hurt you or the bean. Even though she's not a bean anymore."

My heart flutters in my chest with the sincerity in his eyes. "Last night was incredible for me, in case you couldn't tell, and the bean is fine."

He chuckles, then leans down to kiss me. "It was incredible for me too, Roxy."

His intensity as he stares at me makes my whole body warm, like I'm being swallowed by sunlight. I've never experienced anything like it.

I thread my fingers through his hair. "Was it worth waiting to break your no-sex streak?"

"Abso-fucking-lutely. I'd do it all over again just to be with you."

A huge smile erupts on my face. "Want me to cook some dinner tonight? I've been craving lasagna lately." I'm about to list off some other options when my phone buzzes on the nightstand. After I untangle myself, I lift it to read the text. My stomach drops when I see who it is.

Groaning, I toss the phone on the bed and bury my head under the pillow.

"What's wrong?" Billy asks as he rubs my back.

"Abigail. I completely forgot we're supposed to go to dinner with her and Ezra tonight."

"Shit."

"Can I just hide here for the rest of the week?" When he

doesn't say anything, I lift my head to look at him. "I'm so sorry for wrangling you into this situation. You don't have to come. I'm sure spending time with them is the last thing you want to do."

"The hell I won't come."

I'm caught off guard by the edge to his voice.

He clears his throat. "Sorry, Roxy. I don't mean to sound like an asshole, but I'm not sending you into the lion's den by yourself. I'll take you. No apology necessary. We'll handle this together."

Together. It's such a foreign concept to me. I've never had someone who was my person. Someone who stuck with me through thick and thin. While my parents are supportive, they have each other, and my dad is really focused on my brother's football career. I'm realizing I want something, someone, for myself.

The way Billy's been here for me these last few weeks warms my heart.

"Deep down, I think I want Ezra to see I'm okay. That I don't need him. That I never did."

Billy nods. "Makes sense. And I'm here for all of it." He kisses my forehead and jumps out of bed.

I'm momentarily at a loss for words as I watch this beautiful, naked man as he moves through the room, gathering his clothes.

After the way he worked me over last night, I'm not sure how I have anything left in my tank right now, but suddenly, my core is throbbing.

He looks at me over his shoulder and freezes. "Fuck, Rox, I really want to come back to bed right now."

Slowly, I drag down the sheets to give him a good look. His eyes heat as they travel over me, and his cock jerks against his stomach. He reaches down to give it a tug and smirks. "Tonight, when we're having dinner with that fool, I'm gonna be thinking about how my cum is probably still dripping out of you."

My mouth drops open, and I laugh. "Billy!"

He jogs over and plants a kiss on my lips. "Take a nap today, baby, because I plan to fuck you until the neighbors know my name when we get home later."

I nod because that sounds like a good plan.

When he jumps in the shower, I flop back in bed with a huge grin on my face. Nothing about my relationship with Billy is what I expected. He's so caring. So sweet. So thoughtful.

Taking a deep breath, I starfish in bed. *I love him so mu—*

I freeze.

My eyes widen as my heart beats erratically in my chest.

Swallowing hard, I shake my head.

No, I don't love Billy like *that*. I couldn't. Even if I was capable of that sentiment, it's too soon.

After I think it over, I realize I love him like a friend. My best friend. Pregnancy hormones are just making me more emotional than I usually am. I'm simply excited that everything is going smoothly. That we're getting along. That we have such great chemistry. That we have so much fun together.

Because it would be stupid to fall in love with someone who once swore to be a lifelong bachelor.

29

ROXY

Saliva pools in the back of my throat, and I convulsively swallow. *Ugh, girl, don't throw up now.*

A palm slides over my thigh, and Billy's gruff voice whispers in my ear. "Everything will be fine. Don't let him get to you."

I muster a smile for Billy, who's sitting next to me at the bar, and a wave of those butterflies hits me again. It's crazy that I'm debating whether or not it's possible to fall in love with him while desperately trying not to hurl. "Thanks, boo."

He gives me that sexy, crooked smile and squeezes my thigh. Having him here helps.

When I shift in my chair, the little sting reminds me of all the dirty things he did to me last night. The man has some moves.

And yes, a huge member.

If I walk bowlegged today, there's a reason.

"Roxy!"

We turn to see Abigail trotting toward us, waving, while dragging Ezra behind her. He looks thrilled to be here. *Back at ya, asshole.*

"Hey. How's it going?" I hop off the chair to hug her, but

when I let go, Ezra holds open his arms. *As fucking if.* Ignoring him, I motion to my date and turn toward Abigail again. "This is my boyfriend, Billy." God, I love how that sounds. Even if this won't last forever, I'm grateful to have him now.

"Nice to meet you, Abigail." Then he gives Ezra a chin lift. "How's it going?"

"Oh, you know. Shit's kinda busy right now, what with every team in the NFL blowing up my phone."

God, Ezra's such a prick. What the hell did I see in him? Yes, he's attractive, but every time he opens his mouth, I want to punch him in the face.

Abigail squeezes his arm. "Language, babe."

He rolls his eyes and looks away as though he's bored.

I really don't understand why they're together when he seems to resent her, but maybe he's just pissed he had to come tonight.

She either doesn't sense his mood or ignores it and grabs his hand. "I'm so proud of E! Did you know that only fifteen quarterbacks got invited to the scouting combine this year? And E's only a junior, but he got an invitation. Isn't that cool?"

"It's great, Abigail," I say sincerely. I might hate the guy, but he is an outstanding quarterback, thanks in large part to my father, who spent so much time with him refining his skills and shuffling around the team until the offense worked for his QB.

She hops up and down on her toes. "I'm so anxious. I can't believe the combine is less than two weeks away. I might get a stomach ulcer before it's over."

That seems to soften Ezra, who puts his arm around her. "I told you I got this."

Billy is silent through the whole exchange. All this talk about the combine is probably getting to him. I know how much he wants to go pro. There has to be something I can say to my father to open his eyes to Billy's talent.

"Why don't we get a table?" I grab my purse and take Billy's hand when he holds it out. I really love this whole handholding thing. I've never dated anyone who always reached for me.

As we walk through the bar, people call out to us, and Ezra stops to talk to a rowdy table of fans who high-five him and start talking about the draft. He's eating up the attention, and poor Abigail is standing there awkwardly behind him, waiting for him to finish. He doesn't even bother to introduce her to anyone.

Billy and I greet a few people, but we don't stop to talk. When we reach the hostess, she tells us it'll be a little wait, so we lean against the wall. He wraps his arm around my shoulders and kisses my temple.

"You hanging in there?"

"Yeah. I've gotten over the urge to vomit." I'm sure part of the anxiety stems from not having seen Ezra since I crashed his engagement party. Now that I'm not doing cheer, I don't hang out at the field house anymore, and I never see him on campus.

Billy chuckles. "That's good. So what's the plan tonight? Do you want to tell him about the bean or should I keep my big mouth shut?"

"I still think it would be good to wait until the draft to minimize the drama, but I feel like Abigail should know who she's dating sooner rather than later. And if I tell her, I have to assume it'll get back to him. I'm still really conflicted."

"Whatever you decide, I'll follow your lead."

Turning in his arms, I push up on my toes and kiss him. "Thanks for everything. Really," I whisper. "I know this fake dating situation isn't ideal for you, but I want you to know I'll always be grateful for what you've sacrificed to help me get through this pregnancy."

He frowns. "Rox, I—"

"Babcock!" We both turn to the hostess, who ushers us over to a table.

Abigail joins us and gives us a shaky smile. "E can't stop talking to his friends."

I glance over my shoulder and find the douche hugging two girls. As in, they're both plastered to him, and he doesn't seem to be in any rush to detach them.

Ezra has some nerve, letting women hang all over him when he's engaged to Abigail. That's my biggest pet peeve. A guy should respect his fiancée enough to set boundaries with other women. Back when my dad was a big-time baller in the NFL, I remember random women running up to him and trying to hug him. He'd high-five or fist-bump them, but if they grabbed him before he knew they were coming, he'd quickly peel them off.

There was never a doubt in my mind that he's always been one hundred percent committed to my mother. That's relationship goals right there. Being with a pro athlete comes with its challenges, one of the biggest being the temptation to cheat. And if your guy doesn't have the sense to have some boundaries in front of you, what's he doing behind your back?

I already know what Ezra's doing behind Abigail's back. Now I just have to figure out how to tell her.

The three of us peruse the menu as Ezra takes his sweet-ass time to come to the table. I scan the appetizers. "I hear this place has great fried calamari. Does anyone want to share some with me?"

Billy nods. "Get whatever you want. I'll eat anything you don't finish."

"That's so convenient." I laugh, wishing I could spend the rest of the night talking to Billy instead of being on this awkward double date.

But then I remind myself that Abigail asked me to be her friend, so I try to focus on her. "Abigail, how are your classes going?"

"So great!" She flaps her hands excitedly. "I'm taking this classical myth course that's so interesting."

Ezra plops down into the chair between me and Abigail and across from Billy. "Let me guess. She's regaling y'all with notes from her myth class about old dead guys."

The light in Abigail's eyes dims. I could reach over and slap him for being a dick to her. I clear my throat. "I'd actually love to hear more."

She gives me a hesitant smile. "It's probably not that exciting. I'd hate to bore you."

I grab her hand. "I'm a huge geek. Trust me, I won't be bored. Tell me everything."

Abigail looks to Billy, who nods and points to me. "Roxy has historical romances on her bedside table. She loves stories of yore."

Stories of yore? I chuckle. I love that Billy is being so nice to Abigail and helping her feel comfortable. I lean over and kiss him again, promising myself to fuck him straight through the headboard when we get home.

When I sit back, Ezra is staring at me with a strange expression. *Whatever, asshole.*

Abigail explains how her professor has them read a classical myth and then watch a contemporary film that explores similar themes.

"Oh, that *does* sound interesting. What films are you watching this semester?"

"*Raging Bull*, *The Godfather*, *Nosferatu*, and—"

"Really old fucking movies," Ezra says as he flags down our waitress. "Can we order already?"

Jesus, he's rude. Billy told me he's a dick, but I've never seen him like this before. *Maybe that's because he never took you anywhere public. You were his dirty little secret and you didn't even know it.*

Embarrassed that Ezra's dismissing her again, Abigail flushes and looks down at her lap. The urge to stab Ezra in the leg with my fork is strong.

A long awkward silence ensues after we give the waitress our order.

Abigail clears her throat. "I hope this isn't too personal a question, but did I hear you guys were having a baby?"

Oh, Jesus. Here we go. "Yeah, I'm having a little girl."

"That's so cool! We want lots of kids, don't we, E?" When he doesn't say anything, she continues. "Roxy, how far along are you? Because you don't look pregnant at all."

"I'm due August first. I just passed sixteen weeks."

I feel Ezra watching me, and I finally look at him. I can almost see the moment when a light bulb goes off over his head.

With eyes narrowed, he motions between me and Billy. "I had no idea you two were a thing last fall."

That's what he's going with? "Funny, because I didn't know you had a girlfriend back then either." I give him a big, fake smile before I break out my phone and open the notes app. "Abigail, what's that course number? Maybe I can fit it in my schedule next spring. I love old films."

After I jot down the info, I catch sight of Billy's face. He and Ezra are doing some weird staredown. Under the table, I grab his hand to let him know I'm okay.

Once the waitress drops off our appetizers, Billy tilts his head. "So, Ezra, how did you and Abigail meet?"

"High school." Scanning the crowd, Ezra chugs a Heineken.

Abigail gives him an undeserved sweet smile that he doesn't notice. "E was having trouble writing an essay, so I helped him. And one essay turned into two and then three. He finally admitted he didn't need help, but just wanted an excuse to see me."

I smile at her. "That's really sweet." Unless he just fed her that line so she would write his assignments.

Billy nods slowly, still staring at Ezra. "When did you know you'd... *forsake all others* for Abigail because she was *the one*?"

I'm taking a sip of water and almost choke.

Ezra's jaw tightens. "I guess when you know, you know."

Abigail sets down her iced tea. "E told me it was because I always drop everything to help him with his papers. I mean, when are we not video-chatting about his course work?"

I'm wildly curious how much help she gives him.

Ezra shrugs. "Abigail and I started dating when I was a third-string quarterback on a sub-par team, back when I was a nobody. At least I know she's not with me for the NFL paycheck."

"That's super romantic, dude," Billy says sarcastically.

"It's the truth. You can't trust anyone these days," Ezra says as he stares at me with a hard look in his eyes. "At least I know I can trust my fiancée."

He has the balls to talk about trust?

I have to bite my tongue to keep myself from saying anything. Because this is not how I want to unleash the truth on Abigail.

She fiddles with her napkin, and I can see how disappointed she is in Ezra's answer. That he didn't say he was head over heels in love with her or something heartfelt.

Billy sits back in his chair, still eyeballing Ezra like he's a gnat. "Perhaps you can trust her, but can *she* trust *you*?"

Oh, shit. It's a challenge to school my expression. I can't even be upset with Billy for saying that. Ezra's being such a cocksucker.

Ezra smirks. "Such an interesting question, Babcock. Let's turn it around. Can Roxy trust you, the biggest player on campus? Because last I heard, you were having orgies and gangbangs at the Stallion Station." He turns to me with victory all over his face. "You should know what kind of guy you're with, Roxy."

That hypocrite. Billy has never lied to me, never made me promises he didn't keep, and never slept around behind my back.

Red clouds my vision, and I can't bite my tongue any longer. "Interesting *you* should question someone else's morals, Ezra. Because last I heard, you shouldn't go fucking half the women on campus when you're *engaged*."

All the air seems to get sucked out of the room.

Next to me, Abigail makes a pained sound in the back of her throat. "Wha... what are you talking about?"

I'm about to apologize for dropping that bomb on Abigail when Ezra pushes back his chair so hard, it clatters to the ground. "Nothing you need to worry about." Then he mutters underneath his breath, "Just some skank who can't keep her legs together, upset I didn't fuck her at a party."

A fraction of a second later, Billy leaps up and grabs the front of Ezra's shirt. Next thing I know, he hauls back and punches him.

Ezra lands on the floor in a heap and grabs his face. "What the fuck! You broke my nose. I'm gonna sue your ass!"

"I'd like to see you try." The entire restaurant turns to watch us as Billy stares him down. Leaning over him, he hisses, "Let's be clear about one thing, asshole. Roxy has always been out of your league. And if I ever hear you talk about her like that again, you won't be able to get up after I'm done."

Then he grabs my hand, apologizes to Abigail for ruining dinner, and leads me out of the restaurant.

As I follow him through the maze of tables, my heart throbs in my chest like I just ran a marathon. Everyone is staring. Some people have their phones out.

I lift my chin because I will not be ashamed. There's not a single cell in my body that regrets that punch. Billy stood up for me and took down the dirtbag who ruined my college experience.

But in the back of my mind, I hear the question loud and clear, like a foghorn slicing through a quiet night.

What is this going to cost him?

30

BILLY

It doesn't take a genius to know I'm in a shitload of trouble. What kind of dumbass knocks the star quarterback on his ass in the middle of a packed restaurant? If I wanted to show Roxy I'm the kind of man she can rely on, I have a piss-poor way of proving that.

I hiss when Roxy adjusts the ice pack on my hand.

"I'm sorry. Did that hurt?"

"Not more than smashing Ezra's face."

Since we got home, Roxy's been running around the apartment, grabbing first-aid supplies, and fussing over me. I've never had anyone fuss over me before. If my mother did it when I was young, my father flipped out, complaining I'd grow up to be a pussy.

I'm sitting on the couch, staring off, wondering just how bad this is gonna get, when she straddles my lap, grabs my face and presses a hard kiss to my lips. "That was really stupid, Billy."

"Your father is gonna lose his shit when he finds out."

"I don't care what my father has to say about this. I just don't want you to get in trouble. With the school. The cops. Your parents. My father is the least of our worries right now."

"Our?"

She pauses. "What do you mean?"

"How is this *our* problem? I'm the idiot who punched Ezra. This is my problem."

Her beautiful eyes fill with tears. "You're in this situation because of me. You never would've gone on a double date with Ezra and Abigail if it weren't for me. This is my fault."

Shit. I don't want her taking the blame for this.

Tears stream down her face, and I hug her. She wraps around me like a koala bear. "Don't cry, biscuit." I kiss her temple. "I don't regret hitting him. In fact, I enjoyed it. Maybe a little too much. My one regret is where it happened. If I was smart, I would've kicked his ass in a dark corner of campus." I sigh. "But that sounds kinda psycho, and while I'm admittedly reckless sometimes, I'm not a total freak."

She buries her face in my neck. "Thank you for defending me. No one has ever stood up for me like that before." She hiccups. "Except that time you also stood up for me with Coach."

The vulnerability in her voice hits me like a two-by-four. "I really..." *Love you.* The words get caught in my throat.

It's a terrifying thought. Because I swore to myself I'd never get so wrapped up in a woman that I'd lose my shit, and yet that's exactly what happened tonight. It feels like I'm floating on the open sea without a life jacket. I know fuck-all about healthy relationships. My father turned my mom into a shell of a person, and I seriously doubt he's been faithful. What if I'm no better? What if, deep down, I'm the same kind of scum?

I blow out a breath. Roxy barely agreed to fake-date me, so I'm guessing she doesn't want proclamations of love right now. Though, shit, I really didn't need to get so emotionally involved in this situation with her. This is ten times more complicated than I ever expected it to be.

But would I do things any differently?

I consider that scenario. I wouldn't be living with her now. Wouldn't have her in my lap. Wouldn't be able to kiss her whenever I wanted to. Wouldn't be able to cuddle her at night. Wouldn't be having the best sex of my life with a woman I'm crazy about. I'd be living like a heathen at the football house, fucking random chicks and waking up the next morning feeling numb.

So no, I wouldn't do anything different, because now I need to see where this thing goes. I'm all fucking in with this woman. "I care about you, Roxy. I'll always defend you."

"I really care about you too." She sniffles. "Maybe next time, though, don't use your fist."

I smile and squeeze her tight. "It's a deal."

My eye catches on the coffee table, where our phones keep lighting up with texts and calls. We both silenced our ringers on the way home.

"Guess I can't shut out the world forever." I scoot her to the couch and grab my cell.

Not surprisingly, Coach has called me three times. Fuck.

"Has your dad called you?" I ask. After she scans her phone, she bites her bottom lip, looking freaked out. "It's okay, baby. Lay it on me."

"He texted and said you'd better call him ASAP or you're off the team."

My heart drops. I knew Coach would be upset, but kicking me off the team seems excessive.

I pull up his number, but before I can hit call, his name lights up my screen.

Speak of the devil.

When I answer, he doesn't give me a chance to say anything other than hello. "What the hell were you thinking, Babcock?

Did you really punch the number one draft prospect in the middle of a bar?"

"Coach, don't you want to know why I hit him?"

"There's nothing you can say to justify your actions, not one damn thing, so don't fucking try." He starts yelling so loudly, I pull the phone away from my ear.

Roxy whispers, "Do you want me to talk to him?"

I shake my head. What kind of man would I be if I needed to hide behind my pint-sized girlfriend?

When I return the phone to my ear, he's still shouting. "So if you know what's good for you, you'll get your ass to the field house at five a.m. You're running the stadium stairs until I say stop."

Click.

Shit. Coach is pissed.

31

ROXY

I CAN'T HANDLE SEEING Billy like this. He's always such a force of nature, but right now, with his head in his hands, he looks defeated.

Grabbing my phone, I try calling my dad, but it goes straight to voicemail. After several more attempts, I finally text him. **CALL ME BACK! I WANT TO TALK TO YOU!**

Coach hates when my mother sends him all-cap messages. I'll track him down first thing tomorrow. It's way past time for him to hear the truth about Ezra Thomas. Maybe if my dad knows the whole story, he'll go easier on Billy.

I rub Billy's shoulder. "We'll figure this out. Don't let Coach get to you. He's all bluster. He'll calm down in a few days."

Billy gets up, looking dazed. "I'm gonna take a shower. I need some time to think."

That's not an invitation to join him. "Uh... of course." I don't know why that hurts my feelings, but it does.

Billy wants some time alone. That's not an unreasonable request, Roxy.

What sucks is I can never tell these days if I'm being too

sensitive because I'm pregnant or if I have a legit reason to feel butthurt.

Right now, I suspect it's the former.

Maybe I should get ready for bed. That way Billy can hang out in the living room after his shower and get some space.

Fighting the urge to get emotional, I think about my favorite cheerleading routines. Cheer used to be my happy place. I could shut down my brain and focus on the squad and our routines. Not being able to compete this spring at nationals only makes me sadder, so I focus on those times I nailed my stunts. How free I felt when I was flying through the air. How empowered when I tumbled across the stage. How proud to stand at the top of the pyramid.

Will I ever feel like that again?

I'm enjoying helping Paige and giving her tips, but coaching isn't the same as doing something yourself.

Once in my room, I strip out of my clothes and stare at my naked body in the full-length mirror mounted on the wall. From the front, I don't look all that different. I run my hands over my boobs and weigh them. They feel swollen and sensitive, and I swear the areolas are wider, which is weird. My stomach looks the same, until I turn sideways and there's a definite bump that wasn't there before, which makes sense because my jeans are tighter. But my God, when did this happen?

Slowly, I rub my hand over my lower belly and wonder what my daughter will be like. It's bittersweet to know she'll probably never know her father. I'm guessing Ezra won't give two figs about her once he knows the truth, and while I'm grateful he won't be messing up our lives, I'm sad for my bean. I love my dad, stubborn mule that he is, and I want her to have a father figure in her life like I did.

After I dress in a tank top and pajama bottoms, I glance at the moving box in the corner marked CHEER. It has a few medals and awards I've won over the years, photo albums from all the places I've trained since I was a kid, and scrapbooks. It's too painful to look at right now, but when I'm up to it, I want to unbox everything and make peace with the fact it's no longer part of my life.

Not wanting to disturb Billy, I grab some spare toiletries I kept in my cheer travel kit I never unpacked and brush at the kitchen sink and wash my face. Then I tuck myself into bed and grab my historical romance. Only I'm too frazzled to concentrate. After reading the same paragraph five times, I give up.

I flip off the light, turn on my side, and try to sleep, but all of these horrible scenarios keep running through my head. What if Billy really gets in trouble for punching Ezra? What if the school decides to make an example of him and expels him? What if he's put on some kind of probation that affects his eligibility? What happens when scouts get wind of this fight and write him off because they think he's too high-risk?

I groan into my pillow. How did I let this get so out of control?

From the hallway, I hear the bathroom door open, and I hold my breath. Will Billy head back to the living room? Will he sleep on the couch? Did I ruin this thing between us before we even got started?

"Babe, you awake?"

I'm so relieved to hear his voice, I get choked up. "Yeah."

"What's wrong?"

"Just… I hate that you're in this situation because of me." My voice wavers and I sniffle, upset I can't keep my shit together anymore.

He crawls into bed behind me. He's naked. I don't know why, but this makes me relax. Not that we have to have sex, but I'm craving a physical connection with Billy, even if it's just snuggling.

His large hand moves to my belly that's beginning to swell and strokes me gently. "How's our bean?"

A shaky smile pulls at my lips. The baby is about the only thing that could get me to smile right now. "She's good."

Turning me around, he pulls me on top of him. I close my eyes, wrap my arms around his neck, and nuzzle against him. His hair is damp, and he smells like body wash.

In this dark, quiet room, it's easy to be honest with myself. Still, I close my eyes, embarrassed that I've dragged him through my drama. "Billy, I'm sorry for all of this. For making you do this stupid fake-dating thing for me."

He strokes my back. "I'm not sorry."

Sniffling, I open my eyes, surprised he's not royally pissed off at me. "Really?"

"Of course not. Because if you hadn't proposed it, I wouldn't be in your bed right now, and there's nowhere else I'd want to be."

That gets the tears rolling. I'm almost afraid to ask, but if I don't, I'll go out of my mind. "Are we still fake-dating? Or is this... is this real? Because..."

Say it.

But he beats me to it.

"Because this feels real."

"Yeah." My voice wavers.

"Don't cry, biscuit." He palms my face, and in the dim light coming from the streetlamp outside the window, I can make out his handsome face through the tears. "Forget all that fake-dating crap. You're mine, and I'm yours. This is as real as it's gonna get." He takes a deep breath. "I know you said you didn't think you could fall in love, but maybe you could give me a chance. Give us a chance. Because I'm ass-over-head crazy about you."

Hope blooms in my chest. Even though the room is dark, I'm

filled with sunlight. "Are you saying… are you saying you love me?" I hold my breath as I wait for his reply.

"I love you so fucking much, it freaks me out," he says softly as he dries my tears.

"I love you too." In between kisses, I laugh. "I didn't think I had it in me, but you've changed everything."

"Well, I could *put* it in you."

I snort and playfully smack his shoulder. "You horndog."

"Let's put blame where it belongs. My dick is the horndog. It has a mind of its own. The rest of me is much more evolved."

I'm wrapped around his bare chest, and that wayward body part is sticking straight up against my ass. I wiggle back against it, loving the groan that rumbles from his chest. "I suppose we should do something about this."

He threads his fingers through my hair, gently rubs his thumb against my cheek. "We don't have to. I just like lying here with you."

I know what he means. When I'm with him, I don't feel like I need anything else. Like there's a part of me that's always been searching for something, and when we're together, it's like finding that missing puzzle piece.

Leaning down, I graze my lips against his. "Maybe I want to do that with you. Maybe I'd like to have sex with my official boyfriend, seeing how I love him and all."

Those words seem to make something in him snap, and he angles my head to deepen the kiss. His tongue slides against mine as he holds me to his chest, and I almost forget to breathe. But then he pulls back. "Are you sore, baby?"

That throws a damper on things. "Um. Yeah. A little." From that crazy monkey sex in the shower.

"We don't have to—"

"But I want to. Maybe we could go slow?" We haven't even done anything yet tonight, and my body is raring to go, the painful throb in my clit much more insistent than any soreness from last night.

He considers it. "Stay on top. That way you can control things."

I am one hundred percent on board with riding Billy.

Eager to feel him skin to skin, I sit up and strip off my tank top. He helps me wiggle out of my pajama bottoms and undies. Moving back a bit, I straddle that jutting part of him and rub him between my legs.

"You're so wet. I fucking love that." He grips my thighs to help me move. "Wait." Reaching back, he flips on the small bedside lamp. "I want to see you."

I know what he means. Maybe it's how long it took us to get to this point or what happened tonight, but for some reason, I'm almost desperate to have him inside of me. And I want to capture every moment in my mind to relive later.

As I shift my hips, we both look down to see his thick cock head surge between my pussy lips again and again. I rub his weeping tip with my finger as I move back and forth. He squeezes my boobs and pinches my sensitive nipples, which shoots tremors of pleasure through my body. When I can't stand it any longer, I push up on my knees and angle back to take him inside of me.

I love taking him without a condom. It makes this thing between us so much more intimate. Like he's really mine.

It takes a moment to work him in because he's so thick, but the stretch is incredible. When I can't take it all, I collapse on his chest, panting. "I'm stuck."

He chuckles. "You're not stuck."

"I'm stuck on your big jungle dick and can't move. I need one of those Life360 alert necklaces so I can call someone to help me."

He barks out a laugh that makes him swell inside of me, and I groan with delight and rest my forehead on his hard chest.

"Rox, you kill me. In all the best ways." I smile against him as he rubs my back. "Let's roll you."

We twist around until I'm on my side next to him with my thigh over his. He pulls me closer and kisses me until I melt into him. His giant hand grabs my ass cheek, and he helps me move up and down his dick as he finishes working himself into me. "This angle is insane," I pant, loving how the root of his erection rubs against my core. "Don't stop."

"Yes, ma'am."

He takes over, thrusting into me until I shiver. "I'm so close. It feels so good. You're so thick." I make some strangled noise in the back of my throat as he reaches behind me and rubs his finger through my wetness and then back to my asshole. He only circles me a few times before I'm flying apart in his arms. "Oh my God. Billy! Yes!" I shriek and scream with delight.

That sets him off, and he lets out a loud groan as he pulses between my legs, which sets off another round of euphoria in my body.

I'm sweaty and panting and utterly spent. I smile against his chest, and he kisses my forehead. "Love you, Roxy. So much."

My heart swells, and my eyes mist, but I don't mind because they're happy tears. "Love you too, Billy."

After we clean up, he wraps himself around me again, and I swear there's a permanent smile affixed to my face. I know I'm mentally blocking out a lot of stuff we to deal with, but right now, in his arms, it almost feels like we can conquer anything.

32

BILLY

JUMPING out of bed at four thirty in the morning and leaving my warm, naked girlfriend is torture. She reaches for me in her sleep, and I kiss her forehead. I have no idea what today will bring, but knowing I'm coming home to Roxy makes everything okay. I'll get through this morning with Coach, take whatever punishment he doles out, and return to my biscuit. I'll be fine.

It's still dark when I reach the field house. Ominously, there's only one other car in the lot. Coach's.

The moment I step into the locker room, he barks my name. "The stadium. Now."

All righty then. I don't bother saying anything. The murderous look in his eyes tells me exactly where he stands—with Ezra. I'm not surprised, but it bothers me he won't hear me out. He's all talk when he spouts that bullshit about fairness and camaraderie and having each other's backs, because the moment shit goes sideways, he's out for blood.

So there's no point in explaining how I wasn't gonna sit there and let that little prick talk trash Roxy. I suspect Ezra has an inkling the baby *could* be his based on the looks he gave her when she was talking about her pregnancy, which makes what he said even worse. That's the mother of his fucking child. He deserved to have his ass kicked up and down the block and back again.

Unless he thought she was cheating with me the whole time.

Which... doesn't bother me in the least. That fucker is due some bad karma.

Besides, if he really knew Roxy, he'd never draw that conclusion. Rox is the most loyal woman I know.

When we reach the field, Coach points to the stadium stairs. "Go until I say stop."

In other words, I'm running, racing up and down the stairs, with no end in sight. He sits on the bottom bench and texts on his phone as though he's too disgusted to look at me. I watch him rub his chest, like I've caused him some kind of physical pain. After a while, he disappears, probably back to his office.

At first, I'm fine. I'm in great shape. But running stairs takes its toll on your knees, so by the time the sun starts to peek on the horizon, I'm in pain.

I don't say a fucking word. I'll run until I drop, and if Coach thinks otherwise, he doesn't know me.

In my mind, I replay those words Roxy said last night. She loves me. Me. The fucking black sheep on the team. Hell, the black sheep of my family too. Maybe that means I'm not such a loser. Because if Roxy Santos can love me, maybe there's hope for my future after all.

I try to focus on my breath. On being grateful. On all the hard times I've gotten through in the past. Birds chirp merrily like they don't know how the lower half of my body strains with each and every step.

In the distance, the sound of a siren cuts through the quiet morning.

As I turn to go up another flight, I strip off my sweatshirt and t-shirt and drop them to the ground. Even though it's so cold I can see my breath, I'm covered in sweat, and my knees and quads are screaming now. I sprint until I can't anymore, and then I jog. Finally, I walk. It's either that or crawl, but pride keeps me on my feet.

Coach Gates pokes his head up from the tunnel. "Babcock! How long you been out here?"

I open my mouth to say something, but nothing comes out. Coughing, I hold up a hand. "Maybe since five?" Who fucking knows.

His eyes widen, and he tells me to stop.

"Coach Santos said to run until he said otherwise," I wheeze.

"I don't fucking care. Get your ass down here and stretch! Then I want you to ice your knees."

When I reach him, I can barely stay upright. I can't seem to make my legs cooperate and almost fall over. He reaches out to steady me. "Jesus Christ. What the hell is wrong with him? I know you fucked up, but this is insane."

I've never heard one of the assistant coaches disagree with Santos before. I try to shrug, but sway. He wraps his arm around my waist and helps me back to the field house. "Did you eat something this morning?"

"No. Didn't want to puke when I was running."

"Grab some breakfast. Don't want you to pass out from low blood sugar."

When we make it back to the locker area, I see two other assistant coaches talking to a firefighter, who holds up a finger and says something into the walkie-talkie clipped to his shoulder.

My addled brain thinks he's here for me for some reason, but then he says, "The ambulance took Santos."

I grab onto the wall to stay upright. "What's wrong with Coach?"

The special teams assistant rubs his jaw. "He collapsed."

~

WHEN I CAN'T GET AHOLD of Roxy, I race home, but she's not there. Every step makes my knees almost buckle, but now is not the time to be weak.

Not knowing what to do, I call Cam, but he doesn't answer, so I ring Jake.

I don't even give him a chance to talk before I tell him that Coach is in the hospital, and I can't reach Roxy. Then I let out a string of curses, because if I caused the man to have a heart attack, he'll always hate me. And I'm not sure if I can live with Roxy's dad hating me when I'm trying to build a life with her.

Because that's what we're trying to do, right? Build something together?

"Hold on," Jake says. "Let me ask Charlie if she's heard from her." A minute later, he returns. "Sorry, man. They haven't spoken today. I'll let you know if I hear anything, though. Do you know which hospital he's at? Maybe we should go down there."

Would Coach want to see me? Probably not, but there's a chance Roxy's already heard and headed to the hospital, and I could go support her. "That's a good idea. The firefighters said paramedics took him to Charming Memorial. I'll see you there."

I hang up and pace my living room to calm the fuck down. I don't know if it's adrenaline, but suddenly, the pain in my legs is the last thing I'm thinking about.

What the hell am I supposed to tell Roxy? *Sorry, Rox, but your dad got so pissed at me he had a heart attack?* I don't know for sure that's what happened, but I did see him rubbing his chest this morning. Could I have done something then to help? Should I have said something?

As I grab my jacket, I have the fleeting thought that at least today can't get any worse.

Then I open the door.

Two police officers stare at me, hard expressions on their faces. One has his hand up, about to knock.

Oh, fuck. I killed Coach. He was so pissed at me, he dropped dead. Rox will never forgive me for killing her dad.

The taller cop holds out a badge. "William Babcock?"

I probably shouldn't lie right now. "Yes."

"You're under arrest for assaulting Ezra Thomas."

I'm so relieved this isn't about Santos, I almost laugh. That pencil dick Ezra.

As I'm hauled off in handcuffs and jammed in the back of a police cruiser, I consider the silver lining.

Maybe Coach is alive.

33

ROXY

ALL OF THE terrible things I planned to say to my father threaten to choke me as I try not to blow through stop signs on the way to the hospital. It started raining a few minutes ago out of nowhere, and now the roads are slick.

My mother called me crying, telling me that Dad collapsed at the field house this morning. Paramedics told her he had chest pain and felt lightheaded.

I'm halfway there when I realize I left my phone on the nightstand, but I'm too scared to turn around. What if something horrible happens in the meanwhile and I don't get a chance to see my father?

Calm down, Roxy. And don't get a ticket on the way there.

My knuckles grip the steering wheel as I fishtail into the ER parking lot. When I reach the lobby, I head straight for the female nurse sitting behind plexiglass. "Hi, I'm here to see Richard Santos. He was brought by ambulance a little while ago."

"Who are you in relation to the patient?"

"His daughter."

She nods and checks her computer screen. "He hasn't made

it into the system yet. They're probably still admitting him." She points to the waiting area behind me. "I'll let you know when you can head back."

I'm just supposed to wait out here when he could be dying right now? "You don't understand. He collapsed. It's serious. What if he doesn't..." I can't even say the words, much less think them. My voice wavers, and I blink several times. "My mom is back there, and she's expecting me."

"You can call her to come get you."

I could if I had my damn phone.

"Rox."

Turning, I see some of the players and assistant coaches on the other side of the room. Relief almost takes my breath away when I spot Charlotte. I run over to her, and the second Charlie hugs me, I start bawling.

"Roxy, he'll be okay. He's a tough guy."

"How did you find out?" I ask, struggling to pull myself together.

"Billy called Jake and told him your dad collapsed. Jake and I drove here separately, though, because I have to get to a shoot in a few hours. Jake was only a few minutes behind me. He should be here soon."

I'm relieved Billy knows what happened. I'm guessing he'll be here any minute now. He probably tried calling me, but my stupid phone is at home.

"I was so mad at Coach last night." I glance up from her shoulder to see several of my dad's players watching us, so I take her arm and drag her to the corner, where I wipe my eyes. "We had a double date with Ezra and Abigail last night, and Billy punched Ezra. My dad flipped out. Said Billy was off the team if he didn't show up to run stadium stairs this morning."

She winces. "I heard. Everyone's talking about it."

My stomach churns. I hate people knowing my business. "I

was going to track down my dad this morning so he heard our side of the story, but I slept straight through my alarm. Then my mom called, freaking out, and told me to get down here."

Her phone dings with a text. "Jake's here."

I'm glad to see so many players came to support my family, but one person is missing. Actually, two, including Ezra, but maybe he's off licking his wounds. "Where's Billy?" Wouldn't he be here by now since he was at the field house this morning?

She stills, looking uncomfortable all of a sudden.

"What?"

"Are you sure Billy would come after what happened this morning?" She leans close and lowers her voice. "I heard your dad made him run stadium stairs for hours. That Billy was about to start crawling up them when one of the other coaches made him stop."

My heart drops. I knew my dad was pissed, but I've never seen him take out his anger on a player like that. "Are you sure? That doesn't sound like my father." He's all bark and bluster. I figured he'd yell at Billy, make him run for a bit, and then hit him with some community service hours. That's usually his go-to plan when players screw up.

Cam walks in with Jinxy and Jake, who heads for Charlotte and leans down to kiss her.

"Hey, Rox, how are you doing?" Cam says, pulling me into a quick hug.

"I'm hanging in there. Just frustrated that I'm not allowed to go back and see my dad yet."

Cam nods. "I'm sure they'll give you an update soon." He glances around. "Where's Billy?"

"I have no idea." Why isn't he here? Unless he's pissed at my dad for making him run.

"He said he was coming," Jake says, pausing to glance at his phone. "I'm not sure why he's not here yet."

Billy is on his way. I'm finally able to take a deep breath.

"Roxanne."

I turn around and see my mom. Her mascara is smeared, and her eyes are swollen. I run into her arms. "How's Dad?"

She shakes her head. "I'm not sure yet. Let's return to his ER room. I don't want to miss the doctor."

When we get there, I pull back the curtain and rush in, expecting to see my father, but the bed is gone. "Where is he?"

My mother sits me down and then pulls over another straight-backed chair. "He had a blockage and was rushed into the OR." She wipes her eyes. "It's all those damn pork rind chips he eats on Sunday while he watches football. I told him he needs to watch his cholesterol. *Ya no somos niños*."

We're not kids anymore.

Sniffling, I wrap my hand tightly around her cold fingers. "We'll make sure he eats better. I'll start looking for recipes I think he'll like."

We sit side by side, and I watch the clock tick on the wall.

An hour later, a doctor joins us. "The procedure went smoothly, and it was relatively quick, which bodes well for his recovery," he tells my mother, who breaks down. For some reason, my tear ducts are dry. Maybe it's because Mom needs me to be strong. I wrap my arm around her as the doctor continues. "He's in the recovery room. We'll let you know when he's been moved upstairs, and you can join him."

After he leaves, my mom hugs me. "*Mija*, what if *Papi* hadn't gone to campus this morning? He wasn't supposed to go in until noon, and I had a breakfast date with some girlfriends. If this had happened while he was at home, no one would've been there to help him." She swipes at the tears streaming down her face.

I consider that for a minute. If Billy hadn't decked Ezra, this could've been tragic. Unless the stress of that situation was the catalyst, but I won't think about that possibility. It sounds like my dad's heart condition was a ticking time bomb. "I'm just grateful things happened the way they did and that Coach is going to be okay."

She smiles, relief in her eyes. "I'm going to call your brother. Will you go update everyone in the waiting room?"

"Of course."

When I get out there, I look for Billy, but he's still not here. Maybe he's not coming. I don't know how to feel about that. He said he loved me. Wouldn't that mean he'd set aside his differences with my dad to support my family?

I talk to the assistant coaches and let them know my father will be okay. Everyone looks relieved.

Cam motions to me and pulls me aside. "Billy's in trouble."

Of course he is, I think with exasperation. My nerves are shot, and the last thing I want to deal with is more drama. "What happened?"

Cam's lips flatten. "He got arrested for assault."

My stomach drops.

No. Pressing my hand to my mouth, I shake my head. *This is my fault.*

That's when I lean over and throw up all over a potted plant.

34

ROXY

My tires screech to a halt in front of my apartment, and I run in to grab my phone. I want to call out Billy's name, but I know he's not here.

Don't dawdle, Roxy. The faster you do this, the quicker you'll get him home.

Before I can second-guess myself, I gun it to Ezra's house. I'm nauseated, hungry, and pissed off. For Ezra's sake, I hope he hears me out, because I don't know what I'll do if he insists on pressing charges.

I feel guilty for thinking Billy would blow off my dad when he's in the hospital. There are probably messages from him on my cell.

My sweater feels tight, and I pull it away from my neck. I can't stop thinking that if I hadn't dragged him into this situation, he never would've punched Ezra. His agent told him to stay out of trouble, and then this happens. I can't imagine this bodes well for his prospects next year. If I were a scout, I'd start to think Billy was a bad bet.

And wasn't that the whole point of us fake-dating? So I could help him clean up his act? I'm doing a piss-poor job of that.

Which is why I'm here.

I can't let this situation spiral anymore.

If me asking Ezra isn't enough, I need a backup plan. As I pull to a stop in front of that asshole's house, the idea comes to me. I grab my phone, which is all lit up with messages, but I don't have time to go through them. I swipe it open and go straight to the contacts. After a few minutes of furiously tapping at the screen, I'm ready.

This is crazy, even for me, but I owe it to Billy to try.

Before I lose my nerve, I march up to Ezra's house and ring the doorbell several times. His car is here, and the lights are on.

"I know you're in there, Ezra!" I straight-up sound like a lunatic, but I'm too upset to care. When no one opens the door, which is locked—I know because I check—I stomp around to the side of the house. He's going to regret sneaking me into his room.

To think I bought his lies. *Oh, we need to keep this on the down-low so girls don't give you a hard time for dating me. I'm not ready to share you with anyone yet. Let's keep this between us for a while so we can work on our relationship.* What a bunch of bullshit.

I grab hold of the trellis and climb up to the second floor. The window slides open, probably because he's still banging girls on the side. After I climb in, I call out his name, but he's not in the en suite bathroom either.

His room looks the same, except messier. I fling open his bedroom door and storm down the stairs. I find that asshole sitting at the kitchen table. His nose is swollen and his eyes are rimmed in black. It almost makes me smile.

His brows lift when he sees me.

"What? Did you think I'd forget how to climb up the trellis like you taught me when you wanted to fuck me behind Abigail's back?"

Someone sucks in a breath behind me—a female someone

—and I close my eyes. Abigail's here. Shit. Slowly, I turn, and there she is. Her pretty eyes are red-rimmed like she's been crying. "I'm so sorry. I swear I didn't know he had a girlfriend."

She points to my belly as tears swim in her eyes. "Are you... Is that..." I can't blame her for not being able to finish that question.

I nod. "It's Ezra's."

"The hell it is," he bellows, kicking back his chair, and making me flinch. I spin around, and the murder in his eyes makes me take a step back. "You little skank. You slept with Billy last fall when you swore you were just friends, and now you're pretending it's mine."

"That's what we said because I wasn't ready to tell you. You know, after finding out you had a girlfriend the whole time. Why do you think I drove down to San Antonio after the championship game? To congratulate you?" I snort. "No, I fucking went there to tell you I was pregnant. Only to find out you got engaged. To the girlfriend you've been cheating on the whole time you've been at Lone Star!"

"Don't believe a word she says, Abigail." He reaches for her, and she flinches.

"You and Billy weren't lying last night. Were you?" she asks me. "Ezra's been sleeping around."

As much as I loathe Ezra, I hate hurting Abigail, but she needs to know the truth. "We'd never say something like that if it wasn't true."

"What a load of crap," Ezra spits. "Just like you claiming that baby is mine."

"How much are you willing to bet? Because we can go down to the hospital right now and do a blood test." It'll cost an arm and a leg, but it's the only noninvasive method to identify paternity until the baby is born. I'm willing to pay it if I have to, even if it means maxing out my credit card.

The look in Ezra's eyes makes me think he realizes I'm not blowing smoke up his ass. When he doesn't say anything, I have to drill the point home. "Are you willing to bet your first-round draft pick?"

"What does this have to do with football?"

I offer a grim smile. "Did you know that pro teams invest millions of dollars to vet potential drafts? I know this because my father's college roommate is a scout. And he does background checks for a living. So I happen to know that if an athlete has a ton of skeletons, it often just takes *one lead* to unravel the lies. For example, what would happen if I sued you for paternity and then sent those legal documents to every NFL team's recruiting department? That would give them the motivation to look deeper."

He shrugs. "They'll just think you're a gold digger."

"The daughter of one of the most respected coaches in college football? You don't think my family has money?" Well, it belongs to my parents. It's not mine, but if I clarify this point, it'll just add to his belief that I'm after a payday. "You and I both know that I'm only one of many girls. It makes me wonder who else might have a grievance against you." I turn to Abigail. "I'm sorry you had to find out this way, but homie here has been pretending to be single this whole time. Ask anyone. His roommates. The women at their parties. Basically anyone on campus."

She's wiping away the tears. I want to hug her, but I don't think she'd welcome any comfort from me. "That's why he never wanted me to visit."

"Babe, it's not like that," he says, holding out his hands to her. "Roxy's just pissed I wouldn't sleep with her."

Jesus, he's really going to make me say it. "Ezra, your dick curves to the left. When you come, you make this little high-pitched noise that's actually quite unattractive. And you can't find a girl's clit if she drew you a map and highlighted the destination." The only reason I ever got off was if I reached down to rub it myself.

Through her tears, Abigail reluctantly laughs. "Oh my God, I thought it was me."

Ezra's cheeks go red, and I almost feel bad for insulting his sexual prowess until I remember all that slut-shaming he's hurled my way.

"Drop the charges against Billy, and I'll never sue you for paternity. Make it go away, and you and I will go our separate ways. You'll head off for the draft, make all that money, and do your thing. Those NFL teams won't get a whiff of what happened between us even if a private investigator starts sniffing. Come draft day, they'll still think you're that golden boy." Until some unlucky team finds out he's a grade-A asshole, but that's not my problem. "Let Billy off the hook, and I swear on all that is holy that you'll never hear from me again."

Then I consider Ezra's family back in San Antonio. Maybe Ezra has a heart deep down and would actually want to know his child. Or perhaps his parents would. "Unless... unless you want to be involved in my baby's life?"

"Fuck, no."

That shouldn't hurt, but it does. I'm in pain, not for myself, but for my daughter, who's done nothing wrong. I take a deep breath to shake it off. "When people ask why Billy hit you, say it was a prank gone wrong. That you were supposed to duck, but one of the chairs was in the way."

"That's stupid."

"Then make up another excuse, something that doesn't get Billy in trouble. Say someone was recording a prank for TikTok, but Billy misunderstood when he was supposed to *pretend* to hit you."

"But I gave my statement to the police last night."

"Then fucking change it. You're the star quarterback for the most popular college football team in Texas. They'll listen to you. Tell them you weren't thinking clearly. That you were in pain from the punch and had a migraine. That you've gotten your bell rung on the field one too many times and it makes you forget things you shouldn't. I don't know what you need to say, but you need to retract your original statement."

I can tell Ezra's considering my words. He'd better think harder because I have every intention of getting in touch with my inner bad bitch.

His eyes narrow. "How do I know you won't tell your father, and he'll go on some kind of smear campaign?"

"Do you think I want Coach to know you're the father of my child?" I sneer. "Do you think for one minute I want to confess I had an affair with a man who's practically married? Come on. You know my dad. *The Saint* will be so disappointed in me."

Ezra nods slowly. "That's true."

God, he's an asshole. He's like one of those old Polaroid photos that keeps developing, and every new detail that emerges is worse than the last. "This offer is good for twenty-four hours. If the charges aren't dropped by this time tomorrow, get ready for war. And I'm talking a full-out media blitz, the kind that puts your name on the ticker tape at the bottom of the screen on ESPN. I grew up on the sidelines of the NFL, so you'd better believe I know who to call to make this happen."

When he doesn't say anything, I throw the Hail Mary. "Think of it this way, Ezra. You're the only one who stands to lose anything. What will I lose? My reputation? I've never given a damn about that. Cheerleading? It's already over thanks to you knocking me up. My dad's respect? I'm not sure I have much there to lose." Sad, but true. "While you stand to lose the number one draft pick and a hell of a lot of money. I'd think long and hard before turning me down."

I take out my phone and scroll through my contacts, pausing to show him name after name of NFL coaches and staff. I'm bluffing on most of them. I've never met some of these people, but he doesn't know I programmed a few fake contacts while I was parked outside of his house.

His face pales when he sees the name of the head coach from his dream team. "Just because I tell the cops I don't want to prosecute doesn't mean they'll drop the charges."

As I march out the door, I yell, "Then you'd better turn on that golden boy charm and make them listen to you. Twenty-four hours, Ezra!"

If he thinks I'm bluffing about telling the media, he has another thing coming. And while I was fibbing about most of those contacts, that doesn't mean I don't know people who do know them.

He's messing with the wrong girl.

35

BILLY

STILL GROGGY AND sore from sleeping on a bench and running a million stadium stairs yesterday, I stare at Officer Hardy's cup of Dunkin' Donuts. The smell makes me want to hurl.

I know the score. I might not have gone to law school like my brothers, but our father drilled in a few things in case we ever got in trouble. Not because he loved us, but because he was considering a run for Congress at the time.

One, I need to keep my big fucking mouth shut.

Two, I should secure an attorney as soon as possible to negotiate with the district attorney and potentially present evidence on my behalf. He might be able to prevent formal charges from being filed.

And three, if my father doesn't send his guy and no one shows up, I'll get stuck with some court-appointed attorney, and that'll suck.

But the real kicker is if I get formally charged, I can probably kiss my senior year of football goodbye.

A class-A misdemeanor for simple assault will cost four grand in fines and might get me up to a year in prison. Aggravated assault, however, is a felony, and will cost ten grand and up to twenty years in prison.

My father's right. I'm really fucking stupid. I don't know why I wasn't thinking about the legal ramifications of hitting that douchebag the other night.

This is definitely not the way to win over Coach's approval or prove to Roxy that I'm a man she can rely on.

I pinch the bridge of my nose. Shit. I hope Santos is okay. Roxy is probably worried sick over her father, and then I go and get arrested. Fucking brilliant.

"Do ya still want to wait for your attorney?" Hardy slides the cup of coffee over and pushes a box of donuts toward me. "If you make a statement, you can have some breakfast."

This guy must also think I'm an idiot. I don't remind him that it's my constitutional right to remain silent. "Thank you, sir, but I'll wait." My father said he'd come down last night. He's probably trying to teach me some kind of lesson. I get it. I shouldn't punch people in the face in the middle of a crowded restaurant.

I'm sitting with my hands folded. Granted, the cuffs restrict my movement, but I'm using it as a reason to hide my scuffed knuckles.

The door opens again, and a guy in an Armani suit strolls in. "William Babcock? I'm Corbin Shaw. Your father hired me to be your attorney." He turns to Hardy. "A little privacy, please?"

The cop shrugs and shoves half a donut in his mouth before he shuffles off to the other room with his box of snacks.

Shaw tosses a legal pad on the table and takes the seat opposite me. "Anything you say right now is private due to attorney-client privilege. You're looking at a potential assault charge, but whether it's a misdemeanor or felony depends on whether you broke the other guy's nose. Tell me what happened and start at the beginning."

I'm not sure why I was expecting to see my father, but I'm obviously not thinking clearly. He's a divorce attorney, so he hired a criminal attorney. That's some basic law shit I should know growing up in my family.

"Uh, we were on a double date. The other guy, Ezra Thomas, got my girlfriend pregnant." Shaw stops writing to look at me. "This was before we got together. I knew she was pregnant when we started dating."

He doesn't say anything, but based on the expression on his face, he thinks I'm a dumbass for dating Roxy. "Continue." He jots down notes as I relay the story.

He might claim attorney-client privilege, but since my father is footing the bill, I have to assume Shaw is going to share these details with him, and he is not going to be pleased.

When I'm done, Shaw taps his pen. "We could argue that you were defending your girlfriend from a verbal assault, and—"

The door swings open, and Hardy sighs. "Charges have been dropped. Mr. Thomas says you two were just pulling a prank that went sideways. Says those concussions from playing football made his memory a little foggy, but that's off the record." He scratches the back of his head. "You coulda just said it was a prank, you know. Saved us all a lot of time."

A prank? Why the hell would Ezra Thomas say anything in my defense?

I keep my expression impassive, as does my attorney, who tucks away his notepad.

Hardy gives me a stern look. "You're lucky the DA loves the Broncos. He's not willing to press this issue if our quarterback isn't on board." He finally smiles. "By the way, great third quarter interception in the championship game. I was rootin' for ya."

I clear my throat. "Th-thank you, sir. Appreciate it."

After Hardy leaves, Shaw leans forward. "I'm going to do a

little digging just in case. Because a victim has two years to press formal charges after an altercation, and you don't want this to bite you in the ass down the road. So don't say a fucking word about this to anyone, do you understand? No one is your friend right now. You'd be surprised by who will testify against you if this eventually goes to court."

This shit will hang over my head for two more years? I nod, still recovering from the whiplash of the last few minutes.

"And no more fights. I doubt the next one will be as easy to dismiss."

About half an hour later, I'm finally released, but there's no time to celebrate because my father's waiting for me in the lobby.

My attorney's reprimand is nothing like the riot act Warren Babcock reads me on the way out of the precinct.

~

THE WINDSHIELD WIPERS can't come fast enough to clear the rain. They squeak and squish in time with the vein throbbing in my father's temple.

Waiting for me to get out of his Bentley, he taps a finger against the steering wheel. He just spent the drive back to my apartment tearing me a new asshole.

"I'm not breaking up with her." He said I had a nut loose for wanting to date a girl who was pregnant with someone else's baby. I'll admit it's not ideal, but I love the bean, regardless of who her dipshit father is. I haven't mentioned that I told Rox she could name me as the father of the baby on the birth certificate for fear my father might drive me back to jail.

He glances at me sideways. "You have some big post-graduation plans I'm not aware of? Because it looks like your NFL potential is disappearing as we speak. Assuming Santos even lets you play next fall."

He's not wrong. Before I gave the man a cardiac episode, Coach gave me strong "get the fuck off my team" vibes. Like I had personally offended him.

Like I was his biggest disappointment.

That's not a new sentiment. I seem to inspire this emotion in people.

My father shakes his head. "Of all the girls to fuck around with. You had to screw with the Saint's daughter? Why can't you date someone like Samantha Schilling? She's beautiful, smart, motivated, and child-free."

Why the hell's he bringing up Sam?

I'm not going to try to convince the asshole that I'm serious about Roxy in a way I've never been serious about anything, except maybe football. I reach for the door handle. "So you're saying you don't want an invite to Roxy's baby shower?"

"Cut the crap, Billy. What are you going to do? Marry her and raise another man's baby?" He laughs darkly. "Twenty-two percent of marriages fail within the first five years."

"I get it. The odds are stacked against us." But I love her, and I'm not letting her go without a fight.

As my shredded knuckles indicate.

He sighs. "It might not seem like it, but I'm trying to help you. Contrary to what you seem to think, I want you to succeed in life."

It's so foreign to hear him say anything remotely positive to me, I sit there speechless. "I appreciate your concern, I do. If you got to know Roxy, you'd see she's an incredible woman."

He shakes his head. "It doesn't matter how smart, resourceful, or attractive this girl is. You're looking at a long shot at best. When it's fourth and twenty, you punt."

I should be used to his grenades, but this one hits hard. I

scramble to look for a bright side. "You and Mom have made it through hard times."

"By the skin of our fucking teeth, if you want to know the truth."

"Maybe if you spent more time with her—"

"Don't be obtuse. You know how much time I have to put in at the office. Now get out. I have a long drive home."

And I'm dismissed.

The second I close the passenger door, his tires squeal. I stand in the rain and watch his taillights zip down the street like he can't get away from me fast enough.

I trudge up the stairs, resisting the urge to grab the railing. My knees and quads are sore as hell. It didn't help that I couldn't ice them when I was locked up. With the back of my arm, I wipe the rain from my face.

Jesus, I'm ripe. They don't exactly offer you toiletries when you're in lockup.

Pausing in front of the door to our apartment, I take a moment. I need it. I almost fucked myself ten ways to Sunday by hitting Ezra. But now I get to come home to Roxy, and that's everything.

When I open the door, I frown when I see her asleep, hunched over several stacks of paper on our small dining room table.

"Babe." I brush the hair out of her face.

Her eyes flutter open, then widen. "Billy!" She leaps out of her chair and into my arms. "What happened? Are you okay?"

"I'm fine. It's over. For now at least." I kiss her. "How's your father?" *Please don't tell me he died.* But then she probably wouldn't be happy to see me if something horrible had happened.

"He had a blockage, but doctors caught it in time. He should make a full recovery."

Thank fuck. "That's good news, biscuit." Coach is a surly bastard, but that doesn't mean I want him to die.

Leaning back, she takes my face in her hands and kisses me again. "When did you get out?"

"Just a little while ago. Ezra changed his story and retracted his statement. It was the damnedest thing." A triumphant smile spreads over her gorgeous face. "What?"

That smile turns into a smirk. "Let's just say that Ezra and I had a little conversation yesterday."

"Where did this happen? Where'd you see him?"

"I broke into his house." She says it so matter-of-factly, I laugh.

"You broke into his house?"

Her smile widens. "Yeah. And I told him to go back to the cops and change his damn statement or he could expect the story of my cheating baby daddy to land in the hands of every NFL recruiter in the league."

Oh, shit. "So you told him he's the father?" I guess we kinda laid the groundwork for that the other night. "How did he take the news?"

"About as you'd expect. He denied it, but Abigail was there, so I don't know if the denial was for my benefit or hers. Probably both. But at the end of the day, he doesn't want anything to do with the bean, so it doesn't matter."

"Aww, babe. I'm sorry." Not that I want him to be around my girls, but I can imagine being blown off by your baby's father like this sucks. I take her hand and head for the couch, where I pull her into my lap. Having her in my arms feels so good, I can almost ignore the pain in my knees and quads. "I kinda reek, so you won't hurt my feelings if you don't wanna be near me."

She snuggles into me. Pauses to sniff my neck. Shrugs. "You always smell good."

Huh. Pheromones are a weird thing. "Tell me what happened."

"I had a gut feeling Ezra would react this way, and he didn't disappoint. But what matters is that he recanted his statement."

"And that's all it took? A threat to tell recruiters?"

She glances away. "Well, no, I had to make one or two promises."

The hair on the back of my neck stands up. "What kind of promises?"

"Nothing you need to worry about, okay?" When I won't let it drop, she sighs. "I told him I wouldn't ever sue him for child support. That he could go off to play in the NFL, and he'll never hear from me."

Jesus. "Rox."

"What? I'm never asking that man for a damn thing anyway. It's no loss."

I kiss her forehead. "I appreciate that sacrifice. More than you know. I just want you to keep your options open. You never know what kind of obstacles life might throw at you down the road." Pretty sure my mother was head over heels in love with my father until he started treating her like shit. Maybe if she'd had some options she wouldn't have stayed with the asshole.

Roxy grabs my face. "Please tell me you won't get in any more fights."

"I won't."

"You promise?"

"Yes, I swear. Besides, Ezra's only here a few more months through the end of this semester. I won't have to deal with him next fall."

"Thank the good Lord."

As I smooth Roxy's curly hair down her back, I hope I'm the man she can rely on for all the shit Ezra won't be doing.

Because Roxy is endgame.

Somehow, this little pixie cheerleader wormed her way into my heart, and I'll be damned if I let her walk away.

Now I just need to win over her father, but I'll never do that if I keep fucking up.

It's time to get serious. About my life. About football. But most importantly, about Roxy and our bean.

36

ROXY

After he takes a shower, Billy flings off his towel and flops on the bed with a groan. Water droplets glisten on his back and tight ass.

"I'm so fucking sore. I'm gonna sleep for the next year," he mumbles into the pillow. "Wake me up for graduation."

I feel bad about what happened between him and my dad. Making Billy run endless stadium stairs is negligent and cruel, and I've never known my father to be those things. I can only hope he wasn't himself due to his heart issues and inadvertently took it out on Billy.

While I don't have those answers yet, maybe I can make my boyfriend feel better. I perch next to him and draw my finger down his spine, where I connect drops of water. "Do you really want to sleep?"

"Yeah." A minute later, his head jerks up. "Why? What did you have in mind?"

I shrug. "Thought maybe a back massage might make you feel better."

He lifts an eyebrow. "Might it include my ass, hamstrings, and quads?"

Laughing, I nod. "It would be my pleasure to massage those particular parts."

He reaches down under his body with a sheepish grin. "I'm already hard."

My core throbs in response, but that will have to wait. "No funsie naked time before we work on those muscles."

"Can't we start with *that* muscle?"

I smack his ass. "No."

After I grab some body oil and a dry towel, I make him scooch over and lie on it. "Let's start with your back. I'm afraid I'll get sidetracked if we start with your quads."

"Smart."

Billy is very agreeable when naked, I chuckle to myself. "I'll work my way down."

"Down, up, sideways, I'm not picky."

I strip down to my underwear because I'm pretty sure this is going to get messy. I'm wearing a pale pink bra and matching boy shorts.

He watches me undress with hooded eyes.

"Don't distract me with those looks, mister."

"I can't help that you're hot as fuck." He reaches down again and does something that makes him groan.

"Even with this bump?" I turn sideways and show off my slight belly.

"Definitely. Come here." He reaches for me and leans up to kiss my stomach as I tangle my fingers through his hair. "Baby Bean, you need to sleep for the next two hours. And don't listen to a thing I say to your mama. That's not for your innocent little ears."

Oh my God, he's adorable. "Two hours? That sounds ambitious." The expression on his face says he's not kidding. He grabs my ass and growls, but I wiggle out of his hold. "Tsk, tsk. If you wait, the payoff will be better."

"Will this payoff include coming on your tits?"

Billy loves coming on my boobs. I grab the aforementioned body parts and push them together, loving the heated look he gives me. "Wouldn't you rather come *in* me than on me?"

He curses and throws his face into the pillow. "If you keep talking like that, I'm gonna come on your sheets."

"We can't have that." I straddle his back and drizzle massage oil along his shoulders. "Where does it hurt?"

My beautiful man sighs. "Everywhere. I slept on a bench last night and can't turn my head to the right."

"Poor baby." I work my thumbs into his neck and shoulders, and he starts groaning. They sound like sex noises, and it's turning me on. I resist the urge to wiggle and find some relief.

When I'm done with the top half, I start at his feet and work my way to the middle.

"You don't have to massage my mangled feet."

"It doesn't bother me. Cheer sometimes gave me the worst blisters. Besides, you just took a shower." If I'm being really honest with myself, the massage is also for decking Ezra in his ugly face. Not that I want Billy fighting, because I don't. But if that punch had to happen, at least Ezra deserved it.

I dig my thumbs into the sole of Billy's huge foot. He's well proportioned. Everything about him is enormous. My hands are starting to get tired, but I'm getting to the really good stuff now, so I'm confident I can push through it.

He groans again when I reach his hamstrings, so I take my time there. "Spread your legs."

"Why do I feel like we're about to kick off a prison fantasy?"

I laugh and smack his ass again. "I will not violate your booty. Now come on."

Billy complies, and my eyes widen when I see his long, thick erection pressed down between his muscular thighs.

I drizzle oil over his glutes and down to his dick and balls.

Goosebumps break out on his skin, and I smile as I begin to massage it into his ass. I won't lie—my eyes are glued to his steel rod.

Finally, I reach between his legs and jerk him slowly, pausing to rub my thumb over his weeping slit.

"Babe, you're killing me."

"Roll over and I'll do it from the front."

I scoot over and feast on the image before me when he sprawls out on his back. He's breathing hard, his cheeks are ruddy, and his pupils are blown out.

Moving down, I massage up his calves.

"What? No. We can skip that."

Smiling, I shake my head. "We will not skip anything." I glance up his body. It's a masterpiece of sharp planes and valleys. A broad chest, bracketed by chiseled arms. A narrow waist cut with slabs of muscle. That sexy V, which leads down to thick thighs. "The soreness in your legs is why I'm doing this. We can't skip it."

"But you haven't even reached my thighs yet."

"Good things come to those who wait."

Closing his eyes, he tilts his head back, his hands tightening into fists. I'm torturing my sweet man, but I'll make sure he gets a big payoff.

When I reach his thighs, I tap his leg. "Spread."

His dick bounces on his stomach, but I won't rush. We'll get there. I work my thumbs into his inner thighs.

"I don't think I've ever told you this, but you're nicely groomed." His groin is neat and trimmed.

He chuckles. "Remember that first time I slept over and you fell asleep?"

"Don't remind me. I was so embarrassed."

"I was worried I wasn't trimmed well enough and that maybe

you didn't like what you saw. So I had a long talk with Jake about it to get his opinion."

I laugh. "You guys chatted about manscaping?"

"Yup. I guess you could say we bonded over it."

It's such a sweet, vulnerable admission, I give up trying to draw out the torture and reach for the bottle of massage oil. Our heated eyes meet as I drizzle it over that thick muscle bobbing over his stomach. "Let me show you how much I like you, just the way you are."

"Even if I had a crazy man bush?"

"Even if you were wild and wooly." We smile at each other, but when I take him in hand, our expressions grow serious. "I more than liked what I saw that night. You're beautiful. Inside and out."

"I don't think men are supposed to be beautiful."

"You are, so get used to it."

My hand works up and down his length with slow, deliberate strokes as we watch each other.

"Take off your bra." His deep rasp makes me shiver.

I flick the clasp and shrug out of it before I stand up and shimmy out of my boy shorts.

"Speaking of beautiful... Roxy-Roxy, my little foxy-foxy."

Smiling, I sit between his spread legs and resume shuttling my palm up and down his length. "When I'm huge and can't reach my bush, will you shave it for me?"

"Only if I can give you the VIP treatment afterward with my tongue."

At the thought, the pulse between my legs is so insistent, I have to squeeze my legs together.

"Are you wet, Rox?"

"Yes."

"Stick your fingers in your pussy and show me."

Oh my God. Billy has such a dirty mouth. I love it. Of course,

I comply. With two fingers, I stroke between my legs and pull them out.

He takes my hand and smirks at my glistening fingers before he leans up and sucks them into his mouth. "Sit on my face."

As tempting as that is, I'm not done yet. "No."

"No?" His brows lift.

"This is about you. Now lie back." Then I crawl on top of him with my ass in his face and lean over to lick his thick erection.

I'm too short for him to go to town on me in this position. I know this. But I love the tortured groan that rumbles beneath me. "Roxy. Baby, come on."

"Shut up and enjoy the show." I suck his crown, lick up and down his length, gently tug on his balls until they draw up to his body.

His giant hands massage my ass, and after a minute, he drags a thick finger down between my legs and sinks into my pussy, making me shiver. "You're dripping wet."

In answer, I wave my ass at him. I feel his eyes on me as he works me over with two fingers and then three.

It's a tight fit, and it makes me wild. I suck him harder, take him deeper, stroke him faster.

"Baby, I'm going to shoot down your throat if you don't stop."

He sits up behind me, and instinctively I understand what he wants, so with his chest to my back, I position myself over his cock and sink down. Because his thighs are so much bigger than mine, this angle really spreads my legs. It takes a second to work my way down him, but the reward is worth it.

"Fuck, you feel so good," he mumbles in my ear as he reaches around to massage my clit. His other hand squeezes my breast and pulls at my nipple.

I thread my fingers through his hair, loving how he bites my neck. Tiny nibbles that get harder in perfect rhythm with his strokes along my core.

I'm so, so close. He lightly pinches my clit, and I fly apart. "Oh God!" I squeeze my eyes shut and bright lights flicker behind my lids.

He grunts in my ear. "I can feel you squeezing my dick. It's incredible, Rox. God damn."

His hands tighten on my hips as he pushes up, once, twice, and the third time he comes. His hot release is so intense, it seeps down my thighs.

We're a sticky tangle of limbs when we collapse on the bed.

A few minutes later, after we clean up, I'm wrapped around him with my head on his chest and my thigh tossed over his. "If I weren't pregnant already, I'm pretty sure that sex would've knocked me up."

He laughs and kisses my forehead. "I love you, Roxy. Maybe... maybe one day we'll have more babies."

"I love you too. So much." Leaning up, I kiss him again. "We should definitely have more babies someday."

I hadn't really thought I wanted kids, much less several, but I realize I do with Billy.

The night is perfect.

Which makes the news later that week that much more difficult to swallow.

I'm sitting on the couch, eating a breakfast burrito and watching ESPN, when I read the crawler.

"That can't be right." I move closer to the TV in case I'm misreading it.

Junior Ezra Thomas, a potential number one draft pick, will not be attending the NFL Combine next week and has decided to stay at Lone Star State one more year to support his coach, Richard Santos, who suffered a cardiac episode last weekend.

What the holy hell is going on?

37

ROXY

"I CAN'T BELIEVE people are buying this shit," Cam says. Billy grunts in agreement. Jinxy, Jake, and Charlotte stare ahead, riveted to the TV screen.

We're hanging out at the football house, watching Ezra's press conference on *Bronco Nation.*

I squeeze Billy's hand. "He can barely turn to the left. I can't believe no one has picked up on that yet."

My dad is sitting next to Ezra, looking grim. He's only been out of the hospital for a few days, and he has no business doing a damn press conference, but my mom said he wouldn't listen to her.

Still sporting a broken nose, Ezra awkwardly leans toward the mic. "As I'm sure you all know, I've decided to stay at Lone Star one more year."

"Ezra, what prompted this change of heart?" a reporter asks. *"You were projected to be a first-round draft pick."*

"I owe much of my success to Coach Santos. He's like a second father to me." Ugh, he makes me want to puke. "And the moment I heard he had a cardiac situation, it made me realize I wanted to stay here one more year to offer my support and finish out my degree as a Bronco."

What a load of crap.

While his official story is this song and dance about my dad, word on the street is he was injured at one of the frat houses and can't fucking throw a football.

"Does this have anything to do with that fight you had with defensive safety Billy Babcock last weekend?" someone else asks. *"It looks like you have a broken nose."*

I suck in a breath, and Billy freezes next to me.

Ezra laughs awkwardly. Looks down. *That asshole had better not renege on our agreement.* "No, not at all. Billy Babcock and I were just horsing around. It was a prank gone wrong. And it's not broken, just a little bruised." He looks at the camera and smiles. "Kids, don't do TikTok challenges."

The reporters chuckle.

I let out a relieved breath.

"Coach Santos, how do you feel about Ezra's return to Lone Star State to play his senior year?"

"Obviously, I'm thrilled." I laugh out loud because my dad doesn't look thrilled. Maybe he knows more about what's going on with Ezra than I suspected. "Ezra Thomas is a joy to have on my team. He has a fantastic work ethic, a dynamic understanding of the game, and a bullet arm. His teammates are ecstatic."

I look around the living room. The guys definitely don't look ecstatic.

"Coach, how are you feeling? You're just days away from a serious health scare. Shouldn't you be at home?"

My dad musters a smile, but I know he's faking it. "I'm doing much better, and I know how important it is to set the story straight. I have the best college quarterback in the country returning for another season. That's a huge reason to celebrate."

Coach pats Ezra on the back. I'm not sure if anyone notices that Ezra winces, but I do.

Billy clicks off the TV. "Son of a bitch. Now we're stuck with that asshole another year."

Dread fills my chest.

I'm not sure what that means for Billy, but it's probably not good.

38

BILLY

FOUR AND A HALF MONTHS LATER

"DUDE, where do you want the chocolate-filled diapers?" Jinxy asks as he sniffs one of them.

Jake hefts his son Asher on his hip as he side-eyes me, and I shake my head. "Don't look at me like this was my idea. I'm just executing Charlie's suggestions."

Sure, I came up with a few things, but filling a diaper with melted chocolate so it looked like shit and making everyone guess what kind of candy bar it is was not my brainchild.

We're all running around Coach's backyard, prepping for Roxy's baby shower. Several football players came today, including my old roommates, a half dozen cheerleaders from her old squad, two pregnant college students she met at a parenting class, and a few friends from an animal rescue we've both volunteered at with Charlotte.

It's an interesting mix of people, but that's because everyone adores Rox wherever she goes. And I'm grateful as hell Ezra was too stupid to fall in love with her because then she wouldn't be mine.

Roxy's mom drapes a banner behind the gift table. "Don't let anyone give you a hard time, Billy. The shower games you and Charlotte came up with are great. Roxy is going to love them."

Deacon stares at the pregnancy photo of Rox that Charlie took last month. She looked so beautiful, I had it enlarged and mounted. Roxy is glowing, and she's all baby bump. Deacon makes a face and reaches for a balloon to blow up. "Good thing we're doing this now. Roxy looks like she's gonna burst any day now."

Charlotte pokes her head up from under the table to give him the stink eye, which matches mine.

Marlena elbows her son. "You'd better not say that to her, *mijo*. A woman feels self-conscious when she's this pregnant. She held off doing the shower because you were moving last month, and she didn't want to put you out."

Roxy is thirty-six weeks pregnant. I don't know why people describe pregnancy as a nine-month thing. She could go up to forty weeks. That's ten fucking months. And yeah, she kept pushing back the date of her shower. The draft and cheerleading nationals were in April, and she wanted to support our friends. Then we had finals in May, and Deke was moving here in June, and she helped him settle in at his new apartment. My little mother hen has been focused on everyone except for herself.

After he blows up another balloon, Deacon shrugs. "I don't know why I have to be here. I thought baby showers were for women."

He may be Roxy's brother, but he's starting to piss me off. "Bro, do me a favor and pretend to be grateful she held off her shower so you could attend. Because if you say that shit in front of your sister and hurt her feelings, you and I are gonna have a problem."

Everyone gets quiet, and I realize I've just told off Coach's son, but when I look up, Marlena nods in approval.

Mrs. Santos likes me okay, but I'll never be Coach's favorite person.

While he didn't kick me off the team, I'm still on probation. I'm not sure he bought Ezra's official story that we were horsing around at the restaurant, but that jackass didn't get in trouble while I did because of the arrest and Ezra's broken nose.

But Coach did me a solid and talked to the police station. The captain said that because he's a huge Bronco fan and Ezra recanted his story, they'd wipe my slate clean so the media wouldn't get wind of my arrest. If we were in a larger jurisdiction, it would've been harder to keep under wraps, but fortunately, there aren't any reporters who troll our local precinct.

Coach also told me he felt bad for making me run so many stadium stairs. He said he collapsed before he was able to tell me to stop, and no one else knew I was out there. He apologized for making me run so long, but then he had to ruin it by telling me to quit fucking around and get serious about life.

The people who posted footage of the fight only got the tail end, once Ezra was already down on the ground, so there's no video of me clocking him. And the audio was shit, so you can't hear what we're yelling at each other.

Now Ezra has a little notch on the bridge of his nose. It's a reminder of that punch, which I'm pretty fucking fond of, to be honest. Especially now that I have to see him all the damn time since he decided not to declare for the draft.

His cover story about staying to support Santos? Yeah, it's all bullshit.

That idiot fell out of the window of a frat house while he was getting a blow job. Abigail had broken up with him, and he ran out to hook up with someone else like fifteen seconds later. He was getting his knob polished when he leaned back, fell, and landed on his shoulder.

It was only the first floor, so it's not like it would kill him, but he was injured enough that he couldn't throw at the combine the following week. And while not every single person who gets drafted attends the combine, NFL teams would wonder why he didn't show up. Personally, I think he was lucky the girl blowing him didn't bite off his pencil dick when he flipped backwards.

He told Coach he was accidentally pushed down some stairs at a party.

Apparently, Coach was on board with Ezra not disclosing his injury to protect his reputation, and there's not a requirement that he share this information. Coach explained to us that no team wants their opponents to question the strength of their quarterback heading into a new season, so it behooves everyone to shut the fuck up and pretend he's staying "to help his team."

Like Ezra gives a shit about anyone other than himself.

Once the decorations are done and the food is laid out, Charlie tries to get everyone's attention. When people keep milling around the pool and talking, Jake makes Asher cover his ears and then sticks two fingers in his mouth to let out an ear-piercing whistle.

Charlotte laughs at him, her face turning pink. He winks at her, and her blush deepens. She's so fucking gone over that guy. I'm happy those two worked out their shit. And Jake just got drafted by Dallas. He'll get to play with Rider Kingston, who's a kick-ass quarterback and former Bronco. They'll have a solid shot at making it to the Super Bowl next year.

She clears her throat. "I'm going to get Roxy now, so make sure to put your gifts for her on the gift table. Grab a raffle ticket because Mrs. Santos got some really cool prizes, and for the love of God, Jinxy, don't touch the cake yet!"

The guys chuckle as she runs into the house to get our girl.

A few minutes later, the sliding glass door opens, and Coach walks out with a glass of ice water in his hand. Roxy put him on a low-cholesterol diet and banned sodas and beer, which made that goat even grumpier.

He's wearing a polo shirt that's tucked into his dress pants. Honestly, he doesn't look like a dude who'd have a blockage. I've always thought he seemed pretty fit. But I understand why Roxy has spent the last few months cooking special meals for him so he could straighten out his health issues.

My precious girl waddles out behind her dad and hooks her arm in his. She coos over the decorations and lights up when she sees the cake.

She's wearing a pink flowing dress that hugs her belly every time the wind blows. It's true she looks like she's gonna burst any minute, but nothing could get me to admit that to her. Even heavy with her baby, she's still the most beautiful woman I've ever seen. Her gorgeous hair is down and flowing around her shoulders. She's glowing, like someone flipped on a light inside of her.

And don't get me started on her rack. If I could drown between her tits, I totally would.

When she sees me and sends me a sweet smile, my heart knocks hard against my ribs. She drags her father over to me.

"Coach." I nod.

"Babcock." He nods back.

Santos doesn't smile. He just kinda stares off, like he's doing meditation exercises in his mind to stay calm.

I get it, man. I'm a disappointment to you.

Perhaps I'd feel the same way if some jackass knocked up my daughter her junior year of college, but I've bent over backwards to try to be a good boyfriend to Rox and help her get ready for the baby. You'd think that would soften him up, but nope. I'm still persona non grata.

Roxy steps away from her father, and I pull her into my arms. "Happy baby shower day, biscuit."

"Thank you, Billy. Everything looks beautiful." She and I walk around, and she pauses in front of one of the party favor tables. "Oh my God, this is adorable! How did you know I loved those soaps?"

I kiss her forehead. "Because I pay attention."

She picks up the handcrafted soaps that are wrapped with labels that say, "From my shower to yours," with her name and the date of today's party. Each soap is wrapped with a bath loofah and one of those little floaty ducks. All the girls who attend today will get a gift set. The guys will get a bag of gourmet popcorn that says, "Thanks for popping by."

It's corny, but cute. And judging by her huge smile, Rox is pleased. Really, that's all that matters.

Cam and his girlfriend hug Rox, and then the girls wander off to greet other guests.

"You outdid yourself, Daddy," Cam teases.

I give him a look.

"What?" He lowers his voice. "For all intents and purposes, you're gonna be a dad. Are you ready?"

Jinxy jumps on Cam's back, nearly tackling him to the ground. I grab them before they topple into the cake and give me a heart attack.

After I untangle them, Jinxy slaps me on the back. "Hey, hey, Daddy-o! Should we throw you a bachelor party or something?"

"It's not like we're getting married." Yet. But I hope someday I can put a ring on her finger. I'm gonna work like hell this year to show her I'm responsible. That I'm not just gonna fuck off. I plan to focus on school, football, Roxy, and the baby. That's it. Hopefully this plan will help me graduate and get to the NFL. It's a long shot, but I've gotta try.

"Yeah, but now you have a ball and chain and the stork's headed your way. Your single life is DOA, dead on arrival. You should have a night to cut loose and have one last hurrah."

The moment he brings up a strip club, I shut that shit down. Pretty sure Roxy would cut off my balls and shove them down my throat if I did that. My biscuit is fierce. I dig it. I'm pretty fucking protective of her too. While this might not be my baby, nothing else about my relationship with this woman is fake.

Last year, I would've been down for any kind of public debauchery, but the last several months have changed me. The thought of random women shoving their tits in my face doesn't do it for me anymore.

Roxy's tits, though? I get hard just thinking of those beauties.

Cam smacks Jinxy's back in warning. "Don't mind our resident horndog, Billy. Jinxy is just looking for a reason to go to a strip club."

"Jesus." Jinxy reaches back to rub his shoulder. "Take it easy. It was just a suggestion."

"A stupid suggestion," Cam adds, pausing as the sliding glass door opens again. He motions behind us. "Is this gonna be a problem?"

I follow his line of sight. Abigail's here. "I fucking hope not. Rox invited her in passing last week, but she didn't think she'd show."

They've had a few awkward run-ins over the last few weeks, and I know Roxy feels bad about how things went down with her. I think Rox inviting her to the shower was an olive branch. She says Abigail's having a hard time here because she doesn't know anyone, and her ex is a douchebag.

Coach gives the new guest a wide smile. "Hey, Abigail. Welcome." He glances around. "Is Ezra joining you?"

Oh, shit. I guess Ezra never told him he broke up with his fiancée.

Abigail's eyes widen, and she starts wringing her hands. "Uh, no. He, um... He, um... He can't make it."

Roxy threads her arm through Abigail's. "I'm so happy you could join us."

I know my girlfriend is a cheerleader at heart and trained for years to root for the home team, but her enthusiasm for Abigail is one hundred percent genuine. It's not just some rote mechanism that clicks on.

Abigail and Roxy whisper back and forth a few times, and then Abigail starts to relax. If I had to guess, Roxy had to talk her into staying.

Everyone enjoys po' boys and sweet iced tea while we play a few baby shower games. The cheerleaders put a banner around Rox that says "Mama To Be" and place a sparkly tiara on her head. She looks so damn cute when she gives everyone a wave worthy of a queen.

Roxy's friend Paige takes some pics with her phone and shares them with my girlfriend.

Rox and I watched the online coverage of the cheerleaders performing at nationals. Paige spent several weeks training with Roxy beforehand. Sometimes it was just Paige sending her videos of her practices, and Rox would give her pointers and help her get the right mindset for the competition, which she nailed. It was a cool way for Roxy to stay connected to the squad.

After lunch, we gather under a large white tent so Roxy can open her gifts. Charlie jots down who gave what while I hand my girlfriend the gifts. I've never been to a baby shower, but it's kinda fun to be honest.

Her eyes water every time someone gives her a little onesie or pint-sized dress. My girl is gonna be such a great mama. Finally, there's just one gift left—mine.

"Sorry, biscuit, but you're gonna have to get up to open this one." I had a hell of a time moving it here this morning, but the guys helped me.

Her parents gave her a crib and stroller. I wanted to get her something special too. This wasn't on her registry, but I know she wants it.

I help her out of her chair, and she walks around the huge gift as I rub the back of my neck. "I know the wrapping isn't great, but it's an odd shape."

Her brows lift. "This is from you?"

"Yeah."

She laces her fingers through mine. "You didn't need to get me anything."

I scoff and kiss her temple. "Of course I'm gonna get you something. Open it." I got a part-time job this summer at a pizza joint to be able to buy this for her.

Giddy, she pulls off the giant bow and starts tearing at the paper. When she realizes what it is, her mouth forms an O. "It's that rocking chair."

She throws her arms around my shoulders, and I laugh at how much I have to bend over to reach her over her stomach. "Figured you would need something comfortable to feed the bean." It's one of those fluffy gliding rockers she collapsed in when we were working on her registry, the one she said was too expensive to put on her list of potential gifts. She felt funny asking friends to buy it for her.

"Billy, this is too much." Her eyes well, and she starts blinking to keep her emotions locked down.

"It's not nearly enough." I pat her ass. "Open the rest."

"There's more?"

She gives me a watery smile and rips off the rest of the paper and finds the fluffy pink robe and matching slippers. "My mom told me she lived in her robe after she had me and my brothers, and I thought that one looked comfortable. Plus, pink's your favorite color."

Mom was surprisingly cool when she found out about Roxy. I expected her to flip out like my father did, but she said that any woman who won my heart had to be special. Although she couldn't be here today, she wants to meet Roxy soon.

My sweet girl can't hold back the tears now, so I hug her. Damn, I didn't mean to make her cry. I smile awkwardly at everyone. That's when I see her teary-eyed mom. She's elbowing Coach, who has a strange expression on his face.

Roxy waves her hand in front of her face. "Sorry, y'all, I'm pregnant. I'm basically bursting with hormones." Everyone chuckles. "Thank you for all of these lovely gifts. Billy and I are so grateful to have such amazing friends." She rubs her swollen stomach. "We can't wait to introduce you to our bean."

She's due the day before I start training camp. I'm hoping she goes into labor before then so I can spend more time helping out with the baby.

But as everyone knows, I have terrible luck.

39

BILLY

August in Texas is hotter than Satan's asshole. It's so fucking hot, I can feel it through the soles of my shoes. We run one more drill, and I'm lightheaded by the time Coach Gates calls for a break.

I squirt water on my face and watch the quarterbacks take turns throwing to their wide receivers. Deke Santos is a bullet on the field, but he and Ezra aren't gelling yet. The new second-string QB, Nick Silva, is probably cursing pencil dick for staying another year. I'm sure he didn't expect to come here to ride the bench.

I keep waiting for Ezra to say something to me about Roxy or ask how she's doing, but all he does is give me the stink eye as he walks by. He's a little shit for not caring about his baby mama.

Jinxy chugs water and wipes his face with the back of his arm. "Nick has a kid, too, huh? Y'all can have a daddy's club."

Everyone knows the story about Nick Silva. He was engaged to his high school sweetheart, who died in a car crash on the way back from a game. Just like that, he became a single dad.

I can't imagine what the poor guy went through. The

thought of life without Roxy is devastating. I hope I never know what that's like.

For the millionth time this afternoon, I wonder how she's doing. She was due three days ago. Even though I'm supposed to live on campus during training camp, Coach is letting me stay with Rox. During the day, she's with her mom, but I pick her up as soon as I'm done here.

Yes, I'm terrified about her delivering a baby. So much could go wrong. But Roxy is a tough girl. She'll kick ass.

All morning, I do my best to stay positive and keep focused on our drills, but I'm anxious as fuck. Any minute now, Roxy's water is gonna burst, and the bean will be here.

Each day of training camp this week feels like the longest day of my life. When Coach blows the final whistle, I take a lightning-fast shower and book it out of the stadium. When I get to the Santos's house, I find Rox sprawled out on the couch, fanning herself with a magazine.

"Hey, babe." I lean over to kiss her and rub her beautiful belly. Our wiggle worm is getting antsy in there. "How you doing? How's the bean?"

"I'm so hot, and I keep getting kicked in the kidney. I'm afraid I'm going to pee my pants."

I chuckle and push the hair out of her eyes. It's actually pretty cold in her parents' house, but my poor girl's always uncomfortable. "Would ice cream make you feel better?"

"Oh my God, yes." Her eyes light up and she holds out her hands. I help her up.

"This looks good on you." She's wearing one of my t-shirts.

"I'm stretching it out."

Glancing around to make sure her mom isn't around, I whisper in her ear. "If you're a good girl, I'll stretch *you* out when we get home."

Her eyes go hazy, and she nods enthusiastically. "Sex is supposed to stimulate my parts and encourage labor."

I kiss her again. "I would be happy to stimulate your parts."

Someone clears his throat behind me. I close my eyes. *Goddamn it. Why does Santos always sneak up on us like that?*

Turning around, I do my best to keep my expression bland. Because if I look guilty of perving on his daughter, that'll only piss him off more. "Hey, Coach. I'm taking Rox for some ice cream. Can we bring some back for you and the missus?"

Roxy elbows me, and I remember myself. *Sorry,* I mouth to her. I forget about his diet sometimes.

Coach waves us off. "It's okay, Billy. I shouldn't have any ice cream, but thanks for the offer." Him calling me by my first name is new. I nod and grab Roxy's purse for her. Coach coughs. "Good hustle on the field today. I know it must be tough to concentrate right now, but you're doing a commendable job."

Getting a compliment from him is so foreign, it takes me a second to realize he's talking to me. When the words sink in, my head jolts up. "Th-thank you. Sir."

Roxy gives me a wide smile. "Dad, did Billy tell you he set up everything in the nursery? He painted the room, assembled the crib, and washed and folded all the baby clothes. He even installed the car seat."

Coach smiles. "Sounds like we're ready for liftoff. I'm getting excited to meet my grandbaby. Think it'll happen tonight?"

"I haven't had any contractions since last weekend."

"Damn."

Roxy and I laugh. We both know he placed bets in that pool. Everyone's been trying to get info from me, like I have a clue when the bean will pop out.

"I'm going to win!" Marlena calls out from the other room. "Call it grandma's intuition."

On our way out, I nod at Coach. "I'll call you if anything happens."

He nods, his expression serious. "Marlena and I will both have our cell phones by the bed."

After we grab two pints of ice cream and some cones, we head home. I have a feeling Rox might want more than just one scoop, so I figured it would be handy if we have extra.

I get her comfortable on the couch while we enjoy our scoops. When we're done, her head tilts back and she lets out a sigh.

"What's wrong?" I ask as I grab the lotion she likes to rub into her skin so she doesn't get stretch marks. I squirt some in my hand and slowly work it over her stomach.

She chews on her bottom lip. "Can I ask a favor? You can say no."

"Of course."

"Remember when we joked about having a wild bush?" When I nod, she motions to her crotch. "I don't want to go into the hospital like this, but I can't reach that far."

Is she asking me to shave her?

I grab her hand and kiss the back of it. "I love your pussy, bush or no bush. Runway or forest." 'Cause sometimes she has a sexy little strip. "If you want it shaved, though, I'm happy to do it."

"Really?"

"Sure. Just tell me what you want."

"It's more comfortable bare, and I really like how sex feels when it's like that."

My dick is on board. "Babe, I ask this only because I don't wanna get too excited if we're not going to fuck—and it's totally okay if you don't wanna go there, but it'll help to know so I can calm down my junk."

In response, she reaches between my legs and strokes me. "Oh, we'd better have sex afterward."

Fuck yes. "Your wish is my command."

It's easier said than done. She's *very* pregnant. If she lies in the tub, I can't reach her pussy. So I get a large bowl of hot water and throw a towel down on the closed toilet seat, so it's not so hard, and then I get her undressed. We'll jump in the shower when we're done to get off all the shaving cream.

She leaves on her bra but shimmies out of her underwear.

"Sit and spread 'em."

She laughs. "Why is everything you say so dirty?"

"Part of my charm, babe." I nibble on her neck as I rub her stomach. Because she was in such great shape to begin with and has continued doing light workouts when she's able to, she really is all baby. Well, all tits and ass and baby.

Leaning back, she slowly lowers herself. The sweet look she gives me makes my insides go haywire. I have to remind myself I have a job to do before we fuck.

Kneeling, I part her legs and lean down to kiss her thigh. "Want me to shave your legs too?"

"Would you?"

"No prob." I grab her dainty foot and place it on my thigh. I work some shaving cream along her smooth skin and follow it with the razor. Each stroke is slow and deliberate because I'm trying hard not to nick her. By the time I've finished both legs, my mouth is watering at the thought of going down on her. I've been trying to avoid looking at her pussy, but it's right there in my face, and she smells so fucking good.

As I reach between her legs to squirt some shaving cream, she squirms. "This is turning me on."

"I'm glad I'm not the only one." I point to my groin where my erection presses tightly to the zipper of my jeans. "We're almost done. Then we'll get to the good stuff."

She leans back and spreads her legs, and I barely hold back my groan. This is one of the hottest things I've ever done in my life.

Roxy is obviously turned on too. Her breath is sawing in and out of her chest and her cheeks are bright pink.

After I spread more shaving cream on her, I shave all the hair along the top first because it's the easiest to reach. Then I move lower.

"Don't shave off my clit. I kind of need it," she teases.

I was fine doing this until she uttered those words. "Give me your hand." I take her finger, lick it, and press it to her clit. "We need a clit shield. Don't want any accidents."

By the time I do both sides, she's slowly circling her fingers between her legs.

"That's it, Foxy. Make yourself feel good."

After I wipe off the rest of the shaving cream with a damp towel, I remove her hand and replace it with my face, where I lick her like one of those dripping ice cream cones.

"You're so wet, baby," I mumble between swipes of my tongue.

Her hand threads into my hair as her soft cries fill the bathroom. She comes within a minute. Afterward, we take a quick shower, and then I dry her off and lay her down in bed.

I cuddle her from behind, fully prepared to ignore my raging hard-on, when she pushes her ass into me.

"You sure?" I ask as I run my hand along her stomach.

"I'd rather induce the labor with sex than with some pill or shot."

"So the doctor said you need a good dicking?"

She snort-laughs. "That's *exactly* what she said. How did you know?"

"Just a lucky guess." I nibble her earlobe. Lick down her neck. Nuzzle her shoulder. "From behind?"

"I don't think I can roll over, so yeah." We both laugh. Sex with Rox is always like this. I find myself laughing at the weirdest times. But it's always so damn good.

Reaching down, I position myself at her entrance. It's a snug fit, and after a few minutes of trying to wedge myself in there, I haven't had any success.

"Lift your leg over mine." I help her adjust and then I grab her ass cheek and spread it. "Don't worry. I'm not headed for brown town." I'd never do that without lube. "Just trying to make some room."

She giggles and reaches back to scratch the back of my head.

I work my way in. Slow and steady. Pausing just to enjoy the sensation of being burrowed deep inside.

Leaning up on one arm, I arch over her and cup her face to kiss her. I'm worried as fuck about what happens when Rox goes into labor, but I shove that outta my head to focus on her.

Her hips move faster, and I take the hint, grabbing onto her thigh to keep her in place as I thrust harder.

She's moaning, her pussy squeezing me. Fuck. I push two fingers against her clit to rub tight circles, and she flies apart in my arms.

I'm right there. So close.

I come on a deep thrust that turns her moan into an ear-piercing shriek. Heart hammering, I still, but my dick's pulsing.

There's water everywhere.

Shit.

What did I just do?

It takes my dumb ass a hot minute to figure out what's going on with my dick still jerking inside of her.

Holy fuck. Is the baby coming?

Jesus, I'm probably hurting her. I slowly slide out.

"Baby, what do you nee—"

She sobs in pain, and I pull her into my arms and try to

comfort her, but she shoves me away. "It hurts. So bad. Make it stop."

It hits me all at once. How I don't know what the fuck I'm doing.

I rush around the bed to get dressed. To help Roxy clean up and find clothes. To get her to the hospital. My heart is beating so hard, I'm wondering if I'm going to be one of those assholes who passes out at the delivery.

She's crying and worried and upset, and I don't know what to say to make this better. I'm so far out of my depth, I can't tell what's up or down.

So I call the one person I know we can count on. Coach.

40

BILLY

Brow furrowed, Coach pats me on the back. "She'll be okay, Billy. These things take longer than you'd think. I bet she'll ask for you in a little while."

We're in the waiting room where I've been pacing for the last hour. The doctor wanted to examine her and asked everyone to leave. Told Rox she could keep one person.

She wanted her mom.

I can't say I blame her, but in my mind, today didn't play out this way. Why'd Roxy have me go to Lamaze class if she didn't want me by her side? Or have me go to all of her doctor appointments? Or have me rub her belly with lotion every night?

The doctor walked out a while ago, but her mom's still in there.

Rox cried all the way to the hospital and wouldn't let me hold her hand.

I feel sick, like I fucked her up when we had sex. Like I was too busy thinking with my dick to help her. Like I'm fulfilling all of Coach's worst thoughts about me.

Her father is being shockingly nice. It makes me uncomfortable. I'm not used to him smiling or patting me on the back.

Cam jogs through the doors to the maternity ward and holds up a bag of takeout. "I brought burgers. Jinxy will be here soon with more snacks. Figured we'd hang out and keep you company."

I force a smile. "Thanks, bro. Appreciate it." The guys aren't supposed to leave the dorms after practice during training camp, but I guess Coach is making an exception.

"How's she doing?"

Shrugging, I look down the hallway. I want to tell him I got kicked out a little while ago, but that sounds petulant.

Thankfully, Marlena sticks her head out of Roxy's room and motions to come. Is she talking to me?

I look behind me, and Coach nods. "See? I told you Roxy would want you. Go on."

My stomach tightens. I have no idea what I'm about to walk into. But she needs me to be strong. *She's the one who's about to push out a baby, dude. Don't be a fucking wuss.*

Right.

When I reach Marlena, she gives me a worried mama smile and grabs my shoulder. "*Mijo*, she's going to get an epidural, which should help with the pain."

That's a shot into her spine.

I blink a few times, feeling lightheaded. Fuck. If I pass out right now, I'm gonna kick my own ass. "What do I do?"

"What you've done for her this whole time. Be there for her. Love her through this." She chuckles. "She might not be very nice. I was a beast toward my husband when I had the kids, but he took it all."

I nod. I can do that.

She ushers me in, and Rox turns toward me. She looks so small in that hospital bed. Except for the giant round bulge in her midsection. *Ezra's such a fool,* I think for the millionth time. How could he give her up?

Her eyes are swollen and her face is flushed. She looks as terrified as I feel. This is probably a good time to fake it 'till I make it.

"Hey, biscuit. How you doing?" I give her a reassuring smile and reach for her hand. Thankfully, she lets me hold it this time.

"My uterus feels like it's going to explode. Remember that movie *Alien* where that creature busts through that man's chest?"

I nod hesitantly. My older brothers love horror films.

"It's like that, only lower. Like there's something gnawing its way out of my guts."

My stomach lurches, but I swallow and try to keep my shit together.

A contraction hits her, and her eyes squeeze shut as her whole body tightens. The machines around her beep. One is her heart rate, which speeds up every time she gets a contraction, and one is connected to a strap around her waist and predicts the contractions a few seconds before they happen.

The nurse stacks towels on the table opposite the bed.

I head over to her. "Excuse me. Can I get some ice water and washcloths?" I remember one of the moms at that birth class said she liked having cool cloths and needed to drink lots of water. Roxy is sweating up a storm. Bet that might make her more comfortable.

"Of course." The nurse returns a minute later with the supplies I asked for.

After I wash my hands in the en suite bathroom, I dampen a washcloth. "Rox, think this might help?" I hold it up and wipe her face and neck.

"That feels so good. Thanks."

I let out a breath of relief. Maybe I won't be a fucking idiot today.

It hurts to watch her writhe in pain. It makes me put a pin in the idea that she'll want more kids someday because I don't know why she'd subject herself to this kind of torture again. I hold her hand through every contraction. "Good thing I'm not a quarterback anymore," I joke and shake it out after a few minutes.

"Oh, sorry."

I lean over to kiss her sweaty forehead. "I'm good, babe. Just do your thing."

Finally, an anesthesiologist arrives to give her that epidural.

He has her turn on her side, and I crouch down to talk to Roxy while he does the procedure. I don't tell her that I might pass the fuck out if I have to watch him slide that enormous needle into her vertebrae.

"Did you decide on a name?" I whisper as I stroke her head and push the hair out of her eyes. It's piled on top of her head, but several strands have escaped and are sticking to her sweaty skin.

Baby names is one of our favorite topics, and I'm hoping it'll distract her.

She shakes her head. "I can't decide. How do you choose a name? It's forever, and that's a lot of pressure. I don't want to get it wrong."

"You're right. A name is important." I lace my fingers through hers and squeeze her hand until the procedure is over. "Maybe when you meet her, it'll come to you, and you'll just know."

Her brows pull tight. "Billy, speaking of names, there's something I want to talk to you about." She chews on her bottom lip. "I did some research, and—"

She pauses as a contraction overpowers her. She cries out, and I look at the nurse, worried. "I thought the epidural was supposed to make the pain better."

Each wave seems stronger than the last, and she barely has time to recover before the next one hits. Watching her suffer is excruciating.

I don't know how long this goes on. It feels like hours. The nurse and I reposition her a few times to get more comfortable, but then, all of a sudden, the contractions start coming even faster.

The nurse says she's going to update the physician, and a few minutes later, several people rush in all at once.

"Daddy, why don't you stand up there while I examine her," the doctor says as he puts on gloves.

Daddy. Never thought I'd love the sound of that, especially when I can't fucking stand my own father. But our little bean changed everything. Roxy changed everything.

Tears stream down her face, and I gently squeeze her hand. "You got this, baby. You're doing great."

The doc reaches between her legs to check dilation. "Looks like your daughter is eager to join us, Roxy. I think you're ready to push."

Her eyes widen when the nurse brings this bar over to the bed and asks her to sit up. "You can hold on here. This position is great because gravity helps you."

I steady her and hold her up to the bar. It all happens so fast. She pushes and screams and cries.

When I glance down, my eyes widen. *Holy shit. There's the baby's head. Like, right there.*

Then a little wail joins Roxy's.

The nurse wipes off the bean and clears her mouth with this suction tool. Wraps her in a striped hospital blanket and places her on Roxy's chest after she collapses back on the bed.

"You did great, biscuit. She's beautiful." The baby has huge eyes and a head of dark hair. Something mysteriously like tears burn my eyes, and I wipe them with the back of my hand.

The doctor smiles. "She's indeed a beauty. And I hate to ruin this moment, but we still need to deliver the placenta. You'll experience more contractions until that happens. I'll press on your lower abdomen to move things along."

Birth is a messy ordeal, but as I stare at the munchkin on Roxy's chest, she seems one hundred percent worth it.

I grab her little hand. "Hey, baby biscuit. You're just as beautiful as your mom." Leaning over, I kiss Roxy on the forehead. "You kicked ass, babe."

She's crying, but these look like happy tears. "Hey, little one. What am I going to call you?"

The baby's serious eyes land on her mom, and my nose stings again. "Want me to take some pics?"

Roxy nods and I whip out my phone and take several, making sure to keep the focus well above her waist 'cause the doctor is still down there prodding. Roxy winces from time to time until he pulls out this bloody purple blob that turns my stomach.

I look away and swallow several times. "Hey, should I get your parents?" I ask when I'm sure I won't hurl.

"Yes, please."

As I walk around her, I notice the nurse whisking away all of the bloody chunks. Pretty sure Roxy would die twice if she knew she pooped in the middle of all those contractions. But she pushed a whole person out of her body, so I'm not surprised a little extra came with it. The birthing class prepared us for that sort of thing.

Before I reach the other side of the room, the doors burst open, and Roxy's parents rush in. After I take some photos of them each holding the baby, I realize it's after three in the morning.

"Coach, it's late." With his health issues, he probably shouldn't be up right now.

He smiles down at the baby in his arms. "Look at this sweet angel." His eyes go misty, and then he coughs. "I sent the guys back to the dorms, but I'll let them know our little princess arrived." To my surprise, he gives me a huge smile. "You did good, son. I can give you a day off, but then you need to get back to training camp. Wish I could give you more time, but..."

"I understand. Thanks, Coach."

He pats me on the back. "I'm proud of you and Roxy."

My throat gets tight, and I have to swallow to keep my shit together. I don't remember the last time someone told me that besides Roxy. I clear my throat. "She's the one who did all the hard work."

The nurse ushers everyone out so Roxy can breastfeed. It's such an incredible moment. "Look at you. You're such a natural."

The beaming smile she gives me as she cradles the bean hits me right in the solar plexus. "Thanks for everything, Billy. I mean it." She holds out her hand, and I lace our fingers together.

Once she's done feeding the baby, I place her in a clear bassinet next to Roxy's bed and then I crash on the narrow couch. The next day is full of learning how to bathe the bean and tips on feeding and changing her. Tests to make sure she's healthy. And a ton of visitors.

At one point, the nurse asks me to take off my shirt and hold the baby skin to skin. Apparently, that's good for them. So I hold my little sweetheart to my bare chest and softly sing to her as I watch her beautiful mama sleep.

When I finally get back to training camp, my mind is on the bean and Roxy. The guys congratulate me like I had something to do with Roxy kicking ass. I smile and promise to pass along the well wishes. I'm proud as hell of that woman.

But the coolest thing is when my teammates call me Daddy. They all think she's mine. In my heart, she is. I puff up like a rooster and strut around practice all day.

At one point, Ezra looks like he wants to say something to me, but he's too chicken shit to do it.

Roxy's mom is staying with her while I'm away. She'll be released from the hospital this evening. I don't know how I'm going to handle being away from my girls so much this fall.

As I think about my schedule—football and classes and training—I wonder if I'll ever sleep again. But it's all worth it for the bean.

After practice, I return to the hospital. I poke my head in the room, but Roxy is asleep. I look for the bassinet, but it's not there.

I head for the nursery. It's a large glass room where they place the babies when the mothers need to rest. A nurse points to the corner.

"Marley Santos is right here."

Roxy decided on a name, then. Marley. It's beautiful.

But then my attention snags on the last part.

Santos.

Not Babcock.

Nodding slowly, I try to take a deep breath, surprised by how difficult it is to fill my lungs. "Th-thanks."

I guess Roxy decided she didn't want to use my last name. Of course, this is her baby and she can call her whatever she wants. She's the one who gestated this kid for ten months. I'm not even the sperm donor.

This shouldn't bother me, but the tightness in my chest suggests it does.

As I attempt another breath, I realize this is a wake-up call. Because I'm not really the father. I'm just the stand-in. A placeholder.

Makes me wonder if I'll ever be more.

41

ROXY

My mom packs up my hospital room while Coach holds Marley and my brother baby-talks to her.

"Who's your favorite uncle? That's right, cutie. Your Uncle Deke." He turns to me. "I'd better get going. Some jerk is giving me a curfew at the dorms, and I still need to pick up Subway sandwiches for the guys." After some stink-eye to our dad, who's too busy doting on the baby to pay attention to the salty attitude, my brother takes off.

My pulse skyrockets the moment the door closes. I fist my hands by my side so they don't tremble. "Guys, there's something I wanted to talk to you about before Billy gets here." Not because I don't want him to be a part of this conversation, but because it's time I do the right thing on my own without his help. Because Billy has helped me with *everything* for the last several months. I honestly don't know how I would've gotten to this point without his support.

But this? This I need to do on my own.

Billy texted that he stopped by earlier today when I was sleeping, and he's heading out to run a few errands, but he'll return to take me and Marley home in an hour.

My mom stops folding my clothes and comes to stand next to the bed, where I'm sitting and trying to motivate myself to get dressed.

Coach hands me Marley. "What's up, honey? Is everything with you and Billy okay?"

"Yes, he's wonderful. It's not about him." That's not exactly right. "I'm not saying this correctly. Actually, I haven't been honest with you two about something, and now that Marley's here, I see how wrong that was." I drag a finger over her dark hair that looks so much like Ezra's. "I want to be the kind of parent she can be proud of, and lying isn't the way to do that."

Mom tilts her head. "This sounds serious. Let me grab some chairs."

I brace myself. I should've done this a long time ago.

My parents sit down, and I take a deep breath. "Billy isn't Marley's father."

They look at each other. At me. Blink. Finally, my mom's eyes bug out. "*Mija*, does Billy know this?"

"Of course. He's known from the beginning."

Coach shakes his head again and again. "But that day in my office when I first found out you were pregnant, he told me he was the father."

"He was upset that you yelled at me in front of half of the football team and made me cry. He was trying to protect me."

My mom elbows my father in the gut. "You made her cry? You never told me this."

"You don't need to get mad at Dad. I should've come to you guys long before then. The truth is Marley's biological father doesn't want to be involved. While I didn't know that then, I had a strong hunch. And that made me ashamed. So Billy stepped in."

Coach looks like he's going to explode. There's an angry vein in his temple that's a little scary. "Roxanne." He wipes his mouth. "I gave that boy so much shit this year because of you."

My face flames in embarrassment. "I know, and it was totally unwarranted. He's a really good guy who was just trying to stand up for me."

Mom holds up her hand. "I'm confused. So are you two really dating?"

"It didn't start out that way, but we're together now."

"Oh, good. Because I really like him."

I smile. "I do too." A knot forms in my throat as I think of all the ways Billy has supported me. "He was even willing to let me put his name on the birth certificate."

My mom's eyes water. "He's such a sweet boy."

"Marlena, that's called fraud, and it's illegal," my father says, ever the pragmatist.

"You both will be relieved to know I finally came to my senses. That wasn't the right way to go about things." When Marley and I hopefully take Billy's last name someday, it won't be because we're fudging a birth certificate.

Coach motions to the baby. "So who's the father?"

I bite my bottom lip. "I can't say, Dad."

Silence.

"Is it one of the players on my team?" he asks in a deadly quiet voice.

"I'm not telling you. Just know that he couldn't care less that I had his baby."

Coach points at me like I just dropped a touchdown pass in the end zone. "That's too fucking bad. He created this problem, so he needs to man up and be responsible. He should be paying you child support."

"Dad, lower your voice. Studies show that stress can affect babies." I snuggle Marley closer to my chest. "Besides, my baby is not a 'problem.' She's the sweetest little angel on Earth, and I'm honored to be her mother. And I'm not chasing after a man who doesn't care about our child. That's on him. All I can do is love my daughter and try to give her the best life possible. Besides, Billy loves the bean. And he loves me. He treats me like a princess."

My mom nods. "He really does. I can tell he loves you."

Dad reluctantly agrees, but then sighs. "Billy's been a stand-up young man through this whole pregnancy." He tugs at the neckline of his shirt. "I feel like an asshole." I laugh and Mom snorts.

"Then make it up to him," I suggest. "You can start by looking at his QB stats in high school. And consider how hard he's worked at every position he's had at Lone Star, roles he didn't ask for. Every time the team got a new coach, he got the shaft. But he worked his ass off to fill those roles. He could've transferred, gone to a different program, but he stayed here because he's loyal and loves the Broncos. Aren't those the very characteristics you're always touting?"

Coach's lips flatten as he considers what I'm saying. "Since Ezra is staying, I have more quarterbacks than I know what to do with this fall."

I do my best to not flinch when he says that name. "A wise man once told me you can never have too many QBs." I smirk because he used to say that all the time.

He rolls his eyes. "I'll see what I can do, but at this point, I wouldn't be doing Billy any favors to switch him back to offense. NFL recruiters want to see consistency, not a player who gets shoved in any available position."

Here's a novel thought. "Why don't you ask him what he wants?"

~

BILLY'S quiet on the drive home from the hospital. Maybe he's nervous. Marley looks like a rag doll in this car seat, even with the extra baby bumper. I swear I feel every pothole in the road, and each one fills me with worry that it'll be too jarring for her.

I'm sitting in the back seat next to the baby, who's facing backwards, but I keep glancing at Billy in the rearview mirror as he drives. "Is everything okay?" I finally ask.

"Yup." Then silence.

"That doesn't really sound like everything's okay."

"Just thinking."

"Is it camp? I know things must be hard since you're not staying with the guys on campus. Would it help if you moved back?" I'd hate that, and I'd miss him like crazy, but the team's camaraderie is built during these summer training days, on and off the field.

His eyes dart to mine in the mirror. "Trying to get rid of me?"

"What? No, of course not. I was just thinking it'll be nice to finally be home so I can sleep in the same bed with you, but I'd understand if that's what you felt you needed to do."

His responding grunt isn't exactly the enthusiasm I was hoping for.

I don't know what's going on, but maybe this will cheer him up. "I have some good news. I talked to my parents this afternoon, and I told them the truth. My dad feels bad for giving you shit, as he should."

"You told them the truth about what?" he asks, his knuckles white on the steering wheel.

"About Marley. About you not being the father. I want to get off on the right foot here and be the mom I know I should be." He doesn't say anything, which makes me frown. "I thought you'd be happy. You were always encouraging me to talk to my parents." Again, no response. "You didn't even tell me if you liked her name. I thought Marley was the perfect nickname for Marlena."

"It's a beautiful name for a beautiful baby," he says gruffly.

When he doesn't say anything else, I know something's really wrong. "Billy, what's going on? You're acting... so cold. Like I don't matter."

He lets out a brittle laugh. "Roxy, all I've done since January is make you a priority in my life. You were pregnant and needed a stand-in father, I volunteered. You needed a roommate to make your parents happy, I stepped in. You needed a ride to doctor appointments, I gladly took you. You wanted to use my dick to break your water, I did the job."

Flinching at the tone of his voice, I whisper, "You were never just a dick or a roommate or a chauffeur."

"Funny, because that's how I'm feeling right now."

Tears quickly fill my eyes, and I inwardly curse that I'm such a faucet. When will these hormones settle down? I swipe at my face, angry that I can't keep my emotions under control. "You're my best friend, and I love you. Please don't be angry with me. If I did something to make you feel unappreciated, I'm so sorry. I've been overwhelmed. I thought you'd be happy I told my parents the truth. You've been my rock, and I'd be heartbroken to know I've hurt you."

The SUV slows down, and he pulls onto the shoulder of the road. We're on a back road, so there's no traffic. He looks down at his lap for several moments. Then he unsnaps his seat belt and throws open the door.

Oh my God. Is he leaving?

Relief pours through my body when he stalks back to my door and flings it open. "Come here." Hesitantly, I unlock my seat belt, and next thing I know, I'm in his arms. "I'm sorry, biscuit. I got butthurt over something stupid, and I'm not handling it well."

I squeeze him tight. "You've barely slept this week." I hiccup into his chest. "You're training all day and up with Marley and me at night. This baby thing is so much harder than I thought. But please don't be mad at me. I can't take that right now."

He apologizes again. "This afternoon, I came by to see you and stopped off at the nursery. I saw that you had named the baby. It just caught me off guard."

"You don't like the name Marley?"

"I love Marley. I just wasn't expecting you to name her Santos, which is stupid because that's your name. I guess... I thought you were still going to put me down as the father on the birth certificate and give her... give her my last name."

"Aww, babe." Hot tears roll down my face. "I was going to. Up until the last minute. I've been debating it all week. It's what I wanted to talk to you about the day I went into labor, but I got sidetracked by contractions. I finally researched paternity laws in Texas, and if I put you down on the birth certificate and had you sign all of the paperwork, you'd have to sue to get taken off. We'd have to go before a judge. It's this whole ordeal with the state, and reading about it freaked me out. I hope you and I are together forever, but I didn't want to put that on you."

Sniffling, I look up at him and grab his handsome face. "The name doesn't change anything between us, okay? I just don't want to start her life with a lie. I'm done lying. It's juvenile, and when I think of all the energy I wasted being scared of telling my parents the truth, I want to smack myself."

"Guess having a baby puts a lot into perspective." He kisses me on the forehead. Gives me a hug.

But the look in his eyes is still remote, like he's guarded.

That's when I realize how selfish I've been. This whole time, I've been worried about myself without a thought to how Billy would take this.

If I have to look at the silver lining, it's getting to date this incredible man. I'm not sure we'd be together if he hadn't jumped in to defend me to my dad back in January. He's been amazing.

And me? Well, I haven't been on my best behavior. That's obvious. But maybe I can make it up to him. Now that I'm out of the hospital, now that I've had Marley, Billy and I will have more time together.

We'll be able to work through this.

42

ROXY

I WILL NOT CRY, damn it.

Leaning over, I kiss Marley. Ugh, I hate leaving her.

"Can we go over the plan again?" I'm so anxious about my first day of school, which started two weeks ago. I've been doing class virtually, and while I could've gotten more time off, it'll be hard enough to catch up as it is. I'm worried that all of the good assignments in broadcast journalism will be doled out, and I'll get stuck doing something dull.

My mom gives me a patient smile as she cradles my daughter. "I've got her until noon, and then Billy will pick her up and bring her to you for lunch."

I'm supposed to be free after twelve, but I need to stop by the financial aid office and sign some paperwork. I can take Marley with me for that.

I nod, kiss the baby again. "Mom, do you think there's enough breast milk? I wanted to pump some more last night but fell asleep."

"It's just one morning, *mija*. There's plenty in the refrigerator."

My mom gives me a fierce hug before I step out of the apartment. When I close the door, I wait to see if Marley cries, but she doesn't.

"You can do this," I tell myself. "You can step away from her for a few hours. It's not the end of the world."

Tell that to my heart. It feels like it's cracking into a million pieces.

As I drive to campus, I blast the radio and try to focus on the music to get out of my head. It also helps me ignore the burning sensation in my vagina, which still feels like someone used it as a punching bag.

My doctor wanted me to take more than two weeks before returning to school, but the thought of losing that much time sent me into a tailspin. I want to make the most of my senior year, so I assured her I could do it. But right now, when I feel something suspicious leaking between my legs, I wonder if this was the right thing to do.

After I waddle to the bathroom, where I'm relieved to find I'm not bleeding out, I clean up and get to my first class. Pre-pregnancy Roxy did not appreciate how awesome her body was. Right now I'd kill to have boobs that don't leak or private parts that don't feel like shredded roast beef.

Broadcast is the one course I've been dying to take since I got here. The local affiliates broadcast LSSU-TV's student coverage from time to time, particularly if it deals with sports. *Bronco Nation* covers all the major Lone Star State teams, so I'm hoping I can cover cheer and football.

It's a small class of about twenty other students, and we all sit around a large conference table.

Professor Fowler hands me a syllabus and a packet of papers before he heads to the front of the class. "Roxy, since you're just now joining us, you'll need to pick a beat to cover. We still have the annual Nut Festival and the work that goes into preparing for it. The weekly city council meetings. And the new beautification plans for the downtown area, which includes those new artsy bronco installations."

My heart sinks when he doesn't mention anything sporty. "Sir, are there any teams that need coverage? Football, basketball, or volleyball?"

"They've already been assigned."

"What about cheerleading?"

Everyone laughs, and my stomach tightens into a ball.

Professor Fowler chuckles with the class. "I'm not sure there's much demand to cover cheerleading. It's not really much of a sport."

My hackles rise. *Do not argue with the professor on the first day, Roxanne.*

I chew on the inside of my cheek to keep my temper in check. "With all due respect, sir, Division I cheerleaders are elite athletes. Have you ever watched them during halftime? They're not just doing dance routines. They're doing advanced tumbling skills and stunts. In fact, the squad just won a national championship last spring."

Some guy across the table smirks. "They're fucking hot."

Professor clucks. "Language, Douggie. There will be no cursing in class. If you can't curb yourself in here, how can I trust you to do live coverage?"

"Sorry," Douchey—I mean, Douggie—says, not looking very contrite.

I raise my hand. "Could I possibly do one segment on cheerleading? And if you don't think it's newsworthy, I could cover something else?"

Fowler considers it. "If you cover the bronco art installations, you can do one segment on cheer."

Did I just talk my way into doing more work than necessary? It's too late to back out, though, so I nod as I scan the syllabus. "Thank you."

"It's more interesting than it sounds. Those broncos are supposed to be like Chicago's 1999 CowParade, which featured fiberglass bulls that were decorated by local artists and later raffled off for charity. But a few mischievous Charming residents, who I'm guessing are Lone Star students, took it upon themselves to rearrange some of our statues."

I start scribbling down notes on the back of the syllabus. If I have to do a segment on this, I want to make sure I understand the history behind the event.

Douchey laughs. "This morning, the horses were humping on Main Street in front of the library."

And now I'm doing a segment on horny statues. Great.

Fowler taps on the desk. "As for football..." My head jerks up. "Any chance you could get Douggie access to your father or some of the marquee players after the games?" Glancing around the table, he motions to me. "Roxy is Coach Santos's daughter."

Ugh, why is he telling everyone? Usually, I don't mind. I'm proud of my dad, but it sucks when people only want to get to know you because of who your father is.

As though he can read my mind, Fowler points to the second page of the syllabus. "If you read through my handout, you'll see the personal questionnaire you'll need to complete online. It will be shared with your peers in this class. You'll have access to theirs. The reason we do this is because you never know who might have connections or affiliations you'll need to access."

"I'm happy to introduce student reporters to my father after a game..." *Do it, Rox. Don't chicken out.* "Especially if I could do a football segment too. I know all of the players and coaches."

That sounds braggy, but I feel like I need to negotiate to get caught up to everyone who's been in class for the last two weeks.

"I generally don't allow children of parents or coaches to cover their events due to conflicts of interest." I understand his rationale, but damn, that sucks. "But let's play it by ear."

So, no. He just doesn't want to shoot me down. Probably because he wants me to give the class better access to the team.

I suppose I have enough on my plate.

If he's worried about conflicts of interest, he probably wouldn't be a fan of me being a former cheerleader if I plan to cover the sport. If he asks, I will emphasize the *former* aspect. Besides, no one can appreciate how hard we work more than someone who has done it.

After class, I drag myself across campus. My crotch is stinging like a mofo, and I'm so tired, I could curl up under a tree and sleep for the next week. Seeing Marley and Billy is the only motivation that keeps me going.

Billy and I took a look at our schedules and realized we would never see each other if we didn't try to meet up during the day. We're hoping to squeeze in lunch three times a week before he has to head to practice.

He had a great game last weekend, and we won even though the offense struggled to get into a rhythm. Ezra looked shaky out there, but we somehow pulled out a win.

When I reach the student union, I scan the cavernous room. I finally spot Billy.

He's surrounded by women.

They're all making goo-goo eyes at my baby. Though I'm guessing this is really about flirting with my boyfriend, who looks fucking delicious right now. His dirty blond hair is tousled, and his jaw is scruffy. His skin is golden brown from spending so much time outside. His jeans and t-shirt fit snugly, putting all of his muscles and tattoos on display.

The fact that Marley is strapped to his chest is the icing on the thirst-trap cake.

A cake I want to devour.

Except I have to wade through his fans to get to him first.

I press a finger into my twitching eye as I stand there and wait for him to see me.

"She's gorgeous, Billy," one girl says as she squeezes his shoulder.

"Aww, you're so good with her!" another one squeals.

"I always knew he'd be a great dad," a familiar voice says.

Grr, it's Vicky, his former friend with benefits. She's leaning close to him, pressing her boobs into his arm, to feign looking at Marley. It makes me want to yank that girl's hair until she gets away from my baby and boyfriend.

I clear my throat.

No one fucking hears me.

"Excuse me."

Finally, one of the girls turns around. She eyes me up and down. "I was here first."

I laugh. "That's my kid."

Her brows pull tight. "You're Billy's mom?"

Dear Lord Almighty, please don't let me stab this idiot with a rusty fork.

"Babe. Hey." Billy nudges everyone out of his way and gives me a one-armed hug so he doesn't squish the baby. I can't bring myself to hug him back. "I was just introducing Marley to some friends."

"Yeah. I caught that. Listen, I'm going to head out. Let me get Marley's stuff, and I'll take her off your hands."

Concern lines in his handsome face. "Can't you stay a little longer? We can grab a quick lunch."

"I'll keep you company, Billy," Vicky says as she tugs on his elbow, and I legit feel my blood pressure rise.

"Maybe some other time, Vic. I miss my girl." *Some other time?* He slings his arm around my shoulders and moves me to an empty table several feet away. "Sorry about that. Just got caught up showing everyone how cute Marley was. She's had a great day, by the way. Hasn't cried at all. Your mom said she took her early nap like a champ. And don't worry. I didn't let anyone touch her. Don't want her to catch some cooties." He kisses the top of her head with adoration as he slides into a booth.

He loves my daughter. That's clear as day. Even if she's not his, he treats Marley like she is. That says a lot about a man. That he would give his heart to a baby, especially one spawned by his enemy.

I let out a breath. It would be dumb to be upset because of those women. Billy is dating me. There's no need to be insecure. I don't want to be *that* girl. The one who says he can't have female friends and accuses him of things he hasn't done.

But Vicky is a former friend with benefits. That's a little different, isn't it?

When I sit across from him, I can't bite my tongue any longer. "Are you really going to hang out with Vicky?"

"No. I just didn't want to be a dick about it."

I nod slowly. "Okay."

"Don't be jealous. I'm in love with you."

Our eyes meet, and my chin starts to wobble. "I miss you. I feel like we never see each other anymore, and the season has only just started. What's going to happen in a few months?"

He gets up, careful not to jostle Marley, and comes to my side of the booth. "Scoot over."

When I do, he slides in next to me and tugs me to his chest. "Let's be honest here. This semester is going to suck. We both have a lot of responsibilities. We just need to steal whatever time we can. These lunches will help."

I wipe my eyes and nod against him. "This is hard."

"I know, baby. Hang in there. This won't last forever. We just had Marley. It's going to take us time to adjust."

Breathing in his scent relaxes me, and I'm about to tell him what happened at class when his phone rings. "We Are the

Champions" by Queen blares from his back pocket. That's my dad.

"Hold on." Billy pulls out his cell. "Hey, Coach. What's up?" He freezes. Looks at me. Opens his mouth, but nothing comes out.

My dad keeps talking on the other end, and Billy nods. "Yes, sir. I'd like that. Thanks for asking."

Whatever my father is saying makes my boyfriend's whole face light up.

"Sure thing. I can get there in ten minutes."

As soon as the call ends, he starts unstrapping Marley from his chest. "Sorry, biscuit. Gotta run."

"Everything okay?"

"Yeah. It's kinda crazy, but your dad asked if I'd like to work on some offensive drills. Said he wants to go over a couple of things before practice."

Billy conditions in the early mornings before class, then has practice in the late afternoons and early evenings. He's gone all day Saturday for games, and if it's an away game, he might have to leave the night before.

And yet my dad wants him to do *more* during the only spare time he has. I shake my head. Football interrupts my life once again.

At least Billy will get to do something on the offense. He looks excited.

As I watch him walk away, I try to remind myself this is just a one-time thing. Except when Billy gets home that night, he says he's practicing drills with a few of the guys during lunch for the next few weeks and can't meet in the afternoons anymore.

I tell myself it's not the end of the world.

It just sometimes feels like it is.

43

BILLY

"I FEEL like we're doing something illegal," Nick Silva, one of the transfer quarterbacks, says under his breath as we make our way out of the tunnel and onto the field.

The guy has a hell of an arm. He's a senior but redshirted his sophomore year because his girlfriend died in that tragic car crash. He says he's not looking to return another year, though. He's got a three-year-old at home, and that has to be tough. I get wanting to graduate and move on.

And while I might never get to play quarterback again, I find that doesn't bother me when Nick's throwing instead of Ezra.

"I'm sure Coach has something up his sleeve." This is our second week of practicing trick plays and formations with me, Nick, Deke, Cam, and a few of the guys who don't click with Ezra's offense. "Coach wants us to see if we have any chemistry before he moves forward."

These aren't sanctioned practices. Coach can't even attend, but we're encouraged to report back to him and give him our thoughts. He and I have had long talks about what I think works with this group.

One thing is for sure. The man knows what he's doing.

I almost stumble when I realize how much I trust him. Santos has been strangely nice to me since Marley was born. Maybe he sees I'm really dedicated to my relationship with Roxy? I don't know, but I'm not gonna question it.

It's possible that health scare changed his outlook. Coach is not as quick to yell these days, and he smiles more. And Roxy and Marlena are on his ass to eat healthy because we all want him around for a long time.

Nick pauses and turns to me. "You don't think it's weird as fuck that you're a defensive player coming in to practice offensive plays during our lunch?" He scans the field. "That we're supposed to keep this top secret?"

We have to lock the tunnel entrance after we arrive, so no one accidentally stumbles in on our sessions.

I chuckle. "Yeah, I do. And yes, a two-way player in college is rare, but if it makes you feel any better, I was a QB in high school and wide receiver freshman year."

His brow quirks up. "How'd you end up on defense?"

"That's a long story." I smack him on the back. "C'mon, let's go before we're late and piss off Coach."

"As long as you watch my back and keep me from getting sacked, D-man."

"I'll do my best." I motion to him. "Hey, how's your daughter doing? Is she handling the transition to Charming okay?"

He scrubs his face, suddenly looking exhausted. "No, she's not, but keep that between us. I don't want Coach to think I can't handle my responsibilities."

"I get that, more than you probably know. My girlfriend just had a baby, and while that kid is cute as hell, I don't think I've slept since early August."

He laughs. "All these dudes complaining in the locker room about how hard DI football is? I want to tell them it's nothing compared to being a father."

"I got shit on this morning by a ten-pound angel, so I couldn't even be mad, but I feel you. You're handling it well, but if you ever need anything, you and your daughter are always welcome at our place."

"Thanks, man. Appreciate that."

We spend an hour working on different formations and handoffs. A few different trick plays. It's fun as hell. I forgot how awesome football can be when you don't hate your teammate.

Roxy's right. I have to get back to what made me love the game. It changes everything.

Sure as shit doesn't hurt that Ezra has no clue I'm helping the quarterback who's gunning for his starting position.

While we've won our first two games, Ezra's struggled throughout. Solid defense and the strength of the rest of the team nabbed those wins. Certainly not the interceptions he's thrown.

To look at him, you wouldn't guess he's the guy who took us to the championship game last year.

I almost feel bad for him until I remember how he treated Roxy like crap and hasn't bothered to ask about Marley, and then I'm over it.

In the locker room, I see him rubbing his shoulder a lot. I'm guessing he's not a hundred percent. Serves him right for being such a prick. At the same time, I don't want the team to suffer.

Roxy has been worried about Deacon getting his chance at a national championship, and with Nick wanting to graduate in the spring, her concern isn't unfounded.

We break a half hour before the team meets, but Coach waves me aside. "What do you think of Silva?"

"He has a strong arm, and he and Deke gel well. Their timing is spot on."

"That's what I was thinking." He tugs at the neckline of his shirt. "Billy, I've been meaning to tell you something."

Oh, shit. Now what? I brace myself for something terrible.

"Well," he says, squinting into the sun, "I just want to let you know how much I appreciate you looking after Roxy and my grandbaby. You're doing a commendable job with everything. And... I'm sorry for being so hard on you last spring. Sometimes when you have kids, you lose perspective. But I want you to know I think you've been a stand-up young man."

My eyes sting. Then my nose. My throat closes up. What the hell is going on right now? I nod and blink. Then nod some more. "Thank you, sir. I love my girls."

"Good." He faces me. "Then maybe you can tell me who Marley's father is."

I freeze. Wait. What? "No. Sorry. Can't do it, Coach. I won't betray Roxy's confidence. She's trying to protect you in her own way."

"What does that mean?"

How do I say this without spilling the beans? "One, she doesn't want you to flip out and do something you'd regret. Two, she knows how much this team means to you, and she doesn't want to be responsible for saying something that could mess up the camaraderie you have with your players. And three, she wants the team to have the best chance to reach the playoffs for Deke."

He watches me carefully. I feel like I just got my leg caught in a bear trap. "So what you're saying is Marley's biological father is one of my players."

Motherfucker. Did he not know this already? I blow out a breath and put my hands on my head. "Coach, don't ask this of me."

He takes off his Bronco baseball cap and wipes his sweaty forehead. "My daughter is going to be the death of me. You'll see some day. When Marley comes home and tells you she has her first boyfriend or she's going on a date or to prom or whatever the hell kids are doing."

"Any asshole who wants to date Marley will have to go through me." I cross my arms. "Pretty sure Roxy and I are in agreement that there will be no dating until Marley's twenty."

Coach chuckles and pats my shoulder. "I like your attitude."

Something no one has ever said to me.

Then he stalks off.

I DRAG my ass in our apartment, drop my shit at the door, and collapse on the couch. "Rox." She might not be able to hear me since I'm face-down in a cushion.

"Hey, you're home early."

It's nine at night. That's a sad state of affairs. "You have a good day?"

"Douchebag Douggie wants me to take him onto the field for our next home game. Introduce him around. I'm trying to have a good attitude, but it's tough when I feel like I know more about football than he does."

"Who's Douggie again?" When she doesn't say anything, I lift my head, and she's giving me that look. The one that says I fucked up. "Sorry. I know you told me."

"It's okay. You're busy. I get it." She's wearing a t-shirt with stains and sweatpants. Her hair is tied up in a messy bun that's falling. And Marley is snuggled on her shoulder. They're both so fucking adorable.

"Bring me that baby." I roll over and hold open my arms. Roxy places her on my chest, and I kiss her forehead. "Look at you, Starley Marley. Smelling fresh."

"I just gave her a bath. It's past her bedtime, but I thought if I kept her up a little later, maybe she wouldn't wake up at two in the morning and I could stretch out the time between feeds."

"It's worth a try." I pat Marley's butt. "Should I be keeping her up or putting her to bed?"

"Bed. Actually, would you mind watching her while I take a shower? I have puke and pee on me, and a mustard-brown spot I'm scared is poop."

"Sexy."

She laughs. It's good to see her smile. "I swear I'll just be five minutes."

"Take your time."

"Are you hungry? There's lasagna in the fridge."

My mouth waters. "I'm always hungry."

"I can reheat it for you as soon as I get out of the shower. Actually, I could go for a snack too."

"Sounds good, biscuit." We might live together, but we rarely get to hang out anymore. I want to make the most of tonight. Maybe we can watch a movie or something, even if it's just for an hour.

Roxy gives me a sweet smile, and my heart kicks in my chest. I love this woman. She has no idea how much. It sucks that we have so much going on because there's nothing else I'd rather do than hang out with her and enjoy her company.

I hold Marley, and she conks out two minutes later, so I place her in the bassinet by Roxy's side of the bed. Yes, there's a nursery, but it doesn't make any sense to put Marley in there when she wakes up at all hours. That just means it takes us longer to get to her.

Though I have to say, now that we have a baby rooming with us, I can't bring myself to sleep naked anymore. Roxy is always breastfeeding, and it would be weird for me to slide into bed with my junk hanging out while she's cradling Marley. So now I sleep in track pants that twist and bind my nut sack, but it's better than traumatizing the kid or, hell, myself. No one wants to come eye to eye with a baby when you're not dressed.

I'll admit that going so long without sex is making me stir crazy. Not that Rox can have sex yet, which I totally get. She's still healing, and I'd never do anything to jeopardize that. Plus, if I'm being honest with myself, I'm still a little fucked up over her water breaking while I was balls deep inside of her.

I would never tell her this, but I've had nightmares about that moment. To remember how she cried out in pain while I was still pulsing in her body freaks me the fuck out. I'm not sure what I have to do to get over it. If I could scrub my brain with bleach to forget, I would.

Don't get me wrong—I still want her. I just... have this weird mental block. All I can hope is that by the time we can get physical again, I'm over my issues.

After I tuck in Marley, I grab the baby monitor and collapse on the couch again. Flip on the TV.

Yawning, I stretch out. My eyes feel so heavy. I'll just close them for a minute. Until Roxy gets out of the shower.

I wake with a start hours later. There's a cold plate of lasagna in front of me and an empty one that must belong to Rox.

Damn, I fell asleep on her.

And I have an away game Saturday that requires an overnight, which means I won't be home tomorrow night. Fuck.

44

ROXY

AM I BUMMED Billy fell asleep on me? Yes.

Am I still upset about it two days later? No.

Well, maybe a little.

Not with him exactly. I'm frustrated that our lives are so misaligned I can't even share one meal with my boyfriend for the entire fucking week. And now he's in Iowa.

Again, not his fault.

I have a sneaking suspicion I'm pissed at my dad, but it's not like he can help it. His entire focus is always about getting the team to the playoffs. That's just who he is. Wanting to change this about him is like hoping to blow over a brick wall with my breath—pointless. My mom has complained about his tunnel vision since I was a child. There's no changing Coach.

Doesn't mean I have to be happy about the demands he makes on his players.

A knock on the door makes me startle. I look at Marley in her bouncer. "Are you expecting someone?"

I laugh to myself. This is my life. I talk to my five-week-old infant.

When I look through the peephole, I can't keep in my gasp of surprise.

Abigail.

I open the door. "Hey. How's it going?" I haven't seen her around much since my baby shower, which she reluctantly attended. I was hoping to introduce her around so she could make some friends.

She gives me a hesitant smile. "I'm okay. Can I come in?"

"Sure." I wave around at the tornado that has exploded in my living room. "Please ignore the mess. I swear this room was clean two days ago. Then… I don't know what happened."

Actually, I do know. Billy left and I fell into a funk and wanted to wallow.

Which is really fucking sad.

I'm the girl who gets depressed when her boyfriend goes out of town.

That's just great.

I promise myself to get my ass in gear. As soon as the Iowa game is over.

After I move a pile of clean laundry off the couch, Abigail and I sit down.

"I brought something for the baby." She hands me a small gift bag.

"That's so sweet of you." I dig under the decorative tissue paper and pull out a little sundress that's going to look adorable on Marley in the spring. "This is beautiful, Abigail. Thank you for thinking of her. I've been meaning to tell you she loves that blanket you gave us at the baby shower. I always use it to snuggle her after her baths."

Abigail, who's sitting at the very edge of my couch, wrings her hands. "I'm sorry I dropped by unannounced. Honestly, I don't know what I'm doing here."

"I can't imagine what you're going through. I want you to

know how touched I am that you would get Marley something and that you came to our shower."

Her eyes turn red, and she sniffles. "Is it sad that the only friend I have here is the girl my boyfriend cheated on me with?"

My stomach knots. "I'm so sorry."

"No, please don't apologize anymore. I wish I could hate you. Honestly, that would make my life easier, but you're the bright lining here. You didn't know he had a girlfriend." Marley gurgles from her bouncy recliner, and I lift her out and cradle her in my arms. Abigail leans over to grab Marley's hand. "Your daughter is so beautiful."

"Thank you." She has a dark head of hair like her father.

Abigail tilts her head in thought. "She looks a lot like Ezra."

"Yeah. There's not much I can do about that."

She and I look at each other and laugh. "At least the asshole is attractive."

"There's that."

Her brow wrinkles. "Has he reached out to you at all to see the baby?"

"No, and I'm fine with that."

"That's what I don't understand. How he could be so removed. He told me he wanted us to have a big family, but if he's able to treat you and Marley this way, he's not the man I thought he was. Not that I would ever get back together with him."

"Marley is one hundred percent mine, just the way I like it. I don't want some guy involved in her life who won't commit to her the way she deserves."

"And Billy's that, for the two of you."

I smile. "He is. I mean, I never see the man because he's always at football, but he adores Marley. You should see him sing to her. I swoon every time." I catch a glance at the clock and reach for the remote. "Do you want to stay and watch the Iowa game with me? I was going to order a pizza, and I'd love the company, but I totally understand if you can't."

She looks down at her lap and sighs. "I'd love to. Is it okay if I curse at Ezra, though?"

"Absolutely." I grab my phone. "What do you want on the pie?"

After we put in our order, I place Marley back in her bouncy chair and pop on the TV to watch the game.

"We should have this in the bag, but Ezra's been wonky since that injury," I say, not thinking.

"What injury?" Abigail asks, her eyes wide.

Of course he didn't tell her.

"This is top secret, because the team never announced it, but Ezra hurt his shoulder last spring being an idiot. Coaches aren't required to disclose injuries, and my dad doesn't want to give other teams leverage in knowing how to tackle him."

"Makes sense."

When the Broncos charge out of the tunnel, my chest fills with pride. I love this team, and I'm so proud of what my father and Billy and his friends have accomplished. I hope they're able to go all the way this year too.

But we struggle during the first half. Ezra gets sacked twice and throws two freaking interceptions, which he's never done before as a Bronco. At halftime we're down by fourteen points. In the third quarter, Coach substitutes Nick Silva at QB, who connects with Deke for a touchdown.

I cheer for my brother even though he can't hear me through the TV screen.

By the fourth quarter, we're still down by six points and can't seem to get any traction. I sit on my hands so I don't chew my nails. With less than two minutes left in the game, Iowa commands their way down the field on every down.

"Oh my God. I can't watch." I almost cover my face because

I'm sure they're going to throw for a touchdown. After the snap, the Iowa QB drops back and checks his options. It looks like he has a clear shot to his wide receiver, who's open and booking it down field.

No!

The QB reaches back. Throws. My stomach clenches as I watch the ball slice through the air.

At the five-yard line, his receiver stretches out his arms.

But then a Bronco leaps between him and the ball.

"That's Billy!" I shout so loud, I startle Marley, who cries out. "Sorry, baby."

I'm jumping up and down as Billy intercepts it. After he hauls the ball to his chest, he races toward the Bronco end zone.

It's ninety-five yards away.

Defenders fly at him, try to drag him down, tangle in his legs at one point, but he manages to evade them all as he zigzags and strong-arms them, even leaping over a player.

He clears the last defender around the ten-yard line and sails in for a touchdown.

"YES!" Abigail cheers with me and lets me hug her as I freak out. "Ninety-five yards!" Billy is definitely making the ESPN highlight reel.

I immediately text him. **Great game! So proud of you!**

Of course, I remember my promise to him about back massages to reward each interception, and while I haven't gotten the green light yet from my doctor to have sex, that doesn't mean I can't help Billy find his o-zone.

Excited to see him after such a big game, I make him enchiladas while I research that bronco art installation my professor is so excited about.

But by eleven o'clock, when Billy's still not home, I start to get worried. They're flying in from Iowa, and sometimes their flights get delayed.

I break out my phone to send him another message. **Hey. When will you be back?**

Hanging out with the guys. That okay? I was gonna head home, but we just got burgers, and I'm famished. Want one?

I press my finger to my eye. It's twitching.

I didn't think I had to tell my boyfriend I wanted to spend time with him after the game, but I suppose I should have.

Doesn't make me any less annoyed, though.

I reply, **Nope. Enjoy.**

And then I toss the enchiladas in the fridge and go to bed.

45

BILLY

IT ISN'T until someone cannonballs naked into the pool that I realize how late it's gotten.

I only stopped by the Stallion Station to grab a celebratory beer with Cam and Nick after the game. Nick has been having trouble finding a babysitter and wanted to take advantage of the fact that he had one tonight.

He's kind of a standoffish guy at first, so I wanted to make sure he felt welcomed. He had a decent first game. Not quite the explosive start I thought he'd have, but he did better than Ezra, and we won, so that's all that matters.

"What time is it?" I yell to Cam over the music. My phone died a few hours ago.

He looks at his watch. "Almost two."

I wince. "I'd better get going."

"Roxy gonna be pissed you're out so late?"

My guess is yes, but that's my business. "She's probably asleep. Still, I want to get home in case she needs help with Marley."

The apartment is dark when I get home. I try to be quiet. Accidentally waking the baby is the worst feeling in the world.

When I get to our bedroom, there's a side lamp on. Rox and the baby are asleep, which is a relief. Maybe she won't realize it's so late. Not that I was doing anything I shouldn't. Just... I'm new to navigating my social life while having a girlfriend, and I really don't know if how I handled tonight is cool. I'll ask her in the morning.

I strip out of my clothes and pull on some track pants before I slide into bed. Rox is curled up on the far side, next to the bassinet. Inching over, I wrap my arm around her to pull her to my chest when she goes stiff.

"You smell like stale beer and cigarettes."

"Sorry. I know it's late," I whisper. She doesn't respond, which is probably a bad sign, right? "Are you mad?"

"That you didn't come home until after two, that you smell like you've been partying, or that you'd rather hang out with your bros than with me after a big win?"

Oh-kay. I blow out a breath and flop back. "Rox, come on. I haven't hung out with my friends after a game *at all* this semester." Really, I haven't seen much of them since Roxy and I started dating, but I don't want to make her feel bad.

"It's only the third game."

"And I came straight home after the first two. I didn't think having a few beers tonight would be a big deal. Sorry if I upset you."

"I'm not upset. I'm realigning my expectations."

That doesn't sound good. I shouldn't ask the question, but I can't help myself. "So now you have new expectations?"

"Yes. I won't expect you home at a decent hour after a game, which means I won't bother making you enchiladas and flan next time."

Damn. Her flan is fucking orgasmic. "You cooked for me?"

"You made a ninety-five-yard return after an interception. You were the defensive player of the game. You made ESPN. So yes, I cooked. I thought we could celebrate. It's in the fridge. You can eat it whenever."

"Shit. I'm sorry. You should've told me you were making dinner."

"That's not really the point, Billy." Her voice is thick, and I hate myself for making her emotional.

"Come here, biscuit."

"No. I'm really tired, and I just want to go to sleep."

Of course it's at this moment that Marley lets out a loud cry. Roxy huffs and kicks off the covers.

I'm exhausted, but I'm sure Roxy is too. "I can feed her. Let me warm up a bottle."

She shakes her head and reaches for the baby. "I can't use the stash in the freezer at night or I might not have enough to cover next week when I'm at class. I need to pump more, but I haven't had the time."

And she spent all evening cooking for me.

I feel like an asshole.

THE NEXT MORNING, I yawn. I must've slept like the dead because it's almost noon. I stretch, marveling at how good it feels to sleep in this late.

My eyes snap open.

There's a reason I never sleep in anymore. I bound out of bed, worried. Usually, I get up around five-thirty or six for conditioning, so I change and feed Marley before I go. And since I'm used to getting up that early, I try to do that on the weekends to help Roxy get a little sleep.

When I peer over the edge of the bassinet, it's empty.

I dart out to the living room, but no one's here.

There's a Post-it in the kitchen with a note from Roxy. All it says is, "Going to my parents'. See you later."

She usually invites me over for things like that, but I'm guessing she's still pissed about last night. I hope she doesn't tell her dad. He's just beginning to not hate me, and it would suck if he got another bug up his ass.

I open the fridge. There's a huge casserole dish of enchiladas. They're untouched. Like she baked them and didn't want to eat without me.

Feeling like shit, I grab my phone and text her.

Thanks for the food, babe. Looks amazing. Want to hang out tonight?

Sundays are literally my only night free, and so far, something has always come up.

My heart sinks when I read her response.

I can't. I have that segment I'm recording, remember? I told you about it last week.

I groan. Now it's all coming back to me. Her mom is gonna babysit Marley so Roxy can do something for broadcast this evening.

That's probably why she wanted to hang out last night.

"Nice job, Babcock. Way to blow off your girlfriend."

46

BILLY

"I CAN'T BELIEVE I forgot this appointment. I'm so sorry, Billy," Marlena says as she darts around her living room, gathering baby supplies.

"I got this. Marley will probably sleep during the whole morning anyway." I pause to consider what we're doing. "Are you sure Roxy won't mind?"

"Why would she mind?"

Well, aside from her still being upset with me? I mean, I'm guessing she is. I've barely seen her, and when I do, she seems so standoffish. It didn't help that I had another away game last weekend.

I feel like I'm screwing up everything, and I don't know how to fix it. There's nothing I can do about my football schedule.

Now that Coach is confident he can use Nick as a starter and he's having me work on trick plays during our official practices, we don't have secret lunchtime drills. On the bright side, Ezra is riled up as hell about it. On the downside, Rox can't meet then anymore because she's always recording broadcast assignments. In other words, our schedules are a total clusterfuck.

Remembering that Marlena asked me a question, I rub the

back of my neck. "She might not be crazy about me taking Marley to class."

"She won't care as long as someone responsible is babysitting."

Grandma Lena overrules. Fine by me.

Because I'm running late to class, the only spot is down at the front, and I'm afraid if I take it, Murphy's law says Marley will wake up and cause a ruckus. Plus, it's right next to Vicky, and I don't want to encourage her.

So I stand in the back of the huge lecture hall with Marley strapped to my chest and sway side to side. My little bean is sound asleep.

"Mr. Babcock," Professor Leonard calls out. "Are you planning to join us?"

The entire room turns to look at me. Why is everyone acting like they've never seen a man with a baby before?

"I'm listening, sir." I point to my binder that's sitting on the back window ledge. "And I have my notes here."

"Why did you bring a random child to my class?"

I almost make a joke about how this *is* Child Development, so what better way to learn about kids than to have one on hand? But I don't. Because Coach Santos taught me not to fuck around and be an idiot.

"She's not random. She's..." I want to say "my daughter," but I can't. While a lot of people assume she's mine, I generally avoid the subject. It's a little reminder of who I am to Marley. At the end of the day, I'm no one. Fucking Ezra Thomas has a bigger claim on her than I do. I clear my throat. "I promise she won't cause a problem."

"See that she doesn't."

After class, a few people come up to chat. One girl says she's from the school newspaper and asks me how I learned to hold a baby.

"She's like a football. Cradle her like she's precious, and watch the handoff."

Everyone laughs. I'm feeling pretty good about myself since I managed to pay attention in class while keeping my little sweetheart comfortable.

Fortunately, Marley slept through most of class, and when she woke, she wasn't fussy. When I fill in Roxy on my day, she says she's just grateful I could babysit.

But when a photo gets printed in the *Bronco Times* two days later of me in the back of class with Marley, her eye gets that twitch. "Baby cradled by star football safety." Her eyebrows hike up her forehead. "Did you know you're on the cover of the school newspaper?"

I'm sprawled out on our couch, reviewing some notes. It's one of the rare times we've both been home at the same time in ages. Wish I didn't have to study for a test. "Funny, isn't it?"

She sighs. "You and your fans."

That doesn't sound like enthusiasm. "What do you mean?"

"Look at this pic. You're basically being mobbed. When you walk through campus holding Marley, you're catnip to single women everywhere."

I smirk. "Yeah, but am I catnip to you?"

When she doesn't say anything, I realize our problems are bigger than me trying to make her laugh with some smartass remark.

"Roxy. Come here."

She finally looks at me. "Don't you have to study? It's getting late."

"Get your ass over here before I get up and toss you over my shoulder." That makes her crack a smile, and she wanders closer. Close enough for me to whip my arm out and pull her into my lap. "Stubborn woman."

I sink back on the couch and wrap my arms around her.

When she rests her head on my shoulder, I start to relax. Maybe this is all we need. Some time together to just fucking hang out without so much damn pressure.

It's been so long since I've held her, I almost don't know what to say. But I finally pull my head out of my ass. "I'm sorry about not coming home early after that game." I booked it home last weekend once we got back from Wisconsin, but she was sound asleep, and although I had a stellar game, there were no enchiladas waiting for me in the fridge.

She shakes her head. "I'm sorry I overreacted. Of course you can hang out with your friends after a game. You don't need my permission," she says softly, playing with a button on my shirt. "Everything seems like a big deal to me right now. It's like I'm watching TV, and everything is loud, and I can't turn down the sound."

"I know what you mean. This semester's been intense."

"I don't know how to get through this. I feel like fun Roxy, the cheerleader, got buried in the backyard, and I'm the *Pet Sematary* version with demon eyes who wanders around her apartment in stained sweats and yells at everyone."

"Aww, babe. You're sleep-deprived and exhausted."

She's so small in my arms. Every protective instinct in me roars to life. Along with an uncomfortable erection. And since she hasn't gotten the green light to have sex yet, I don't want her to feel pressured.

I scoop her up and set her down next to me. She looks surprised. I feel like it's an inappropriate time to bring up my dick, so I motion to the coffee table. "Better get back to studying."

Her face falls. "Sure. Sorry."

Damn. I'm not doing this right. "Rox, I'm sorry, but—"

"Of course you need to study."

We're both apologizing, but I don't know that this fixes

anything. I almost groan when I remember that call I got from my father this afternoon. "Babe, I hate to do this to you, but I need to go home this weekend." Sucks, because it's a bye weekend, and I'd love to spend it with Roxy. "My family is doing some dinner thing for my mom's birthday, and I'd like to check in on my grandmother, seeing how no one else does."

Grandma always has a list of shit she needs done, and if I get there early Saturday, I can probably bang it all out. Mow her lawn. Change her light bulbs. Bathe her mangy dog. Coach gave us Saturday off—which never happens—and said we can work out on our own as long as we check in with the trainers.

"You're going home? Overnight?" There's an odd note to her voice.

"Yeah. Sorry, I know it's a bye weekend, and it would be great to hang out here. But I haven't seen my mom or grandma in a while. I thought I'd go Friday night after practice and come back Sunday morning. Think you could get your parents to help you with the baby?" I hate leaving her alone, but no one ever looks in on my grandma, and she sounded lonely when I called her last week.

Roxy nibbles her bottom lip. "I don't want to impose, but could Marley and I join you?"

Shit. She looks so hopeful, and I hate disappointing her. "I asked if I could bring you, but my father said it was just family."

"Oh. Okay... I, uh, Marley and I can hang out with my parents."

I'm about to ask if she wants to study with me when she wanders back to the bedroom and shuts the door.

Yeah, I'm fucking this up.

I just don't know what to do to fix this.

47

ROXY

RUSHING INTO OUR APARTMENT, I book it to the kitchen. Billy and Marley watch me race by. "My boobs are about to explode. I have to pump before I… leak everywhere." Too late. "Damn it."

Of course Billy is here to witness this. I was hoping my mom had worked out her conflict and could stay this afternoon.

I'm still a little hurt I can't go home with him to visit his parents this weekend. I feel like he knows my family well when I've never even met his. It just feels imbalanced, like we're not on the same page.

With a fistful of paper towels pressed to my chest, I bite the bullet and trudge back into the living room. He's already seen me in more embarrassing situations, I suppose, and I'm too raw to bottle this up. "How do women handle everything? How do they breastfeed and live their lives? I forgot my essay this morning, the one I stayed up half the night writing. Then I almost ran out of gas on the way home. When I turned on Main Street, I hit the curb because I took the corner too sharp. My brain is mush!"

"Sorry, babe. That sucks. Bet this will make your day better —guess who smiled today?"

"No, she didn't." *Please tell me I didn't miss Marley's first smile.*

"She totally did. Watch this." He waves me closer, and I stand behind his shoulder so we're both looking down at Marley. "Who's my pretty girl?" She looks up at him, coos, and gives him a toothless smile.

She smiled at Billy. I'm not surprised. He's so good with her.

He tickles her, and her grin widens. "Who's the smartest seven-week-old baby I know? That's you, Starley Marley. Yes, it is."

Billy says her eyes twinkle like she has stars in them.

He kisses her on the forehead and hands her to me. "Sorry, biscuit, I gotta jet. If I'm late to practice again, your dad said I'm cleaning out the urinals for a month." He laughs like he's amused.

That's new. My dad still gives him shit, but I think it's out of affection because Billy genuinely thinks it's funny now.

I watch him grab his gym bag. He's so handsome, it hurts to look at him. Especially now. I was a fool to think we'd have more time together after I had Marley. We're so rarely home at the same time. Billy either has practice or conditioning or classes or a study group. When I'm not at school or taking care of Marley, I have to record broadcast segments or do homework. And we're both constantly doing laundry. It's never-ending.

The only time I ever see Billy these days is if I roll over in bed. But now he's never naked. He wears track pants.

And he doesn't reach for me.

I get it—I still haven't gotten the go-ahead from my doctor to have sex. And I'm still wearing a few extra pounds. Except I thought our relationship was based on more than sex. I mean, he'll snuggle me if I ask him to, but before I had Marley, I never had to ask. He would just grab me and tuck me to his chest.

Something has changed. I can't quite put my finger on it. All I know is things are different now.

Granted, I'm exhausted because Marley does not sleep well

yet. Billy tries to wake up, but after training all day, he basically falls into a coma. He offered to set an alarm clock so he could get up to do a late-night feed, except it's hard to tell when Marley will be hungry. He already gives her a bottle when he gets up at five or six in the morning. Asking him to do another feed feels like I'm taking advantage of him.

Plus, Marley is my responsibility. Billy already watches her sometimes when my mom can't stay, like this afternoon when he came home to babysit during his lunch break. He changes her diapers. Feeds her. Bathes her. Basically anything she needs. All that on top of his grueling football schedule. So no, I won't make him set an alarm in the middle of the night to feed my baby.

"You okay?" he asks.

I was so in my head, I didn't realize he was standing right in front of me. "Um, yeah. Just tired." This is too much to lay on him right before he leaves for practice.

I'm learning that communication is important, but how the hell do you discuss something like this? I barely understand how to describe the problem. I just know that there's distance. Distance I'm not sure how to bridge.

My throat tightens when I think about how he's going home this weekend. When he mentioned it yesterday, I nearly had a panic attack. I had to remind myself that he's not Ezra. That Billy's really going home to help his granny and see his mom. I can trust him.

"Maybe y'all can grab a nap together." He leans over and kisses my cheek, then the baby's. "Be good, Marley-cakes."

When the front door closes, my chin wobbles and my eyes sting.

I love Billy, and he loves me. We can work through this.

But there's a little voice in my head that questions whether love is enough.

48

BILLY

The Aberdeen Country Club in Austin is as pretentious as it gets. I'm sure we're here because my father wants to hobnob with his friends and not because he wants to treat Mom. If it were up to her, she would've picked the Olive Garden, but that's not highbrow enough for dear old Dad.

I pull at my collar.

The other thing that sucks, besides the snooty waitstaff and snootier clientele, is the fact that I have to wear a suit.

Maybe it's a good thing I didn't bring Roxy. This wouldn't have been a fun night for her, and I can't imagine bringing Marley here.

My mom looks uncomfortable, so I put my arm around her shoulders as we wait in the lobby. "Getting excited for some overpriced food that leaves you hungry afterward?"

She laughs and pats my arm. "I'll meet you in the kitchen at midnight and reheat some sliders."

"I always knew I was your favorite." While she doesn't say anything, because she'd never admit she likes me more than my brothers, she's having a hard time not smiling. "Oh, Grandma said she found your Pyrex. Whatever that is." I spent the whole day cleaning Grandma's house. She hurt her back and couldn't walk her dog, so he crapped everywhere. Good times.

"I'll swing by to get it. How's she doing?"

"Not great. Why doesn't Dad visit her more? Why doesn't he get her some help?"

She sighs. "Julia is a proud woman. She only lets you do things for her because you're so persistent."

I explain how Grandma hurt her back and her dog made a mess. My mom frowns. "I'll stop by to check on her this week and bring her some lunch."

"Thanks." I kiss her cheek.

"Honey, how's your girlfriend doing?"

I tell her about all of the segments Roxy's been shooting for her broadcast course. How she juggles everything while being such a great mother.

"She sounds lovely. When do I get to meet her?"

"I wanted to bring her tonight, but Dad said it was just family."

Her face goes flat. "Hmm."

We're waiting for my father to finish talking to one of his golfing buddies when a familiar face rounds the corner. Samantha Schilling, a tall blonde with a bubbly personality, waves as soon as she sees me.

"Sam. Hey." I give her a hug. She and I were friends in high school. "It's been ages. Are you meeting your family?" Our fathers are both partners at their law firm.

"It's so good to see you, Billy! Your dad invited me. I'm one of his interns, and he said I did a great job on a project this week, so this is my reward."

My eyes dart to him, and he gives me a nod. He's inviting interns, and I couldn't bring my fucking girlfriend? It's nice to see Sam, but I don't understand why I had to leave Roxy at home.

When my brothers stroll in with their dates, I'm fuming. So it wasn't about not bringing girlfriends. My father just didn't want me to bring *my* girlfriend.

We're seated at a round table, and since I'm now with three other couples, being the odd man out, there's an empty chair next to me, so Sam sits there.

She puts her hand on my arm. "How's Lone Star? I watch all of your games. You're kicking ass this season."

Some of my anger wanes. I shouldn't take out my temper on Sam. She's an innocent bystander. "Thanks. Coach wants another championship, so we'll either get there or die trying."

As much as Santos pisses me off sometimes, I have to admit he's a damn good coach, and I kinda love him. He's the sort of man I wish my father was. And now that I have Marley in my life, I understand why he was so upset with me last January. I'd lose my shit too if some cocky fuck knocked up my daughter.

Sam and I catch up over dinner. It's better than talking to my brothers, who just want to gloat about their law careers. They're now both employed by our dad and basically get paid to kiss his ass.

I lean over to Sam. "It doesn't annoy you to work for my father?"

She laughs and shakes her head. "He's so good at his job. You should come by and see him in his element."

I'd rather eat a brick, but since we're playing happy family tonight, I make some noncommittal sound and change the subject. I'll admit it's hard to hate on my father since he got me a kick-ass attorney when I was arrested. But I feel like he's setting me up on a date tonight when he knows I have a girlfriend, and that's fucked up.

Sam tells me about school and our old friends. We laugh about the dumb things we did in high school. I forgot how cool she is. We were good friends for a while back then but ended up going to different colleges and lost track of each other.

When dinner is over, the waiter brings out a huge cake. The look on my mom's face is priceless. I'm shocked my father is actually doing something nice for her. We all break out our phones and take pics and video of her blowing out the candles.

Sam leans into me. "Your mom has always been such a sweetheart. I bought her a shawl. Do you think she'll like it?"

"She'll love anything you get her. It's the thought that counts for her."

The moment those words leave my mouth, it hits me hard. How I haven't done anything special for Roxy in a long time. She had Marley, and next thing I knew, I was focused on training camp, and then school started. We've been in a mad dash ever since.

Maybe that's how I fix shit between us. I can start doing special things for her and let her know I care. That I love her.

After we enjoy cake and Mom opens her gifts, we gather around her to take a few photos.

Sam tugs on my sleeve. "I'd better get going."

"Nonsense," my father says. "We're all headed out to play putt-putt golf. You should join us."

For some reason, my mom loves putt-putt. I think it's her attempt to do something my father enjoys, but he never invites her to golf.

I can't remember when we last all hung out like this. My mom must be in heaven. So even though I want to beg off and head back to Roxy's tonight instead of tomorrow, I'll do anything to keep that smile on my mother's face.

Sam turns her head up to me. "Is it okay if I tag along?"

I shrug. "Sure. The more the merrier." Hanging with Sam is better than talking to my brothers or their girlfriends, who haven't stopped yammering about designer handbags for the last hour.

We all meet up at Pirate's Cove Putt-Putt. My mom is nailing her shots, and it's pissing off my dad, who's not a great putter despite all the time he spends at the golf course. The irony is sweet.

Sam shivers, and I frown. "Are you cold? I'm actually burning up, so you can have my suit jacket if you want."

"Really? Thank you."

I hand it to her and blast that little golf ball so hard, it hits some Captain Jack Sparrow lookalike statue in the eye before it lands right next to the hole. "Yes!"

That was a lucky shot because this is boring as hell.

I much prefer playing with my big balls. Heh.

Sam takes her turn, but accidentally loses her ball behind a shipwreck. I help her over some shrubs, and we retrieve it.

We straggle behind my family because they're all talking about some case my dad just won. Sam and I get into a deep conversation about her last boyfriend, who graduated a few months ago and took off to New York—without her.

"That had to suck. I'm sorry." Her eyes get misty, and I give her a quick hug. "If he can't see a good thing when he has it, fuck him."

She laughs as she wipes her eyes. "Yeah. Fuck him."

We join my family for the last two holes. My mom wins, and Sam and I dance with her to the reggae music piped through the speakers.

On the way out to the parking lot, Sam says she wants to meet Roxy.

"Come on up for a visit anytime. You're going to love her daughter. Marley and her mom have both stolen my heart."

She chuckles. "I never thought I'd see the day when Billy Babcock fell in love. I'm happy for you."

I feel my ears go hot, and I make a face. "Okay, stop giving me shit. And hey, if you're into football players—"

She nudges me. "You know I am."

Stepped into that one. I laugh awkwardly. "Well, I have a few friends you might like. I swear I'll only introduce you to the ones who aren't dogs."

"I'd love that."

I give her my number, and she texts me. **Don't forget that date! I need me a football player!**

I look up at her. "How do you feel about quarterbacks? I think Nick Silva is single." Although... now that I think about it, he might not be the best option.

As soon as Sam drives off, my father pulls me aside. "What the hell are you doing?"

Wasn't it obvious? "I was hanging out with Samantha like you clearly wanted me to."

"No, I mean why are you setting her up with your teammates?"

"Why is that a problem?" I watch my brothers drive away while my mom waits patiently for my father in his car.

"I invited her tonight for you, dumbass."

I knew it. "Why would you do that when you know I have a serious girlfriend?"

He scoffs. "I'd suggest you reserve that role for a woman who didn't get knocked up by another man minutes before dating you."

My jaw goes tight as I stare down at the pavement. "I love Roxy. I know you find this to be a difficult concept."

He adjusts his cufflink. "Look, she might be a hot piece of ass, which is doubtful after pushing out a kid, but you're delusional if you think I'm going to welcome her with open arms. Klein told me point blank that he won't take you on his roster in January if you're all wrapped up with some trashy girl and her kid. He said you could have the best season of your life, but the optics don't work for him."

The optics don't work for him.

Hands clenched, I take a deep breath so I don't break his nose too. "You know how they say money can't buy happiness? Apparently, it can't buy class either. Tell Klein he can go fuck himself. And you can join him."

I stalk toward my car as my father yells, "Get rid of her before she ruins your career!"

Heart pounding, feeling sweaty, I drive aimlessly.

I still hear my father's voice, telling me that now, when I'm so close to achieving my dream, I'm going to flush it down the drain. But that can't be right. In what world would I have to give up the woman I love to play a game I love?

At some point I realize it's getting late.

There's no way I'm crashing at my parents' house tonight.

But then I remember I need to swing by to collect my text-books. I got a ton of homework done on Friday night after I ate dinner with my mom, but it won't do me much good if I don't bring it to class.

Fortunately, everyone's asleep, so I duck into my room and shove all my crap into my bag. Hopefully I didn't forget anything.

Then I hit the road again. I don't want to go to Roxy's because she'll take one look at me and know I'm upset. I can't tell her what happened with my father because she'll be crushed.

So I head to the Stallion Station. The guys will let me crash there so I can get my shit together.

49

ROXY

WHEN THE DOOR to the apartment opens late Sunday morning, I try to keep my good news in check. I had a follow-up doctor appointment with my OB-GYN on Friday afternoon, and she gave me the go-ahead to have sex.

I'm not sure I'm ready to dive into the deep end of that pool right away, but I'd love to dip in my toe. Maybe that would help bridge this weird distance between me and Billy. While sex can't fix everything, it certainly couldn't hurt.

I wanted to give Billy the news in person, and since he left after practice on Friday to visit his parents, this is the first chance I've had to talk to him.

I expect a smile and a big hug since he's been gone for two days, but his solemn expression immediately sets off warning bells.

"How was your trip?"

He shrugs and dumps his gym bag by the door, where his suit jacket is probably balled up. "Mom was happy. My father was a dick. What's new?"

He heads straight for the kitchen and rummages around in the fridge. I suck in a breath, a little hurt he didn't notice I dressed up. Well, clean clothes and makeup, which constitutes getting dressed up for me. My hair is done. For once I feel like a woman and not a baby-wearing robot.

I finally fit in my old jeans. They're snug, but it felt so good to get some of my body back, I did a little jig in the living room this morning to celebrate.

Of course, my shape is different. I'm only about ten pounds heavier than I was before I got pregnant, but my boobs, thighs, and ass seem way bigger than that. I hope Billy likes my new normal because I'm definitely thicker than I used to be.

Walking over to him, I motion behind me. "Marley is with my parents this afternoon."

"That's nice." He piles lunch meat and bread on the counter and slaps together sandwiches.

"I thought maybe we could hang out. I got the go-ahead from my doctor for, you know."

"Cool."

Cool?

Did he not understand? "My doctor said I could have sex."

He doesn't say anything. Just keeps piling meat on four pieces of bread.

"Billy."

He finally looks at me. His expression is tight and there are dark circles under his eyes.

"What's up with you? Why do you look like you've been up all night drinking?"

He's wearing his suit pants, but his dress shirt is untucked and wrinkled. *What the hell is that?* I grab his collar. "Why is there lipstick on your shirt?"

His eyes widen, and a look of horror crosses his face. "I don't know. It's probably my mom's."

We stare at each other, and a strong wave of déjà vu hits me. I remember confronting Ezra and how he looked at me like I was crazy when I asked if he was sleeping with other girls after he swore he was committed to me.

Words I haven't even formed in my head yet spill from my lips. "Are you sleeping with someone else?"

He scoffs. "Calm down, biscuit. I'd never do that. Don't get your panties in a twist because I hugged my mother."

The confidence in his voice soothes my ruffled feathers, but I can't let go of the feeling that something happened this weekend. "Billy, I need you to swear on Marley that you're not playing the field. That you're not banging other girls. Because I've already been down that road, and—"

"Roxanne." He grabs my shoulders and stares into my eyes. "I swear on Marley that I'm not cheating." He kisses me on the cheek, and I sink into him, but all too quickly, he lets go and returns to those damn sandwiches.

I almost ask to see his phone, but I don't want to be that girl. The paranoid one who invades his privacy.

But why is he being so standoffish and weird? "How... how's your mom? Did she have a fun birthday?"

"She was happy to have us all together. We went to this dumb country club and played putt-putt golf afterward. It was great to see her smile. Although my grandmother's damn dog crapped all over her house, and I spent most of Saturday afternoon cleaning it."

Listening to him talk about what he did makes me feel better.

But I know something's wrong.

I just wonder why he won't tell me what it is.

50

ROXY

For such a tiny peanut, Marley sure does weigh a ton right now. I hoist her higher on my shoulder while I push the stroller, which is loaded with her diaper bag and my backpack, with my other hand.

My mom dropped her off with me this afternoon. Marley joined me in the library so I could do some research.

"You've been such a good girl today," I whisper against her downy soft head. "I hate leaving you to go to class, but someday you'll understand. I'm working hard to make sure I have a career someday because a girl has to rely on herself. I think I want to be a sports broadcaster. I like journalism even though my professor this semester gets on my nerves. But I guess things don't always go the way you expect them to. I'm learning that right now."

Let's take Billy, for example. I thought after a weekend with his family, he'd be rested and relaxed, but he's been so cagey this week during the few times I've seen him.

It scares me.

What if he did something I can't forgive?

Because it's obvious he's hiding something.

I hope I'm wrong.

By the time I get to my car, Marley's getting cranky, so I scoot into the back seat and feed her. She makes these little growly sounds when she's at my boob. You'd think I starved her with how she's going at it.

"There's plenty of milk, pumpkin. Take your time."

I curl her dark hair with my finger. She's so tiny and beautiful. How could Ezra not want her? I keep expecting to run into him, but haven't yet. I guess that's a blessing in disguise because I have no idea what I'll say to that man.

Marley's eyes close, her face blissed out from a milk coma.

"Okay, little mama. Let's get going." I gently place her in her car seat and strap her in.

Really, I should've waited to feed her until we got home, but my boobs were starting to hurt, and I didn't want to leak all over the place again.

When I get home, I regret not waiting because as soon as I pick her up, she pukes all over my shirt.

Ugh. Jesus, take the wheel.

I grab a cloth diaper and clean her face. "Poor girl. I'm so sorry. I should've burped you."

Sometimes I feel like I have everything figured out with Marley and then do something stupid like forget to burp her.

Once I'm confident I'm not going to burst into tears, I load up the stroller and carry everything upstairs. I'm sure I'm a sight, dragging the stroller with one arm while holding Marley with the other. On the bright side, it's helping me get back in shape.

When we get inside, I clean her up. I'm about to situate her on the couch when someone knocks on the door.

I glance through the peephole. I don't recognize the older man, but he looks familiar somehow. Tall. Broad. And dressed in a designer suit.

Since he doesn't look like an ax murderer, I open the door. "Hi. Can I help you?"

He eyes me and the baby like we're old food in the fridge he forgot to throw out.

I glance down and remember my shirt is wet because Marley hurled on me. Shit. I strategically move her so you can't see my chest.

"I'm Billy's father, Warren Babcock."

Oh my God. And here I am, a mess. "Hi. It's so nice to meet you. I'm Roxy. Are you looking for Billy? Because he's at practice." Billy's not fond of his father, but I can't be unwelcoming to someone I've never met before.

"Actually, I'm looking for you." That catches me off guard. "It'll only take a minute."

He moves toward me, and I back up instinctively, not because I want him to come inside but because I don't want him to run into us.

Mr. Babcock takes that as an invitation to come in.

Inside my head, all of my alarms are going off. "Um, have a seat, I guess. Do you want something to drink? I have ice water or juice."

"No. Like I said, I won't be here long." He sits in the middle of the sofa, drops his briefcase on my coffee table, and unsnaps it. Reaching in, he pulls out a stack of papers.

I sit on the edge of my recliner. Why in the world does Billy's dad want to talk to me?

Mr. Babcock tilts his head as his hawklike gaze sears through me. "Let's cut to the chase, shall we? I have a top-notch agent who's interested in my son, but he says the optics of Billy dating a single mother looks terrible. Especially when the child isn't his."

I open my mouth, but nothing comes out.

I clear my throat. "What are you saying? That you want me to break up with him?"

"That's exactly what I'm saying. And I'll make it worth your while."

What the hell?

I'm so incensed, I can barely breathe. "Look, Mr. Babcock, you might not approve of us dating, but we love each other, and—"

"Darling, I'm a divorce attorney. You're barking up the wrong tree if you think you can convince me of some romantic sentiment. I'm looking out for my son's future, which hinges on the success of his senior year on the gridiron. He should be eating and breathing football, not playing house with a girl who got knocked up by another player." A look of disgust crosses his face. "Why don't you work things out with your baby's father and leave my son out of this? Why is Billy getting your leftovers? Don't you think he has better things to do than change diapers or fight your ex-boyfriend in a crowded restaurant?"

His words slice like sharp blades flung from across the room. I do my best not to cry, but my face flushes.

He flips through a packet of paper. "I can see I've made my point, but like I said, I'll make this worth your time. I'm not trying to be callous. I'm trying to help Billy, who won't help himself. He can't hack law school, so football is it. My son has one last chance to make it to the NFL."

When I'm sure my voice won't wobble, I clear my throat again. "I'm the one who got Ezra to drop the charges."

"Which was the least you could do, considering you're the reason those two fought in the first place. Did you know that this one lapse in Billy's judgment could've landed him in prison for twenty years on aggravated assault charges?"

Holy shit. I feel the blood drain from my face. Good thing Marley's sleepy because I couldn't handle having this conversation if she was fussy. "No, I didn't know that."

"If I hadn't hired the best defense attorney in the state, things could've turned out differently."

Maybe I didn't have much to do with Billy's release from jail after all.

"Miss Santos, I know who you are. I'm well aware that your father is the coach. And maybe you think that entitles you to use my son the way you are, but—"

"I'm not using him. Billy asked me to go out with him months before I got pregnant."

"So you didn't ask him to fraudulently sign your baby's birth certificate?"

His words suck the air out of the room. How does he know that? Billy says he doesn't talk that much to his father. I can't imagine they had some heart-to-heart. Unless that's a lie.

"Mr. Babcock, I don't know what you and Billy have discussed, but I did not put him on the birth certificate of my child. You know, since he's not the father."

The man doesn't look convinced. I can't believe I have to do this. "Fine. I'll prove it to you." I carry Marley into the bedroom and settle her in the bassinet. Then I quickly throw on a sweater to hide my chest, run over to the stack of files on my desk, and reach for the one with my daughter's name on it.

My hands are trembling when I return to the living room and hand him the paper. "Here's her birth certificate. Note that her name is Marley *Santos* and that there is no father listed on the bottom."

He flips it around. Holds it to the light. Jesus, now he thinks I'm a forger.

"That's a relief. Especially after I read this." The man pulls out a crumpled old napkin.

It takes me a second to realize it's the contract Billy and I wrote in that coffee shop. "Where did you get that?"

"My son threw it away in his trash can last weekend. The

maid saw it when she was cleaning and brought it to me because she was concerned."

Billy threw it away?

That lump in my throat returns. I hoped to frame that one day as a keepsake. I thought it would be sweet, something to remember how we started. I guess Billy didn't view it with the same sentimentality. "You don't have to worry about the paternity stuff. As you can see, I didn't name him on the certificate."

He taps the napkin on my coffee table. "Doesn't this prove to you that this is just some stupid game Billy is playing? Who writes a contract on a napkin?" I'm about to tell him that was *my* idea and that's *my* handwriting when he levels me with that ice-cold gaze again. "This may be hard to hear, but my guess is he just wanted sex and played the long game with you. Because Billy does not get attached to women. Ask any of the girls he's hooked up with since he's been at Lone Star. As I'm sure you know, there've been plenty. Just look up his name on that old gossip blog."

That damn blog again. I'm well aware of it. That's one of the things that torpedoed Billy's relationship with my father in the first place.

My chin wobbles. "He's not like that," I whisper. "Not—"

"Not anymore?" The bastard laughs. "Darling, take it from a pro—they all say that. My guess is he has one foot out the door as we speak. Is it possible he wants to break up with you but doesn't know how to do it?" He pauses. "I'm guessing he didn't tell you about his date last weekend with Samantha."

Who the hell is Samantha? Was that her lipstick on his collar and not his mother's?

And oh my God, what if Billy really does want to break up?

But I can't bring myself to doubt my boyfriend to his father.

"Billy would never date someone behind my back." My voice doesn't have the kind of conviction I hoped it would.

"You know what always works well in court? Evidence. And I have plenty of it for you." He pulls out his phone and swipes a few times. Then angles it toward me.

My heart crumbles with every image. It's obvious they're from last weekend. From the dinner Billy swore was only for family. Pic after pic of my boyfriend with a beautiful, statuesque blonde. Hugging her. Dancing with her. Sitting with her at dinner. She's even wearing his suit jacket.

"Don't they make a lovely couple? I'm pretty sure our agent can get behind *these* optics. For the record, Billy left with her Saturday night. Why don't you take care of yourself and your daughter and accept my proposal while you still can? I'll give you fifty grand to go your separate ways."

I'm going to be sick. "Get out."

He shakes his head. "You're a beautiful girl." That disgusting man looks me up and down. "I can see why Billy wanted to be with you, but let's get real here. You just had a baby. You're probably still packing extra weight. You're sleep-deprived and covered in sour breast milk. Are you really going to provide the kind of sexual activity my son is accustomed to?"

My whole body trembles in disgust and shame. I'm a giant bullseye and his words are arrows, each accusation hitting its aim. Because even though I told Billy I could have sex, he hasn't gotten near me all week.

And while I hate Mr. Babcock for talking to me this way, I'm more troubled by the truth of his claims.

Because I *am* heavier. I *am* covered in puke. I *am* a hot mess.

And I'm not entirely sure Billy wants me in his bed anymore.

Did he really go home with Samantha Saturday night?

"Get the fuck out of my house." I stand and point to the door. "If you set foot on my doorstep again, I'm calling the police. How would those 'optics' look?"

He drops a stack of paper on the coffee table. "You're upset right now, but think it over. Once you calm down, I'm sure you'll reconsider. My offer still stands. Think of it as a parting gift." Turning away, he pauses, then faces me again. "And before you go running to Billy to tell him about his big bad father, ask yourself if you want to be responsible for ruining our relationship. He and I have not had the easiest time getting along. Until now. So think long and hard about that."

Then that asshole strolls out of my apartment like he hasn't just upended my world.

51

BILLY

EXHAUSTION MAKES MY EYELIDS HEAVY, but I still need to finish an assignment before I can crash. I trudge up the stairs to our apartment. It's late, so I quietly unlock the door. The living room is dark, so I flip the lights on.

"Holy shit, Rox. You scared me." I hold my hand to my chest. "Why are you sitting there in the dark?"

She gives me the strangest look. "Just wondering when you were getting home."

"I told you I had a study group for psych class." I drop my backpack and gym bag by the door. I'm about to head over to the kitchen to grab some water when her words make me freeze.

"You had a study group from eight to ten. It's almost midnight."

I guess it is kinda late. "I went for a burger with people after we finished studying for that test next week."

"Oh. Did you bring me something? A doggy bag maybe?"

Shit. "No, sorry, biscuit. I didn't think you'd be up this late. You're usually asleep by now." When I get closer, I realize her eyes are red-rimmed and swollen. "What's going on? Is everything okay? Is the baby all right?"

"Marley's fine." Her voice is raspy. "I can't say the same about myself."

After I sit next to her, I grab her hand. It's cold and clammy. "Babe, what's wrong?"

She drags her hand back to her lap. "Just wondering where you've been. You didn't answer my texts."

"My battery died." I dig it out of my back pocket to show her. "Forgot to charge it last night."

Her face is blank. Emotionless. "Can I ask who you went to dinner with?"

"The people from our group."

"And they would be?"

Not sure why she's giving me the third degree, but it is late, and I don't want her to be concerned. I shrug. "Jinxy, that guy Carlo and his cousin Marc, a girl named Sarah, and Vicky."

She stares at me a long moment. "Vicky? Your ex? That Vicky?"

"We didn't really date."

"No, you just slept with her from time to time. Yes, perhaps we should clarify that." She lets out a breath while I try to catch mine. Where is this going? "Why didn't you tell me you had a class and were in a study group with your former friend with benefits?"

"I don't know. Because you didn't ask? It didn't seem relevant."

Her eye twitches, and she rubs it. "So if I wanted to do a late-night study group and have dinner with someone I used to fuck, that would be okay? Like, let's say Ezra was in my study group, and I was out with him until almost midnight."

"What the fuck is going on right now?"

"Funny, because I wanted to ask you the same thing."

I stare at her for a minute while I try to gather my thoughts. I know she's suspicious because of the lipstick on my collar last weekend, but that probably did belong to my mom. It wasn't like I made out with Samantha or anything, and bringing her up now would only piss off Roxy more. "If you don't trust me, why don't you just say that?"

"Okay, I don't trust you."

Damn. That hurts. I let out a caustic laugh. "Fuck, Roxanne. After everything we've been through? What have I ever done to make you not trust me?"

"Where's your jacket?"

I squint at her, unable to keep up with this conversation. "My jacket?"

"The suit jacket you wore last weekend. Where is it?"

Shrugging, I motion toward the bedroom. "Probably in the closet."

"It's not in the closet. Nor is it in your laundry. So unless it's balled up in your gym bag, I'd like to know where it is."

This is seriously starting to piss me off. "I haven't a fucking clue. Why are you acting like this?"

"Like what?"

"Like a jealous girlfriend who can't deal with the fact that I have a life outside of this apartment."

Her chin wobbles, and I feel like an ass, but then she says, "I'm acting like this because I heard you went on a *date* last weekend with someone named Samantha. That you went *home* with Samantha."

I stare at her, confused. "How the hell do you know about Sam?"

Her eyes narrow into sharp slits. "So you *did* go on a date? Was all of that stuff about going to Austin for your mom's birthday just bullshit? Or was the part about not being able to bring me bullshit?"

"Calm down, Roxanne. I didn't invite her. My father did. She's just a friend."

Her wild laugh is unnerving. "A friend? She didn't look like a friend in those photos."

"What photos?"

"Did you fuck her?"

"Jesus, no." She doesn't look like she believes me.

"You're saying you've *never* slept with her?"

Fuck. I wince, hating that the truth is going to flip her out, but I won't lie to her. "It was a long time ago."

She stands and shouts at me. "What? Like last week? Last month? When? What does 'a long time ago' mean?"

"It was in high school. Calm down."

"Don't fucking tell me to calm down. Why didn't you tell me you came back to Charming Saturday night?"

I look down at the ground, pissed she doesn't trust me, but also angry at myself for letting shit get to this point. "How do you know that?"

She swipes at the tears running down her face. "If you're not going to be honest with me, why should I be honest with you?"

My jaw tightens. "What can I say to make you believe me?"

She holds out her hand. "Let me see your phone. If you have nothing to hide, then I should be able to go through your messages, right?"

"It needs to charge."

"That sounds like an excuse."

I'm not trying to give her excuses, but I do need a minute to think about what's on my phone. I haven't flirted with anyone since I started dating Roxy. Haven't sexted anyone. Haven't sent any dirty photos.

But my mind snags on that message Sam sent me. *Don't forget that date! I need me a football player!* That could sound incriminating without any context, and I'm not sure Roxy would believe me if I told her I was setting Sam up with one of my teammates.

"You know what? You say you're not cheating, but you look guilty as hell. Why is that?"

"I—I don't know, Roxy. Just..."

She stares at her hands. She's so still, it almost looks like she's not breathing. I'm pissed but also worried. Roxy isn't herself. "You don't reach for me."

"What?"

"You never reach for me anymore."

"What does that mean?"

When her eyes meet mine, they're welling with tears. "In bed. You never reach for me. In fact, I don't remember the last time you kissed me on the mouth. Maybe the night I went into labor. Why don't you kiss me anymore? I had Marley two months ago."

I scoff. "You can't even have sex yet. It'll be at least another few weeks before you can do it."

She shakes her head. "I told you last weekend the doctor gave me a thumbs-up, but it was like you didn't even care."

Shit. She did mention that.

Do I tell her I haven't recovered from when we broke her water using my dick and she screamed in pain? I get turned on by her all the time, but the thought of actually having sex with her puts my head in a bad place. How the fuck do I phrase that?

I rub the back of my neck. "I kiss you. Just the other day, in fact. When I was leaving to go get us a pizza."

"I kissed you."

"What?"

"*I* kissed you. You were standing in the kitchen, and I walked over to you, got in your face, and kissed you. You didn't kiss me. And when you do, it's a peck on my cheek, the same kind you give Marley."

I hold up my hands. "Okay, I guess. I didn't realize I needed to keep track of who kissed who and how I did it. Sorry."

"No, don't do that. Don't act like everything is fine between us. You know as well as I do that it's not. You never reach for me at night anymore. You don't sleep naked anymore. You never kiss me anymore. We're not fucking fine."

I cover my mouth, a little stunned. "It's not like that." I mean, I don't think it is. Sure, things are different between us, but she just had a damn baby. We're both up to our eyeballs with school. I'm up at five thirty in the morning for football conditioning. Any spare time I have, I'm helping with Marley. And the last time we had sex, I broke her water and freaked myself out. What the fuck does she want from me?

"And then I come to find out that you have a class with Vicky and see her all the time. And you're out late having dinner with her. And you took another woman for dinner with your parents."

"For the last time, I didn't invite Sam. And it wasn't *just* Vicky tonight. There were other people."

"Did she sit next to you?"

That question makes me bristle. "So now I can't sit next to another woman I used to date?"

"You just told me you didn't date, you only had sex."

"Jesus, Roxy. Yes, she sat next to me, but Jinxy was on my other side. Are you worried about him too? Think we pulled a gangbang behind the dumpsters afterward?"

"Gangbangs are your specialty."

What the fuck? I'm done.

I stalk over to the front door, grab my backpack and gym bag, and pull my keys out of my pocket. "This is bullshit, and you know it. I'll talk to you when you're done accusing me of crap that's never even crossed my mind."

I slam the door behind me, questioning my sanity.

Turns out I still have no clue what a healthy relationship looks like.

52

ROXY

THE SLAMMING DOOR makes me flinch.

A second later, a furious cry comes from the bedroom. Damn him. Billy woke her up.

I run to the crib and pick up Marley. "I'm sorry." I cradle her in my arms and cry with her.

After a few minutes, I sit in the rocker and try to breastfeed her, but she doesn't want the nipple.

Angrily, I wipe my face with the sleeve of my sweater. "Maybe I shouldn't have said some of those things like that, but I was so upset," I tell my daughter, whose plaintive wails break my heart.

I was going crazy tonight waiting for Billy to come home. All evening I stewed on the bombshells his father had dropped on me. And I finally had an idea. Billy had left me his mother's cell phone number in case I had an emergency while he was gone. So I called her and introduced myself. I asked her if Billy had accidentally left his jacket there Saturday night. I told her I was worried because he would need it for his next game, which is totally true.

I'll admit I feel guilty for misleading her with the way I

phrased everything, but I didn't know what else to do. He hadn't called me back or responded to any of my texts. I felt like I was out of options.

Then I said, "Oh, wait. Did he come back Saturday night? I'm so sleep-deprived, I can't remember."

She said, "He didn't stay with us Saturday night, dear. He left after playing putt-putt."

Hearing those words was worse than what Billy's father told me. Because his mom wasn't trying to hurt me.

So where did Billy sleep that night?

I'm not sure, but it wasn't with me.

I didn't mean to ask him about why he never reaches for me anymore. I guess I thought this was my last chance to get everything on the table. Because that had been bothering me long before his father waltzed through my door.

But as I think back about the sad way I cried to Billy, like I was begging him to touch me, I feel pathetic.

I'm starting to think having him in the delivery room and watching me push out a kid changed how he views me.

I rock Marley and rock her some more. She won't stop crying, and I feel like I might throw up.

I guess none of it matters. It's obvious this is over, probably when he threw our contract in the trash.

Billy doesn't love me anymore. Maybe he never did.

53

BILLY

As I toss and turn on the couch at the Stallion Station, I can't stop replaying that argument in my head. Roxy knew all of the buttons to push, and I let her.

It's as clear as day—I should've come home Saturday night and told her what happened with my father. That he invited Sam. That he was being an asshole. That he wanted me to break up with Roxy.

Because now, she'll never believe me.

In the moment, it was easy to react, but since I've had some time to calm my ass down, I get why she jumped to those conclusions. One, I don't exactly have a stellar past. Two, I suppose I have been distant lately. And three, Ezra spouted off a million lies while he fucked everything with two legs, all while having a very serious girlfriend at home.

So what did I do? I gave her every reason to doubt me.

Nice job, Babcock. Way to fuck things up.

I break out my phone. No messages. I'm not surprised. Roxy is a stubborn woman. Tenacious. It's something I love about her. When she sets her eye on something, she goes after it with a vengeance.

But the flip side of that is I'm headed for an uphill battle if I want her to forgive me.

When I can't stand it any longer, I text her.

You're right. I haven't been completely honest with you about something. But it's not what you think. I'D NEVER CHEAT ON YOU. Call me when you get this.

I finally doze off around three in the morning, only to have my alarm go off at five thirty.

Sitting up, I groan. I miss my bed. I miss my woman, and I miss Starley Marley.

Cam walks down in his underwear. "Hey, man. Rough night?"

I rest my head in my hands. "You have no idea."

"Problems at home?"

"Rox and I got in an argument." His eyebrows lift, and I nod. "A big one."

"You do something dumb?"

I blow out a breath. "Sorta, but then I wasn't honest with her, and when she cornered me about it, I doubled down, and she rightfully flipped out." Because if the roles were reversed, I'd probably be pissed too.

I'm on my way to class a few hours later when my phone finally buzzes with a message. I scramble to yank it out of my pocket.

When can you get your stuff? Coordinate it with my mom and give her your key.

Damn. I guess she doesn't want to talk it through.

My chest gets tight when I think of everything I just lost.

What have I done?

54

ROXY

Looking into my rearview mirror, I dab more concealer under my puffy eyes. I miss Billy so much it hurts to breathe, but I'd have to be an idiot to ignore all of those red flags. I did that with Ezra and regret not listening to my gut more.

The fact that Billy couldn't answer any of my questions is crushing. If I had known he was going to do this to me, I never would've dated him. It feels like I just got handed off from one heartbreaker to another.

If I'm going to be a good mom to Marley, I need to be smarter than that.

I suppose that's what today is about. Instead of wallowing in bed like I want to, I'm doing a broadcast segment on cheer.

After I make sure I'm presentable, I rehearse the questions one more time and then haul all of my recording equipment out of my car.

On the way into the gym, the smell hits me, and as strange as this sounds, it feels like home.

Debbie spots me and waves. "Roxy! It's so good to see you!"

We hug, and she asks to see pics of Marley. After we catch up for a few minutes, I track down Paige.

This squad is one of the most highly decorated teams in the country, and yet they rarely get any media coverage. At a school this size, it's easy to get overshadowed by football and other popular sports, but I'm hoping my coverage gets them more recognition.

Paige stretches on the mat while I set up the camera I borrowed from Professor Fowler. No one tells you how unglamorous broadcast is when you have to shoot all of your own footage. Broadcast is not just sitting at an anchor desk in an air-conditioned studio.

I'm interviewing her in a spare room off the main gym where the squad will meet for practice later this afternoon.

"There's nothing to be nervous about," I remind her. "Just tell me your story like you did last spring and how cheer helped you."

She nods.

I check to make sure I'll be in the shot and hit record. I'll edit out our chitchat later.

After I stand next to her, I clear my throat. "Are you ready?"

She nods, sending her ponytail bouncing. I turn to the camera with a smile. "I'm here with Paige Lewis, who's a Bronco cheerleader. The squad recently won their tenth national championship last spring.

"Paige, I'd like to talk about your training because some people have the misconception that cheerleaders just jump around and yell. Some even claim that cheerleaders are not real athletes. How would you respond to that?"

She laughs. "It isn't unusual for us to spend five or six hours training. *Every day.* Because those of us in cheer eat, live, and breathe the sport. There's no way to be one of the best squads in the country without that kind of dedication. It takes a high level of athleticism and stamina to be able to perform our two-and-a-half-minute routines. Most of us are also gymnasts, and many have been training since we were kids."

"What exactly do you do on the squad? What's your position?"

"I'm a flyer. That means I get tossed in the air."

"Are you ever afraid up there? Because sometimes you're being tossed to the top of a very tall pyramid, correct?"

"It can be scary, yes. But you have to prepare yourself mentally, and you have to learn to trust your teammates, in your bases and spotters."

I keep my face serene even though I'm grinning on the inside, proud that she's taken my advice to heart. "It's been a long road for you to get to this point. Can you describe some of the challenges you've faced along the way?"

"Gymnastics and cheer are expensive activities, and my family could never afford them. When I was about nine or ten, I started helping our coaches clean up the gym equipment after practice and do odd jobs so I could keep taking lessons."

"Why was it so important for you to stick with it?"

"I've always been a shy girl, but when I'm out here on the mat? When I'm flying through the air? When I'm at the top of the pyramid? I know I can overcome any obstacle. I've overcome bruises and fractured bones and financial hardship to be on this mat today. All of that has made me tougher."

"What would've happened if you hadn't had this activity growing up?"

Her head tilts as she considers my question. "Honestly? I'm not sure I would've graduated from high school, much less gone to college. Being in cheer made me care about school because we couldn't attend events if we didn't have the grades."

"How did it feel to win nationals in Daytona last spring?"

"It was amazing, but knowing that my family and old

coaches were back home watching on TV was definitely a highlight of my life. I'll never forget it."

"The squad cheers for the Bronco football team, which also won a national championship last year and was widely covered in the media, whereas the cheerleaders did not get much recognition. Do you ever resent football for getting so much attention?"

"Not at all. I love our football team. I just think there's enough room for all of us to shine."

That was a great answer. "Do you have any parting words for the naysayers who don't think cheerleaders work very hard?"

She gives me a big grin. "I'd say, 'Bless your heart.'"

We both chuckle. "Thanks for joining me today, Paige. This is Roxy Santos with *Bronco Nation*. Back to you in the station."

When I stop the camera, she squeals. "That was so fun! You're such a cool cucumber under pressure, Roxy."

"That's because I rehearsed those questions fifteen thousand times before I got here." I grab the camera and the bag. "Come on. I need to record your routine again, but this time close up."

Fifteen minutes later, I'm kneeling near the pyramid, but not so close that I get kicked in the face, as I record the routine. This year's cheer squad is tight, and while I miss this like crazy, I wouldn't give up Marley for the world.

And that's the biggest revelation. Every sacrifice I've made in the last year, every tear, every sleepless night has been worth it because of my daughter.

I wouldn't give her up for anything. Not even cheer.

When the routine comes to an end, Paige flips off the pyramid and lands in the arms of her bases before she sticks the landing with a triumphant look on her face.

It feels good to know I played a small part in helping her achieve her goal.

I spend much of the next day editing the cheer footage.

Afterward, as I drive home from campus, the football game is letting out. It took everything in me not to watch the Broncos play this afternoon, but I need some space to process what happened this week.

"Hope you won, Dad," I say out loud to my empty car. "Billy, I hope you got some interceptions, you asshole."

I wipe the tear that escapes. Even though I'm still irate with him, I want him to achieve his dreams.

Because maybe we just weren't meant to be.

55

BILLY

I'M ABOUT to slink out of our post-game meeting when Coach shouts my name.

I had a crappy game. Good thing Nick kicked ass out there, because I let Oklahoma snag a touchdown when I misread a play. The only bright side is that Coach took Ezra out for the second half of the game, and he's over there all pissed off.

Frankly, I would have done the same thing. Ezra hasn't been the same since that injury.

I run over to Coach and prepare myself for an ass-kicking. Instead, he grabs my shoulder. "What was up with you today? Why were you all thumbs and two left feet?"

"Sorry, Coach." I've had two sleepless nights on the couch at the football house while I've debated what to do. I've been fucking miserable. The thought that my girl thinks I'd do her dirty tears me up. I haven't been sleeping. Barely been eating. And as Coach so aptly put it, I was totally ham-handed out there on the field today.

"Does this have anything to do with why my daughter and Marley are staying at my house? Why Roxy has been crying her eyes out until she falls asleep?"

Fuck. She's been crying?

"We broke up, sir." I mean, I guess that's what she means by telling me to get my shit out of her apartment. Cam was gonna help me move my stuff tomorrow night, but I was hoping Roxy and I could talk first. See if I could get her to understand. I've stopped by her apartment twice, but she's never around.

"I gathered that based on the fact that you look like hell. But why? I thought you were crazy about her."

"I am crazy about her. But—"

"No buts. You either love her or you don't, and if you do, you need to fix whatever it is you broke."

I give him a look. "I thought you didn't like me dating your daughter, sir."

He crosses his arms. "I can admit when I'm wrong. I think you've helped her get through a very difficult time when most men wouldn't bother. That says a lot about you."

"She thinks I cheated." His eyes go glacial, and I hold up my hands. "I didn't. I would never. Ever. I swear on football and both my nuts."

After a second, he chuckles. "Son, I'm not going to say she's hormonal, because she'd strangle me, but I will say that her body is going through the most change she's ever experienced as an adult. So if I could give you any advice, it's that she needs a lot of reassurance that you still love her."

He clears his throat. "This is awkward, so I'm not gonna sugarcoat it, but women... sometimes... uh... They want to know you don't view them any differently because..." With a grimace on his face, he waves his hands. "Because you saw all the things you likely saw in the delivery room."

I nod. Yeah, that shit was intense. That's something Roxy mentioned, that she thinks we've been off since Marley was born, and I guess she's not wrong. "Yes, sir. I gotchu."

"Good. *And* it takes time for those pregnancy hormones to

regulate again. I speak from personal experience. Marlena and I were never closer to breaking up than when the kids were newborns. Add football, and it's a pressure cooker. Only the strongest survive. But if it means anything, I think you two have what it takes to get through this."

"Thank you, Coach. But Roxy wants me to get my stuff tomorrow and move out."

He considers that. "Then maybe you have to move out, but that doesn't mean you have to give up. If you show her you still love her, maybe she'll give you another chance." Lowering his voice, he says, "All I know is that she's heartbroken. She might put on a tough girl act, but she loves you. So dig deep, guard your balls, and go see her."

I chuckle. "Yes, sir. Thank you." Something like hope springs in my chest. Maybe I have one more shot to make this right.

56

ROXY

WITH A SIGH, I push the food around my plate.

"Do you not like dinner, *mija*? *¿Por qué no comes?*" my mom asks from across the dining room table, concerned why I'm not eating.

"Sorry, Mom." I shovel in a bite and try to smile. "It's great."

She sends my dad a worried look. Marley cries on the monitor, and I start to stand, but my mom shakes her head. "I'll get her. You stay put."

Then it's just me and my dad. I can feel him staring at me. "What?"

"Have you talked to Billy yet?"

I shake my head. "I don't know what to say. Have you ever felt like something important was too broken to fix?"

"That's what everyone told me I was getting when I took the head coaching job here at Lone Star. That I was getting a football team beyond repair. Krugman really made a mess of things."

"How did you know what to do?"

"I had to look beyond the problems. Consider the team I wanted to have instead of the one fumbling on Saturday afternoons." He takes a drink of his water. "When you consider your relationship with Billy, if you could get past whatever disagreement you had, could you envision something long-term with him?"

My eyes sting, and my throat gets tight, but I nod. "I'm just not sure how to get past everything. We said some pretty horrible things to each other. Plus..." I haven't told anyone about Billy's father approaching me, but I could really use some advice right now.

My mom rejoins us, and I decide to tell them. "Billy's dad came to the apartment earlier this week and offered me fifty thousand dollars to break up with him."

The fork falls out of my father's hand. "Please tell me that's not why you kicked him out. Roxanne Santos, I thought I taught you better than that—"

"No, Dad. That's not why we broke up. I'm not taking that money. I would *never* take that money." This is the hard part. "If I tell you what happened, I don't want you to hate Billy again, okay? I need to talk to my father right now, and not the coach of the football team."

"I'm sorry, Roxy. I never meant to hate on Billy. I was just disappointed in his behavior. When I first got here, he was such a little shit. Always so damn mouthy. Always with some smartass quip. Always on that damn gossip blog being an idiot."

"I know, but he's not that guy anymore."

And that realization makes me still. How can I be so confident he's changed and then, in the next breath, accuse him of so much wrongdoing?

My father nods. "I agree. He's not that punk anymore."

With my heart in my throat, I tell my parents what happened. How he's been acting distant since I had Marley, and how he has a class with Vicky, someone he used to hook up with. "I'm just setting the stage, though. That's where we were before he went home last weekend."

My mom comes around to sit next to me and grabs my hand. "*Mija*, when someone goes through delivering a baby with you, it's an intensely personal thing. Not every man knows how to handle that. But based on how I've seen him around you and Marley, I'd guess that he's very devoted to the two of you. He's made a lot of sacrifices to be with you."

Sniffling, I nod. "Don't think I don't feel guilty about that, because I do." I clear my throat. "His father told me there's a top-notch agent who's interested in Billy, but the agent won't take on Billy in January if he's still dating me then. Because he doesn't like the 'optics' of Billy dating some 'trashy girl' who had some other man's baby."

"*Pinche cabrón*. Did he really say that?" my dad asks.

My eyes widen because my father never curses like that. "He really said that. But here's the part that tripped me out. Mr. Babcock showed me photos of Billy out on a date with some blonde last weekend. Billy told me he couldn't bring me, that it was family only, but then he was sitting with this beautiful girl. Dancing with her. Smiling. Hugging. It looked like a date. But Billy swore his father invited her."

I tell them the rest. How she was wearing his suit jacket, the one he couldn't find at home. That he didn't stay with his parents Saturday night like he said he would, but he didn't come back to our apartment either. That they had a *thing* in high school.

When I'm done, my father pinches the bridge of his nose. "Why do you always get into so much trouble, Roxy?"

My mother reaches down the table and smacks his arm. "Do not blame her for this. You wanted honesty, and she gave it to you. Even when it was painful for her to talk about."

Dad lets out a sigh. "You're right. I'm sorry. Well, did you ask Billy to explain what's going on?"

"He said it's not what I think it is. That he would never cheat on me. But he was so cagey and weird, and when I asked him to prove it by showing me the messages on his phone, he looked like a deer in headlights. It was like dating Ezra all over again."

I freeze when my father's eyes snap to mine.

Oh, shit.

I slap my hand over my mouth and frantically shake my head. "No. Forget I said that last part."

He braces his arms on the table and looks down. We sit in silence for several minutes. "I wondered if Ezra was Marley's father. She has his dark hair. And Billy punched him in the face. The better I got to know Billy, the more I realized he wasn't just a loose cannon, that he must've had a good reason for doing that, but I didn't want to believe the kid I treated like my own son would get you pregnant and then bail on you." Finally, he looks at me. "I'm assuming you told Ezra the truth?"

It's a sad day when my father wonders whether I told the father of my baby I was pregnant. After how I behaved back then, I guess I deserve that doubt. "Of course."

"And he didn't want to be involved?"

"His response was basically, 'Fuck no, I don't want a baby.'" I take a deep breath. "Swear to me you won't say anything. Because I promised Ezra I wouldn't tell you the truth if he dropped the charges against Billy."

When my father doesn't say anything, I press on. "Dad, Billy could've gotten charged with a *felony* and been sentenced to up to twenty years in prison for breaking Ezra's nose. So please, *please* don't do anything that could jeopardize Billy, okay? I'm just telling you because I can't deal with any more secrets." I might be upset with Billy right now, but that doesn't mean I want to ruin his life.

My dad taps on the table. "Again, I ask how you get in the middle of these situations."

"I don't know, okay? Ezra told me he was single and swore he was committed to me. But then I found out he was sleeping around, so I broke things off with him. When I realized I was pregnant, I drove all the way to San Antonio to tell him, and I basically busted in on his engagement party."

"Dios mio," my mother says, her eyes bugging out.

I toss up my hands. "I know. Trust me. I hate being in the middle of this soap opera. And Abigail is such a sweetheart. It killed me to have to tell her that Ezra was a cheating asshole."

My mom nods. "He really is a cheating asshole. That boy had me fooled."

I look at Dad. "He fooled a lot of people. Did you know that the day Abigail broke up with him, Ezra fell out of a window at a frat house while being..." How do I put this? "While being *serviced* by some random girl? *That's* how he hurt his shoulder."

"That little liar. He told me he got pushed down some stairs." He rubs his forehead. "Okay, then I'm going to stop feeling guilty about cutting his game time." Tilting his head one way, then the other, he smiles. It's not Dad's usual smile. No, it's Coach's stone-cold smile, the one he gets when he talks about kicking some rival team's ass. "If Silva starts next weekend, I don't think the boosters will care, given how Ezra's been performing."

"Do what's best for the team. I want y'all to win. I want you and Deke to get your championship this year. And if that means Ezra plays, so be it."

"I would never let my personal feelings toward a player affect whether I played him—much."

I'm not entirely sure how to interpret that statement, but Ezra made his bed. Now he can sleep in it.

My father taps the table again. "As for Billy, hear him out.

Don't jump to conclusions, and for the love of God, don't get so caught up *making up* that you get pregnant again."

"Dad!"

"What? Do you know how many women get pregnant right after they had a baby?"

My mom laughs and covers her mouth. "Guilty. Roxy, you were just a baby, and your father and I had this huge argument. To apologize, he brought me flowers. He was so sexy with that sweet smile of his, and then he started kissing my neck, which I couldn't resist." She starts muttering sweet nothings to him in Spanish, and my eyes widen.

Oh God. "I really don't need to hear how Deacon was conceived." I cover my ears, and my parents laugh.

After dinner, I'm staring out the front bay window, debating what to do, when my mom wraps her arm around my shoulders. "Billy will be by your apartment at eight to pick up his things. He's expecting me, but I think he'd be much more pleased to see you. I'll watch the baby tonight so you can take your time and talk."

I turn to her, worried. "What if we can't overcome this?"

She gives me a sad smile. "Then you can say you gave it your best shot."

I wonder if that'll be enough.

57

ROXY

WITH MY HEART pounding in my chest, I turn the lock to my apartment. Sitting on the couch are Billy and Cam.

Anticipation makes my stomach flutter. I've missed Billy so much. Part of me wants to leap into his lap, but I manage to tamp that down because we have a lot to talk about.

He has something spread out across the coffee table.

Cam nudges him, and he finally looks up. I'm caught off guard by the anger in his eyes.

"What the hell is this?" Billy waves one of the pages at me. I'm guessing that's his father's contract.

"Nice to see you too." Maybe my parents got this wrong, and Billy and I won't have some big heart-to-heart. Here I am, trying to have an open mind so we can talk, and he's barking at me like I committed a crime. My walls instantly go up. "That's a gift from your father, who was also kind enough to share all those photos he took of you and Sam at your mom's birthday dinner."

Billy's jaw goes tight. "Are you going to sign this?"

"Of course not."

"This isn't why you broke up with me?"

"We broke up because you *lied* to me. Because you stayed out all night that Saturday, presumably with Sam, who you fucked in high school. Because she's in all these photos wearing your suit jacket, the one you can't find. And because you wouldn't prove your innocence by showing me your phone."

Cam makes a face. "Bro, that sounds pretty bad."

Billy glares at him. "I had reasons."

I cross my arms and give him a look. "You wanted to talk, so here I am. Are you planning to share those reasons anytime soon or do you just want to get your stuff?"

He takes several deep breaths like he's debating what to say.

The silence stretches out as humiliation crawls up my neck.

Fuck this. "You know what, why don't you just get your crap and go. It's obvious you don't want to hash this out. Or maybe you can't defend what you did."

"It's not like that, Roxy."

"Then just spit it out. What's so bad that you can't say it? Did your father tell you he thought I was a trashy girl the way he told me? How I'm basically a slut for sleeping around? How your potential agent doesn't like how I look with you because Marley isn't yours? Is that what you're hiding? Because I've already heard it straight from the horse's mouth."

Billy's eyes widen, but I'm not done. "Apparently, the going rate for getting rid of your son's girlfriend is fifty grand. He said that since I probably can't satisfy you sexually because I just pushed out a kid, someone like Samantha could."

His jaw tightens. "That motherfucker. Are you serious?"

"So did she? Satisfy you?"

"Rox. Come on."

"This is the part that stumps me. Where did you go after dinner that night? Why was Samantha wearing your damn jacket? If everything was so innocent, why couldn't you show me your phone? And why the hell were you dancing with her?"

"I never danc—" He stops suddenly. "Hell. Maybe I did."

"Get your shit and go." I move to the kitchen to get some water. I need something to do with my hands before I strangle him. Why won't he just be straight with me?

I hear the guys muttering for a minute before Cam sticks his head in the kitchen. "Roxy, I'm gonna take off. You two obviously have a lot to discuss." He gives me a hug and whispers, "Hear him out. He's crazy about you."

My nose stings, and I shake my head. "Doesn't seem like it at the moment."

Cam looks me in the eyes and says, "He stayed with us Saturday night. There were no shenanigans, I swear." With one hand, he crosses his heart. "Don't know why he won't just say that." He squeezes my shoulder and leaves.

I've always trusted Cam, and the fact that he's vouching for Billy's whereabouts on Saturday night calms me down a little.

But all of Ezra's buddies covered for him too, a little voice whispers in my head.

Frustrated, I pour two glasses of ice water and return to the living room where Billy has his head in his hands. I put one down in front of him and sit in the rocker.

He clears his throat and sits back. "How's Marley? Sorry, I should've started there instead of making accusations."

"She misses you."

"Yeah?" He cracks a smile that dims quickly. "Roxy, I just need you to not jump to conclusions. I'm not explaining any of this well, but that doesn't mean I've been up to anything nefarious."

I nod, hoping he can untangle everything. "I'm sorry I yelled at you just now. I... I've been really upset by this whole thing." My throat gets tight, and my eyes well, and I take a moment to calm down. "I hate that we're on the outs, that we can't seem to talk. That everything we've worked so hard to build seems to be crumbling when you and Marley are the most important people in my life. Not seeing you every day breaks my heart."

He reaches over and yanks me into his lap, where I burrow my face in his neck and cry. "I'm sorry, baby. Please believe me when I say that I never meant to hurt you. I just couldn't... I couldn't bring myself to tell you about the argument I had with my father. That asshole basically unleashed a similar diatribe with me that night once the party was over. I knew you'd take one look at me, see that I was pissed off, and want to know why. The thought of uttering those words to you shredded me. He's right—I didn't go back to my parents' house, but that didn't mean I went to Samantha's. I drove to the football house, where I had a beer and crashed on the couch."

"So what about all of those photos?"

He shrugs. "My family took pics because it was Mom's birthday. Sam sat next to me because that was the one seat available. The dancing happened because she and I were dancing with my mom, who was conveniently cropped out. I held Sam's hand because we had to jump over some shrubs to get her golf ball, and I hugged her hello and goodbye, but it was no different than you hugging Cam just now."

Sitting back so I can see his face, I give him a look. "Except I haven't slept with Cam."

He has the decency to look embarrassed. "True. And I'm sorry about that, but I swear to God our vibe was purely platonic that weekend. I spent the whole night talking about you and Marley. The reason I froze when you asked to see my phone is because Samantha and I had been talking about setting her up with one of the guys on my team, and I gave her my number so I could follow up on that. But I thought if you just read her message—which was something like, 'I need me a football player'—I didn't think you'd be cool with that without any context."

Pulling out his phone, he hands it to me and gives me the password. "I haven't erased anything. Look at whatever you want, whenever you want to. I have nothing to hide."

I scroll through his messages with Sam since that night. He's right—that first message would've tripped me out. But later, she messages him again, and they discuss the different single guys on the team he thinks she'd like.

"We can call her if you want. I'd hoped we could go on a double date, so she wouldn't be uncomfortable meeting one of my friends on her own. She wants to meet you, but if that's too weird because of my past with her—which, I just want to emphasize, was a one-time thing back in high school, like junior year—I completely understand."

I consider everything. "When you lay it all out like that, I feel foolish for freaking out."

He hugs me and kisses my forehead. "If the roles were reversed, and I was in your shoes, I'd probably have the same reaction. But don't feel foolish. I never want you to shove down your feelings. We have to be honest with each other, and I'm sorry I didn't know how to break this all down."

"I hate that we argued."

"This is just a bump in the road, babe." After I wipe my eyes, he cups my face. "Tell me what you're comfortable with, Roxy. Are you cool with me being friends with Sam? Because I would never want to do something you're not down with."

Sniffling, I shrug. "I'd like to meet her, but if she's dating one of your teammates, then yeah, I think it's okay."

"You can check my phone whenever you want if you get weird vibes. Given how much temptation there is for the guys on the road, I want you to feel confident in us."

"I don't want to be that paranoid person who's constantly monitoring my boyfriend. That's not the kind of relationship I want to have. If I have questions, I'll ask you. But I appreciate you offering."

He lifts an eyebrow. "Is this where we kiss and make up?"

58

BILLY

I'M ABOUT to lean in and plant one on her when she holds up her hand. "What about the other stuff I mentioned? Why you stopped reaching for me and how you don't sleep naked. You never kissed me anymore. I felt like we did a one-eighty after I had Marley."

Shit. "I was hoping to bypass that part." I scrub my face with one palm. "Uh… I'm just gonna put this all out there, and I hope none of it hurts your feelings."

"That doesn't sound promising." She scoots off my lap and sits next to me. "I can't handle being so close to you when you say things like that."

"Understandable." I take a drink of water. Clear my throat. Wipe my hands on my thighs.

"Does this have something to do with being there for the delivery? Because I took a dump on the floor at some point and didn't even realize it?"

I chuckle. "No. Strangely, that didn't flip me out."

"Then what did?"

"It was coming, balls deep inside of you, when your water broke and hearing you scream out in pain." I grab my junk and shudder. "Even now, my sack wants to crawl up inside my body."

"Ugh, that makes so much sense. I'm so sorry. I didn't realize that could traumatize you."

"How could you? We were just trying to get Marley out, and I thought sex sounded like an awesome way to do that. Just wasn't prepared for everything to work the way it did. And then Marley's always in bed with us when you're breastfeeding. It feels wrong to slide into bed naked with you when she's there."

"I didn't even think about that."

"Plus..." I wince. "I hate getting boners when you're breastfeeding. It's just... your tits are so great, and I basically wanna die smothered between them."

She busts out laughing, and I pull her into my lap again, relieved she doesn't hate me. I grab her beautiful face and kiss her.

After a minute, her eyes flutter open. "What about the kisses? Why did you stop kissing me?"

"'Cause I'm a moron." I kiss her again, and the taste of her lips makes me groan. "I guess that other stuff just took its toll on me. Maybe I was subconsciously trying to put some distance there because I didn't know how to deal with everything."

I'm trying to think of all the issues we fought about because I want to get it out now. Then it comes to me. Vicky.

"So, um. I also want to address your concern about Vicky..."

Roxy lifts her eyebrows but doesn't say anything, so I continue.

"Yes, she's still interested in me, but aside from our group going to get a bite to eat, I haven't sat next to her, not even in class. I've told her, in no uncertain terms, that I have a girlfriend, and I make a point to sit somewhere else so I don't encourage her." I hand her my phone. "Check my phone if you want."

She shakes her head. "I believe you."

My whole chest puffs up like a damn rooster. "Really?"

"Yeah. And if we're going to make this work, I think I need to trust you more." She bites her bottom lip. "I'm sorry for accusing you of doing a gangbang with Jinxy and Vicky."

I laugh and kiss her again. "There's only one woman I wanna bang these days, and she's this cute little cheerleader I've had my eye on for ages."

Her arms wrap around my neck, and she straddles me. Fuck yes, please let this lead to naked things. My cock is a sundial pointing to high noon, ready to bust through my zipper.

Huh. I guess talking about everything really does work because I have zero reservations about fucking Roxy until she screams my name.

Hold up, asshole. She just had a baby two months ago. She might not be ready for that.

I try to keep a lid on my expectations. The bottom line is while I would love to have sex with her, I'm just so fucking thrilled we're over all our baggage. I want to love up on my woman whether she has clothes on or not.

She takes my face in her hands and licks my bottom lip. "Billy."

"Hmm?" I'm drunk off her presence and high off the feel of her in my arms. I crack open my eyes.

"I probably can't handle all of you right now. Your dick's too big."

"Baby, that's probably the nicest thing you've ever said to me."

She laughs and threads her fingers through my hair. "I love you, you crazy man."

"Love you too, biscuit. So fucking much."

The first taste of her tongue on mine makes me groan. My hand travels up her shirt. I fill my palm with her tit and give it a gentle squeeze that makes her squirm in my lap. "Let me make you feel good, Foxy."

Her nose brushes against mine as she nods.

Undressing her feels like unwrapping a gift on Christmas morning. Finally, she's beautifully bare and lying beneath me.

Shyly, she looks up at me from beneath her lashes. "I don't look like I did before Marley."

"No, you don't. You're somehow more beautiful." I kiss her collarbone, between her gorgeous full breasts that I shape with my hands, and down her slightly rounded stomach. "All of you is precious to me."

I lean back and kiss the inside of her knee, one, then the other, and am about to slide down her slender thighs when she tugs on my shirt. "Take this off."

Reaching back behind my neck, I yank it off and drop it to the floor.

Her hair is tossed back and dangles down the side of the couch. She's beautifully disheveled as she watches me with hooded eyes.

Gently, slowly, I part her legs wider, but she suddenly covers her pussy with her hand. "It's a jungle down there."

I chuckle. "I don't care what it looks like as long as I can make your kitty purr."

She smiles, and it hits me so hard. How much I love this woman.

I kiss her palm, then move it out of my way so I can graze her swollen clit with my tongue. I take my time, savoring her sweet taste. Loving the sounds she makes as her chest starts to heave.

"Can I put my finger inside you?"

She nods. "Just go slowly."

I spread her wetness around her opening and work my way inside her, making sure her sounds reflect pleasure. There's no hint of discomfort, and I take that as a sign to keep going.

Soon, she's thrashing. Writhing beneath me. Mewling with sounds that make me so fucking hard.

"Billy. I want you. All of you."

"No, baby. We'll do that some other time. I don't wanna hurt you."

"I can take it. Please."

Christ. My resistance wears thin when she opens her dark eyes that plead with me. Her face is flushed, her swollen nipples sharp little points.

I swallow, so tempted. "What if I try two fingers? If you can handle that, then maybe."

She frantically nods, and her desperation makes me crazy. I remind myself to be gentle as I push in a second finger. She's wet and so damn tight.

"That okay?"

"Yes! More!"

My hand moves faster as her hips counter me. The sucking sounds coming from between her thighs almost make me lose it.

With my other hand, I reach down and unzip my jeans. My cock springs out, its weeping head eager to be reintroduced, but there's no way I'm pressuring her to do more. I'll be happy jerking off.

As I bury my face between her legs, I shuttle my fist over my length, feeling just as desperate for a release.

Roxy urges me up. I slowly remove my hand from her pussy and slide over her lush body. "Are you sure?"

"Yes. Please don't make me wait."

I wipe my face with my arm before I settle between her thighs. My cock grinds against her, and she arches into me.

Jesus, her tits are insane. I lick one, and she shivers beneath me. "Is it okay if I suck them?"

Because I need to ask, right? I don't know the protocol for

this kind of thing. I have no idea if milk is gonna shoot me in the eye, but I'm willing to take the risk.

In answer, she holds up those two perfect mounds, and I nearly blow right then and there. I lick around her areola. Nibble it. Drag my lips across that swollen nipple. Before I suck.

Her milk is sweet just like the rest of her.

I groan and suck harder.

"Billy." She thrusts her hips up, and I take the hint and slide my cock through her damp folds.

Her knees pull up, and I reach down to guide myself into her pussy.

It's a tight fucking fit. "Rox. Baby, are you sure?" I'm a few inches in, but I don't wanna hurt her.

"It's snug, but it feels amazing."

"Good, okay. Just tell me if it doesn't, and I'll stop immediately."

She smiles at me and cradles my face with her hand. "I know you will. I trust you."

I groan and kiss her. We're suddenly in a frenzy to get closer. She sucks on my tongue. Scratches my back. Arches her hips.

It takes everything in me not to pound into her. But she's so slick that I eventually wedge my way in.

It's fucking heaven.

"Baby. God. You feel so good." I pause because I need a minute, and I know she needs to get used to my size.

Once I know she can handle it and I won't nut early, I start to move. Our damp bodies slap together, and she sings a chorus of *yes* and *more* and *right there.* When I think she's close, I reach between us to rub her clit. With a sharp cry of pleasure, she arches and throbs so hard, I let go and chase my own release.

It only takes a few thrusts before I'm pulsing in her tight pussy.

Out of breath and nearly robbed of sight, I almost collapse

on top of her. I somehow manage to keep some of my weight off her.

Her arms and legs wrap around me as we come down off our orgasms, and I burrow my face in her neck.

"I never want to let you go," I murmur against her skin.

"Then don't."

I'm blissed out, ready to sleep until next week, when my eyes fly open. "Babe, did we need to use a condom?"

Her head jerks up to look at me. "Oh my God. What if I get pregnant again?"

For a minute, I think about that.

"Just means I'll get to marry you sooner." Her brilliant smile tells me we're good. No, we're fucking great. I press my lips to hers again. "I'll get some for next time, though. I'm guessing you don't wanna pop out another baby for a while."

Though... I'm really looking forward to this baby-making thing.

I think we'll be damn good at it.

And when she's ready, it'll be game on.

59

ROXY

"One cotton candy, please." I hand the vendor my money before I turn around to scan the giant field where half the town meanders between hundreds of booths.

The Nut Festival is a three-day event that citizens of Charming take very seriously because it brings in revenue for local businesses that helps them get through the slower winter months.

I bounce Marley in my arms as I wait for my sweet treat. Billy dropped us off at the entrance while he went to find a parking spot.

Things with Billy are good. Incredible, actually. We're insanely busy, but as soon as he comes home, we make a point to talk about our day. And if I'm too tired to bone—it happens—he snuggles me, which is heavenly. We agreed that our bare minimum is half an hour a day to talk, snuggle, eat together, whatever. But we need that time to reconnect.

Although it's only been two weeks since we talked things out, I think we're on the right path.

When I get my cotton candy, I take a bite. "This is a one-time thing," I tell Marley. "Mommy rarely eats sugar, but tonight I'm letting myself have cotton candy and a praline. Because how can we go to the Nut Festival without having something with nuts?"

"That's solid logic," a familiar voice says next to me.

I turn.

And freeze.

Ezra.

I can't believe I haven't seen him all semester. Leaving cheer meant not being around the field house, and that was a blessing in disguise because it meant I got to avoid him.

I hold Marley tighter and turn her away from him. Not that I think he'd hurt her. It's just, after all the horrible things he said to me, I don't want to share her.

Which... I'm not sure is fair since he did donate half her DNA, but here we are.

He clears his throat. "Hey, Roxy. How've you been?"

"Fine." I look around, hoping Billy will be back soon.

"Look, I don't want to bother you. I just want to say I'm sorry for all the shit I gave you. Losing Abigail was a wake-up call. I figured that girl would stay with me come hell or high water. Never thought she'd dump me. I'm a pretty good catch, you know?"

"Are you serious right now? Why don't you check that ego." I almost say something snarky about him not being able to throw a touchdown anymore, but that seems cruel. And even though he's been an asshole to me, I won't sink to his level.

He hangs his hands on his hips and nods. "I just wanted to see how the baby was doing. Is she healthy?"

My hackles are still aflutter, and I frown. But I keep myself from insulting him because this is the first time he's asked about her since I told him I was pregnant. "She's great."

A large presence moves next to me, and relief hits me hard. I look up at Billy and see the concern on his face. "He just wanted to know if Marley was doing okay."

Billy wraps his arm around my shoulders, and I lean into him. "She's a happy baby," he says. "Because Roxy busts her ass."

Ezra nods slowly. "Can I… can I see her?"

Everything in me screams no, but I see regret in his eyes. I don't know what this means, if he wants to be involved now or how I feel about that. I guess I'm getting ahead of myself.

"Sure." I angle her toward him so he can see Marley's face.

She's sleeping peacefully, her little bow lips pursed. Her short dark hair is gathered in a spiky bow on top of her head. She's all snuggled in a blanket because it's chilly. Her eyes flutter open, and she stares up at him.

"She's beautiful. Wow." For a moment, Ezra's cocky mask slips. "Hey, Marley. It's… it's me. Uh…"

Is Ezra about to call himself Daddy? I feel my blood pressure rise. Because that role belongs to Billy. He's the one who held my hand during labor. Who rubbed lotion on my stretch marks. Who wiped my tears when I thought birthing her was going to break me in half. Who feeds her at dawn before he goes to practice.

Ezra coughs. "It's Uncle E, pretty girl."

Emotion makes my throat tight. "Uncle" is okay, I suppose.

He almost touches her cheek, but then backs away. Swallows. "Look, Rox, I can't be involved, but I want you to know that's because of me and my issues. Not you. You're great, and she's a beauty." He jams his hands in his pockets. "If you or she ever need anything—"

"They won't," Billy says, stepping closer to me. "I've got them."

Ezra nods slowly. "Thanks, man. Then, uh, then I guess I'll let you guys get back to the festival."

When Ezra turns and leaves, Billy immediately wraps me and Marley in a hug. "You okay?"

I sniffle. "No, but I will be." He kisses my forehead, and I melt into him. "Why was that so hard?"

"Because Marley is the center of our universe, and he's a threat to that."

She *is* the center of our universe. "Thank you." I look up at him and kiss his chin, since that's what I can reach. "Thank you for loving her like she's yours."

He gives me a crooked smile. "In my heart, she belongs to me."

I grasp his face with my palm. "I love you so much. And someday when you put a ring on my finger, you can make Marley officially yours. I mean, if you want to." I'm not surprised Ezra won't be around, since he hasn't bothered to try to see her before now. And I'm good with that. My daughter already has a stand-up man in her life. She doesn't need someone who's not committed to her the way she deserves.

"I definitely want to." Laughing, he lifts me and Marley in a hug and spins us around. "I'm gonna hold you to that."

"Don't squish her."

"I'm not. I'm holding you by your ass." He sets me down, kisses me, and pats my butt. "How about we go get some matching t-shirts so we can make our friends gag?"

"Let's do it." I don't know how Billy does that, how he gets me in a good mood after that interaction with Ezra, but he does.

He takes Marley from me and rests her on his broad shoulder as we stroll through the vendors. My eyes keep drifting to him. He's wearing jeans, a t-shirt, and his letterman jacket. He's so damn handsome with that baby in his arms. I sigh at the gentle way he pats her back.

We pause by a stand of t-shirts.

"Did you know that pecans are an every-other-year nut?"

Billy hums. "I'm more of a daily-nut kind of man."

I laugh and shove him a little. "Goof."

The slogans are hysterical. Several have squirrels who are holding pecans with slogans like, *Don't touch my nuts*, or *I'm nuts about you*, or *I love big nuts and I cannot lie.* And my personal favorite features a squirrel dangling off a tree that says, *It's all fun and games until someone loses a nut.*

We laugh at a poster that says, *The Charming Nut Festival. I came. I saw. I nutted.*

I hold up a t-shirt to my chest. "What about this one?" It has a football next to a pecan and says, *Charming, Texas, home of big ballers and bigger nuts.*

Billy chuckles. "Is it safe to assume I'm the baller and you're the nut?"

I frown at him with mock indignation. "Pfft. I'm the baller."

"Whatever you say, biscuit."

Snickering, I poke him in the ribs. "I'm totally a baller. Did you see my segment last weekend?" While my professor was hesitant to run it, my cheer story got such a great response, he said I could have my pick of human interest stories for the rest of the semester.

Billy pats my ass again. "You killed it. After watching your piece, Coach said he felt a little ashamed he hadn't personally thanked the cheerleaders for always coming to our games."

Aww. "Speaking of my dad..."

My parents are strolling toward us, arm in arm. I've never really appreciated how in love my parents are. They're smiling at each other like the lovesick fools they are. It's helped them get through my dad's career in the NFL and several cross-country moves. I hope Billy and I can always be head over heels for each other the way my parents are.

When my mom sees us, she heads straight for Marley. "How's my grandbaby?" Marley gives her a big, toothless grin. "Look at that smile. Come here, darling."

Billy hands over the baby.

My mom kisses my daughter, then turns to us. "Why don't you two go enjoy yourselves for a while? Daddy and I can watch Marley."

"Are you sure? You guys could probably use a night out."

Dad nods. "Go on, honey. Enjoy yourself. We know how hard you've been working. And in case I haven't told you lately, I'm so damn proud of you. People have been coming up to me all week, praising your cheerleading piece. I can't wait to see what else you're going to do."

My eyes sting, but I'm smiling. "Thanks, Dad. That means a lot to me."

Billy wraps his arm around me. "Wanna go up the Ferris wheel?"

"Yes, but let's get our baller shirts first."

After I give my mom Marley's diaper bag and we pay for our t-shirts, we head for the area with the rides. I shiver as we wait in line for the Ferris wheel.

"You cold, baby?"

"A little," I say. He strips off his letterman and drapes it across my shoulders. "Won't you be cold?"

"Nah. I'm fine. As you're always telling me in bed, I'm hot-blooded." He waggles his eyebrows, and I laugh.

When we get our seats on the ride, I immediately scoot into him, and he wraps his arms around me.

We slowly rise into the night, and the lights of Charming twinkle in the distance.

I take a deep breath, feeling really lucky. I can't begin to describe the range of emotions I experienced in the last year, but somewhere in there, Billy became my other half, and I'm so grateful to call him mine.

I take his rough hand in mine. "You played great today. I thought I was going to lose my voice from screaming. Wish I could've been there." I had to shoot another assignment, and this afternoon was the only time I could do it, but I caught the second half when I got home.

"Your assignments are just as important as mine. Besides, there are more games left in the season."

"Are you worried about the draft? I still feel bad about that agent losing interest."

"It'll be fine, biscuit. Don't lose sleep over that asshole."

I'm tempted to ask about his father, but that's still a sore subject. They had it out last weekend when Billy went home to get a few things, including our napkin contract, which Billy says must've fallen out of his textbook. It now sits in a scrapbook I'm making.

"You're going to be on ESPN tonight with that crazy interception." He had another huge day. "And now that all of my parts have healed, I have to get back to my promise to reward you with back massages." Which we both know is code for something else.

His eyebrows lift. "It *was* a great return."

I laugh. "Maybe we could go home right after this."

He grabs the back of my head and tilts my face so he can kiss me. "Have I ever told you how motivated I am by rewards?"

My hand drifts down his hard chest, and my blood heats. "How do you feel about naked rewards?"

He gazes into my eyes. "Draft or no draft, I already have the best reward, more than I probably deserve, with you and Starley. Love you, biscuit."

"Love you, Billy." So, so much.

EPILOGUE

ROXY

IT'S BITING COLD, I can't feel my face, and my toes are frozen, but none of that matters because we're down three points against UT with less than a minute remaining.

"Come on, Broncos!" I scream, my voice hoarse. "Let's do this!"

The stands are full. Seventy thousand fans are freaking out just like I am at the last game of the regular season.

I'm standing on the sideline, trying not to lose my mind. I'm so into the game, I almost drop my mic.

I had tickets to this game, but Douggie got mono and couldn't cover it at the last minute, so my professor asked me to do it. No one had to twist my arm, obviously. Given how popular the team is, I never thought I'd get a chance to cover them. Today really is a dream come true.

Professor Fowler said I could cover it as long as I disclosed that Coach is my father and explain to viewers how I'm providing a unique perspective. I recorded that as soon as we got here today and did a whole behind-the-scenes segment in the locker room before the game started.

The cool thing about football is I get a cameraman and don't have to shoot everything myself. Tater, who got his nickname because he's always snarfing down Tater Tots in class, is huge, which means his footage won't get obstructed.

"Maybe edit out all of my screaming," I tell him, and he chuckles.

I know I'm supposed to be unbiased, but this is *my* team. That's my boyfriend on the sidelines, having the game of his life. That's my dad talking wildly into his headset, and my brother huddled up next to the QB, hopefully ready to score.

Turning to the stands, I wave at Billy's mom, who's sitting in the first row with one of her friends.

After Mrs. Babcock found out what Billy's dad had said to me and that disgusting way he tried to pay me off, she was so upset, she left him. Apparently, he's been sleeping around behind her back for years, but this was the straw that broke the camel's back. She made a point to meet me for dinner and told me she'd never seen her son so happy and that we had her support. It meant more to me than she'll ever know.

Billy says he's relieved his parents are divorcing because his father treated his mom like crap, and our situation only proved to him that his sperm donor isn't someone he wants in his life.

All of this only makes me that much more determined to make him feel welcomed by my family. Given how he, my dad, and brother spent last Sunday planning a fishing trip in the spring, I think they're on the right track.

When I turn back to the field, my attention snags on Ezra, who's sitting on the sideline looking grim. He's been benched for the last few games. My father swears that decision had nothing to do with me and everything to do with Ezra's lackluster performances since he injured his shoulder. Since ESPN agreed giving

Nick Silva a shot at QB1 was the right thing to do, who am I to question it?

Seeing the devastated expression on Ezra's face, I almost feel bad for him.

Almost.

Abigail says she was hoping he'd get a permanent case of erectile dysfunction, but this is even better. She swears this is the universe's way of paying him back for being such a douche. I can't say I disagree. His decision to hook up against an open window with some random girl, only hours after Abigail dumped him, likely cost him his dream of being drafted and a shot at the NFL.

As for Abigail, she and I have decided that our friendship is the silver lining in this whole screwed-up situation. Ezra did us both dirty, but she and I are grateful to have found each other.

Tater elbows me. "Think Silva has another touchdown in him?"

I hold up my hand and cross my fingers. Silva is a solid quarterback, but the rest of the team has really leveled up, which has kept us undefeated thus far. But this game has been fierce.

The Longhorns are our biggest rivals since they're our nearest neighbor, and the toughest competition in our conference this season. They're undefeated too.

Billy has had a great game, but I know that doesn't matter to him if the team doesn't get the win.

The Broncos have possession at the forty-five-yard line.

"Why is Babcock heading out there?" Tater yells.

My eyes widen. Sure enough, there's Billy, the team's *defensive* safety, joining Nick in the huddle.

Billy told me he's practiced a few trick plays on offense, but my dad isn't a fan of those because it's too easy to miscommunicate in high-pressure situations. So I never thought they'd actually try to execute one.

And yet there's Billy, getting in formation at the line of scrimmage.

With the offense.

I'm so anxious, my stomach does a flip-flop. *Don't throw up, Roxy!*

"Maybe he'll block for Nick or get a lateral pass," I say to myself as I bite my nail. "My dad knows Billy's tough *and* fast and could run in the ball."

That's not what happens.

Nick gets the snap and looks downfield as he charges toward the sideline to hand it to my brother. They're still behind the line of scrimmage, and I expect Deke to run.

Instead, he heads back toward the other side, where he hands it off to Billy in a classic double reverse.

"He's definitely running it in," Tater says, trying to read the play.

Because yeah, Billy's one of the fastest safeties in the country. I've seen him strong-arm giants. And while it's a bold move to use a defenseman on offense, it's not a stretch to use Billy, who used to be a wide receiver, which is what he's playing now.

Billy dodges one defender. Then another.

Damn. This doesn't look good.

Somehow, he breaks free, running laterally, toward the sideline again.

Then looks downfield.

Cocks his arm.

Releases the ball.

Holy shit, he's passing it.

Time slows as the ball sails through the air, and Bronco fans collectively hold our breath, because *oh my God.*

If he nails this, we win and go to the playoffs.

The ball starts its descent.

One lone Bronco, Cam, sprints to the end zone, but a

defender is hot on his heels. Cam leaps into the air, arms outstretched.

And snags the ball.

"Touchdown!"

I'm screaming, along with seventy thousand other fans. Because Billy just threw the biggest Hail Mary of his life, in what had to be a fifty-yard pass, and nailed it.

Then we get the extra point.

Except there's still time on the clock.

When our defense heads back out onto the field for the remaining ten seconds, everyone is tense. It's possible they could score. They're a phenomenal team.

But I'm smiling because Billy stays on the field to freaking play defense too.

"Your boy's a stud," Tater says.

"He sure as hell is."

Every single person in the stadium is on their feet when the ball snaps. We're blitzing, meaning our guys are rushing the UT quarterback.

He gets the ball off at the last second.

It's a long pass.

"Oh God! No!" I'm freaking out because if the UT receiver catches it, there's a chance he could run it in and score, and there's no time to recover.

At the last second, Billy leaps up next to him. Stretches out. And nabs the ball. He carries it ten yards before he's tackled, but the clock is out.

Billy just won the game.

I'm jumping up and down, screaming. Fans rush the field. It's pandemonium.

As a journalist, I know I'm supposed to stay uninvolved, but fuck it. I'm too ecstatic to care about rules right now.

Tater waves his phone at me and reads a text message from

our professor. "We need interviews with your dad, Nick, Cam, and Billy."

Right now, all I want to do is celebrate, but I have to tamp down my euphoria and do my job.

We make our way through the crowd, and I high-five several of the Broncos. I finally spot my father, who's being interviewed by ESPN, so Tater and I wait in line.

After we interview Cam and Nick, I finally get to Coach.

"Great job, Dad!" I hug him, and he's smiling from ear to ear. "I need a minute to interview you."

He motions toward the tunnel. "Join me in the media room for the post-game press conference. I'll give you a chance to get your questions in, but I need to get back there to talk to one of the scouts."

I nod and scan the field for Billy, but can't find him.

"Billy will join us. Come on, Roxy. I don't want to keep these guys waiting."

Smiling because my father read my mind, I reluctantly follow along with Tater, wishing I could've talked to Billy on the field. He was so amazing today, and I can't wait to leap into his arms, but that will have to wait until I'm done with my interviews.

By the time we get to the media room, it's wall-to-wall press, and Tater and I have to squeeze in along the back. But the Bronco media liaison spots us and waves us forward, and we end up near the front, which is really cool because I couldn't see over all of the cameras.

When Billy enters the room, my heart skips a beat. He's sweaty and dirty and likely exhausted, but when our eyes connect, I don't care that he looks like he just rolled around in the grass. That man is mine, and I'm so damn proud of him.

He smiles, and I grin back, not caring that I'm wearing my heart on my sleeve.

The players sit at the table with my dad—Nick, Cam, Billy, Deke, and one of the defensive linemen.

Just like on the field, I have to wait my turn to ask a question. I swear every other station gets to go first. I'm starting to get a cramp in my arm from holding it up when my dad finally calls on me.

"Coach, congrats on the win. What prompted you to use Billy Babcock, a safety, as a wide receiver?"

My dad chuckles. "Someone reminded me last summer that Billy was a standout quarterback in high school, and that perhaps I wasn't utilizing him as much as I could. But not only does he have a great arm, Billy Babcock is one of the best college safeties in the country. Today's interception was his eighth, and that ties him for first. But he's more than just a great defenseman. He's quick, has great hands, and has a high aptitude for the game. We're lucky to have him."

Billy turns to my dad. "Thanks, Coach. You're not so bad yourself."

Everyone laughs. Even my dad.

Someone else asks, "Billy, who do you hope drafts you in the spring?"

He swallows, looks down, and I have to bite my bottom lip to keep the tears at bay because this is the first time a reporter has asked him about that. I hope he knows he truly has major draft potential now.

Billy leans in toward the mic. "I'd be thrilled to play in the NFL, period. If there are teams out there who want me, they should know they'll be getting someone who loves the game. Someone who gives their heart and soul out there every day."

My dad pats him on the back. "I'll vouch for the kid. We didn't always see eye to eye, but he's grown by leaps and bounds and is a leader on the team and on the field. Any NFL team who drafts Billy Babcock will be lucky."

Inside I'm beaming. I'm so damn proud of my boyfriend. And so grateful to my father for giving him another chance.

Another reporter says, "Billy, back to that incredible offensive play. What was going through your mind as you made that pass?"

"That I'd better not screw up or Coach would kill me." My dad nods, but he's smiling. Billy clears his throat. "Plus, it would suck to lose. I couldn't exactly ask my girlfriend to marry me after a loss."

Wait.

What did he just say?

Stunned, I stand there like a concrete pillar as Billy gets up and comes around the table.

All the cameras in the room swivel with him as he stops in front of me and drops to one knee.

My mouth drops open, and I slap my hand over it.

Billy grabs my other hand and kisses the back of it. He gives me that sexy smile that makes me melt. "Roxy, you're the light of my life. You brighten every day, and I never want the sun to set without seeing your beautiful face before I go to sleep. Will you do me the greatest honor and marry me?"

He holds out his other hand, and Cam drops a little black box in it.

My eyes are saucers as Billy opens it and pulls out a diamond ring that he slides on my finger.

"This belonged to my grandmother. She wants you to have it."

I wipe the tear that escapes. "You know this is forever, right?" I whisper.

His smile goes soft. "I'm not sure that's long enough."

I grab his handsome face and kiss him. "Yes, I'll marry you."

Everyone cheers, and he picks me up in a hug.

So much for being objective, but I can't bring myself to care.

The man of my dreams just asked me to marry him, and I couldn't be happier.

~

IT TAKES a while to leave the stadium. Billy wants me to wait for him, but he has to shower and get his stuff. I swear, he's the last one out of the locker room.

While I wait, Tater shows me the footage of Billy proposing, and I want to let out a girlie squeal at the sweet expression on Billy's face. I can't believe he coordinated this.

My dad made a point to pull me aside afterward to let me know Billy had asked him for his permission—to marry me and pop the question at the press conference. Coach told him the only way he'd go along with the post-game proposal was if they won today.

Coach says that definitely put an extra fire in the furnace.

I gave my dad a look, and he hugged me and whispered he would've let Billy propose whether we won or lost.

After the press conference, Billy's driving us home when he turns off early.

"We have to go pick up Marley from the babysitter's," I remind him.

"Don't worry, biscuit. This won't take long." We pull into the parking lot of the Yellow Rose Bar & Grill. "Let's grab some dinner to go."

I hop out of his car and hook my arm in his. I'm so happy, I suspect my feet are floating off the ground. Coming here today reminds me of our first "official" date after we signed our napkin contract. We danced to slow music, and Billy sang in my ear.

I don't know who I was fooling, but he nabbed my heart right then and there.

"I'm really excited to be your wife." Skipping alongside him, I grin at him like a fool, unable to contain my excitement.

"Good, because you're stuck with me." He winks and opens the door for me.

"Congrats!" everyone shouts.

My mouth drops open again. All of our friends are here. My parents and brother. His mom. Dozens of Billy's teammates. My cheer coach. Paige and Abigail. Even Charlie and Jake and a few of our friends who graduated the year before last.

Across the back of the room, it says, "Congrats, Billy and Roxy!"

My mom brings me Marley, and I snuggle her to me as Billy wraps his arm around us.

I press my face to his chest where I finally let out all the happy tears. "Thank you. This is so thoughtful."

How did he know I would want an engagement party? Something to replace that terrible memory from last January?

Billy lifts my chin and gently wipes the tears before he presses a tender kiss to my lips. "Thanks for being my forever. You and Starley mean everything to me."

Marley opens her arms for him, and he picks her up and blows raspberries on her belly, which makes her giggle.

"We might need a new contract to replace the old one," I tease as I watch him hold her.

He nods. "We should add your enchiladas and flan."

"To our marriage contract?"

"Absolutely. Food is the basis for a solid marriage."

"What about more snuggling?"

"I definitely need more snuggling."

"And slow-dancing on Friday nights?"

"Hell yes. And maybe reading those historical romances out loud. The last time was fun." He winks.

I remember that night in vivid detail. I read him a spicy

passage, and the second I put down the book, we mauled each other.

I beam. "We might need a bigger napkin this time."

He kisses my forehead. "Grab a big-ass piece of paper. I have ideas." Then he turns to our friends and families, holds up my hand, and yells, "I'm king of the world! Roxy Santos said she'll marry me!"

They cheer and clap and hoot.

Laughing, I shake my head. "What about your Hail Mary today and your game-winning throw? Might that have contributed to your king of the world status?"

Leaning down, he whispers, "That's just icing on the cake, biscuit. You're the real prize, and everyone here knows it."

That night, after we get the baby to bed, and we're intertwined, sweaty and naked, I sigh happily as I graze my nails along his forearm that's wrapped around my belly. "How will you know which agent to choose?"

Three top agents contacted him today, wanting to represent him at the draft.

"I hope to meet with each one over the holidays, but I need to get some input from your dad first."

"Smart."

Billy whispers, "Let's not talk about Coach while I have an erection."

I snicker and reach back to scratch his head. "Another one?"

"Earlier was just an appetizer, biscuit."

"What's the main course?"

He nibbles my neck. "You."

I giggle. And then a thought hits me. "How would you have proposed if Douggie hadn't gotten sick?"

"I paid that kid a hundred bucks to sideline his ass today."

Gasping, I turn around. "What?"

"I had no idea if your prof would let you cover the game in his place, but I was hoping."

"That's kinda crazy." I think about our "big ballers and bigger nuts" t-shirts and laugh. "And totally us."

He kisses my nose. "Thought so."

Sinking into his embrace, I sigh happily. "By the way, I finished that historical romance, the one about a rakish duke and the daughter of his archnemesis."

"What happened at the end?"

"She ended up with the man of her dreams."

Just like me.

EPILOGUE TWO

FOUR MONTHS LATER

ROXY

I squeeze Billy's hand. "You got this."

His expression is somber as he watches the TV screen. "Thanks, babe."

Mrs. Babcock gives me a worried smile from across my parents' living room. She's sitting with Billy's grandma, and my mom and dad.

Today is the last day of the draft. And so far, despite the incredible stats Billy had this season, despite the number of interceptions he had, despite that heart-stopping Hail Mary he threw in the UT game, and despite having a top agent, no team has picked Billy yet.

He even spoke to two NFL coaches this week to discuss their interest.

And yet he still hasn't been drafted.

It pisses me off. How can teams not see how incredible he is?

Is it because he switched positions twice in college? Because of his rowdy past? Because he comes across a little carefree?

Out of the two hundred and fifty-nine picks, there were just fifteen safeties drafted last year, and so far, fourteen have already been picked.

I'll be sick if Billy's not drafted. I stare at the potted plant on the other side of the room, because there's a strong likelihood I'm going to puke on my mother's philodendron.

Internally, I'm freaking out, but on the outside, I hope I appear calm. Billy doesn't need me to lose it right now. He needs me to be supportive.

I squeeze his hand again. "You're next. It's going to happen." It had better fucking happen, or I'm going to Hulk out and... I don't know what I'm going to do, but it won't be pretty because Billy absolutely deserves a shot at the NFL.

Marley grabs my hair to try to stand in my lap. "Up! Up!" My daughter is the only thing that can bring a smile to my face right now. "Up" and "Mama" are the only two words she says, but she knows what they mean.

I stand her in my lap, and she holds her arms open for Billy. "Do you want to go to Daddy?"

"Da."

Billy's head jerks around as his eyes widen. "Did she just say..."

"Dada!" she yells and bounces up and down.

I give him a watery smile. I know how much this means to him. Someday, when Marley gets a little older, we'll explain that she has a biological father too. We won't hide that from her. But she'll know she has a daddy who will always be by her side.

Billy's eyes get shiny as he pulls her into his lap. "Hey, baby. Whatcha got for me?"

She plants a slobbery kiss on his cheek, and my heart melts at the sweet look he gives her as he sits her in his lap. Then he grabs my hand and laces his fingers through mine and pulls me close. "Love you, biscuit."

"Love you too, baby."

When he kisses me on the forehead, I sigh. We'll get through this, no matter what. But I hope with everything in me that Billy can achieve his dream.

I look around the room, and my dad winks at me. I smile back, grateful that Billy and I have the support of my family.

My parents are hosting this three-day draft party for the team, since we have several players who declared for the draft. Tater and Douggie have been here the whole time to get local coverage. Douggie interviewed my brother, and I interviewed Cam. When Billy gets drafted—please, Jesus—Douggie will interview him too, since I can't now that we're engaged.

My mom, ever the hostess, comes by with a tray of hors d'oeuvres, which she sets down on the coffee table, swapping them out for Marley, who now wants her grandma to pick her up.

Cam, who got picked in the first round, is here with his girlfriend. My brother declared as a junior and got drafted yesterday, and he's out back grilling burgers. Nick is here too, though he decided to use his last year of eligibility and return to Lone Star State in the fall.

Although we won our bowl game and made it to the championship game, Nick struggled throughout, and no amount of defense could carry a win.

I try to look on the bright side. At least Billy, Deke, and Cam played great, and my dad felt the guys gave it their best shot. Forever the optimist, he said there's always next year.

Nick joins us on the couch with his adorable daughter Hazel, who's almost four.

"Can I ask you guys a question?" Nick says over the top of Hazel's head. "Do you know any good babysitters? I need someone for the summer."

It pops into my head so fast, if I were standing, I'd trip over myself. "Do you know Abigail Dawson? She's an early ed major, and she's looking for a nanny job right now."

He frowns. Looks around. Lowers his voice. "As in Ezra's ex?"

Ezra. Who hasn't been drafted either and likely won't be. Though he's not here, thank God.

"The very one. Abigail's such a sweetheart, and she's so good with Marley." For some reason, he's not jumping at my suggestion. "Have you guys met? She's coming later today."

That's when I hear the magical words on the TV.

"Chicago selects Lone Star State safety Billy Babcock."

The whole room erupts in cheers. Billy and I leap up, and a second later, he lifts me into his arms.

"You did it, baby! I'm so proud of you!"

He kisses me. Spins me around. Shouts and high-fives our friends and family, all the while carrying me with his other arm. I cling to his shoulders, laughing.

Billy had been hoping Chicago would pick him because his old roommate Olly plays there. He and his lovely wife Maggie have twin boys, and it'll be really cool for our kids to grow up together.

After everyone congratulates Billy, Tater and Douggie interview him. When it's over, Billy turns to me. "So tell me, biscuit, how do you feel about Chicago?"

I tap my chin. "Are you going to be there?"

He chuckles. "Yes."

Pushing up on my toes, I kiss him. "Then there's nowhere else I'd want to be."

BONUS CHAPTER

ONE YEAR LATER

Roxy

Pulling back the curtains, I smile into the bright sunshine.

Today's the day I'm marrying my best friend. The man of my dreams. The one who stole my heart when I wasn't looking.

And Chicago's star rookie defensive back.

The team might not have picked Billy until day three of the draft, but he kicked ass his first year.

I knew he could do it.

"It's a great day to get married," I say to the hotel room, not caring who hears me.

My bridesmaids agree as they flutter around me, pinning my hair up and fluffing my dress. I'm too excited to worry about what I'm wearing or make sure my hair looks just right. Charlotte calls my name, and I turn.

She snaps a photo and grins. "You look so beautiful standing there in the window. I know you said no more photos, but I couldn't help it."

"My face was starting to hurt from smiling, so that's why I

told the wedding photographer to give me a break, but you're welcome to take as many as you want."

My mom peeks in the room. "Roxy, it's time."

I press my hand to my stomach. The excitement is starting to get to me. *Please don't throw up on your wedding day.*

"Does anyone have some crackers?" I ask. "Or some ginger ale?"

My mother gives me a look, and I pretend I don't notice. Paige hands me something ice cold and bubbly.

"Thank you." I take a few sips, and the nausea starts to subside.

Maggie, who's married to Billy's teammate Olly, comes up to me with her compact. "Can I dab a little of this on your nose?"

"Yes, please. Can't be shiny on my wedding day. Oh, and in case I haven't told you lately, everyone keeps saying how beautiful those wedding invites were that you designed for us. I've been giving out your info left and right."

"I'm so happy you like them." She dabs my nose and then hands me my lipstick for another coat.

"I might have another event soon, so pencil me in for early fall."

She nods. "Whatever you need."

Maggie and Olly both attended Lone Star State too, but it wasn't until Billy and I moved to Chicago that Maggie and I really spent time together. I feel like I discovered a long-lost sister. She's spunky and kind, and her twin boys are adorable. It's so nice to have a mommy friend who knows what I'm going through with a toddler.

I pause by the full-length mirror to make sure my boobs are still tucked away where they should be. This dress fit perfectly a month ago. Now, everything's just a little tighter than it should be.

But I'm getting married today, so I'm not going to let anything bother me.

Charlie hands me my bouquet, and I keep it away from my face in case the smell is too much.

We all pile into the elevator, and Paige breaks out her phone and starts playing "Crazy In Love" by Beyoncé, so naturally we start dancing.

"Y'all, I'm marrying Billy Babcock today!"

Everyone yells excitedly.

I don't care that I'm acting like an idiot. I'm too in love to care.

Our first year in the NFL is in the books. Although our senior year at Lone Star was incredibly trying, being able to work through those challenges helped us prepare for what was to come.

The night before his first road trip, Billy handed me a piece of paper that had all of his passwords, his hotel rooms, and his coach's number. He said it was for security, in case I had an emergency, but also so I could always have confidence in his commitment to me. He also reiterated his open phone policy.

And then we put the baby to bed and ripped each other's clothes off.

Now that I think about it, we did that a lot this year. When he gets home from his away games, he's ravenous for me. I can't seem to get enough of him either. I thought we'd slow down after the season ended, but I guess we're having too much fun now that his schedule isn't as jam-packed.

Which is why I'm barely squeezing into my wedding dress.

"Don't mess up your hair," my mom warns me as I dance with my girls. She's squished in the corner of the elevator, taking a video of us looking like fools.

The elevator doors open, and we scuttle out into the hotel lobby where my wedding coordinator ushers us to the exit.

We're getting married across the street at the Charming Arbory, which is a hundred-year-old warehouse that's been converted into this industrial-chic wedding venue surrounded by lush gardens.

My bridesmaids look so beautiful in their glittery pink cocktail dresses. Dusk is starting to fall, and twinkle lights criss-cross overhead. I'm standing behind a pillar, so I can't see Billy.

A few minutes later, we're all lined up ready to head out into the gardens when my dad joins us. "Don't look at me," he says gruffly.

I laugh as I straighten his boutonniere. "Why's that?"

"Because you're going to make your tough old dad cry."

I jut out my lower lip that's starting to quiver. "Not fair. You can't say something like that. Because if you cry, then I'll cry."

Maggie turns to my dad and tuts. "Coach, if you make her tear up and screw up her mascara, I'm going to have a bone to pick with you."

He smiles. Sniffles. Nods. "I'm okay."

Aww. I kiss him on his cheek. "Remember the game plan, Coach. We're headed straight for the goalpost. Don't deviate from the route."

He laughs and hugs me.

That's when Billy's mom Brenda comes up to us holding Marley, who's decked out in a poofy white dress. My girl loves twirling in it.

Her eyes widen when she sees me. I lean over to kiss her. "Remember, toss one flower petal at a time, and don't eat them this time."

Brenda sets her on the ground, gives her the basket of pink rose petals, and my other flower girl takes Marley's hand.

It's possible none of those flowers will land in the right place. Marley might dump them on her head and flop on the ground, but Billy and I don't care. We just want her to have a special place in the ceremony.

From where I'm standing, I can't see the groomsmen, but I'm able to watch the girls start down the aisle. A few petals get tossed. And then I hear, "Daddeee!" and the pounding of little feet as Marley bolts down the aisle toward Billy.

Everyone laughs, and I smile.

The Wedding March starts, kicking my heart into high gear. "Dad, don't let me trip."

He pats my hand. "This is the biggest handoff of my life. I'm ready."

We move to the aisle, and my heart catches in my throat when I finally see Billy.

My devastatingly handsome fiancé smiles, and I can't take my eyes off him. His hair is trimmed short on the sides but is longer on top. His jaw has his signature scruff, and he fills out that black tux to perfection.

I can't believe I get to spend my life with this man. I'm so excited to see him, I'm tempted to run down the aisle too.

"Billy loves you so much," my dad whispers. "You were right about him."

I'm too choked up to say anything, but I nod.

I don't remember walking down the aisle but I must have. When I reach Billy, he and my dad do a half hug thing, and then my soon-to-be husband takes my hand.

He leans close and whispers a little too loudly, "You're a fucking vision."

The minister coughs, and Billy holds up his hand. "Sorry."

The groomsmen laugh. Everyone looks so handsome in their tuxes. Cam, Jake, Olly, Deke, and two of Billy's teammates stand next to him. When we turn to the audience, I smile at my mom, who's now holding Marley.

"Mama! Daddeeee!" she yells excitedly as she waves her fluffy tulle skirt at us. "Purdy dwess!"

Billy chuckles. "Looking good, Starley."

By the time we get to the vows, I'm trembling with excitement.

Billy takes my hands in his and grins. "Roxy, you're my best friend, my favorite cheerleader, and the best mother to Marley. Our relationship is something I never dreamed I could have. You've made me believe in things I didn't know I wanted. I promise to always have that same faith in you. To be the man you think I can be. To be the father Marley needs me to be. I promise to always comfort you if you're sad, to cheer your accomplishments, and to share in your joys. I'll bring you sweet tea on Sunday afternoons and coffee first thing in the morning."

My smile widens. "And if you're at an away game?"

"I'll set the coffee timer."

The audience chuckles.

He swallows. Squeezes my hand. Kisses my forehead. "You have my heart, body, and soul."

I nod and blink rapidly so I don't cry. "Billy, you stole my heart that night at the Yellow Rose by singing in my ear during a slow dance. We've had a whirlwind romance, and even though everyone said we were crazy, you've always believed in us."

He gives me a sweet smile, and I melt.

I take a deep breath. "When I was young, I used to dream of the kind of man I'd marry someday. I wanted him to be bigger than life, strong and kind, gentle with me and our kids, but fiercely protective. I wanted the love of a lifetime, the one for storybooks. That's what I have with you. You're the man in those dreams. I promise to always have faith in us, to always cheer the loudest at your games, and to give you pointers if you need them."

He laughs and nods.

"Billy, you stole my heart, body, and soul, but they're yours to keep. Always."

Leaning in, he kisses me.

The minister says, "We're not there yet."

Everyone laughs again.

We then say more traditional vows.

"I, William James Babcock, take you, Roxanne Amara Santos, to be my wife, to have and to hold, from this day forward, for better or worse, for richer or poorer, free agent or contracted..."

I smile, so grateful I get to marry my best friend. And I love that we've made our day exactly what we want it to be.

When he places his grandmother's ring on my finger, I glance over at her, and she winks.

By the time we get to the actual wedding kiss, I can't contain my excitement anymore, so when the minister says, "You may kiss the bride," I leap into my husband's arms.

The groomsmen hoot and holler as Billy dips me in a kiss.

When he lifts me, he kisses me again. "Hello, wife."

"Hello, husband."

"Are you ready to start forever?"

I grab his hand and grin. "Let's do this."

Billy

My wife is a vision. I watch her hug our guests and take photos with everyone. I can't take my eyes off her.

"You're a lucky man," Olly says with a clap to my back. We're sitting at the banquet table, enjoying a beer. "Never thought I'd see the day when Billy Babcock settled down."

"My mother says it's a miracle." Probably as much a miracle as me getting along with Roxy's dad.

But the fact that he took me and Deacon fishing again a few weeks ago is evidence that I'm officially part of the family. Because that man does not let just anyone go fishing with him.

Even though Coach was tough on me at Lone Star, I can honestly say I appreciate it. I'm not sure I would've been drafted without him hounding my ass to get my shit together. But it took his daughter to make me believe I had a shot at actually achieving my dream.

Playing in the NFL has been a blast. It's tough and has its challenges, but with Roxy by my side, I feel like I can do anything.

When we moved to Chicago, I heard my new team needed a social media person to create content, someone to cover the games and interview players for our fans online. Roxy jumped at the opportunity and had the entire team impressed with her skills when several of her TikToks went viral.

While it's not the broadcast job she dreamed of, she says she's having too much fun to worry about that, and she's planning to use her social media momentum to build her own platform and cover the more serious topics she cares about.

Because it's a flexible gig, she can still spend lots of time with Marley and coach a cheer camp on occasion.

My wife is a boss. I couldn't be prouder of her. And the fact that she knows football inside and out gives me major bragging rights in the locker room.

"You got a little drool on you." Olly motions to my shoulder.

I glance down at Marley, who's wrapped around me like a monkey. She passed out a few minutes ago. My mom is going to watch her tonight, but we wanted our girl to enjoy the festivities for a while. "Come on, baby. Let's get you to bed."

My mother must have a sixth sense because she's there in a flash. "Want me to take her now?"

"Thanks, Mom. Appreciate it." I give her a hug with one arm before I hand her Marley.

She and Marlena will be babysitting for the next few days while Roxy and I head to Port Aransas, a small Texas beach town we both like. We considered going somewhere more exotic, but we wanted to be close in case we had to book it home for Marley. We're leaving tomorrow morning.

Roxy sees us and comes over to check in with my mom. "Call us if you need anything. We can be home in five hours."

My mom chuckles. "Honey, I had three little hellraisers. I can handle one small angel. Besides, Marlena's going to swing by every day and she said she can take Marley overnight if I need a break. You don't need to worry. I want you two to enjoy your honeymoon and get some rest."

I glance at Roxy as her face flushes, and I laugh to myself.

Rest might not be on the agenda.

After my mom leaves, we check in on my grandmother. "You doing okay? Do you need to go to bed?"

"I'm old, not dead." She smirks. "There are some good-looking men here. I plan to enjoy the eye candy."

Since my mother divorced my dad, she moved my grandma in with her. I think Grandma likes her more than she likes her own son. Who wouldn't?

I didn't bother inviting my father to our wedding, and since my idiot brothers also gave me shit for getting with Roxy, they didn't get invites today. No loss. My real family is here.

My grandma and Roxy hug, and then I take my wife on the dance floor.

"Can I give you my present soon?" I ask as I twirl her around. We took couples' lessons this spring, and I can bust out a waltz if needed.

Her fingers play with the hair at the nape of my neck. "I have two gifts for you."

"Two?" I lift an eyebrow. "I distinctly remember us saying we would just do one."

She leans up on her toes and kisses my chin. "The second gift was a surprise to me too."

Now I'm intrigued.

After the dance, we head back to the banquet table, and I pull the square blue box out of my coat pocket.

"Tiffany's? Baby, you spent too much."

"If I can't lavish my beautiful wife with a special gift on our wedding day, then why am I working so hard?" I realize that now. Without my girls, what does playing in the NFL really mean?

She grins. "For the record, I love Tiffany's."

I smile, knowing she'd been eyeing this bracelet, but she's not the kind of person to buy it for herself.

The look on her face when she opens the box is priceless. "I've been wanting an ID bracelet. This is so beautiful." It's a delicate gold band with diamonds. She holds it out to me so I can help her put it on.

"Look at the inscription." It says Santos-Babcock.

She's taking my last name, but I know how much her family means to her. Her eyes water. "Thank you. I love it so much."

After I put it on and kiss her, she hands me an envelope. "This is not as fancy as what you gave me."

"I don't care about that." But I am curious. Carefully, I break the seal and pull out what looks to be a contract.

They're adoption papers for Marley.

A knot forms in my throat, and my eyes sting.

Roxy takes my hand and kisses my rough knuckles. "You're already her father in spirit. Let's make it official."

I nod, touched more than I can say. "Thank you, Rox. It would be my honor. I love her so much." I pull my beautiful wife into my lap and kiss her.

"There's that surprise gift too."

I look around the table, not spotting anything. "Are you going to give me a clue?"

"You're holding it."

"You are a gift, that's true." I chuckle.

"How does it feel to have a family of three?" Are we still talking about the surprise? Before I can answer, she takes my hand and places it on her stomach. "Because we're about to become a family of four."

I'm glad I'm sitting because I get lightheaded. "Are you serious? Holy shit, that's awesome." When I'm sure I won't topple over, I jump up and spin her around. We said we wanted to have our children while we had the energy to run around after them, but this is indeed a surprise. "When are you due?"

"Late December."

Lacing our fingers together, I kiss her forehead. "That's the best wedding gift ever."

She hangs her arms over my shoulders and gives me a heated look. "I might have one more gift for you, but it's lacy and sheer, and you'll need to rip it off with your teeth later tonight."

"Goddamn, I'm ready for this." We've spent the last few days apart to make tonight extra special, and I am ready to go. I glance around. "I'm not sure it's appropriate to sport a boner at my wedding reception, wife. I'm a married man now."

With a coy look, she drags a finger down my chest. "I brought the massage oil."

That's it.

I grab her hand and jokingly march her to the exit. She pulls me back, laughing.

Swinging her in my arms, I kiss her and all of our friends and family cheer us on.

"Can I tell them our news?"

She nods.

We face everyone, and I'm sure I have the biggest, cheesiest grin on my face, but I don't care. I call out, "Mom! Marlena! Coach!" When I have their attention, I ask, "Do y'all like being grandparents?"

"Heck yes, son!" Coach yells back.

"Good, 'cause you're about to get another grandkid. Mark your calendars for late December! Marley's getting a brother or sister."

The whole room erupts, and I turn back to my beautiful wife. "I love you, wife."

"I love you more, husband," she says with a teasing smile on her lips.

My whole chest swells with pride and happiness, and I smile. "That's not even possible."

WHAT TO READ NEXT

Thanks for reading! If you enjoyed Heartbreaker Handoff, I hope you'll consider leaving a review. I try to read each one.

To stay up-to-date with my new releases, be sure to subscribe to my newsletter, which you can find on my website, www.lexmartinwrites.com.

Next up is Abigail and Nick's book! Let's just state the obvious—these two have a lot of baggage. Their journey to an HEA will not be easy, but it'll definitely be steamy! You can get your copy of **Blindside Beauty** on my website.

And if you want to start at the beginning of the Varsity Dads series, be sure to check out The Varsity Dad Dilemma, which is a USA Today bestseller. Keep flipping to read the synopsis.

THE VARSITY DAD DILEMMA

A USA TODAY BESTSELLER

What's worse than having Rider Kingston, the star quarterback, give you the big brush-off because he doesn't want to get serious? You'd probably think living across the street from him where you get a firsthand view of his hookups, right?

That's what I thought. Until someone drops off a baby with a note pinned to her blanket that says one of those jocks—either Rider or one of his roommates—is the father. The problem? Baby mama doesn't mention which of these numbskulls is the sperm donor.

I wouldn't care about their paternity problems—not the slightest bit—except my brother lives there too. Which means that adorable squawking bundle might be my niece, and there's no way I'm leaving her unattended with those bumbling football players.

They need my help, even if they don't know it yet. Once we solve this dilemma and figure out who's the daddy, I'm out.

I'll just ignore Rider and those soul-searing looks he gives me every time I reach for the baby. He broke my heart three years ago. He won't get a second chance.

~

The Varsity Dad Dilemma **is a sexy, small-town sports romance novel from USA Today best-selling author Lex Martin. Readers are raving about this passionate, angst-filled enemies-to-lovers romance, and the smoking-hot chemistry between Gabby, the slightly nerdy Latina with a take-charge attitude, and her surprisingly sweet former fling, Rider. Who knew that he actually had a heart of gold underneath that deliciously ripped, well-defined exterior?**

"Gabby and Rider have great chemistry and their banter is HOT. While she had loathed everything about Rider since freshman year, there was no denying the physical attraction they had towards each other... If you are looking for a college romance that brings the laughter, with loads of sexual tension and plenty of heart melting moments, check this book out!" – Reader Review

ACKNOWLEDGMENTS

I hope you enjoyed Billy and Roxy's book as much as I loved writing it! Heartbreaker Handoff was my happy place to escape life during the last part of 2023. My father was gravely ill, and I spent several weeks with him in the hospital and then months caring for him at home. By the third trip to the hospital, I was sure the universe was conspiring against me to thwart my plans for this book.

Alas, I made it! And I'm happy to say my father is doing much better. (He's currently propped up in bed at my house, eating dinner, and watching Neflix.)

Fortunately, Billy and Roxy made it easy for me to dive back in to writing. These two characters jumped off the page for me when I was drafting Second Down Darling, and I knew I wanted to give them a special story. Not only was I totally engrossed with their romance, that Billy/Coach arc was really fun to explore too.

Full disclosure—I took some creative license with the draft declaration timeframe. I won't bore you with the details, and unless you really care about those dates, it shouldn't impede your enjoyment of the story.

A very special thanks to my husband who let me cry all the tears on his shoulder when I was afraid I wouldn't be able to finish this book in time. Then he made me pancakes, pat me on the ass, and told me to get my shit done. Lol. Hugs to my twins, who knew I was super stressed and encouraged me along the way.

I have a great team that helps me reach the finish line: my agent Kimberly Brower, editor RJ Locksley, proofreader Julia Griffis, photographer Lindee Robinson, cover designer Najla Qamber, alternate cover designer Janett Corona, Kylie and Jo from Give Me Books, and Candi at Candi Kane PR. Thank you for everything you do for me!

My PA and dear friend Serena McDonald is my right hand gal. Her feedback and encouragement are invaluable. She also reminded me about Billy's notorious hashtag, which we had laughed about several months ago, and then I promptly forgot. So you have her to thank for that, along with dozens of other details in the story she helped me hammer out.

My lovely friend Leslie McAdam is my sounding board when I need to talk out plot. I always get stuck at some point, and she helps me kick the tires until the storyline reemerges. She never complains when I text her five thousand times to ask her dumb questions at midnight.

Along with Serena and Leslie, I have a fantastic team of beta readers who are so generous with their time and help me craft the best books possible. Victoria Denault, Christine Yates, Jess Hodge, and Amy Vox Libris—thank you for all of your feedback!

A huge thanks also to Chelle Sloan for proofing my football scenes, Janett Corona for double checking my Spanish, and Kristie at Read Between the Wines for that fantastic brainstorming session.

I want to send love out to my readers in Wildcats, my ARC

team, author friends, fans, bloggers, and influencers who've spread the word about my books. You have my deepest appreciation.

Next up is Blindside Beauty! Get ready for Abigail and Nick's story!

ALSO BY LEX MARTIN

Varsity Dads:

The Varsity Dad Dilemma (Gabby & Rider)

Tight Ends & Tiaras (Sienna & Ben)

The Baby Blitz (Magnolia & Olly)

Second Down Darling (Charlotte & Jake)

Heartbreaker Handoff (Roxy & Billy)

Blindside Beauty (Abigail & Nick)

Texas Nights:

Shameless (Kat & Brady)

Reckless (Tori & Ethan)

Breathless (Joey & Logan)

The Dearest Series:

Dearest Clementine (Clementine & Gavin)

Finding Dandelion (Dani & Jax)

Kissing Madeline (Maddie & Daren)

Cowritten with Leslie McAdam

All About the D (Evie & Josh)

Surprise, Baby! (Kendall & Drew)

ABOUT THE AUTHOR

Lex Martin is the *USA Today* bestselling author of Varsity Dads, Texas Nights, and the Dearest series, books she hopes readers love but her parents avoid. A former high school English teacher and freelance journalist, she resides in Texas with her husband, twin daughters, a bunny, and a rambunctious Shih Tzu.

To stay up-to-date with her releases, stop by her website and **subscribe to her newsletter**, or join her Facebook group, **Lex Martin's Wildcats.**

www.lexmartinwrites.com